KT-442-852

DANIEL SILVA

The Fallen Angel

HarperCollins*Publishers*

HarperCollins*Publishers*
77–85 Fulham Palace Road,
Hammersmith, London W6 8JB

www.harpercollins.co.uk

Published by HarperCollins*Publishers* 2012
1

A catalogue record for this book
is available from the British Library

ISBN: 978 0 00 743334 6

Printed and bound in Great Britain by
Clays Ltd, St Ives plc

MIX
Paper from
responsible sources
FSC **FSC™ C007454**
www.fsc.org

Find out more about HarperCollins and the environment at
www.harpercollins.co.uk/green

THE FALLEN ANGEL

Also written by Daniel Silva

The Unlikely Spy (1996)

For Louis Toscano, who has been
there from the beginning. And,
as always, for my wife, Jamie, and
my children, Lily and Nicholas.

I warn you against shedding blood,

indulging in it and making a habit of it,

for blood never sleeps.

SALADIN

VATICAN CITY

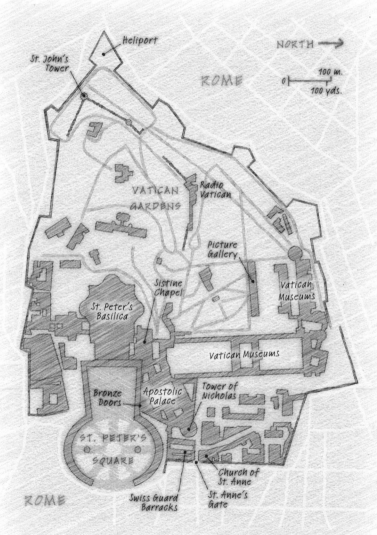

Heliport

St. John's Tower

NORTH →

ROME

0 100 m.
   100 yds.

Radio Vatican

VATICAN GARDENS

Picture Gallery

Sistine Chapel

Vatican Museums

St. Peter's Basilica

Vatican Museums

Bronze Doors

Apostolic Palace

Tower of Nicholas

ST. PETER'S SQUARE

Church of St. Anne

St. Anne's Gate

Swiss Guard Barracks

ROME

OLD CITY of JERUSALEM

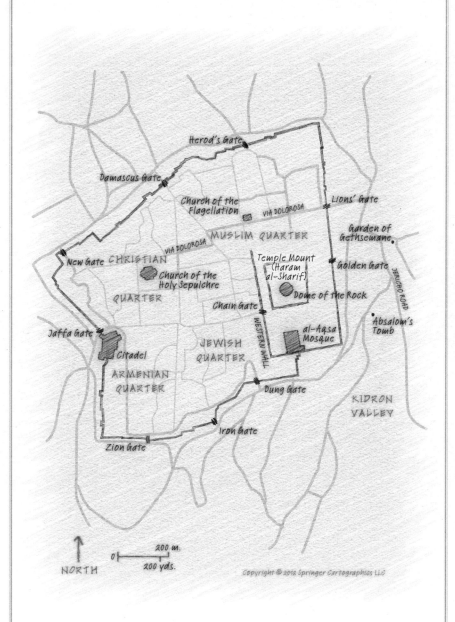

Copyright © 2012 Springer Cartographics LLC

PART ONE

CITY
OF THE
DEAD

VATICAN CITY

IT WAS NICCOLÒ MORETTI, CARETAKER of St. Peter's Basilica, who made the discovery that started it all. The time was 6:24 a.m., but owing to a wholly innocent error of transcription, the Vatican's first official statement incorrectly reported it as 6:42. It was one of numerous missteps, large and small, that would lead many to conclude the Holy See had something to hide, which was indeed the case. The Roman Catholic Church, said a noteworthy dissident, was but one scandal away from oblivion. The last thing His Holiness needed now was a dead body in the sacred heart of Christendom.

A scandal was the last thing Niccolò Moretti had been expecting to find that morning when he arrived at the Vatican one hour earlier than his usual time. Dressed in dark trousers and a knee-length gray coat, he was scarcely visible as he hurried across the darkened piazza toward the steps of the Basilica. Glancing to his right, he saw lights burning in the third-floor windows of the Apostolic

Palace. His Holiness Pope Paul VII was already awake. Moretti wondered whether the Holy Father had slept at all. The Vatican was swirling with rumors he was suffering from a crippling bout of insomnia, that he spent most nights writing in his private study or walking alone in the gardens. The caretaker had seen it before. Eventually, they all lost the ability to sleep.

Moretti heard voices behind him and, turning, saw a pair of Curial priests materialize from the gloom. They were engaged in animated conversation and paid him no heed as they marched toward the Bronze Doors and melted once more into the shadows. The children of Rome called them *bagarozzi*—black beetles. Moretti had used the word once as a child and had been scolded by none other than Pope Pius XII. He'd never said it since. When one is chastised by the Vicar of Christ, he thought now, one rarely repeats the same offense.

He hiked up the steps of the Basilica and slipped into the portico. Five doors led into the nave. All were sealed except for the one at the far left, the Door of Death. In the opening stood Father Jacobo, an emaciated-looking Mexican cleric with strawlike gray hair. He stepped aside so Moretti could enter, then closed the door and lowered the heavy bar. "I'll come back at seven to let in your men," the priest said. "Be careful up there, Niccolò. You're not as young as you used to be."

The priest withdrew. Moretti dipped his fingers in holy water and made the sign of the cross before setting out up the center of the vast nave. Where others might have paused to gaze in awe, Moretti forged on with the familiarity of a man entering his own home. As chief of the *sampietrini*, the official caretakers of the Basilica, he had been coming to St. Peter's six mornings a week for the past twenty-seven years. It was because of Moretti and his men that the Basilica glowed with heaven's light while the other great churches of Europe seemed forever shrouded in darkness. Moretti considered himself not only a servant of the papacy but a partner in the enterprise. The popes were entrusted with the care of one billion Roman Catholic souls, but it was Niccolò Moretti who looked after the mighty Basilica that symbolized their earthly power. He knew every square inch of the building, from the peak of Michelangelo's dome to the depths of the crypt—all forty-four altars, twenty-seven chapels, eight hundred columns, four hundred statues, and three hundred windows. He knew where it was cracked and where it leaked. He knew when it was feeling well and when it was in pain. The Basilica, when it spoke, whispered into the ear of Niccolò Moretti.

St. Peter's had a way of shrinking mere mortals, and Moretti, as he made his way toward the Papal Altar in the gray coat of his uniform, looked remarkably like a thimble come to life. He genuflected before the Confessio and then tilted his face skyward. Soaring nearly one hundred feet above him was the baldacchino, four twisting columns of bronze and gold crowned by a majestic canopy. On that morning, it was partially concealed by an aluminum scaffolding. Bernini's masterpiece, with its ornate figures and sprigs of olive and bay, was a magnet for dust and smoke. Every year, in the week preceding the beginning of Lent, Moretti and his men gave it a thorough cleaning. The Vatican was a place of timeless ritual, and there was ritual, too, in the cleaning of the baldacchino. Laid down by Moretti himself, it stated that once the scaffolding was in place, he was always the first to scale it. The view from the summit was one that only a handful of people had ever seen—and Niccolò Moretti, as chief of the *sampietrini*, demanded the privilege of beholding it first.

Moretti climbed to the pinnacle of the front column, then, after attaching his safety line, inched his way on all fours up the slope of the canopy. At the very apex of the baldacchino was a globe supported by four ribs and crowned by a cross. Here was the most sacred spot in the Roman Catholic Church, the vertical axis running from the exact center of the dome straight down into the Tomb of St. Peter. It represented the very idea on which the enterprise rested. *You are Peter and upon this rock I will build my church.* As the first crepuscular rays of light illuminated the interior of the Basilica, Moretti, faithful servant of the popes, could almost feel the finger of God tapping him on the shoulder.

As usual, time slipped from his grasp. Later, when questioned by the Vatican police, he would be unable to recall exactly how long he had been atop the baldacchino before he saw the object for the first time. From Moretti's lofty perspective, it appeared to be a broken-winged bird. He assumed it to be something innocent, a tarpaulin left by another *sampietrino* or perhaps a scarf dropped by a tourist. They were always leaving their possessions behind, Moretti thought, including things that had no business being in a church.

Regardless, it had to be investigated, and so Moretti, the spell broken, maneuvered himself cautiously around and made the long descent to the floor. He set out across the transept but within a few paces realized the object was not a discarded scarf or tarpaulin at all. Moving closer, he could see the blood dried on the sacred marble of his Basilica and the eyes staring upward into the dome, sightlessly, like his four hundred statues. "Dear God in heaven," he whispered as he hurried down the nave. "Please take pity on her poor soul."

The public would know little of the events immediately following Niccolò Moretti's discovery, for they were carried out in the strictest tradition of the Vatican, in complete secrecy and with a hint of Jesuitical low cunning. No one beyond the walls would know, for example, that the first person Moretti sought out was the cardinal rector of the Basilica, an exacting German from Cologne with a well-honed instinct for self-preservation. The cardinal had been around long enough to recognize trouble when he saw it, which explained why he neglected to report the incident to the police, choosing instead to summon the true keeper of the law inside the Vatican.

Consequently, five minutes later, Niccolò Moretti would bear witness to an extraordinary scene—the private secretary to His Holiness Pope Paul VII picking through the pockets of a dead woman on the floor of the Basilica. The monsignor removed a single item and then set out for the Apostolic Palace. By the time he reached his office, he had settled on a course of action. There would have to be two investigations, he concluded, one for public consumption, the other for his own. And for the private inquiry to be successful, it would have to be carried out by a person of trust and discretion. Not surprisingly, the monsignor chose as his inquisitor a man much like himself. A fallen angel in black. A sinner in the city of saints.

2

PIAZZA DI SPAGNA, ROME

THE RESTORER DRESSED IN DARKNESS, silently, so as not to wake the woman. Posed as she was now, with her tousled chestnut hair and wide mouth, she reminded him of Modigliani's *Red Nude*. He placed a loaded Beretta pistol next to her on the bed. Then he tugged at the duvet, exposing her heavy, rounded breasts, and the masterpiece was complete.

Somewhere a church bell tolled. A hand rose from the bedding, warm and lined from sleep, and drew the restorer down. The woman kissed him, as always, with her eyes closed. Her hair smelled of vanilla. On her lips was the faintest trace of the wine she had drunk the previous evening in a restaurant on the Aventine Hill.

The woman released him, murmured something unintelligible, and drifted back to sleep. The restorer covered her. Then he wedged a second Beretta into the waistband of his faded blue jeans and slipped out of the apartment. Downstairs, the pavements of the

Via Gregoriana shimmered in the half-light like a newly varnished painting. The restorer stood in the doorway of the building for a moment while pretending to consult his mobile phone. It took him only a few seconds to spot the man watching him from behind the wheel of a parked Lancia sedan. He gave the man a friendly wave, the ultimate professional insult, and set off toward the Church of the Trinità dei Monti.

At the top of the Spanish Steps, an old *gattara* was dropping scraps of food into the sea of skinny Roman cats swirling at her feet. Dressed in a shabby overcoat and headscarf, she eyed the restorer warily as he headed down to the piazza. He was below average in height—five foot eight, perhaps, but no more—and had the spare physique of a cyclist. The face was long and narrow at the chin, with wide cheekbones and a slender nose that looked as though it had been carved from wood. The eyes were an unnatural shade of green; the hair was dark and shot with gray at the temples. It was a face of many possible origins, and the restorer possessed the linguistic gifts to put it to good use. Over the course of a long career, he had worked in Italy and elsewhere under numerous pseudonyms and nationalities. The Italian security services, aware of his past exploits, had tried to prevent his entry into the country but had relented after the quiet intervention of the Holy See. For reasons never made public, the restorer had been present at the Vatican several years earlier when it was attacked by Islamic terrorists. More than seven hundred people were killed that day, including four cardinals and eight Curial bishops. The Holy Father himself had been slightly wounded. He might very well have been among the dead had the restorer not shielded him from a shoulder-fired missile and then carried him to safety.

The Italians had imposed two conditions upon the restorer's return—that he reside in the country under his real name and that he tolerate the presence of occasional physical surveillance. The first he accepted with a certain relief, for after a lifetime on the secret battlefield he was anxious to shed his many aliases and to assume something of a normal life. The second condition, however, had proved more burdensome. The task of following him invariably fell to young trainees. Initially, the restorer had taken mild professional offense until he realized he was being used as the subject of a daily master class in the techniques of street surveillance. He obliged his students by evading them from time to time, always keeping a few of his better moves in reserve lest he find himself in circumstances that required slipping the Italian net.

And so it was that as he made his way through the quiet streets of Rome, he was trailed by no fewer than three probationers of varying skills from the Italian security service. His route presented them with few challenges and no surprises. It bore him westward across the ancient center of the city and terminated, as usual, at St. Anne's Gate, the business entrance of the Vatican. Because it was technically an international frontier, the watchers had no choice but to entrust the restorer to the care of the Swiss Guard, who admitted him with only a cursory glance at his credentials.

The restorer bade the watchers farewell with a doff of his flat cap and then set out along the Via Belvedere, past the butter-colored Church of St. Anne, the Vatican printing offices, and the headquarters of the Vatican Bank. At the Central Post Office, he turned to the right and crossed a series of courtyards until he came to an unmarked door. Beyond it was a tiny foyer, where a Vatican gendarme sat in a glass box.

"Where's the usual duty officer?" the restorer asked in rapid Italian.

"Lazio played Milan last night," the gendarme said with an apathetic shrug.

He ran the restorer's ID badge through the magnetic card swipe and motioned for him to pass through the metal detector. When the machine emitted a shrill pinging, the restorer stopped in his tracks and nodded wearily at the gendarme's computer. On the screen, next to the restorer's unsmiling photograph, was a special notice written by the chief of the Vatican Security Office. The gendarme read it twice to make certain he understood it correctly, then, looking up, found himself staring directly into the restorer's unusually green eyes. Something about the calmness of his expression—and the hint of a mischievous smile—caused the officer to give an involuntary shiver. He nodded toward the next set of doors and watched intently as the restorer passed through them without a sound.

So, the gendarme thought, the rumors were true. Gabriel Allon, renowned restorer of Old Master paintings, retired Israeli spy and assassin, and savior of the Holy Father, had returned to the Vatican. With a single keystroke, the officer cleared the file from the screen. Then he made the sign of the cross and for the first time in many years recited the act of contrition. It was an odd choice, he thought, because he was guilty of no sin other than curiosity. But surely that was to be forgiven. After all, it wasn't every day a lowly Vatican policeman had the chance to gaze into the face of a legend.

Fluorescent lights, dimmed to their night settings, hummed softly as Gabriel entered the main conservation lab of the Vatican Picture Gallery. As usual, he was the first to arrive. He closed the door and waited for the reassuring thud of the automatic locks, then made his way along a row of storage cabinets toward the floor-to-ceiling black curtains at the far end of the room. A small sign warned the area beyond the curtains was strictly off-limits. After slipping through the breach, Gabriel went immediately to his trolley and carefully examined the disposition of his supplies. His containers of pigment and medium were precisely as he had left them. So were his Winsor & Newton Series 7 sable brushes, including the one with a telltale spot of azure near the tip that he always left at a precise thirty-degree angle relative to the others. It suggested the cleaning staff had once again resisted the temptation to enter his workspace. He doubted whether his colleagues had shown similar restraint. In fact, he had it on the highest authority that his tiny curtained enclave had displaced the espresso machine in the break room as the most popular gathering spot for museum staff.

He removed his leather jacket and switched on a pair of standing halogen lamps. *The Deposition of Christ*, widely regarded as Caravaggio's finest painting, glowed under the intense white light. Gabriel stood motionless before the towering canvas for several minutes, hand pressed to his chin, head tilted to one side, eyes fixed on the haunting image. Nicodemus, muscular and barefoot, stared directly back as he carefully lowered the pale, lifeless body of Christ toward the slab of funerary stone where it would be prepared for entombment. Next to Nicodemus was John the Evangelist, who, in his desperation to touch his beloved teacher one last time, had inadvertently opened the wound in the Savior's side. Watching silently over them were the Madonna and the Magdalene, their heads bowed, while Mary of Cleophas raised her arms toward the heavens in lamentation. It was a work of both immense sorrow and tenderness, made more striking by Caravaggio's revolutionary use of light. Even Gabriel, who had been toiling over the painting for weeks, always felt as though he were intruding on a heartbreaking moment of private anguish.

The painting had darkened with age, particularly along the left side of the canvas where the entrance of the tomb had once been

clearly visible. There were some in the Italian art establishment—
including Giacomo Benedetti, the famed Caravaggisto from the
Istituto Centrale per il Restauro—who wondered whether the
tomb should be returned to prominence. Benedetti had been forced
to share his opinion with a reporter from *La Repubblica* because
the restorer chosen for the project had, for inexplicable reasons,
failed to seek his advice before commencing work. What's more,
Benedetti found it disheartening that the museum had refused to
make public the restorer's identity. For many days, the papers had
bristled with familiar calls for the Vatican to lift the veil of silence.
How was it possible, they fumed, that a national treasure like *The
Deposition* could be entrusted to a man with no name? The tem-
pest, such as it was, finally ended when Antonio Calvesi, the Vatican's chief conservator, acknowledged that the man in question
had impeccable credentials, including two masterful restorations
for the Holy See—Reni's *Crucifixion of St. Peter* and Poussin's
Martyrdom of St. Erasmus. Calvesi neglected to mention that both
projects, conducted at a remote Umbrian villa, had been delayed
due to operations the restorer had carried out for the secret intelligence service of the State of Israel.

Gabriel had hoped to restore the Caravaggio in seclusion as
well, but Calvesi's decree that the painting never leave the Vatican
had left him with no choice but to work inside the lab, surrounded
by the permanent staff. He was the subject of intense curiosity,
but then, that was to be expected. For many years, they had believed him to be an unusually gifted if temperamental restorer
named Mario Delvecchio, only to learn that he was something
quite different. But if they felt betrayed, they gave no sign of it.
Indeed, for the most part, they treated him with a tenderness that
came naturally to those who care for damaged objects. They were
quiet in his presence, mindful to a point of his obvious need for

privacy, and were careful not to look too long into his eyes, as if they feared what they might find there. On those rare occasions when they addressed him, their remarks were limited mainly to pleasantries and art. And when office banter turned to the politics of the Middle East, they respectfully muted their criticism of the country of his birth. Only Enrico Bacci, who had lobbied intensely for the Caravaggio restoration, objected to Gabriel's presence on moral grounds. He referred to the black curtain as "the Separation Fence" and adhered a "Free Palestine" poster to the wall of his tiny office.

Gabriel poured a tiny pool of Mowolith 20 medium onto his palette, added a few granules of dry pigment, and thinned the mixture with Arcosolve until it reached the desired consistency and intensity. Then he slipped on a magnifying visor and focused his gaze on the right hand of Christ. It hung in the manner of Michelangelo's Pietà, with the fingers pointing allegorically toward the corner of the funerary stone. For several days, Gabriel had been attempting to repair a series of abrasions along the knuckles. He was not the first artist to struggle over the composition; Caravaggio himself had painted five other versions before finally completing the painting in 1604. Unlike his previous commission—a depiction of the Virgin's death so controversial it was eventually removed from the church of Santa Maria della Scala—*The Deposition* was instantly hailed as a masterwork, and its reputation quickly spread throughout Europe. In 1797, the painting caught the eye of Napoléon Bonaparte, one of history's greatest looters of art and antiquities, and it was carted over the Alps to Paris. It remained there until 1817, when it was returned to the custody of the papacy and hung in the Vatican.

For several hours, Gabriel had the lab to himself. Then, at the thoroughly Roman hour of ten, he heard the snap of the automatic locks, followed by Enrico Bacci's lumbering plod. Next came Donatella Ricci, an Early Renaissance expert who whispered soothingly to the paintings in her care. After that it was Tommaso Antonelli, one of the stars of the Sistine Chapel restoration, who always tiptoed around the lab in his crepe-soled shoes with the stealth of a night thief.

Finally, at half past ten, Gabriel heard the distinctive tap of Antonio Calvesi's handmade shoes over the linoleum floor. A few seconds later, Calvesi came whirling through the black curtain like a matador. With his disheveled forelock and perpetually loosened necktie, he had the air of a man who was running late for an appointment he would rather not keep. He settled himself atop a tall stool and nibbled thoughtfully at the stem of his reading glasses while inspecting Gabriel's work.

"Not bad," Calvesi said with genuine admiration. "Did you do that on your own, or did Caravaggio drop by to handle the inpainting himself?"

"I asked for his help," Gabriel replied, "but he was unavailable."

"Really? Where was he?"

"Back in prison at Tor di Nona. Apparently, he was roaming the Campo Marzio with a sword."

"Again?" Calvesi leaned closer to the canvas. "If I were you, I'd consider replacing those lines of craquelure along the index finger."

Gabriel raised his magnifying visor and offered Calvesi the palette. The Italian responded with a conciliatory smile. He was a gifted restorer in his own right—indeed, in their youth, the two men had been rivals—but it had been many years since he had actually applied a brush to canvas. These days, Calvesi spent most of his time pursuing money. For all its earthly riches, the Vatican was forced to rely on the kindness of strangers to care for its extraordinary collection of art and antiquities. Gabriel's paltry stipend was a fraction of what he earned for a private restoration. It was, however, a small price to pay for the once-in-a-lifetime opportunity to clean a painting like *The Deposition*.

"Any chance you might actually finish it sometime soon?" Calvesi asked. "I'd like to have it back in the gallery for Holy Week."

"When does it fall this year?"

"I'll pretend I didn't hear that." Calvesi picked absently through the contents of Gabriel's trolley.

"Something on your mind, Antonio?"

"One of our most important patrons is dropping by the museum tomorrow. An American. Very deep pockets. The kind of pockets that keep this place functioning."

"And?"

"He's asked to see the Caravaggio. In fact, he was wondering whether someone might be willing to give him a brief lecture on the restoration."

"Have you been sniffing the acetone again, Antonio?"

"Won't you at least let him *see* it?"

"No."

"Why not?"

Gabriel gazed at the painting for a moment in silence. "Because it wouldn't be fair to him," he said finally.

"The patron?"

"Caravaggio. Restoration is supposed to be our little secret, Antonio. Our job is to come and go without being seen. And it should be done in private."

"What if I get Caravaggio's permission?"

"Just don't ask him while he has a sword in his hand." Gabriel lowered the magnifying visor and resumed his work.

"You know, Gabriel, you're just like him. Stubborn, conceited, and far too talented for your own good."

"Is there anything else I can do for you, Antonio?" asked Gabriel, tapping his brush impatiently against his palette.

"Not me," Calvesi replied, "but you're wanted in the chapel."

"Which chapel?"

"The only one that matters."

Gabriel wiped his brush and placed it carefully on the trolley. Calvesi smiled.

"You share one other trait with your friend Caravaggio."

"What's that?"

"Paranoia."

"Caravaggio had good reason to be paranoid. And so do I."

3

THE SISTINE CHAPEL

THE 5,896 SQUARE FEET OF the Sistine Chapel are perhaps the most visited piece of real estate in Rome. Each day, several thousand tourists pour through its rather ordinary doors to crane their necks in wonder at the glorious frescoes that adorn its walls and ceiling, watched over by blue-uniformed gendarmes who seem to have no other job than to constantly plead for *silenzio*. To stand alone in the chapel, however, is to experience it as its namesake Pope Sixtus IV had intended. With the lights dimmed and the crowds absent, it is almost possible to hear the quarrels of conclaves past or to see Michelangelo atop his scaffolding putting the finishing touches on *The Creation of Adam*.

On the western wall of the chapel is Michelangelo's other Sistine masterwork, *The Last Judgment*. Begun thirty years after the ceiling was completed, it depicts the Apocalypse and the Second Coming of Christ, with all the souls of humanity rising or falling to meet their eternal reward or punishment in a swirl of color and anguish. The fresco is the first thing the cardinals see when they enter the chapel to choose a new pope, and on that morning it seemed the primary preoccupation of a single priest. Tall, lean, and strikingly handsome, he was cloaked in a black cassock with a magenta-colored sash and piping, handmade by an ecclesiastical tailor near the Pantheon. His dark eyes radiated a fierce and uncompromising intelligence, while the set of his jaw indicated he was a dangerous man to cross, which had the added benefit of being the truth. Monsignor Luigi Donati, private secretary to His Holiness Pope Paul VII, had few friends behind the walls of the Vatican, only occasional allies and sworn rivals. They often referred to him as a clerical Rasputin, the true power behind the papal throne, or "the Black Pope," an unflattering reference to his Jesuit past. Donati didn't mind. Though he was a devoted student of Ignatius and Augustine, he tended to rely more on the guidance of a secular Italian philosopher named Machiavelli, who counseled that it is far better for a prince to be feared than loved.

Among Donati's many transgressions, at least in the eyes of some members of the Vatican's gossipy papal court, were his unusually close ties to the notorious spy and assassin Gabriel Allon. Theirs was a partnership that defied history and faith—Donati, the soldier of Christ, and Gabriel, the man of art who by accident of birth had been compelled to lead a clandestine life of violence. Despite those obvious differences, they had much in common. Both were men of high morals and principle, and both believed that matters of consequence were best handled in private. During their long friendship, Gabriel had acted as both the Vatican's protector and a revealer of some of its darkest secrets—and Donati, the Holy Father's hard man in black, had served as his willing accomplice. As a result, the two men had done much to quietly improve the tortured relationship between the world's Catholics and their twelve million distant spiritual cousins, the Jews.

Gabriel stood wordlessly at Donati's side and gazed up at *The Last Judgment*. Near the center of the image, adjacent to the left foot of Christ, was one of two self-portraits Michelangelo had hidden within the frescoes. Here he had depicted himself as St. Bartholomew holding his own flayed skin, perhaps a not-so-subtle rejoinder to contemporary critics of his work.

"I assume you've been here before," said Donati, his sonorous voice echoing in the empty chapel.

"Just once," said Gabriel after a moment. "It was in the autumn of 1972, long before the restoration. I was posing as a German student traveling Europe. I came here in the afternoon and stayed until the guards forced me to leave. The next day . . ."

His voice trailed off. The next day, with Michelangelo's vision of the end times still fresh in his mind, Gabriel entered the foyer of a drab apartment building in the Piazza Annibaliano. Standing before the elevator, a bottle of fig wine in one hand and a copy of *A Thousand and One Nights* in the other, was a skinny Palestinian intellectual named Wadal Zwaiter. The Palestinian was a member of the terrorist group Black September, perpetrators of the Munich Olympics massacre, and for that he had been secretly sentenced to death. Gabriel had calmly asked Zwaiter to say his name aloud. Then he had shot him eleven times, once for each Israeli butchered at Munich. In the months that followed, Gabriel would assassinate five other members of Black September, the opening act of a distinguished career that lasted far longer than he ever intended. Working at the behest of his mentor, the legendary spymaster Ari Shamron, he had carried out some of the most fabled operations in the history of Israeli intelligence. Now, blown and battered, he had returned to Rome, to the place where it all began. And one of the few people in the world he could trust was a Catholic priest named Luigi Donati.

Gabriel turned his back to *The Last Judgment* and gazed down the length of the rectangular chapel, past the frescoes by Botticelli and Perugino, toward the little potbellied stove where ballots were burned during papal conclaves. Then he recited, " 'The House which King Solomon built for the Lord was sixty cubits long, twenty cubits wide, and thirty cubits high.' "

"Kings," said Donati. "Chapter six, verse two."

Gabriel lifted his face toward the ceiling. "Your forefathers built this rather simple chapel to the exact dimensions of the Temple of Solomon for a reason. But why? Did they wish to pay tribute to their elder brothers the Jews? Or were they declaring that the old law had been superseded by the new law, that the ancient temple had been brought to Rome, along with the sacred contents of the Holy of Holies?"

"Perhaps it was a little of both," said Donati philosophically.

"How diplomatic of you, Monsignor."

"I was trained as a Jesuit. Obfuscation is our strong suit."

Gabriel pondered his wristwatch. "It's rather late in the morning for this place to be empty."

"Yes," Donati said absently.

"Where are the tourists, Luigi?"

"For the moment, only the museums are open to the public."

"Why?"

"We have a problem."

"Where?"

Donati frowned and tilted his head toward the left.

The stairwell leading from the glory of the Sistine Chapel to the most magnificent church in Christendom is decidedly ugly. A gray-green tube with slick cement walls, it deposited Gabriel and Donati into the Basilica, not far from the Chapel of the Pietà. In the center of the nave, a yellow tarpaulin was spread over the unmistakable form of a human corpse. Standing over it were two men. Gabriel knew them both. One was Colonel Alois Metzler, commandant of the Pontifical Swiss Guard. The other was Lorenzo Vitale, chief of the Corpo della Gendarmeria, the Vatican's 130-member police force. In his previous life, Vitale had investigated government corruption cases for Italy's powerful Guardia di Finanza. Metzler was retired Swiss Army. His predecessor, Karl Brunner, had been killed in the al-Qaeda terrorist attack on the Vatican.

The two men looked up in unison and watched Gabriel crossing the nave at the side of the second-most powerful man in the Roman Catholic Church. Metzler was clearly displeased. He extended his hand toward Gabriel with the cold precision of a Swiss timepiece and nodded his head once in formal greeting. He was Donati's equal in height and build but had been blessed by the Almighty with the jutting, angular face of a hound. He wore a dark gray suit, a white shirt, and a banker's silver necktie. His receding hair was shorn to the length of stubble; small, rimless spectacles framed a pair of judgmental blue eyes. Metzler had friends inside the Swiss security service, which meant that he knew about Gabriel's past exploits on the soil of his homeland. His presence in the Basilica was intriguing. Strictly speaking, dead bodies at the Vatican fell under the jurisdiction of the gendarmes, not the Swiss Guard—unless, of course, there was an element of papal security involved. If that were the case, Metzler would be free to poke his snout anywhere he pleased. Almost anywhere, thought Gabriel, for there were places behind the walls where even the commander of the palace guard was forbidden to enter.

Donati exchanged a look with Vitale, then instructed the police chief to remove the tarpaulin. It was obvious the body had fallen from a great height. What remained was a split sack of skin filled with shattered bone and organs. Remarkably, the attractive face was largely intact. So was the identification badge around the neck. It stated that the bearer was an employee of the Vatican Museums. Gabriel didn't bother to read the name. The dead woman was Claudia Andreatti, a curator in the antiquities division.

Gabriel crouched next to the body with the ease of someone used to being in the presence of the newly dead and examined it as though it were a painting in need of restoration. She was dressed, like all the laywomen of the Vatican, professionally but piously: dark trousers, a gray cardigan, a white blouse. Her woolen overcoat was unbuttoned and had arranged itself across the floor like an unfurled cape. The right arm was draped across the abdomen. The left was extended in a straight line from the shoulder, the wrist slightly bent. Gabriel carefully lifted a few strands of the shoulder-length hair from the face, revealing a pair of eyes that remained open and vaguely watchful. The last time he had seen them, they had been appraising him in a stairwell of the museum. The encounter had occurred a few minutes before nine the previous evening. Gabriel was just leaving after a long session before the Caravaggio; Claudia was clutching a batch of files to her breast and heading back to her office. Her demeanor, though somewhat harried, was hardly that of a woman about to kill herself in St. Peter's. In fact, thought Gabriel, it had been mildly flirtatious.

"You knew her?" asked Vitale.

"No, but I knew who she was." It was a professional compulsion. Even in retirement, Gabriel couldn't help but assemble a mental dossier on those around him.

"I noticed you were both working late last night." The Italian managed to make it sound like an offhand remark, which it wasn't. "According to the log at the security desk, you exited the museum at 8:47. Dottoressa Andreatti left a short time later, at 8:56."

"By then, I'd already left the territory of the city-state via St. Anne's Gate."

"I know." Vitale gave a humorless smile. "I checked those logs, too."

"So I'm no longer a suspect in the death of my colleague?" Gabriel asked sardonically.

"Forgive me, Signor Allon, but people do have a way of dying whenever you show up at the Vatican."

Gabriel lifted his gaze from the body and looked at Vitale. Though he was now in his early sixties, the police chief had the handsome features and permanent suntan of an aging Italian movie idol, the sort who drives down the Via Veneto in an open-top car with a younger woman at his side. At the Guardia di Finanza, he had been regarded as an unbending zealot, a crusader who had taken it upon himself to eliminate the corruption that had been the scourge of Italian politics and commerce for generations. Having failed, he had taken refuge behind the walls of the Vatican to protect his pope and his Church. Like Gabriel, he was a man used to being in the presence of the dead. Even so, he seemed incapable of looking at the woman on the floor of his beloved Basilica.

"Who found her?" asked Gabriel.

Vitale nodded toward a group of *sampietrini* standing halfway down the nave.

"Did they touch anything?"

"Why do you ask?"

"She's barefoot."

"We found one of her shoes near the baldacchino. The other was found in front of the Altar of St. Joseph. We assume they came off during the fall. Or . . ."

"Or what?"

"It's possible she dropped them from the gallery of the dome before jumping."

"Why?"

"Perhaps she wanted to see whether she really had the nerve to go through with it," Metzler suggested. "A moment of doubt."

Gabriel looked heavenward. Just above the Latin inscription at the base of the dome was the viewing platform. Running along the edge was a waist-high metal balustrade. It was enough to make suicide difficult, but not impossible. In fact, every few months, Vitale's gendarmes had to prevent some poor soul from hurling himself into the blessed abyss. But late in the evening, when the Basilica was closed to the public, Claudia Andreatti would have had the gallery entirely to herself.

"Time of death?" asked Gabriel quietly, as though he were posing the question to the corpse itself.

"Unclear," replied Vitale.

Gabriel looked around the interior of the Basilica, as if to remind the Italian of their whereabouts. Then he asked how it was possible there was no established time of death.

"Once each week," Vitale answered, "the Central Security Office disables the cameras for a routine system reset. We do it in the evening when the Basilica is closed. Usually, it's not a problem."

"How long does the shutdown last?"

"Nine to midnight."

"That's quite a coincidence." Gabriel looked at the body again. "What do you suppose the odds are that she decided to kill herself during the time the cameras were switched off?"

"Perhaps it wasn't a coincidence at all," said Metzler. "Perhaps she chose the time intentionally so there would be no video recording of her death."

"How would she have known about the cameras being shut down?"

"It's common knowledge around here."

Gabriel shook his head slowly. Despite numerous outside threats, terrorist and otherwise, security inside the borders of the world's smallest country remained startlingly lax. What's more, those who worked behind the walls enjoyed extraordinary freedom of movement. They knew the doors that were never locked, the chapels that were never used, and the storerooms where it was possible to plot, scheme, or caress the flesh of a lover in complete privacy. They also knew the secret passageways leading into the Basilica. Gabriel knew one or two himself.

"Was there anyone else in the Basilica at the time?"

"Not that we're aware of," replied Vitale.

"But you can't rule it out."

"That's correct. But no one reported anything unusual."

"Where's her handbag?"

"She left it up in the gallery before jumping."

"Was anything missing?"

"Not that we know of."

But there *was* something missing; Gabriel was certain of it. He closed his eyes and for an instant saw Claudia as she had been the previous evening—the warm smile, the flirtatious glance from her brown eyes, the batch of files she had been clutching to her breast.

And the cross of gold around her neck.

"I'd like to have a look at the gallery," he said.

"I'll take you up," answered Vitale.

"That won't be necessary." Gabriel rose. "I'm sure the monsignor will be good enough to show me the way."

4

ST. PETER'S BASILICA

T HERE WERE TWO WAYS TO make the ascent from the main level of the Basilica to the base of the dome—a long, twisting stairwell or an elevator large enough to accommodate two dozen well-fed pilgrims. Donati, an unrepentant smoker, suggested the elevator, but Gabriel headed for the steps instead.

"The elevator is shut down in the afternoon after the last group of tourists is admitted. There's no way Claudia could have used it late at night."

"That's true," Donati said with a morose glance at his handmade loafers, "but it's several hundred steps."

"And we're going to search every one."

"For what?"

"When I saw Claudia last night, she was wearing a gold cross around her neck."

"And?"

"It's no longer there."

Gabriel mounted the first step with Donati at his heels and climbed slowly upward. His careful search of the stairwell produced nothing but a few discarded admission tickets and a crumpled flier advertising the services of a less-than-saintly enterprise involving young women from Eastern Europe. At the top of the stairs was a landing. In one direction was the roof terrace; in the other, the viewing gallery for the dome. Gabriel peered over the balustrade at the now-miniaturized figures of Vitale and Metzler, then set out slowly along the catwalk with his eyes lowered toward the time-worn marble. After a few paces, he found the cross. The clasp was intact, but the thin gold chain had been snapped.

"It's possible she tore it off before climbing over the balustrade," Donati said, examining the broken chain by the light of one of the dome's sixteen windows.

"I suppose anything is possible. But the more likely explanation is that the chain was broken by someone else."

"Who?"

"The person who killed her." Gabriel was silent for a moment. "Her neck was snapped like a twig, Luigi. I suppose the break could have occurred on impact, but I believe it happened up here. Her killer probably didn't notice he broke the chain of Claudia's cross as well. He did notice the shoes, though. That's why they were found so far apart. He probably hurled them over the barrier before making his escape."

"How certain are you that she was murdered?"

"As certain as you are." Gabriel studied Donati's face carefully. "Something tells me you know more than you're saying, Luigi."

"Guilty as charged."

"Is there anything you wish to confess, Monsignor?"

"Yes," said Donati, peering down at the floor of the Basilica. "It's possible the person responsible for Claudia Andreatti's death might be standing right in front of you."

They headed out onto the roof terrace of the Basilica to walk among the apostles and the saints. Donati's black cassock billowed and snapped in the cold wind. In one hand, entwined around his fingers like the beads of a rosary, was Claudia's gold necklace.

"She was conducting . . ." Donati paused for a moment, as if searching for the appropriate word. "An investigation," he said at last.

"What sort of investigation?"

"The only kind we ever do around here."

"A secret investigation," said Gabriel. "Ordered by you, of course."

"At the behest of the Holy Father," Donati added hastily.

"And the nature of this investigation?"

"As you know, there's been a debate raging within the art world and the curatorial community over who owns antiquity. For centuries, the great empires of Europe looted the treasures of the ancient world with reckless abandon. The Rosetta Stone, the Elgin Marbles, the great temples of ancient Egypt—the list goes on and on. Now the source countries are demanding the symbols of their cultural heritage be returned. And they often turn to the police and courts for help in getting them back."

"You were afraid the Vatican Museums were vulnerable?"

"We probably are." Donati paused along the façade of the Basilica and pointed toward the Egyptian obelisk in the center of the square. "It's one of eight here in Rome. They were built by craftsmen from an empire that no longer exists and brought here by soldiers of an empire that also no longer exists. Should we send them back to Egypt? What about the Venus de Milo or the Winged Victory of Samothrace? Would they really be better off in Athens than in the Louvre? Would more people see them?"

"You sound like a bit of a hawk on this issue."

"My enemies often mistake me for a liberal who's trying to destroy the Church. In reality, despite my Jesuit education, I am as doctrinaire as they come. I believe that great treasures of antiquity should be displayed in great museums."

"Why Claudia?"

"Because she disagreed with me vehemently," Donati replied. "I didn't want the report to be a whitewash. I wanted the potential worst-case scenario, the unvarnished truth about the source of every piece in our possession. The Vatican's collection is among the oldest and largest in the world. And much of it is completely unprovenanced."

"Which means you don't know exactly where it came from."

"Or even when it was acquired." Donati shook his head slowly. "You might find this hard to believe, but until the 1930s, the Vatican Library had no proper catalog system. Books were stored by size and color. *Size* and *color*," Donati repeated incredulously. "I'm afraid the record keeping at the museums wasn't much better."

"So you asked Claudia to undertake a review of the collection to see whether any of the pieces might be tainted."

"With a special emphasis on the Egyptian and Etruscan collections," Donati added. "But I should stipulate that Claudia's inquiry was completely defensive in nature. In a way, it was a bit like a campaign manager who investigates his own candidate in order to uncover any dirt his opponent might find."

"And if she'd discovered a problem?"

"We would have weighed our options carefully," Donati said

with lawyerly precision. "Lengthy deliberation is our specialty. It's one of the reasons we're still around after two thousand years."

The two men turned and started slowly back toward the dome. Gabriel asked how long Claudia had been working on the project.

"Six months."

"Who else knew about it?"

"Only the director of the museum. And the Holy Father, of course."

"Had she given you any findings?"

"Not yet." Donati hesitated. "But we had a meeting scheduled. She said she had something urgent to tell me."

"What was it?"

"She didn't say."

"When were you supposed to meet?"

"Last night." Donati paused, then added, "At nine o'clock."

Gabriel stopped and turned toward Donati. "Why so late?"

"Running a church of one billion souls is a big job. It was the only time I was free."

"What happened?"

"Claudia called my assistant and asked to reschedule the meeting for this morning. She didn't give a reason."

Donati removed a cigarette from an elegant gold case and tapped it against the cover before igniting it with a gold lighter. Not for the first time, Gabriel had to remind himself that the tall man in black was actually a Catholic priest.

"In case you're wondering," Donati said, "I did not kill Claudia Andreatti. Nor do I know why anyone would want her dead. But if it becomes public that I was scheduled to meet with her the evening of her death, I'll be placed in a difficult position, to say the least. And so will the Holy Father."

"Which is why you haven't mentioned any of this to Vitale or Metzler."

Donati was silent.

"What do you want from me, Luigi?"

"I want you to help protect my Church from another scandal. And me, as well."

"What are you suggesting?"

"Two investigations. One will be carried out by Vitale and the gendarmes. It will be short in duration and will conclude that Dottoressa Andreatti took her own life by throwing herself from the gallery of the dome."

"Rome has spoken; the case is closed."

"Amen."

"And the second investigation?"

"Will be carried out by you," Donati said. "And its findings will be presented to only one person."

"The private secretary to His Holiness Pope Paul VII."

Donati nodded.

"I came to Rome to restore a painting, Luigi."

"You wouldn't be in Rome if it wasn't for the intervention of my master and me. And now we need a favor in return."

"How Christlike of you, Monsignor."

"Christ never had to run a church. I do."

Gabriel smiled in spite of himself. "You told the Italian security services you needed me to clean a Caravaggio. Something tells me they won't be pleased if they find out I'm conducting a murder investigation."

"So I suppose we'll have to deceive them. Trust me," Donati added, "it won't be the first time."

They paused along the railing. Directly below, in the small

courtyard outside the entrance to the Vatican necropolis, the body of Claudia Andreatti was being placed in the back of an unmarked van. Standing a few feet away, like a mourner at the side of an open grave, was Lorenzo Vitale.

"I'll need a few things to get started," Gabriel said, watching the Vatican police chief. "And I need you to get them for me without Vitale knowing."

"Such as?"

"A copy of the hard drive of the computer in her office, along with her telephone records and all the documentation she assembled while conducting her review of the Vatican collection."

Donati nodded. "In the meantime," he said, "it might be wise to have a look inside Claudia's apartment before Vitale can obtain clearance from the Italian authorities to do so himself."

"How do you suggest I get through the front door?"

Donati handed Gabriel a ring of keys.

"Where did you get these?"

"Rule number one at the Vatican," Donati said. "Don't ask too many questions."

5

PIAZZA DI SPAGNA, ROME

B Y THE TIME THE VATICAN PRESS OFFICE confirmed that Dr. Claudia Andreatti, the esteemed curator of antiquities, had committed suicide in St. Peter's Basilica, rumors of her demise had thoroughly penetrated the gossipy little village known as the Holy See. Inside the restoration lab, work ceased as the staff gathered around the examination tables to ponder how they had missed the signs of Dr. Andreatti's emotional distress, how it was possible to work with someone for years and know so little about her personal life. Gabriel murmured a few appropriate words of sympathy but for the most part kept to his private corner of the lab. He remained there, alone with the Caravaggio, until late afternoon, when he hiked back to the apartment near the Piazza di Spagna through a freezing drizzle. He found Chiara leaning against the kitchen counter. Her dark hair was held in place by a velvet ribbon at the nape of her neck. Her eyes were fixed on the television, where a reporter for the BBC was recounting a story

of a tragic suicide under a computer-generated banner that read
DEATH IN THE BASILICA. When a still photograph of Claudia appeared on the screen, Chiara shook her head slowly.

"She was such a beautiful girl. Somehow it always seems harder
to understand when they're pretty."

She removed the cork from a bottle of Sangiovese and poured
out two glasses. Gabriel reached for his, then stopped. Dark and
rich, the wine was the color of blood.

"Is something wrong?"

"Donati asked me to have a look at the body."

"Why ever would he do that?"

"He wanted a second opinion."

"He doesn't think she committed suicide?"

"No. And neither do I."

He told Chiara about the broken necklace, about the shoes that
landed too far apart, about the quiet review of the Vatican's antiquities collection. Lastly, he told her about the urgent meeting that
was supposed to take place in Donati's office.

"Now I understand the problem," Chiara said. "Attractive female curator is supposed to meet with powerful private secretary.
Instead, attractive female curator ends up dead."

"Leaving every conspiracy theorist in the world to speculate
that the powerful private secretary was somehow involved in the
curator's death."

"Which explains why he's asking you to help with a cover-up."

"That's not how I would describe it."

"How would you?"

"A private fact-finding mission, like the ones we used to carry
out for King Saul Boulevard."

King Saul Boulevard was the address of Israel's foreign intelligence service. It had a long and deliberately misleading name that

had very little to do with the true nature of its work. Even retired agents like Gabriel and Chiara referred to it as the Office and nothing else.

"This has all the makings of yet another Vatican scandal," Chiara warned. "And if you're not careful, your friend Monsignor Luigi Donati is going to drop you right in the middle of it."

She switched off the television without another word and carried their wineglasses into the sitting room. On the coffee table was a tray of assorted bruschetta. Chiara watched Gabriel intently as he selected one smeared with artichoke hearts and ricotta cheese and washed it down with the Sangiovese. Her eyes, wide and oriental in shape, were the color of caramel and flecked with gold. They tended to change color with her mood. Gabriel could see she was troubled. She had a right to be. Their last assignment for the Office, an operation against a jihadist terror network, had been a particularly violent affair that ended in the Empty Quarter of Saudi Arabia. Chiara had hoped the Caravaggio restoration would prove to be the final stage of Gabriel's long and difficult recovery, the start of a new life free from the gravitational pull of the Office. It was not supposed to include an investigation carried out on behalf of the pope's private secretary.

"Well?" she asked.

"It was delicious," said Gabriel.

"I wasn't talking about the bruschetta." Chiara rearranged the pillows at the end of the couch. She always rearranged things when she was annoyed. "Have you considered what the Italian security service is going to do if they find out you're freelancing for the Vatican? They'll run us out of the country. *Again.*"

"I tried to explain that to Donati."

"And?"

"He invoked the name of his master."

"He's not *your* pope, Gabriel."

"What should I have said?"

"Find someone else," she replied. "They're three lovely little words you need to learn."

"You wouldn't say that if you'd seen Claudia's body."

"That's not fair."

"But it happens to be the truth. I've seen many dead bodies in my life, but I've never seen one that had fallen more than a hundred and fifty feet and landed on a marble floor."

"What a terrible way to die." Chiara watched the rain pattering on the little terrace overlooking the Spanish Steps. "How certain are you that Donati is telling you the truth?"

"About what?"

"About his relationship with Claudia Andreatti."

"If you're asking whether I think they were romantically involved, the answer is no."

"You grew up with a mother who never told you about the things that happened to her during the war."

"Your point?"

"Everyone keeps secrets. Even from the people they trust the most. Call it female intuition, but I've always felt there was more to Monsignor Donati than meets the eye. He has a past. I'm sure of it."

"We all do."

"But some of us have more interesting pasts than others. Besides," she added, "how much do you really know about his personal life?"

"Enough to know that he would never do anything as reckless as having an affair with an employee of the Vatican."

"I suppose you're right. But I can't imagine what it's like for a man who looks like Luigi Donati to be celibate."

"He deals with it by giving off an aura of absolute unavailability. He also wears a long black skirt and sleeps next door to the pope."

Chiara smiled and plucked a bruschetta from the tray. "There is at least *one* fringe benefit to accepting the case," she said thoughtfully. "It would give us a chance to take a look at the Church's private collection of antiquities. God only knows what they really have locked away in their storerooms."

"God and the popes," said Gabriel. "But it's far too much material for me to review on my own. I'm going to need help from someone who knows a thing or two about antiquities."

"Me?"

"If the Office hadn't got its hooks into you, you'd be a professor at an important Italian university."

"That's true," she said. "But I studied the history of the Roman Empire."

"Anyone who studies the Romans knows something about their artifacts. And your knowledge of Greek and Etruscan civilization is far superior to mine."

"I'm afraid that's not saying much, darling."

Chiara arched one eyebrow before raising the glass of wine to her lips. Her appearance had changed noticeably since their arrival in Rome. Seated as she was now, with her hair tumbling about her shoulders and her olive skin aglow, she looked remarkably like the intoxicating young Italian woman Gabriel had encountered for the first time, ten years earlier, in the ancient ghetto of Venice. It was almost as if the toll of the many long and dangerous operations had been erased. Only the faint shadow of loss fell across her face. It had been left there by the child she had miscarried while being held as ransom by the Russian oligarch and arms dealer Ivan Kharkov. They had not been able to conceive since. Privately, Chiara had resigned herself to the prospect that she and Gabriel might never have a child.

"There is one other possibility," she suggested.

"What's that?"

"That Dr. Claudia Andreatti climbed to the top of the Basilica in a state of emotional turmoil and threw herself to her death."

"When I saw her last night, she didn't look like a woman in turmoil. In fact . . ." Gabriel's voice trailed off.

"What?"

"I got the sense she wanted to tell me something."

Chiara was silent for a moment. "How long will it take for Donati to get us her files?" she asked finally.

"A day or two."

"So what do we do in the meantime?"

"I think we should get to know her a little better."

"How?"

Gabriel held up the ring of keys.

She lived on the opposite side of the river in Trastevere, in a faded old palazzo that had been converted into a faded old apartment house. Gabriel and Chiara strolled past the doorway twice while determining that their usual complement of Italian watchers had decided to take the night off. Then, on the third pass, Gabriel approached the door with the easy confidence of a man who had business within the premises and ushered Chiara inside. They found the foyer in semi-darkness and Claudia's mailbox bulging with what appeared to be several days' worth of uncollected post. Gabriel removed the items and placed them into Chiara's handbag. Then he led her to the base of the wide central staircase and together they started to climb.

It did not take long for Gabriel to feel a familiar sensation spreading over him. Shamron, his mentor, called it "the operational buzz." It caused him to walk on the balls of his feet with a slight forward tilt and to draw his breath with the evenness of a ventilator. And it compelled him to instinctively assume the worst, that behind every door, around every darkened corner, lurked an old enemy with a gun and an unpaid debt to collect. His eyes flickered restlessly, and his sense of hearing, suddenly acute, locked onto every sound, no matter how faint or trivial—the splash of water in a basin, the diminishment of a violin concerto, the wail of an inconsolable child.

It was this sound, the sound of a child weeping, that followed Gabriel and Chiara onto the third-floor landing. Gabriel walked over to the door of 3B and ran his fingertips quickly round the doorjamb before inserting the key into the lock. Then, soundlessly, he turned the latch and they slipped inside. Instantly, they realized they were not alone. Seated in a pool of lamplight, weeping softly, was Dr. Claudia Andreatti.

6

TRASTEVERE, ROME

T HE WOMAN WAS NOT CLAUDIA, of course, but the like-
ness was unnerving. It was as if Caravaggio had painted
the curator's portrait, and then, pleased with his creation,
had produced an exact copy down to the smallest detail—the same
scale and composition, the same features, the same sandstone-
colored hair, the same translucent blue eyes. Now the copy appraised Gabriel and Chiara silently for a moment before wiping a
tear from her cheek.

"What are you doing here?" she asked.

"I'm a colleague of Claudia's from the museum," Gabriel answered vaguely. He realized suddenly that he was staring too intently at the woman's face. Earlier that morning, on the way out of
the Basilica, Luigi Donati had mentioned something about a sister
who lived in London, but he'd left out the part about an identical
twin.

"You worked with Claudia in the antiquities division?" she asked.

"No," replied Gabriel. "I was asked to collect some files that she borrowed from the archives. If I had known you were here, I never would have intruded on your privacy."

The woman appeared to accept the explanation. Gabriel felt an uncharacteristic stab of guilt. Though he was trained in the fine art of lying, he was understandably apprehensive about telling an untruth to the wraith of a dead woman. Now the wraith rose to her feet and came slowly toward him through the half-light.

"Where did you get those?" she asked, nodding toward the keys in Gabriel's hand.

"They were found in Claudia's desk," he said as the knife of guilt twisted slowly within his chest.

"Was anything else found?"

"Such as?"

"A suicide note?"

Gabriel could scarcely believe she hadn't said *my* suicide note. "I'm afraid you'll have to ask the Vatican police about that," he said.

"I intend to." She took a step closer. "I'm Paola Andreatti," she said, extending her hand. When Gabriel hesitated to grasp it, her eyes narrowed thoughtfully. "So it's true, after all."

"What's that?"

"My sister told me that you were the one who was restoring the Caravaggio, Mr. Allon. I have to admit I'm rather surprised to see you here now."

Gabriel grasped the outstretched hand and found it warm and damp to the touch.

"Forgive me," she said, "but I was doing the dishes before you arrived. I'm afraid my sister left quite a mess."

"What do you mean?"

"Everything in the apartment was slightly out of place," she said, looking around. "I've tried to restore some semblance of order."

"When did you speak to her last?"

"A week ago Wednesday." The answer came without hesitation. "She sounded busy but entirely normal, not at all like someone who was about to . . ."

She stopped herself and looked at Chiara. "Your assistant?" she asked.

"She has the great misfortune of being married to me."

Paola Andreatti smiled sadly. "I'm tempted to say you're a lucky man, Mr. Allon, but I've read enough about your past to know that's not exactly the case."

"You shouldn't believe everything you read in the newspapers."

"I don't."

She studied Gabriel carefully for a moment. Her eyes were identical to the ones he had seen earlier that morning staring lifelessly into the dome of the Basilica. It was like being scrutinized by a ghost.

"Perhaps we should begin this conversation again," she said finally. "But this time, don't lie to me, Mr. Allon. I just lost my sister and my closest friend in the world. And there's no way the Vatican would send a man like you to collect a few stray files."

"I won't lie to you."

"Then please tell me why you're here."

"For the same reason you are."

"I'm trying to find out why my sister is dead."

"So am I."

The ghost seemed relieved she was no longer alone. She stood her ground for another moment as if guarding the passageway to her secrets. Then she stepped to one side and invited Gabriel and Chiara to enter.

The sitting room was a place of academic disarray, of shelves sagging beneath the weight of countless books, of end tables piled high with dog-eared files and hulking monographs. It had an air of urgency, as though its occupant had been in pursuit of something and had been struggling to meet a deadline. Paola Andreatti was right about one thing; everything in the apartment looked slightly askew, as though it had been moved and hastily put back into place. Gabriel walked over to the cluttered writing desk and switched on the lamp. Then he crouched and examined the surface of the desk in the raked lighting. In the center was a perfect rectangle, about ten inches by fifteen inches, where no dust was present. He picked up a half-drunk cup of coffee and carried it into the kitchen, where Chiara and Paola Andreatti stood before the sink finishing the last of the dishes. Neither woman spoke as he placed the cup on the counter and sat at the tiny café-style table.

"Was your sister a believer?" he asked.

"She was a devout Catholic. I'm not so sure whether she actually believed in God." She looked up from her work at the sink. "Why do you ask?"

"She wore a cross."

"It belonged to our mother. It was the one possession of hers that Claudia wanted. Fortunately, it was the one thing I *didn't* want."

"You don't share your sister's faith?"

"I'm a cardiologist, Mr. Allon. I'm a woman of science, not faith. I also believe that more evil has been carried out in the name of religion than any other force in human history. Look at the terrible fate of your own people. The Church falsely branded you as the murderers of God, and for two thousand years you've suffered the consequences. Now you've returned to the land of your birth only to find yourself locked in a war without end. Is this really what God had in mind when he made his pact with Abraham?"

"Perhaps Abraham forgot to read the fine print."

Chiara fixed Gabriel with a reproachful stare, but Paola Andreatti managed a fleeting smile. "If you're asking whether my sister would be reluctant to kill herself because of her religious beliefs, the answer is yes. She also regarded St. Peter's Basilica as a sacred place that was inspired by God. Besides," she added, "I'm a physician. I know a suicidal person when I see one. And my sister was not suicidal."

"No trouble at work?" asked Gabriel.

"Not that she mentioned."

"What about a man?" asked Chiara.

"Like many women in this country, my sister hadn't managed to find an Italian man suitable for marriage or even a serious relationship. It's one of the reasons I ended up in London. I married a proper Englishman. Then, five years later, he gave me a proper English divorce."

She dried her hands and began returning the newly clean dishes to the cabinets. There was something mildly absurd about her actions, like watering a garden while thunder cracked in the distance, but they seemed to give her a momentary sense of peace.

"Twins are different," she said, closing the cabinet. "We shared everything—our mother's womb, our nursery, our clothing. You might find this rather strange, Mr. Allon, but I always assumed my sister and I would share the same coffin."

She walked over to the refrigerator. On the door, held in place by a magnet, was a photograph of the sisters posed along the railing of a ferry. Even Gabriel, who had an artist's appreciation of the human form, could scarcely tell one from the other.

"It was taken during a day cruise on Lake Como last August," said Paola Andreatti. "I was recently separated from my husband. Claudia and I went alone, just the two of us. I paid, of course. Employees of the Vatican can't afford to stay in five-star hotels. It was the best vacation I'd had in years. Claudia said all the appropriate things about my pending divorce, but I suspect she was secretly relieved. It meant she would have me to herself again."

She opened the refrigerator, exhaled heavily, and began placing the contents in a plastic rubbish bin. "As of this moment," she said, "several hundred million people around the world believe my sister committed suicide. But not one of them knows that Gabriel Allon, a former Israeli intelligence agent and friend of the Vatican, is now sitting at her kitchen table."

"I'd prefer to keep it that way."

"I'm sure the men of the Vatican would, too. Because your presence suggests they believe there's more to my sister's death than merely a soul in distress."

Gabriel made no response.

"Do you believe Claudia killed herself?"

"No," Gabriel said. "I do not believe Claudia killed herself."

"Why not?"

He told her about the broken necklace, about the shoes, and about the perfect rectangle on her sister's desk where no dust was present. "You weren't the first person to come here tonight," he said. "Others came before you. They were professionals. They took anything that might be incriminating, including your sister's laptop computer."

She closed the refrigerator and stared silently at the photograph on the door.

"You did notice the computer was missing, didn't you?"

"It's not the only thing," she said softly.

"What else?"

"My sister never went to sleep at night without writing a few lines in her diary. She kept it on her bedside table. It's no longer there." Paola Andreatti looked at Gabriel for a moment without speaking. "How long will it be necessary to allow this terrible lie about my sister to persist?"

"For as long as it takes to discover the truth. But I can't do it alone. I'm going to need your help."

"What kind of help?"

"You can start by telling me about your sister."

"And then?"

"We're going to search this apartment together one more time."

"I thought you said the men were professionals."

"They were," said Gabriel. "But sometimes even professionals make mistakes."

They moved into the sitting room and settled amid Claudia's books and papers. Paola Andreatti spoke of her sister as though she were speaking of herself. For Gabriel, it was like interviewing a corpse that had been granted the ability to speak.

"Did she use any other e-mail address besides her Vatican account?"

"Everyone at the Vatican keeps a private account. Especially the priests."

She recited a Gmail address. Gabriel didn't need to write it down; his uncanny ability to mimic the brushstrokes of the Old

Masters was matched only by the precision of his memory. Besides, he thought, when one is pitted against professionals, it is best to behave like one.

The interview complete, they searched the apartment. Chiara and Paola Andreatti saw to the bedroom while Gabriel handled the desk. He searched now as he imagined it had been searched in the hours after Claudia's death—drawer by drawer, file by file, page by page. Despite his thoroughness, he found nothing to indicate why anyone might want to kill her.

But the men who had come before Gabriel had indeed made one mistake; they had left the building without emptying Claudia's mailbox. Now Gabriel withdrew the post from Chiara's handbag and quickly flipped through it until he found a credit card bill. The charges were a glimpse into a typical Roman life, preserved for-ever, like archaeological debris, in the memory banks of a main-frame computer. All the expenditures appeared unremarkable except for one. Two weeks before her death, it appeared that Clau-dia had spent the night in a hotel in Ladispoli, a drab seaside resort just north of Rome. Gabriel had passed through the town once in another lifetime. He recalled little of the place other than mediocre restaurants and a beach the color of asphalt. He returned the bill to its envelope and sat there for several minutes, a single question turning over in his mind. Why would a woman like Claudia An-dreatti spend the night in a hotel on the Italian coast, just thirty minutes from her own apartment, in the middle of winter? He could think of only two possible explanations. The first involved love. The second was the reason she was dead.

7

VATICAN CITY

THEY HELD THE FUNERAL MASS on the third day, in the Church of St. Anne. The Holy Father did not attend, but after much quiet debate, it was decided somewhere within the halls of the Apostolic Palace that the papal private secretary would officiate. Gabriel entered the church as Donati, cloaked in white vestments, led the mourners in the recitation of the Penitential Act. Paola Andreatti sat silently in the second row, her face expressionless. Her presence made Claudia's colleagues visibly uneasy; it was as if the soul of the departed had decided to attend her own burial. At the conclusion of the mass, as she followed the casket slowly into the Via Belvedere, she passed Gabriel without a glance. A few seconds later, Donati did the same.

The restoration lab was officially closed that day, but Gabriel decided to use the opportunity to spend a few uninterrupted hours alone with the Caravaggio. Shortly after four o'clock, he received a text message from Father Mark, Donati's assistant, asking him to come to a café just beyond the walls of the Vatican on the Borgo Pio. When Gabriel arrived, the young priest was contemplating the screen of his BlackBerry at a table near the window. Father Mark was an American from Philadelphia. He had a face like an altar boy and the eyes of someone who never lost at cards, which was why he worked for Donati.

"A gift from the monsignor," he said, handing Gabriel a small plastic bag from the Vatican bookstore.

"A collection of the Holy Father's encyclicals?"

Father Mark frowned. He didn't like jokes about His Holiness. He didn't like Gabriel much, either.

"It's all of Dr. Andreatti's research into the entire antiquities collection, just as you requested."

"All in this little bag? How miraculous."

"Thumb drives," the priest explained pedantically. Father Mark might have had a sense of humor once, but it had been scrubbed away by eight years of seminary training.

"What about her phone records?"

"I'm working on it."

"E-mail?"

"This is the Vatican we're talking about. These things take time." Nothing registered on the young priest's angelic face. Even Gabriel couldn't tell whether he was holding a straight flush or a pair of deuces. "The monsignor would like to know how you intend to proceed with your inquiry," he said, checking his Black-Berry.

"The first thing I'm going to do is go blind reading several thousand pages of documentation regarding the provenance of your antiquities collection."

"And then?"

"Tell the monsignor he'll be the first to know."

The priest stood abruptly and, citing an urgent matter requiring his attention, headed back to the Vatican. Gabriel slipped the plastic bag into his coat pocket, hesitated for a moment, and then autodialed a number on his BlackBerry. A gruff male voice answered in Hebrew. Gabriel murmured a few words in the same language and quickly severed the connection before the man at the other end could object. Then he sat there as night fell over the narrow street, wondering whether he had just made his first mistake.

There were few more thankless jobs than to be the declared chief of an Office station in Western Europe. Shimon Pazner, head of the generously staffed post inside the Israeli Embassy in Rome, had borne that burden longer than most. His tenure had coincided with a precipitous slide in Israel's public standing among Europeans of every stripe. Where once his country was regarded as a minor irritant, Europeans now viewed the Zionist enterprise with almost universal contempt and scorn. Israel was no longer a beacon of democracy in a troubled Middle East; it was an illegitimate rogue, an occupier, and a threat to world peace. Famously undiplomatic, Pazner had done little to help his cause. High on the list of Italian grievances was his conduct during meetings. His standard response when questioned about Israeli tactics and operations was to remind his brethren that, were it not for the deplorable conduct of Europeans, there would be no Israel at all.

Gabriel found Pazner seated alone on a stone bench outside the Galleria Borghese. Short and compact, he had gunmetal gray hair and a face like pumice. He offered Gabriel a perfunctory greeting in Italian, then suggested it might be better if they walked. They headed westward across the gardens along a footpath lined with umbrella pine. The cold air was heavy with the scent of damp leaves, wood smoke, and cooking—the smell of Rome on a winter's night. Pazner spoiled it by lighting a cigarette. His mood seemed worse than usual, but it was always a little hard to tell with Pazner. Rome annoyed him. As far as Pazner was concerned, it would always be the center of the empire that had destroyed the Second Temple and scattered the Jews to the four winds of the diaspora. He was a man with a long memory who held grudges. Gabriel was the object of several.

"I suppose it's fortuitous you called," he said finally. "We needed to have a word with you."

"We?"

"Don't get nervous, Gabriel. No one at King Saul Boulevard has any intention of calling you out of retirement again, not after what you went through in Saudi Arabia. Even the old man seems content to leave you in peace this time."

"Are you sure we're talking about the same Ari Shamron?"

"Actually, he's not the same, not anymore." Pazner was silent for a moment. "Far be it from me to tell you how to live your life," he said at last, "but it might be a good idea to pay him a visit the next time you're in town."

"When did you see him last?"

"A few weeks ago when I was in Tel Aviv for the annual meeting of the station chiefs. Shamron made his traditional appearance at dinner on the last night. He used to stay up to all hours regaling us with stories about the old days, but this time I had the sense he was just going through the motions. All I could think about was how things were when we were kids. Do you remember what he was like back then, Gabriel? The ground seemed to tremble whenever the old man entered a room."

"I remember," said Gabriel distantly, and for a moment he was striding across the courtyard of the Bezalel Academy of Art and

Design in Jerusalem, on a sun-bleached afternoon in September 1972. Seemingly from nowhere there appeared a small iron bar of a man with hideous black spectacles and teeth like a steel trap. The man didn't offer a name, for none was necessary. He was the one they spoke of only in whispers. The one who had stolen the secrets that led to Israel's lightning victory in the Six-Day War. The one who had plucked Adolf Eichmann, managing director of the Holocaust, from an Argentine street corner.

As usual, Shamron had come well prepared that day. He had known, for example, that Gabriel descended from a long line of gifted artists, that he spoke fluent German with a pronounced Berlin accent, and that he was married to a fellow art student named Leah Savir. He had also known that Gabriel, having been raised by a woman who had survived the Nazi death camp at Birkenau, was a natural keeper of secrets. "The operation will be called Wrath of God," he had said that day. "It's not about justice. It's about vengeance, pure and simple—vengeance for the eleven innocent lives lost at Munich." Gabriel had told Shamron to find someone else. "I don't want someone else," Shamron had said. "I want you."

It was but one of many arguments Shamron would eventually win. Time and time again, he had managed to manipulate Gabriel into doing his bidding, always coming up with some excuse, some minor operational errand, to keep his gifted prodigy within reach of the Office. It had been Shamron's wish that Gabriel assume his rightful place in the director's suite at King Saul Boulevard. But Gabriel, in one final act of defiance, had turned his back on the offer, handing the job instead to an old rival named Uzi Navot. For a time, it seemed Navot would be willing to act merely as Shamron's puppet. But now, having established his hold over the Office, Navot had banished Shamron to the Judean Wilderness, thus severing the old man's ties to the intelligence service he had created in his own image. Shamron lived now in something akin to internal exile at his villa overlooking the Sea of Galilee. The politicians and generals who used to seek his advice no longer beat a path to his door. To fill the empty hours, he repaired antique radios and tried to concoct some way to convince Gabriel, whom he loved as a son, to come home again.

"How often does he call to check up on me?"

"Never," replied Pazner, shaking his head for emphasis.

"How often, Shimon?"

"Twice a week, sometimes three. In fact, I just got off the phone with him before you called."

"What did he want?"

"King Saul Boulevard is in an uproar. They're convinced something is about to come down. Something big."

"Is there anything specific on the target?"

Pazner took a final pull at his cigarette and sent the ember arcing into the darkness. "It might be an embassy or a consulate. It might be a synagogue or a community center. They think it's going to happen in the south, probably Istanbul or Athens, but they can't rule out Rome. We've barely finished rebuilding from the last time we were hit." Pazner glanced at Gabriel and added, "Something tells me you remember that attack well."

Gabriel didn't respond directly. "Is it al-Qaeda?"

"After your last operation, there's probably no al-Qaeda network or cell capable of carrying out a major attack in Europe. And since the Palestinians have no interest in hitting us here at the moment, that leaves only one other candidate."

"The Iranians."

"Acting through their favorite proxy, of course."

Hezbollah . . .

They had reached the edge of the Piazza di Siena. The broad

dusty oval was awash with pale moonlight, and the sound of the traffic along the Corso was but a whisper. It was almost possible to imagine they were the last two men alive in an ancient city.

"What's the source?" asked Gabriel.

"Sources," countered Pazner. "It's a mosaic of intelligence, both human and signals. It appears the Qods Force of the Revolutionary Guard is running the operation. Department Five of VEVAK is apparently involved as well."

VEVAK was the Persian-language acronym of the Ministry of Intelligence and National Security, Iran's formidable intelligence service. Department Five was among its most important divisions, for it dealt exclusively with the State of Israel.

"According to one of our assets in southern Lebanon," Pazner continued, "a team of Hezbollah operatives left Beirut about six weeks ago. We think it's a straight revenge operation. Frankly, we've been expecting something like this for some time. They have good reason to be angry at us."

For much of the past decade, the Office had been waging a not-so-secret war against the Iranian nuclear weapons program. Scientists had been assassinated, destructive computer viruses had been introduced into labs and facilities, and faulty parts had been cleverly inserted into Iran's nuclear supply chain—including several dozen sabotaged industrial centrifuges that destroyed four secret enrichment facilities. The operation had been one of Gabriel's finest. Fittingly, it had been code-named Masterpiece.

"Has my name come up in any of the intel?"

"Not a whisper. But that doesn't mean they don't suspect you were the one behind it. Anyone who underestimates the Iranians does so at his own risk, you included."

"I've never underestimated them. But I have no intention of spending the rest of my life in hiding."

"No one's suggesting that."

"What *are* you suggesting?"

"Jerusalem is lovely this time of year."

"Actually, it's miserable. But that's beside the point. I'm too busy to leave Rome."

"So I've heard. I've also heard that your friend the monsignor asked you to have a look at the suicide in the Basilica while the body was still in situ."

"Very impressive, Shimon. How did you know I was there?"

"Because Lorenzo Vitale told one of his old friends in the Guardia di Finanza. And that friend told one of *his* friends in the Italian security service. And the friend from the Italian security service told me. He also told me that if you step out of line, he'll put you on the first plane out of town."

"Tell him I'm living up to the letter and spirit of our agreement."

"Is that why Donati's assistant invited you to coffee this afternoon?"

"I see you're monitoring my mobile phone again."

"What makes you think I ever stopped?" Pazner walked in silence for a moment. "I don't suppose that woman actually threw herself from the dome of the Basilica, did she?"

"No, Shimon, she didn't."

"Any idea why she was killed?"

"I have a theory, but I can't pursue it without help."

"What kind of help?"

"Forensic help," replied Gabriel. "I need Unit 8200 to have a look under her fingernails."

Unit 8200 was Israel's signals intelligence service, the equivalent of the National Security Agency in the United States. Though formally under the command of the military chief of staff, it carried out tasks for all the Israeli intelligence and security agencies,

including the Office. Its alumni included some of the most successful entrepreneurs in Israel's thriving high-tech industry.

"Let me see if I understand this correctly," Pazner said. "The
State of Israel is currently facing existential threats too numerous
to count, and you would like the Unit to expend valuable time and
effort data-mining a dead Italian woman?"

Gabriel said nothing. Pazner exhaled heavily.

"How far back do you need them to go?"

"Six months. E-mails, browsing histories, data searches."

Pazner ignited another cigarette and blew smoke at the moon.
"If I had an ounce of common sense, I'd drop this down a very
deep hole, and you with it. But now you owe me one, Gabriel. And
I never forget a debt."

"How can I ever possibly repay you, Shimon?"

"You can start by telling your wife to stop dropping my watchers when she's running her errands. I put them there for her own
good."

"I'll see what I can do. Anything else?"

"If you happen to spot a team of Hezbollah operatives walking
around Rome, give me a call. But do me a favor, and leave your
gun in your pocket. I have enough problems."

8

PIAZZA DI SPAGNA, ROME

T HEY APPROACHED THE CASE THE way they did most things in life, with the alert, operational calm of a covert team working in a hostile land. Their target was the killer of Claudia Andreatti. And now, with the arrival of her files from the Vatican, they had the means to begin their search. Still, they braced themselves for the prospect of disappointment. The files were a bit like intelligence. And Gabriel and Chiara knew that intelligence was often incomplete, contradictory, misleading, or a combination of all three.

They worked under the assumption that others were watching their every move, and conducted themselves accordingly. Gabriel in particular had no choice but to maintain his busy daily routine. He was a man of many faces and many different missions. To the youthful Swiss Guards who greeted him each morning at St. Anne's Gate, he was a fellow soldier, a secret sentinel, and a sometime ally. To his colleagues in the restoration lab, he was the gifted but melancholic loner who spent his days behind his black curtain, alone with his Caravaggio and his demons. And to the Italian watchers who trailed him home each afternoon, he was a legendary operative with a past so tangled they knew only bits and pieces of the story. Upon entering the apartment, he would invariably find Chiara hunched over a stack of printouts. Gabriel would work by her side for several more hours before taking her into the streets of Rome for a late supper. They ate only in small restaurants frequented by locals and never spoke of the case outside the walls of the flat.

With each passing day, Claudia Andreatti slipped further from the public's consciousness. The doubts surrounding the publicly stated circumstances of her death diminished, the stories disappeared from the newspapers, and even the most conspiracy-minded Web sites reluctantly concluded it was time to allow her troubled soul to rest in peace. But in the little apartment above the Spanish Steps, the questions persisted. Regrettably, the files given to Gabriel by Father Mark provided not a single answer. The institution they portrayed had been blessed by the fact that, for more than a millennium, the popes held direct sovereign rule over the Papal States, an archaeologically fertile land bursting with Etruscan, Greek, and Roman antiquities. Still, like traditional museums, the Vatican had supplemented its vast holdings by purchasing or inheriting private collections. Here was a potential area for trouble. What if, for example, a private collection contained material that had been illegally excavated or had no clear provenance? But after a thorough investigation, it appeared that Claudia had discovered nothing that would present the Vatican with any legal or ethical problems. In fact, according to the documents, the hands of the Holy See were remarkably clean.

"I suppose there's a first for everything," Chiara said. "It looks as though the Vatican has the only museum in the world without a stolen statue hidden somewhere in its basement."

"They have enough other problems," said Gabriel.

"So what do we do now?"

"We wait for the Unit to fill in the missing pieces of the puzzle."

It would not be a long wait. Indeed, the following evening, one of Shimon Pazner's underlings drew alongside Gabriel on the Via Condotti and handed over a flash drive containing six months' worth of e-mail from Claudia Andreatti's accounts. The next night, it was the browsing history from her IP address, along with a complete list of her Internet searches. The material provided a shockingly intimate window into the life of a woman whom Gabriel had known only in passing—news stories she had read, video clips she had watched, the secret desires she had confessed to the little white box of Google. They could see that she preferred French undergarments to Italian, that she enjoyed the music of Diana Krall and Sara Bareilles, and that she was a regular reader of the *New York Times*, as well as the Web log of a well-known Catholic dissident. She seemed intrigued by the prospect of traveling to New Zealand and the west coast of Ireland. She suffered from chronic back pain. She wanted to lose ten pounds.

Wherever possible, Gabriel and Chiara averted their eyes, but for the most part, they pored over her online musings as though they were fragments of stone tablets from a lost civilization. They found nothing to suggest that she was contemplating suicide or that anyone might want her dead—no jealous lovers, no debts, no personal or professional crises of any kind. Claudia Andreatti, it seemed, was the most contented woman in all of Rome.

The final batch of material from the Unit contained the records from Claudia's mobile phone. They revealed that during the final weeks of her life, she placed several calls to a number in Cerveteri, a midsize Italian town north of Rome known for its Etruscan tombs. Perhaps not coincidentally, it was just a few miles inland from the seaside resort of Ladispoli. At Gabriel's request, the Unit tracked down the name and address of the person associated with the number: Roberto Falcone, 22 Via Lombardia.

Late the following morning, Gabriel and Chiara walked to the bustling Stazione Termini and boarded a train to Venice. One minute before departure, they calmly exited the carriage and returned to the crowded ticket hall. As expected, the two watchers who had followed them from the Piazza di Spagna were gone. Now free of surveillance, they made their way to a nearby parking garage where Shimon Pazner kept an Office Mercedes sedan on permanent standby. Twenty minutes elapsed before the car finally came squealing up the steep ramp, though Gabriel uttered not a word of protest. To be a motorist in Rome was to suffer minor indignities in silence.

After crossing the river, Gabriel followed the walls of the Vatican to the entrance of the Via Aurelia. It bore them westward, past mile after mile of tired-looking apartment blocks, to the A12 Autostrada. From there it was only a dozen miles to Cerveteri. Gabriel spent much of the drive glancing into his rearview mirror.

"Anyone following us?" asked Chiara.

"Just five of the worst drivers in Italy."

"What do you think is going to happen when that train arrives in Venice and we're not on it?"

"I suspect there will be recriminations."

"For them or us?"

A road sign warned that the turnoff for Cerveteri was approaching. Gabriel exited the motorway and spent several minutes driving through the town's ancient center before making his way to the house located just beyond the city limits at 22 Via Lombardia. It was a modest two-level villa, set back from the road, with a flaking ocher exterior and faded green shutters that hung at a slightly drunken angle. On one side was an orchard; on the other, a small vineyard pruned for winter. Behind the villa, next to a tumbledown outbuilding, was a battered station wagon with dust-covered windows. A German shepherd snapped and snarled at them from the trampled front garden. It looked as though it hadn't eaten in several days.

"All in all," said Gabriel, staring morosely at the dog, "it's not the sort of place one would normally expect to find a museum curator."

He dialed Falcone's number from his mobile phone. After five rings without an answer, he severed the connection.

"What now?" asked Chiara.

"We give him an hour. Then we come back."

"Where are we going to wait?"

"Somewhere we won't stick out."

"That's not so easy in a town like this," she said.

"Any suggestions?"

"Just one."

The Necropoli della Banditaccia lay to the north of the city, at the end of a long, narrow drive lined with cypress pine. In the car park was a kiosk-style coffee bar and café. A few steps away, in a featureless building that looked oddly temporary, were an admissions office and a small gift shop. The lone attendant, a birdlike woman with enormous spectacles, seemed startled to see them. Evidently, they were the first visitors of the day.

Gabriel and Chiara surrendered the modest admission fee and were given a handwritten map, which they were expected to return at the end of their visit. Playing the role of tourists, they descended into the first tomb and gazed at the cold, empty burial chambers. After that, they remained on the surface, wandering the labyrinth of beehive-shaped tombs, alone in the ancient city of the dead.

To help pass the time, Chiara lectured quietly on the subject of the Etruscans—a mysterious people, deeply religious but rumored to be sexually decadent, who treated men and women as social equals. Highly advanced in the arts and sciences, Etruscan craftsmen taught the Romans how to pave their roads and construct their aqueducts and sewers, a debt the Romans repaid by wiping the Etruscans from the face of the earth. Now little remained of their once-flourishing civilization other than their tombs, which is precisely what they had intended. The Etruscans had fashioned their homes of transitory materials, but their necropolises were built to last forever. In the rooms of the dead they had placed vessels, utensils, and jewelry—treasures that now were displayed in the world's museums and in the drawing rooms of the rich.

After completing the tour, Gabriel and Chiara dutifully returned the map and headed out to the parking lot, where Gabriel dialed Roberto Falcone's number a second time. Once again, there was no answer.

"What now?" asked Chiara.

"Lunch," replied Gabriel.

He walked over to the kiosk and bought a half-dozen premade sandwiches in plastic wrappers.

"Hungry?" Chiara asked.

"They're not for us."

They climbed into the car and headed back to Falcone's villa.

9

CERVETERI, ITALY

W ITHIN THE FRATERNITY OF WESTERN intelligence, Gabriel's fear of dogs was as legendary
as his exploits. It was not an irrational fear; it was
supported by a vast body of empirical evidence gathered during
violent encounters too numerous to count. It seemed there was
something in Gabriel's very appearance—his catlike demeanor,
his vivid green eyes—that caused even the most docile of dogs
to revert to the feral, prehistoric beasts from which they all had
sprung. He had been stalked by dogs, bitten by dogs, mauled by
dogs, and, once, in a snowbound valley in the mountains of Inner
Switzerland, the Alsatian guard dog of a prominent banker had
broken his arm. Gabriel had survived the attack only because he
had shot the dog in the head with a Beretta pistol. Gunplay was
surely not the preferred option here in Cerveteri, but the current
agitated state of Falcone's dog meant that Gabriel would not be
able to rule it out entirely. The shepherd's mood seemed to have

deteriorated in the hour since they had last seen it. There was only one reason to keep such a disagreeable creature—Roberto Falcone was obviously hiding something on his property, and it was the dog's assignment to keep the curious at bay. Fortunately for Gabriel, it appeared the animal had been mistreated, which meant he was ripe for recruitment. Thus the large bag of sandwiches from the café at the Etruscan necropolis.

"Maybe you should let me do it," said Chiara.

Gabriel gave her a withering glance but said nothing.

"I was just thinking—"

"I know what you were thinking."

Gabriel turned into the property and headed slowly up the pitted gravel drive. The dog set upon the car instantly—not the passenger side, of course, but Gabriel's. It galloped alongside the front tire, pausing every now and again to drop into an aggressive crouch and bare its savage teeth. Then, when the car came to a stop, it launched itself toward Gabriel's window like a missile and tried to bite him through the glass. Gabriel regarded the animal calmly, which incensed it even more. It had the pale yellow eyes of a wolf and was frothing at the mouth as though it were rabid.

"Maybe you should try talking to it," suggested Chiara.

"I don't believe in negotiating with terrorists."

Gabriel sighed heavily and removed the plastic wrapper from one of the sandwiches. Then he cracked the window and quickly shoved the sandwich through the gap. Six inches of Parma ham, fontina, and bread disappeared in a single ravenous bite.

"He's obviously not kosher," said Chiara.

"Is that a good sign or bad?"

"Bad," she replied. "Very bad."

Gabriel slipped another sandwich through the window. This time, the dog's incisor nicked the tip of his finger.

"Are you all right?"

"It's a good thing I'm ambidextrous." He quickly fed the dog three more of the sandwiches in assembly-line fashion.

"The poor thing is starving."

"Let's not start feeling sorry for the dog just yet."

"Aren't you going to give him the last one?"

"Better to keep it in reserve. That way I'll have something to fling at him if he decides to go for my throat."

Gabriel unlocked the door but hesitated.

"What are you waiting for?"

"A declaration of his intentions."

He opened the door a few inches and put a foot on the ground. The dog growled low in its throat but remained motionless. The ears were up, which Gabriel supposed was a positive development. Usually, whenever a canine was attempting to tear him to shreds, the ears were always back and down, like the wings of an attack aircraft.

Gabriel placed the last sandwich on the ground and emerged slowly from the car. Then, with his eyes still fixed on the animal's jaws, he instructed Chiara to get out. He did so in rapid Hebrew, so the dog wouldn't understand. Partially satiated, it devoured the food at a more decorous pace, its yellow gaze fixed on Gabriel and Chiara as they made their way toward the back door of the house. Gabriel knocked twice but there was no answer. Then he tried the latch. It was locked.

He removed the small, thin metal tool he carried always in his wallet and worked it gently inside the lock until the mechanism gave way. When he tried the latch a second time, it yielded to his touch. Inside was a cluttered mudroom filled with old work clothes and tall rubber boots caked with earth. The utility sink was dry. So were the boots.

He motioned for Chiara to enter and led her into the kitchen. The counters were stacked with dirty dishes, and hanging in the air was the acrid stench of something burning. Gabriel walked over to the automatic coffeemaker. The power light was aglow, and on the bottom of the carafe was a patch of burnt coffee the color of tar. Clearly, the machine had been on for several days—the same number of days, Gabriel reckoned, the dog had gone without food.

"He's lucky he didn't burn the house down," Chiara said.

"I'm not so sure about that."

"About what?"

"The part about Falcone being lucky."

Gabriel switched off the coffeemaker, and they moved into the dining room. The chandelier, like the coffeemaker, had been left on, and five of the eight bulbs had burned out. At one end of the rectangular table was a meal that had been abandoned. At the other end was a cardboard box with the name of a local winery printed on the side. Gabriel lifted one of the flaps and looked inside. The box was filled with objects carefully wrapped in sheets of the *Corriere della Sera*. It was a rather highbrow paper for a man like Falcone, he thought. Gabriel had him figured for the *Gazzetta dello Sport*.

"Looks like he left in a hurry," Chiara said.

"Or maybe he was forced to leave."

He removed one of the objects from the box and cautiously opened the newsprint wrapper. Inside was a concave fragment of pottery about the size of Gabriel's palm, decorated with the partial image of a young woman in semi-profile. She wore a pleated gown and appeared to be playing a flute-like instrument. Her flesh and garment were depicted in the same terra-cotta color, but the background was a luminous solid black.

"My God," said Chiara softly.

"It looks like a portion of a red-figure Attic vessel of some sort."

Chiara nodded. "Judging from the shape and the imagery, I'd say it comes from the upper portion of a *stamnos*, a Greek vase used for transporting wine. The woman is clearly a maenad, a follower of Dionysus. The instrument is a two-reed pipe known as an *aulos*."

"Could it be a Roman copy of a Greek original?"

"I suppose so. But in all likelihood, it was produced in Greece two and a half millennia ago specifically for export to the Etruscan cities. The Etruscans were great admirers of Greek vases. That's why so many important pieces have been discovered in Etruscan tomb rooms."

"What's it doing in a cardboard box on Roberto Falcone's dining room table?"

"That's the easy part. He's a *tombarolo*."

A tomb robber.

"That would explain the dog," said Gabriel.

"And the muddy boots at the back door. He's obviously been doing some digging, probably quite recently." She held up the newspaper. "It's from last week."

Gabriel reached into the box again and withdrew another bundle of newsprint. Inside was another section of the vase. The face of a second maenad was visible, along with the *kylix*, a shallow cup for drinking wine, she held in her hand. Gabriel examined the image in silence before looking at the newspaper. It contained a fragment, too—a fragment of a story about a Vatican curator who had committed suicide by hurling herself from the dome of St. Peter's Basilica. The account neglected to mention that the curator had been conducting a secret inventory of the Vatican's collection of antiquities. It appeared her inquiry had led her here, to the home of a *tombarolo*. Perhaps that alone had been enough to get her killed, but Gabriel suspected there had to be more.

He looked at the fragment of pottery again and lifted it to his nose. There was a trace of a chemical odor, not unlike the smell of the solvents he used to remove varnish from paintings. It suggested the fragment had recently been cleaned of soil and other encrustations, probably with a solution of nitrohydrochloric acid. Even an old man living alone in an unkempt house would find it difficult to be around such a smell for more than a few minutes. He would need to maintain a separate facility where objects could be left for long periods without fear of discovery.

Gabriel placed the fragment of pottery into his coat pocket and looked out the window toward the tumbledown outbuilding at the back of the property. Pacing outside, head down, ears back, was Falcone's dog. Gabriel sighed heavily. Then he went into the kitchen, found a large mixing bowl, and began filling it with anything that looked remotely edible.

There were two padlocks, German made, rusted by rain. Gabriel picked them as the dog supped greedily on a casserole of canned tuna, fava beans, artichoke hearts, and condensed milk. When the door swung open, the animal looked up briefly but paid Gabriel and Chiara no heed as they slipped inside. Here the stench of acid was overwhelming. Gabriel groped blindly, one hand covering his nose and mouth, until he found the light switch. Overhead a row of fluorescent lamps flickered to life, revealing a professional-grade laboratory built for the care and storage of looted antiquities. Its neatness and order stood in stark contrast to the rest of the property. One object looked slightly out of place, a javelin-like iron pike suspended horizontally on a pair of hooks. Gabriel examined the traces of mud near the tip. It was the same color and consistency as the mud on the boots.

"It's a *spillo*," Chiara explained. "The *tombaroli* use it to probe for underground burial chambers. They insert it into the ground until they hear the telltale *clank* of a tomb room or a Roman villa. Then they bring in the shovels and the backhoes and grab whatever they can find."

"And then," said Gabriel, looking around, "they bring it here."

He walked over to Falcone's worktable. Clean and white, it was similar to the tables in the restoration lab at the Vatican Museums. At one end was a stack of scholarly monographs dealing with the antiquities of the Roman, Greek, and Etruscan empires—the same sort of books Gabriel had seen in Claudia Andreatti's apartment. One of the volumes lay open to an image of a red-figure Attic *stamnos* vase decorated with maenads.

Gabriel snapped a photo of the open page with his BlackBerry before making his way over to Falcone's storage shelves. Chrome and spotless, they were lined with antiquities arranged by type: pottery, household utensils, tools, weapons, and bits of iron that looked as though they had been extracted from the basement of time. It was evidence of looting on a massive scale. Unfortunately, it was a crime that could never be undone. Ripped from their original settings, these antiquities now said very little about the people who had made and used them.

At the far end of the building were four large stainless steel pools, approximately five feet in diameter and three feet in height. In the first three vats, there were bits of pottery, statuary, and other objects clearly visible in the reddish liquid. But in the fourth, the acid was opaque and very close to spilling over the side. Gabriel retrieved the *spillo* and inserted it gently into the liquid. Just beneath the surface, it collided with something soft and pliant.

"What is it?" asked Chiara.

"I could be wrong," Gabriel said, wincing, "but I think we just found Roberto Falcone."

10

PIAZZA DI SANT'IGNAZIO, ROME

I N THE HEART OF ROME, between the Pantheon and the Via del Corso, is a pleasant little square called the Piazza di Sant'Ignazio. On the northern side stands a church by the same name, best known for a glorious ceiling fresco painted by the Jesuit brother Andrea Pozzo. On the southern flank, across an expanse of gray paving stones, is an ornate palazzo with façades of creamy yellow and white. Two official flags fly from its third-floor balcony, and above the solemn entrance is the seal of the Carabinieri. A small plaque states that the premises are occupied by the Division for the Defense of Cultural Patrimony. But within the world of law enforcement, the unit is known simply as the Art Squad.

At the time of its formation in 1969, it was the only police organization anywhere in the world dedicated exclusively to combating the lucrative trade in stolen art and antiquities. Italy surely had need of such a unit, for it was blessed with both an abundance of art and countless professional criminals bent on stealing every last bit of it. During the next two decades, the Art Squad brought charges against thousands of people suspected of involvement in art crime and made numerous high-profile recoveries, including works by Raphael, Giorgione, and Tintoretto. Then the institutional paralysis began to set in. Manpower dwindled to a few dozen retirement-age officers—many of whom knew next to nothing about art—and inside the graceful palazzo, work proceeded at a decidedly Roman pace. It was said by the unit's legion of detractors that more time was spent debating where to have lunch than searching for the museum's worth of paintings that went missing in Italy each year.

That changed with the arrival of General Cesare Ferrari. The son of schoolteachers from the impoverished Campania region, Ferrari had spent his entire career battling the country's most intractable problems. During the 1970s, a time of deadly terrorist bombings in Italy, he helped to neutralize the Communist Red Brigades. Then, during the Mafia wars of the 1980s, he served as a commander in the Camorra-infested Naples division. The assignment was so dangerous that Ferrari's wife and three daughters were forced to live under twenty-four-hour guard. Ferrari himself was the target of numerous assassination attempts, including a letter bomb attack that claimed two of his fingers and his right eye. His ocular prosthesis, with its immobile pupil and unyielding gaze, left some of his underlings with the unnerving sense that they were staring into the all-seeing eye of God. Ferrari used the eye to great effect in coaxing low-level criminals to betray their superiors. One of the bosses Ferrari eventually brought down was the mastermind of the letter bombing. After the mafioso's conviction, Ferrari made a point of personally escorting him to the cell at Naples' festering Poggioreale prison where he would spend the rest of his life.

The posting to the Art Squad was supposed to be a reward for a long and distinguished career. "Shuffle paper for a few years," the chief of the Carabinieri told him, "and then retire to your village in Campania and grow tomatoes." Ferrari accepted the appointment and then proceeded to do exactly the opposite. Within days of arriving at the palazzo, he informed half the staff their services were no longer needed. Then he set about modernizing an organization that had been allowed to atrophy with age. He replenished the ranks with aggressive young officers, sought authority to tap the phones of known criminal operatives, and opened offices in the parts of the country where the thieves actually stole art, especially in the south. Most important, he adopted many of the techniques he had used against the Mafia during his days in Naples. Ferrari wasn't much interested in the street-level hoods who dabbled in art theft; he wanted the big fish, the bosses who brought the stolen goods to market. It did not take long for Ferrari's new approach to pay dividends. More than a dozen important thieves found themselves behind bars, and statistics for art theft, while still astonishingly high, showed improvement. The palazzo was no longer a retirement home; it was the place where many of the Carabinieri's best and brightest went to make their name. And those who didn't measure up found themselves in Ferrari's office, staring into the unforgiving eye of God.

A career in Italian government spanning some four decades had left the general with a limited capacity for surprise. Even so, he was admittedly taken aback to see the legendary Gabriel Allon stepping through the entrance of his office early that evening, trailed by his beautiful and much younger Venetian-born wife, Chiara. The chain of events that brought them there had been set in motion four hours earlier, when Gabriel, gazing down at the partially emulsified body of Roberto Falcone, came to the disheartening realization that he had stumbled upon a crime scene that could not possibly be fled. Rather than contact the authorities directly, he rang Donati, who in turn made contact with Lorenzo Vitale of the Vatican police. After an unpleasant conversation lasting some fifteen minutes, it was decided that Vitale would approach Ferrari, with whom he had worked on numerous cases. By late afternoon, the Art Squad was on the ground in Cerveteri, along with a team from the Lazio division's violent crimes unit. And by sunset, Gabriel and Chiara, having been relieved of their weapons, were in the back of a Carabinieri sedan bound for the palazzo.

The walls of Ferrari's office were hung with paintings—some badly damaged, some without frames or stretchers—that had been recovered from art thieves or dirty collectors. Here they would remain, sometimes for many weeks or months, until they could be returned to their rightful owners. On the wall behind his desk, aglow as if newly restored, hung Caravaggio's *Nativity with St. Francis and St. Lawrence*. It was a copy, of course; the real version had been stolen from the Church of San Lorenzo in Palermo in 1969 and had never been seen since. Finding it was Ferrari's obsession.

"Two years ago," he said, "I thought I'd finally located it. A low-level art thief told me he knew the house in Sicily where the painting was being hidden. He offered to tell me in exchange for not sending him to prison for stealing an altarpiece from a village church near Florence. I accepted the offer and raided the property. The painting wasn't there, but we found these." Ferrari handed Gabriel a stack of Polaroid photographs. "Heartbreaking."

Gabriel flipped through the Polaroids. They depicted a painting that had not fared well after more than forty years underground.

The edges of the canvas were badly frayed—the result of the painting being cut from its stretcher with a razor—and deep cracks and abrasions marred the once glorious image.

"What happened to the thief who gave you the tip?"

"I sent him to prison."

"But the information he gave you was good."

"That's true. But it wasn't timely. And in this business, timing is everything." Ferrari gave a brief smile that did not quite extend to his prosthetic eye. "If we do ever manage to find it, the restoration is obviously going to be difficult, even for a man of your skills."

"I'll make you a deal, General. If you find it, I'll fix it."

"I'm not in the mood for deals just yet, Allon."

Ferrari accepted the Polaroids of the lost Caravaggio and returned them to their file. Then he stared contemplatively out the window in the manner of Bellini's *Doge Leonardo Loredan*, as if debating whether to send Gabriel across the Bridge of Sighs for a few hours in the torture chambers.

"I'm going to begin this conversation by telling you everything I know. That way, you might be less tempted to lie to me. I know, for example, that your friend Monsignor Donati arranged for you to restore *The Deposition of Christ* for the Vatican Picture Gallery. I also know that he asked you to view the body of Dottoressa Claudia Andreatti while it was still in the Basilica—and that, subsequently, you undertook a private investigation of the circumstances surrounding her unfortunate death. That investigation led you to Roberto Falcone. And now it has landed you here," Ferrari concluded, "in the palazzo."

"I've been in far worse places than this."

"And you will be again unless you cooperate."

The general lit an American cigarette. He smoked it somewhat awkwardly with his left hand. The right, the one missing two fingers, was concealed in his lap.

"Why was the monsignor so concerned about this woman?" he asked.

Gabriel told him about the review of the Vatican's antiquities.

"I was led to believe it was nothing more than a routine inventory."

"It might have started that way. But it appears that somewhere along the line, Claudia uncovered something else."

"Do you know what?"

"No."

Ferrari scrutinized Gabriel as if he didn't quite believe him. "Why were you sniffing around Falcone's place?"

"Dr. Andreatti was in contact with him shortly before her death."

"How do you know this?"

"I found his phone number in her records."

"She called him from her office at the Vatican?"

"From her mobile," said Gabriel.

"How were *you*, a foreigner residing in this country temporarily, able to obtain the mobile phone records of an Italian citizen?"

When Gabriel made no reply, Ferrari eyed him over the tip of his cigarette like a marksman lining up a difficult shot.

"The most logical explanation is that you called upon friends in your old service to retrieve the records for you. If that's the case, you violated your agreement with our security authorities. And that, I'm afraid, places you in a very precarious position indeed."

It was a threat, thought Gabriel, but only a mild one.

"Did you ever speak to Falcone yourself?" the general asked.

"I tried."

"And?"

"He wasn't answering his phone."

"So you decided to break into his property?"

"Out of concern for his safety."

"Oh, yes, of course," said Ferrari sarcastically. "And once inside, you discovered what appeared to be a large cache of antiquities."

"Along with a *tombarolo* simmering in a pot of hydrochloric acid."

"How did you get past the locks?"

"The dog was more of a challenge than the locks."

The general smiled, one professional to another, and tapped his cigarette thoughtfully against his ashtray. "Roberto Falcone was no ordinary *tombarolo*," he said. "He was a *capo zona*, the head of a regional looting network. The low-level looters brought him their goods. Then Falcone moved the product up the line to the smugglers and the crooked dealers."

"You seem to know a great deal about a man whose body was discovered just a few hours ago."

"That's because Roberto Falcone was also my informant," the general admitted. "My very *best* informant. And now, thanks to you, he's dead."

"I had nothing to do with his death."

"So you say."

A uniformed aide knocked discreetly on Ferrari's door. The general waved him away with an imperious gesture and resumed his doge-like pose of solemn deliberation.

"As I see it," he said at last, "we have two distinct options before us. Option one, we handle everything by the book. That means throwing you to the wolves at the security service. There might be some negative publicity involved, not only for your government but for the Vatican as well. Things could get messy, Allon. Very messy indeed."

"And the second option?"

"You start by telling me everything you know about Claudia Andreatti's death."

"And then?"

"I'll help you find the man who killed her."

11

PIAZZA DI SANT'IGNAZIO, ROME

A MONG THE PERQUISITES OF WORKING at the palazzo was Le Cave. Regarded as one of the finest restaurants in Rome, it was located just steps from the entrance of the building, in a quiet corner of the piazza. In summer the tables stood in neat rows across the cobbles, but on that February evening they were stacked forlornly against the outer wall. General Ferrari arrived without advance warning and was immediately shown, along with his two guests, to a table at the back of the room. A waiter brought a plate of *arancini di riso* and red wine from Ferrari's native Campania. The general made a toast to a marriage that, for the moment, had yet to be consummated. Then, as he picked at one of the risotto croquettes, he spoke disdainfully of a man named Giacomo Medici.

Though he bore no relation to the Florentine banking dynasty, Medici shared the family's passion for the arts. A broker of antiquities based in Rome and Switzerland, he had quietly supplied high-quality pieces for decades to some of the world's most prominent dealers, collectors, and museums. But in 1995, his lucrative business began to unravel when Italian and Swiss authorities raided his warehouse in the Geneva Freeport and found a treasure trove of unprovenanced antiquities, some of which had clearly been recently excavated. The discovery touched off an international investigation led by the Art Squad that would eventually ensnare some of the biggest names in the art world. In 2004, an Italian court convicted Medici of dealing in stolen antiquities and gave him the harshest sentence ever handed down for such a crime— ten years in prison and a ten-million-euro fine. Italian prosecutors then used the evidence against Medici to secure the return of looted artifacts from several prominent museums. Among the items was the renowned Euphronios krater, which New York's Metropolitan Museum of Art reluctantly agreed to return to Italy in 2006. Medici, who was accused of playing a key role in the vessel's looting, had famously posed before its display case at the Met with his arms akimbo. General Ferrari had mimicked the pose on the day the krater was triumphantly placed in its new display case at Rome's Villa Giulia museum.

"All told," Ferrari continued, "Medici was responsible for the looting of thousands of antiquities from Italian soil. But he didn't do it alone. His operation was like a *cordata*, a rope that stretched from the *tombaroli* to the *capi ʒoni* to the dealers and auction houses and, ultimately, to the collectors and museums. And let's not forget our good friends in the Mafia," Ferrari added. "Nothing came out of the ground without their approval. And nothing went to market without a payoff to the bosses."

Ferrari spent a moment contemplating his ruined hand before resuming his briefing. "We didn't spend ten years and millions of euros just to bring down one man and a few of his lieutenants. Our goal was to destroy a network that was slowly pillaging the treasures bequeathed to us by our ancestors. Against all odds, we managed to succeed. But I'm afraid our victory was only temporary. The looting continues. In fact, it's worse than ever."

"A new network has taken the place of Medici's?"

Ferrari nodded and then indulged in a disciplined sip of wine. "Criminals are a bit like terrorists, Allon. If you kill a terrorist, a new terrorist is sure to take his place. And almost without fail, he is more dangerous than his predecessor. This new network is far more sophisticated than Medici's. It's a truly global operation. And, obviously, it's far more ruthless."

"Who's running it?"

"I wish I knew. It could be a consortium, but my instincts tell me it's one man. I'd be surprised if he has any overt links to the antiquities trade. That would be beneath him," the general added quickly. "He's a major criminal who's into more than selling hot pots. And he has the muscle to keep everyone in line, which means he's connected to the Mafia. This network has the ability to rip a statue out of the ground in Greece and sell it at Sotheby's a few months later with what appears to be an entirely clean provenance." The general paused, then added, "He's also getting product from your neck of the woods."

"The Middle East?"

"Someone's been supplying him with artifacts from places like Lebanon, Syria, and Egypt. There are some nasty people in that part of the world. One wonders where all the money is going."

"Where did Falcone fit into the picture?"

"When we stumbled upon his operation a few years ago, I convinced him to go to work for me. It wasn't difficult," Ferrari added, "since the alternative was a long prison sentence. We spent several weeks debriefing him here at the palazzo. Then we sent him back to Cerveteri and allowed him to resume his wicked ways."

"But now you were looking over his shoulder," Chiara said.

"Exactly."

"What would happen when a *tombarolo* brought him a vase or a statue that he'd found?"

"Sometimes we quietly took it off the market and put it away for safekeeping. But usually we allowed Falcone to sell it up the line. That way we could track it as it moved through the bloodstream of the illicit trade. And we wanted everyone in the business to think that Roberto Falcone was a man to be reckoned with."

"Especially the man at the top of this new smuggling network."

"You've obviously done this a time or two yourself," the general said.

Gabriel ignored the remark. "How high were you able to get him into the network?" he asked.

"Only the first rung of the ladder," Ferrari said, frowning. "This new network learned from the mistakes of its predecessor. The men at the top don't talk to people like Roberto Falcone."

"So why was Claudia Andreatti talking to him?"

"Clearly, she must have found something during her review of the Vatican's collection that led her to Falcone's door. Something dangerous enough to get her killed. The fact that Falcone was killed too suggests it had something to do with the network. Frankly, I wouldn't be surprised if a few more bodies turn up in short order."

"Do you realize what you're suggesting?"

Ferrari trained his sightless eye on Gabriel and leaned across the table. "It's not a suggestion," he said. "I'm saying that Dr.

Andreatti discovered a connection between the network and the Vatican. And that means your friend Monsignor Donati has a much bigger problem on his hands than a dead curator. It also means that you and I are pursuing the same target."

"Which is why you're willing to pretend that my wife and I were never in Cerveteri today," Gabriel said. "Because if I can find out who killed Claudia, it will save you the trouble of having to crack the network."

"It *is* a rather elegant solution to our dilemma," Ferrari said.

"Why don't you just hand me over to the security service and pursue the case yourself?"

"Because now that Falcone is dead, the only door into this new network has been slammed in my face. The chances of putting another informant in place are slim. By now, they're well aware of my tools and techniques. They also know my personnel, which makes it difficult for me to send them undercover. I need someone who can help me destroy this network from the inside, someone who can think like a criminal." The general paused. "Someone like you, Allon."

"Is that supposed to be a compliment?"

"Just a statement of fact."

"You overestimate my abilities."

The general gave a knowing smile. "Early in my career, when I was working in the counterterrorism division, I was assigned to a case here in Rome. It seemed a Palestinian translator was shot to death in the lobby of his apartment building. It turned out he was no ordinary translator. As for the man who killed him, we were never able to find a single witness who could recall seeing him. It was as if he were a ghost." The general paused. "And now he sits before me, in a restaurant in the heart of Rome."

"I would have never figured you for a blackmailer, General."

"I wouldn't dream of trying to blackmail you, Allon. I was simply saying that our paths crossed once before. Now it seems fate has reunited us."

"I don't believe in fate."

"Neither do I," Ferrari replied. "But I do believe that if there's anyone who can crack this network, it's you. Besides," he added, "the fact that you are already positioned inside the Vatican gives you a distinct advantage."

Gabriel was silent for a moment. "What happens if I succeed?" he asked finally.

"I will take your information and build a case that will stand up in the Italian courts."

"And what if that case destroys my friends?"

"I am well aware of your close relationship with this pope and with Monsignor Donati," the general said evenly. "But if the Vatican has engaged in misdeeds, it will have to atone. Besides, I've always found that confession can be good for the soul."

"If it's done in private."

"That might not be possible. But the best way for you to look after the interests of your friends is to accept my offer. Otherwise, there's no telling what dirt might turn up."

"That sounds a great deal like blackmail."

"Yes," the general said reflectively, "I suppose it does."

He was smiling slightly, but his prosthetic eye stared blankly into space. It was like gazing into the eye of a figure in a painting, thought Gabriel, the all-seeing eye of an unforgiving God.

Which left only Roberto Falcone—or, more precisely, what to tell the public about his unfortunate demise. Ultimately, it came down to a choice of tactics. The matter could be handled quietly, or, as Gabriel put it, they could announce Falcone's death with a fanfare of trumpets and thus help their own cause in the process. Ferrari chose the second option, for, like Gabriel, he was predisposed toward operational showmanship. Besides, it was budget time in a season of austerity, and Ferrari needed a victory, even an invented one, to ensure the Art Squad's enviable funding levels continued for another fiscal year.

And so late the following morning, Ferrari summoned the news media to the palazzo for what he promised would be a major announcement. It being an otherwise slow news day, they came in droves, hoping for something that might actually sell a newspaper or entice a television viewer to pause for a few seconds before surfing off to the next channel. As usual, the general did not disappoint. Impeccably dressed in his blue Carabinieri uniform, he strode to the podium and proceeded to spin a tale as old as Italy itself. It was a tale of a man who appeared to be of modest means but was in fact one of Italy's biggest looters of antiquities. Regrettably, the man had been brutally murdered, perhaps in a dispute with a colleague over money. The general did not specify exactly how the body was discovered, though he doled out enough of the gruesome details to guarantee front-page play in the livelier tabloids. Then, with the flawless timing of a skilled performer, he drew back a black curtain, revealing a treasure trove of artifacts recovered from the *tombarolo*'s workshop. The reporters let out a collective gasp. Ferrari beamed as the cameras flashed.

Needless to say, the general made no mention of the role played by the retired Israeli spy and art restorer Gabriel Allon or of the somewhat Machiavellian agreement the two men had reached over dinner at Le Cave. Nor did he divulge the name he had whispered into Gabriel's ear as they parted company in the darkened piazza.

Gabriel waited until the end of the general's news conference before ringing her. It was clear from her tone that she had been expecting his call.

"I'm in a meeting until five," she said. "How about five-thirty?"

"Your place or mine?"

"Mine is safer."

"Where?"

"The krater," she said. And then the line went dead.

12

VILLA GIULIA, ROME

I N A CITY FILLED WITH museums and archaeological wonders, the Villa Giulia, Italy's national repository of Etruscan art
and antiquities, somehow manages to keep a low profile. Rarely
visited and easily missed, it occupies a rambling palazzo on the
edge of the Borghese Gardens that was once the country house of
Pope Julius III. In the sixteenth century, the villa had overlooked
the city walls of Rome and the gentle tan slopes of the Parioli hills.
Now the hills were lined with apartment blocks, and beneath the
windows of the old papal retreat thundered a broad boulevard that
pedestrians crossed at their own risk. The weedy forecourt had
been turned into the staff parking lot. The battered fenders and
sun-faded paint bore witness to the low wages earned by those
who toiled within the state museums of Italy.

Gabriel arrived at 5:15 and made his way to the second-floor
gallery where the Euphronios krater, regarded as one of the greatest single pieces of art ever created, resided in a simple glass display

case. A small placard told of the vessel's tangled history—how it had been looted from a tomb near Cerveteri in 1971 and sold to the Metropolitan Museum of Art for the astonishing price of one million dollars, and how, thanks to the tireless efforts of the Italian government, it had finally been returned to its rightful home. Cultural patrimony had been protected, thought Gabriel, looking around the uninhabited room, but at what cost? Nearly five million people visited the Met each year, but here in the deserted halls of the Villa Giulia, the krater was left to stand alone with the sadness of a knickknack gathering dust on a shelf. If it belonged anywhere, he thought, it was in the tomb of the wealthy Etruscan who had purchased it from a Greek trader two and a half thousand years ago.

Gabriel heard the clatter of high heels and, turning, glimpsed a tall, elegant woman coming through the passage from the adjoining gallery. Dark hair fell softly about her shoulders, and wide brown eyes shone intelligently from her face. The cut of her suit suggested a source of income beyond the museum, as did the jewelry that sparkled on the suntanned hand she extended in Gabriel's direction. She held the embrace for a moment longer than was necessary, as though she had been waiting to meet him for some time. She seemed well aware of the impact of her appearance.

"You were expecting someone in a white lab coat?"

"I only know one archaeologist," said Gabriel, "and he's usually covered in dirt."

Dr. Veronica Marchese gave a fleeting smile. She was at least fifty, but even in the unflattering halogen light of the museum she could have easily passed for thirty-five. Her name, when spoken by General Ferrari, had been instantly familiar to Gabriel, for it had appeared dozens of times in Claudia's e-mail accounts. Now he realized her face was familiar, too. He had seen it for the first time outside the Church of St. Anne, at the conclusion of Claudia Andreatti's funeral mass. She had been standing slightly apart from the other mourners, and her eyes had been fixed not on the casket but upon Luigi Donati. Something about her gaze, remembered Gabriel, had been vaguely accusatory.

Now she slipped past Gabriel and peered through the shatterproof glass of the display case at the image on the side of the krater. It depicted the lifeless body of Sarpedon, son of Zeus, being carried off for burial by the personifications of Sleep and Death. The image was strikingly similar to the composition of *The Deposition of Christ*.

"I never tire of looking at it," Dr. Marchese said softly. "It's almost as beautiful as the Caravaggio you're restoring for the Vatican." She glanced over her shoulder and asked, "Wouldn't you agree, Mr. Allon?"

"Actually, I wouldn't."

"You don't care for Greek vases?"

"I don't believe I said that."

Her eyes swept slowly over him, as if he were a statue mounted atop a plinth. "Greek vases are among the most extraordinary objects ever created," she said. "Without them, there would have been no Caravaggio. And unfortunately, there are some men in the world who will do anything to possess them." She paused thoughtfully. "But you didn't come here for a debate about the aesthetic merits of ancient art. You're here because of Claudia."

"I assume you saw General Ferrari's news conference?"

"He had the reporters eating out of his hand as usual." She didn't sound impressed. "But he's obviously been taking lessons in evasion from the Vatican."

The general had warned Gabriel about Dr. Marchese's acerbic wit. A graduate of Rome's La Sapienza University, she was regarded as Italy's foremost authority on Etruscan civilization and had served as an expert consultant to the Art Squad on numerous cases, including the Medici investigation. After the raid on Medici's warehouse in Geneva, she had spent weeks examining the contents, trying to determine the origin of each piece and, if possible, when it had been ripped from the ground by tomb raiders. Working at her side had been a gifted young protégée named Claudia Andreatti.

"The general tells me you were the one who was responsible for Claudia getting the job at the Vatican."

"She was my best friend," Veronica Marchese replied, "but she didn't need my help. Claudia was one of the most talented people who ever worked for me. She earned the job entirely on her own."

"You knew that she had undertaken a review of the Vatican's collection of antiquities. In fact, she consulted with you on a regular basis."

"I see you've been reading her e-mail."

"And her phone records as well. I know that she was in contact with Roberto Falcone before her death. I was hoping you might be able to tell me why."

Veronica Marchese lapsed into silence. "Claudia said she'd discovered a problem with the collection," she said finally. "She thought Falcone could help."

"What kind of problem?"

"Apparently things were missing. Lots of things."

"From the storerooms?"

"Not just the storerooms. From the galleries as well."

Gabriel joined her at the display case, his eyes on the krater.

"And when the Vatican announced that Claudia had committed suicide in the Basilica?"

"I was dubious, to say the least."

"But you remained silent."

It was a statement. She delivered her response not to Gabriel but to the corpse of Sarpedon.

"It was difficult," she said quietly. "But, yes, I remained silent."

"Why?"

"Because I was asked to."

"By whom?"

"By the same man who asked you to quietly investigate her death."

"Monsignor Donati?"

"Monsignor?" She gave a melancholy smile. "I still find it hard to refer to him as that."

The museum's café was housed in an old greenhouse set against the villa's main courtyard. The attendant, a woman of sixty with pins in her gray hair, was in the process of closing down the cash register as they entered, but Veronica managed to cajole her into making two final cups of cappuccino. They sat together at a small wrought-iron table in the corner, next to a trellis of flowering vine. Rain pattered overhead on the glass roof while she examined the fragment of pottery Gabriel had taken from Falcone's house in Cerveteri.

"Your wife has an excellent eye. The figure is clearly a follower of Dionysus. If I had to guess, it's probably the work of the Mene-laos Painter, which means it should be here in the Villa Giulia, not on the kitchen table of a *tombarolo*." She returned the fragment to

Gabriel. "Unfortunately, it was probably intact before it fell into the hands of Falcone and his men."

"How was it broken?"

"Sometimes ceramics are shattered by the *spilli* that the *tombaroli* use to locate the tombs. But other times, the *tombaroli* and their middlemen break vases intentionally. Then they slide the fragments onto the market piecemeal over time so as not to attract unwanted attention. Once all the pieces are in the hands of a single dealer, they pretend a long-lost vase has suddenly materialized." She shook her head slowly in disgust. "They're scum. But they're very clever."

"And dangerous," added Gabriel.

"So it would seem." She started to light a cigarette but stopped. "I'm sorry," she said, sliding it back into the pack. "Luigi told me how much you hate tobacco."

"What else has he told you?"

"He said you're one of the most remarkable men he's ever met. He also said you would have made an excellent priest."

"I minister to paintings, not souls. Besides," he added, "I'm a sinner without hope of redemption."

"Priests sin, too. Even the good ones."

She poured three packets of sugar into her cappuccino and gave it a gentle stir. Gabriel should have been thinking about the case, but he couldn't help but wonder how the life of the Holy Father's private secretary had intersected with a woman like Veronica Marchese. He imagined several scenarios, none of them good.

"I thought spies were supposed to be good at concealing their thoughts," she said.

"I'm officially retired."

"Good. Because you're obviously curious about how Luigi and I know each other. Suffice it to say we've been friends for a long time. In fact, I was the one who first suggested a review of the Church's collection."

"You were concerned it might be tainted?"

"Let's just say that, given current political realities, I thought it wise for Luigi to know more than his potential enemies."

"You would have made a good lawyer."

"I am a lawyer," she said, "as well as an archaeologist."

"Why didn't you volunteer to conduct the review yourself?"

"It's not my collection. Besides, Luigi had a perfect candidate for the job on the staff of the museum."

"Claudia."

Veronica Marchese nodded slowly. "She was a natural detective. Her work was impeccable."

"But when I reviewed her notes and research files, there was no mention of any problem whatsoever. In fact, it appeared she'd given the collection a clean bill of health."

"That's because she was advised not to put any of her findings in writing."

"By whom?"

"Me."

"Did she tell you what was missing?"

"She didn't go into specifics, only that she couldn't account for several dozen pieces. Nothing major," she added quickly, "but they were of great value, exactly the sort of things that can confer instant prestige upon your average Arab sheikh or Russian oligarch. She compiled a list of the items and took it to an old friend who might know where she could find them."

"Roberto Falcone?"

"Exactly."

"How did Claudia know someone like Falcone?"

"He was an associate of her father."

"Are you saying Claudia's father *worked* for Roberto Falcone?"

"No," Veronica Marchese said, shaking her head slowly. "Claudia's father would never work for a man like Roberto Falcone. Falcone worked for *him*."

The woman behind the counter rolled her eyes to indicate she wished to close for the night. Gabriel and Veronica Marchese quickly finished the last of their coffee and then headed outside. Darkness had fallen and a gusty wet wind was swirling in the arcades. Veronica lit a cigarette thoughtfully and proceeded to tell Gabriel things about Claudia Andreatti that had failed to make it into her Vatican personnel file. That she had been raised in Tarquinia, an ancient Etruscan town north of Cerveteri. That her father, Francesco Andreatti, a day laborer of peasant stock, had supplemented the family's meager income with a *spillo* and a shovel. It seemed he possessed a unique talent for extracting antiquities from the mounded fields of Lazio, a talent matched only by his ability to keep the Carabinieri and the Mafia at bay. He grew wealthy from his digging, though everyone in Tarquinia believed he was an ordinary stonemason. So, too, did his twin daughters.

"When did they learn the truth about him?"

"He confessed his sins as he was dying of cancer. He also told them about the buried steel container where he stored his discoveries. Claudia and Paola waited until after the funeral to alert the Carabinieri. They were just sixteen at the time."

"The entire incident seems to have slipped Paola's mind."

"I'm not surprised she didn't tell you. It's not something a daughter likes to think about. Unfortunately, most of us have a criminal somewhere in the family tree. I'm afraid it is the curse of Italy."

"Rather ironic, don't you think?"

"That the daughter of a *tombarolo* dedicated herself to the care and preservation of antiquities?"

Gabriel nodded.

"Actually, it was no accident. Claudia was deeply ashamed of her father and wanted to make up for some of the damage he had done. Needless to say, she guarded her past carefully. If it ever became known in the curatorial community that her father was a thief, it would have hung over her like a cloud."

"But *you* knew."

"She told me during the Medici investigation. She felt that she had to because we were working with General Ferrari." Veronica Marchese paused, then added, "Claudia had an exaggerated sense of right and wrong. It was one of the things I loved most about her."

"Do you know what Falcone told her?"

"She wouldn't tell me. She said it was necessary to protect the integrity of her investigation."

They walked past the shuttered museum bookshop and emerged from the front portico. The rain was coming down in torrents. She fished a set of keys from her handbag and with the click of her remote started the engine of a gleaming Mercedes SL coupe. The car looked out of place at the museum. So did Veronica Marchese.

"I'd offer you a lift," she said apologetically, "but I'm afraid I have another appointment. If there's anything more I can do to help, please don't hesitate to call. And do give my best to Luigi."

She started toward her car, then stopped suddenly and turned to face him. "It occurs to me you have one thing working in your favor," she said. "General Ferrari just took millions of euros worth of antiquities from the men who killed Claudia. That means they'll be anxious to replenish their stock. If I were you, I'd find something irresistible."

"What then?"

"Smash it to pieces," she replied. "And feed it to them slowly."

She lowered herself into the car and then guided it into the frenetic traffic of the Roman evening rush. Gabriel stood there for a moment wondering why Luigi Donati had neglected to mention that he was acquainted with Claudia Andreatti's best friend. Priests sin, too, he thought. Even the good ones.

13

APOSTOLIC PALACE, VATICAN CITY

W HAT'S THE SOUP OF THE day?" asked Gabriel.

"Stone," replied Donati.

He raised a spoonful of the thin consommé to his lips and tasted it warily. They were seated in the Holy Father's austere dining room on the third floor of the Apostolic Palace. The tablecloth was white, as were the habits of the household nuns who floated silently in and out of the adjoining kitchen. His Holiness was not present; he was working at the desk in his small private office located directly across the hall. It had been fourteen years since the diminutive Patriarch of Venice ascended to the throne of St. Peter, yet he still maintained a crushing daily schedule that would exhaust a far younger man. He did so in part to preserve his power. The Church faced too many challenges for its absolute monarch to give the appearance of being incapacitated by age. If the princes perceived that His Holiness was beginning to fail, the positioning for the next conclave would commence in earnest. And the papacy of Pope Paul VII, one of the most turbulent in the history of the modern Church, would come to a grinding halt.

"Why the punishment rations?" asked Gabriel.

"As a result of our reduced financial circumstances, the fare at some of the colleges and religious houses in Rome is starting to suffer. His Holiness has asked the bishops and cardinals to avoid lavish dining. I'm afraid I have no choice but to lead by example."

He held his glass of red wine up to the sunlight slanting through the window and then took a cautious sip.

"How is it?"

"Divine." Donati placed the glass carefully on the table and then pushed a thick black binder toward Gabriel. "It's the final itinerary for our trip to Israel and the Palestinian territories. We've decided to do it over Holy Week, which will allow His Holiness to take the unprecedented step of celebrating Christ's death and resurrection in the city where it actually occurred. He will commemorate the passion on the Via Dolorosa and celebrate Easter Mass in the Church of the Holy Sepulchre. The schedule also includes a stop in Bethlehem and a courtesy call at the al-Aqsa Mosque, where he intends to issue an unequivocal apology for the Crusades. The soldiers of the cross killed ten thousand people on the Temple Mount when they sacked Jerusalem in 1099, including three thousand who had taken shelter inside al-Aqsa."

"And they warmed up along the way by killing several thousand innocent Jews in Europe."

"I believe we've already apologized for that," Donati said archly.

"When do you plan to announce the trip?"

"Next week at the General Audience."

"It's too soon."

"We've waited as long as possible. I'd like you to have a look at the security arrangements. The Holy Father also asked whether you would consider serving as his personal bodyguard during the trip."

"Something tells me it wasn't his idea."

"It wasn't," Donati conceded.

"The best way to place His Holiness in danger is for me to stand next to him."

"Think about it."

Donati raised another spoonful of the consommé to his lips and blew on it pensively—odd, thought Gabriel, because his own soup was already lukewarm.

"Something else on your mind, Luigi?"

"Rumor has it you paid a visit to the Villa Giulia yesterday."

"It's filled with many beautiful objects."

"So I've heard." Donati lowered his voice and added, "You should have told me you were going to see her."

"I didn't realize I needed your permission."

"That's not what I meant."

"When I took this case," Gabriel said, pressing him gently, "you assured me that all doors would be open."

"Not the doors to my past," Donati said evenly.

"What if your past had something to do with Claudia's death?"

"My past had *nothing* to do with her death."

The monsignor's words were spoken with an air of liturgical finality. All that was missing was the sign of the cross and the benedictory amen.

"Would you like some more soup?" he asked, trying to ease the tension of the moment.

"I'll resist," replied Gabriel.

Two nuns entered and cleared the dishes. They returned a moment later with the entrée—a thin slice of veal, boiled potatoes, and green beans drizzled in olive oil. Donati used the change in course as an opportunity to gather his thoughts.

"I asked for your help," he said at last, "because I wanted this inquiry handled with a certain discretion. Now General Ferrari and the Carabinieri are involved, which is exactly the outcome I had hoped to avoid."

"They're involved because my inquiry led me to a dead *tombarolo* named Roberto Falcone."

"I realize that."

"Would you have preferred it if I had fled the scene?"

"I would have *preferred*," Donati said after a moment of deliberation, "that this mess not end up in the lap of Italian authorities who do not always have the best interests of the Holy See in mind."

"That would have been the outcome regardless of my actions," Gabriel said.

"Why?"

"Because it wouldn't have taken General Ferrari long to connect Falcone to Claudia through their phone records. And his next stop would have been Veronica Marchese. Unless she was prepared to lie on your behalf, she would have told the general that, after Claudia's death, you asked her to remain silent. And then General Ferrari would have been knocking on the Bronze Doors of the Apostolic Palace, subpoena in hand."

"Point taken." Donati picked at his food without appetite. "Why do you suppose Ferrari suggested that you meet with her?"

"I've been asking myself the same question," Gabriel said. "I suspect that like any good investigator, he knows more than he's willing to say."

"About my friendship with Veronica?"

"About everything."

Outside a cloud passed before the sun, and a shadow fell across Donati's face.

"Why didn't you tell me about her, Luigi?"

"This is beginning to sound like an interrogation."

"Better me than the Carabinieri."

Donati, still in shadow, said nothing.

"Perhaps it would be easier if I answered for you."

"Please do."

"This entire affair falls under the category of no good deed goes unpunished," Gabriel began. "It started innocently enough when Veronica suggested you undertake a review of the Vatican collection. But Claudia's death presented you with two problems. The first was the motive for her murder. The second was your relationship with Veronica Marchese. A thorough investigation of Claudia's death would have revealed both, thus placing you in a precarious position. So you encouraged an official finding of suicide and asked me to find the truth."

"And now you've discovered a small piece of it." Donati pushed his plate a few inches toward the center of the table and gazed through the open door toward the private office of his master.

"How much does he know?" asked Gabriel.

"More than you might imagine. But that doesn't mean he wants it spilling out in public. Gossip and personal scandal can be fatal in a place like this. And if I am tainted in any way, it could harm his papacy." He paused, then added gravely, "That is something I cannot allow to happen."

"The best way to prevent that from happening is for you to start telling me the truth. All of it."

Donati exhaled heavily and contemplated his wristwatch. "I have thirty minutes until the Holy Father's next meeting," he said. "Perhaps it would be better if we walked. The walls have ears around here."

14

THE VATICAN GARDENS

I T IS SAID THAT THE Vatican Gardens were originally planted in soil from Golgotha transported to Rome by St. Helena, mother of the Emperor Constantine and, according to Christian legend, discoverer of the True Cross. Now, seventeen centuries later, the gardens were a fifty-seven-acre Eden dotted with ornate palaces housing various arms of the Vatican administration. The overcast weather suited Donati's mood. Head down, hands clasped behind his back, he was telling Gabriel about a serious young man from a small town in Umbria who heard the calling to become a priest. The young man joined the intellectually rebellious Society of Jesus, the Jesuits, and became a vocal proponent of the controversial doctrine known as liberation theology. In the early 1980s, during a period of violence and revolution in Latin America, he was dispatched to El Salvador to run a health clinic and a school. And it was there, in the mountains of Morazán province, that he lost his faith in God.

"Liberation theologians believe that earthly justice and eternal salvation are inexorably linked, that it is impossible to save a soul if the vessel in which it resides is bound by chains of poverty and oppression. In Latin America, that sort of thinking placed us squarely on the side of the leftist revolutionaries. The military juntas regarded us as little more than Communist subversives. So did the Pole," Donati added. "But that's a story for another time."

Donati stopped walking, as if debating which direction to proceed. Finally, he turned toward the ocher-colored headquarters of Vatican Radio. Rising above it was the city-state's only eyesore, the transmission tower that beamed Church news and programming to a worldwide flock increasingly distracted by terrestrial matters.

"There was a priest who worked with me in Morazán," Donati resumed, "a Spanish Jesuit named Father José Martinez. One evening, I was called away to another village to deliver a child. When I returned, Father José was dead. The top of his skull had been hacked away and his brain scooped from its cavity."

"He was killed by a death squad?"

Donati nodded slowly. "That's why they took his brain. It symbolized what the regime and its wealthy supporters hated most about us—our intelligence and our commitment to social justice. When I asked the military to investigate Father José's death, they actually laughed in my face. Then they warned me I would be next if I didn't leave."

"Did you take their advice?"

"I should have, but his death made me even more determined to stay and complete my mission. About six months later, a rebel leader came to see me. He knew the identity of the man responsible for Father José's murder. His name was Alejandro Calderón. He was the scion of a landowning family with close ties to the ruling junta.

He kept a mistress in an apartment in the town of San Miguel. The rebels were planning to kill him the next time he went to see her."

"Why did they tell you in advance?"

"Because they wanted my blessing. I withheld it, of course."

"But you didn't tell them *not* to kill him, either."

"No," Donati admitted. "Nor did I warn Calderón. Three days later, his body was found hanging upside down from a lamppost . in the central square of San Miguel. Within hours, another death squad was headed toward our village. But this time, they were looking for me. I fled across the border into Honduras and hid in a Jesuit house in Tegucigalpa. When it was safe for me to move, I returned to Rome, whereupon I was immediately summoned by the head of our order. He asked me whether I knew anything about Calderón's death. Then he reminded me that, as a Jesuit, I was sworn to be obedient *perinde ac cadaver*—literally, to have no more will than my own corpse. I refused to answer. The next morning, I asked to be released from my vows."

"You left the priesthood?"

"I had no choice. I'd allowed a man to be killed. What's more, I no longer believed in God. Surely, I told myself, a just and forgiving God would not have allowed a man like Father José to be killed in such a gruesome manner."

A group of Curial cardinals emerged from the entrance of the Vatican Radio building, trailed by their priestly staffs. Donati frowned and led Gabriel toward St. John's Tower.

"I can only imagine that leaving the priesthood is a bit like leaving an intelligence service," Donati resumed after a moment. "It's a deliberately long and cumbersome process designed to give the wayward priest ample opportunity to change his mind. But eventually I found myself back in Umbria, living alone in a village near

Monte Cucco. I spent my days climbing the mountains. I suppose I was hoping to find God up there among the peaks. But I found Veronica instead."

"She's the kind of woman who could restore a man's faith in the divine."

"In a way, she did."

"What was she doing in Umbria?"

"She'd just completed her doctorate and was excavating the ruins of a Roman villa. We bumped into each other quite by accident in the town market. Within days, we were inseparable."

"Did you tell her you'd been a priest?"

"I told her *every*thing, including what had happened in Salvador. She took it upon herself to heal my wounds and to show me the real world—the world that had passed me by while I was locked away in the seminary. Before long, we began talking about marriage. Veronica was going to teach. I was going to work as an advocate for human rights. We had everything planned."

"So what happened?"

"I met a man named Pietro Lucchesi."

Pietro Lucchesi was the given name of His Holiness Pope Paul VII.

"It was shortly after he was appointed Patriarch of Venice," Donati continued. "He was looking for someone to serve as his private secretary. He'd heard about a former Jesuit who was living like a recluse in Umbria. He arrived unannounced and said he had no intention of leaving until I agreed to return to the priesthood. We spent a week together walking in the mountains, arguing about God and the mysteries of faith. Needless to say, Lucchesi prevailed. Breaking the news to Veronica was the hardest thing I've ever done. She is the only woman I ever loved, or ever will."

"Any regrets?"

"One wonders from time to time, but, no, I have no regrets. I suppose it would have been easier if we'd never seen each other again, but it didn't work out that way."

"Please tell me you're not romantically involved with her."

"I take my vows seriously," Donati said dismissively. "And so does Veronica. We are good friends, that's all."

"I take it she's married."

"Infamously. Her husband is Carlo Marchese. He's one of the most successful businessmen in Italy." Donati paused and looked at Gabriel gravely. "He's also the reason Claudia Andreatti is dead."

Somewhere beyond the walls of the Vatican a car backfired with the sharp report of a gunshot. A squadron of rooks whirled noisily in the trees before flying off in formation toward the dome of the Basilica. Gabriel watched them for a moment as he pieced together the implications of the story Donati had just told him. He felt as though he were wandering beneath the surface of an altarpiece, stumbling upon partial images concealed beneath layers of obliterating paint—here a woman lying dead on the floor of a church, here a tomb robber suffering for his sins in a cauldron of acid, here a fallen priest searching for God in the arms of his lover. He had questions, a thousand questions, but he knew better than to break the spell under which Donati had fallen. And so he walked at the monsignor's shoulder with the austere silence of a confessor and waited for his friend to make a full accounting of his sins.

"Carlo descends from the Black Nobility," Donati said, "the aristocratic Roman families who remained loyal to the pope after the conquest of the Papal States in 1870. His father was part of Pius the Twelfth's inner circle. He was close to the CIA as well."

"In what way?"

"He was involved in the Christian Democratic Party. After the Second World War, he worked with the CIA to prevent the Communists from taking control of Italy. Several million dollars' worth of secret CIA funds flowed through his hands before the election in 1948. Carlo says they used to give his father suitcases filled with cash in the lobby of the Hassler Hotel."

"It sounds as if you and Carlo are rather well acquainted."

"We are," Donati replied. "Like his father, Carlo is a member in good standing of the papal court. He also serves on the lay supervisory council of the Vatican Bank, which means he knows as much about Church finances as I do. Carlo is the kind of man who doesn't need to stop at the Permissions Desk before entering the Apostolic Palace. He likes to remind me that he'll still be at the Vatican long after I'm gone."

"Who appointed him to the bank?"

"I did."

"Why?"

"Because Veronica asked me to. And because Carlo appeared to be the perfect man for the job, a man with long-standing ties to the papacy who was regarded as one of the most honest businessmen in a country known for corruption. Unfortunately, that turned out not to be the case. Carlo Marchese controls the international trade in illicit antiquities. But that's just the tip of the proverbial iceberg. He sits atop a global criminal empire that's into everything from narcotics to counterfeiting to arms trafficking. And he's laundering his dirty money at the Vatican Bank."

"And you, the private secretary to His Holiness Pope Paul the Seventh, helped him get the job."

"Unwittingly," Donati said defensively. "But that small detail won't matter if this explodes into yet another scandal."

"When did you learn the truth about Carlo?"

"It wasn't until I asked a talented curator to conduct a review of the Vatican's collection of antiquities," Donati said. "First she discovered that dozens of pieces had vanished from the Vatican Museums. Then she discovered a connection between the thieves and one Carlo Marchese."

"Why did she want to see you the night of her death?"

"She told me she had evidence of Carlo's involvement. The next morning, she was dead, and whatever evidence she had was gone." Donati shook his head. "Carlo actually rang my office that afternoon to offer his condolences. He had the decency not to show his face at the funeral."

"He had other matters to attend to."

"Such as?"

"Killing a *tombarolo* named Roberto Falcone."

They walked past St. John's Tower and made their way to the helipad in the far southwest corner of the city-state. Donati stared at the walls for a moment, as though calculating how to scale them, before taking a seat on a bench at the edge of the tarmac. Gabriel sat next to him and began mentally sorting through the notes of his investigation. One entry stood out: Claudia Andreatti's final telephone call on the night of her death. It had been placed to the Villa Giulia, to the wife of a man who didn't need to stop at the Permissions Desk before entering the Apostolic Palace.

"How much does Veronica know about her husband?"

"If you're asking whether she thinks Carlo is a criminal, the answer is no. She believes her husband is a descendant of an old Roman family who parlayed his modest inheritance into a successful business."

"Does this successful businessman know you were engaged to his wife?"

Donati shook his head solemnly.

"You're sure?"

"Veronica never breathed a word of it to him."

"What about El Salvador?"

"He knows I served there and that, like most of the Jesuits, I had some trouble with the death squads and their friends in the military. But he has no idea I ever left the priesthood. In fact, very few people inside the Church know about my little sabbatical. Any mention of the affair was purged from my personnel files after I went to work for Lucchesi in Venice. It's as if it never happened."

"Almost like Claudia's murder."

Donati made no response.

"You lied to me, Luigi."

"Mea culpa, mea culpa, mea maxima culpa."

"I don't want your apology. I just want an explanation of why you allowed me to investigate a murder when you already knew the identity of the killer."

"Because I needed to know how much you could find out on your own before moving on to the next step."

"And what would that be?"

"I would like you to bring me incontrovertible proof that Carlo Marchese is running a global criminal enterprise from inside my bank. And then I want you to make him go away. Quietly."

"There's just one problem with that," Gabriel said. "After my visit to the Villa Giulia, I suspect I've lost the element of surprise."

"I concur. In fact, I'm quite sure Carlo knows exactly what you're up to."

"Why?"

"Because you've been invited to an intimate dinner party

tomorrow evening at his palazzo. I've already accepted on your behalf. But do try to find something presentable to wear," Donati said, frowning at Gabriel's leather jacket and paint-smudged jeans. "I don't mind if you walk around the palace dressed like that, but the Black Nobility tend to be a bit on the formal side."

15

PIAZZA DI SPAGNA, ROME

G ABRIEL POSSESSED A SINGLE SUIT. Italian in design, Office in manufacture, it had hidden compartments for concealing false passports and a holster sewn into the waistband of the trousers large enough to hold a Beretta pistol and a spare magazine. After much debate, he decided it would be unwise to bring a firearm to Carlo Marchese's dinner party. He knotted the pale blue necktie that Chiara had bought for him that afternoon from a shop in the Via Condotti and artfully stuffed a silk handkerchief into his breast pocket. Chiara made subtle adjustments to both before slipping into the bathroom to finish putting on her makeup. She was wearing a black cocktail-length dress and black stockings. Her hair hung loosely about her bare shoulders, and on her right wrist was the pearl-and-emerald bracelet Gabriel had given her on the occasion of her last birthday. She looked astonishingly beautiful, he thought, and far too young to be on the arm of a battered wreck like him.

"You'd better put some clothes on," he said. "We need to leave in a few minutes."

"You don't like what I'm wearing?"

"What's not to like?"

"So what's the problem?"

"It's rather provocative," said Gabriel, his eyes roaming freely over her body. "After all, we *are* having dinner with a priest."

"At the home of his former lover." She brushed a bit of powder across her cheekbones that brought out the flecks of honey and gold in her wide brown eyes. "I have to admit I'm curious to meet the woman who managed to penetrate Donati's armor."

"You won't be disappointed."

"What's she like?"

"She would have been the perfect match for Donati if he'd chosen a different occupation."

"It's more than an occupation. And I'm sure Donati had very little to do with choosing it."

"You believe it's truly a calling?"

"I'm the daughter of a rabbi. I *know* it's a calling." Chiara examined her appearance in the mirror for a moment before resuming work on her exquisite face. "For the record, I was right about Donati from the beginning. I told you he had a past. And I warned you that he was hiding something."

"He had no choice."

"Really?"

"If he'd told me the truth, that he wanted me to go to war with a made Mafia man like Carlo Marchese, I would have finished the Caravaggio and left town as quickly as possible."

"It's still an option."

Gabriel, with a glance into the mirror, made clear it wasn't.

"You have no idea what you're getting into, darling. I grew up in this country. I know them better than you."

"I never realized the Jewish ghetto of Venice was such a hotbed of Mafia activity."

"They're everywhere," Chiara replied with a frown. "And they kill anyone who gets between them and their money—judges, politicians, policemen, *any*one. Carlo has already killed two people to protect his secret. And he won't hesitate to kill you too if he thinks you're a threat."

"I'm not a politician. And I'm not a policeman, either."

"What does that mean?"

"It means they have to play by the rules. I don't." Gabriel removed the handkerchief from his pocket and smoothed the front of his suit jacket.

"I liked it better before," Chiara said.

"I didn't."

"They're very fashionable these days."

"That's why I don't like it."

Chiara wordlessly returned the handkerchief to Gabriel's pocket. "I never thought I'd meet a woman whose love life was more complicated than my own," she said, inspecting her work. "First Veronica falls in love with a priest who's lost his faith in God. Then, when the priest dumps her, she marries a Mafia chieftain who's running a global crime syndicate."

"Donati didn't *dump* her," Gabriel replied. "And Veronica Marchese has no idea where her husband gets his money."

"Maybe," Chiara said without conviction. "Or maybe she sees exactly what she wants to see and turns a blind eye to the rest. It's easier that way, especially when there's a great deal of money involved."

"Is that why you married me? For the money?"

"No," she said, "I married you because I adore your fatalistic sense of humor. You always make dreadful jokes when you're upset about something and you're trying to hide it."

"Why would I be upset?"

"Because you came to Rome to restore one of your favorite paintings. And now you're about to make an enemy of a man who could kill you with one phone call."

"I'm not so easy to kill."

Chiara gathered up her hair and turned her back toward Gabriel. He raised the zipper of her dress slowly and then pressed his lips against the nape of her neck. In the mirror he could see her eyes closing.

"Why do you suppose he wants us at his dinner table tonight?" Chiara asked.

"I can only imagine that he intends to send me a message."

"What are you going to do?"

"I'm going to listen very carefully," Gabriel said, kissing her neck one last time. "And then I'm going to send him one in return."

16

THE VIA VENETO, ROME

THE MARCHESES LIVED WITHIN walking distance of the Piazza di Spagna, on a quiet street off the Via Veneto where the ceaseless march of time seemed to have stopped, however briefly, in an age of grace. This was the Rome that travelers dreamed of but rarely saw, the Rome of poets and painters and the fabulously rich. In Carlo's private little corner of the Eternal City, *la dolce vita* endured, if only for the moment.

His home was not a real home but a vast ocher-colored palazzo set amid an expanse of parkland. Surrounding it was an iron fence topped with many security cameras—so many, in fact, the property was often mistaken for an embassy or a government building. A large Baroque fountain splashed in the forecourt, and in the entrance hall loomed an armless statue of Pluto, lord of the underworld. Standing next to it was Veronica Marchese, dressed in a flowing gown of crushed green silk. She greeted Gabriel and Chiara warmly and then led them along a wide corridor hung with Italian Renaissance paintings in ornate frames. Between the canvases, balanced atop fluted shoulder-height pedestals, were Roman busts and statuary. The paintings were museum quality. So were the antiquities.

"The Marchese family has been collecting for many generations," she explained, a note of disapproval in her voice. "I don't mind the paintings, but the antiquities have been a source of some embarrassment for me, since I am on record as saying the collectors are the real looters. It's quite simple. If the rich would stop buying antiquities, the *tombaroli* would stop digging them up."

"Your husband has excellent taste," Chiara said.

"He has an expert adviser," Veronica replied playfully. "But we're not responsible for any of these acquisitions. Carlo's ancestors purchased them long before there were any laws restricting the trade in ancient artifacts. Even so, I'm trying to convince him to give away at least a portion of the collection so the public can finally see it. I'm afraid I still have a bit of work to do."

At the end of the hall was a wide double doorway that gave onto a grand drawing room with tapestried walls. The furnishings were stately and elegant, as were the guests scattered among them. Gabriel had been expecting a quiet dinner for six, but the room was filled with no fewer than twenty people, including the Italian minister of finance, the host of an influential television talk show, and one of the country's most popular sopranos. Donati had cloistered himself at one end of a brocaded sofa. He was dressed in a double-breasted clerical suit and was imparting some well-rehearsed Curial gossip to a pair of bejeweled women who seemed to be hanging breathlessly on his every utterance.

At the opposite end of the room, surrounded by a group of prosperous-looking businessmen, stood Carlo Marchese. He had the square shoulders of a man who had been a star athlete at school, and was groomed as if for a photo shoot. His small wireless spectacles lent a priestly gravity to his even features, and he was gesturing thoughtfully with a hand that had wielded no tool other than a Montblanc pen or a silver fork. His resemblance to Donati was unmistakable. It was as if Veronica, having lost Donati to the Church, had acquired another version of him absent a Roman collar and a conscience.

As Gabriel and Chiara entered the room, several heads turned in unison and the conversation fell silent for a few seconds before resuming in a subdued murmur. Gabriel accepted two glasses of Prosecco from a white-jacketed waiter and handed one to Chiara. Then, turning, he found himself staring into Carlo's face.

"It's a pleasure to finally meet you, Mr. Allon." One hand closed around Gabriel's while the other grasped his arm just above the elbow. "I was in St. Peter's Square when the terrorists attacked the Vatican. None of us who are close to the Holy Father will ever forget what you did that day." He released Gabriel's hand and introduced himself to Chiara. "Would you be kind enough to allow me to borrow your husband for a moment? I have a small problem I'd like to discuss with him."

"I suppose that depends on the nature of the problem."

"I can assure you it's entirely artistic in nature."

Without waiting for a reply, Carlo Marchese led Gabriel up a sweeping central staircase, to the second level of the palazzo. Before them stretched an endless gallery of ancestral treasures: paintings and tapestries, sculptures and timepieces, antiquities of every sort. Carlo played the role of tour guide, slowing every few paces in order to point out a noteworthy piece or two. He spoke with the erudition of a man who knew much about art but also with a trace of discomfort, as though his possessions were a great burden to him. Even Gabriel found the presence of so much art in one space overwhelming; it was like wandering through storerooms filled with the plunder of a distant war. He paused before a Canaletto. The painting, a luminous depiction of the Piazza di San Marco, was vaguely familiar. Then Gabriel realized where he had seen it before. A few years earlier, the work had been stolen. Its successful recovery, announced with much fanfare by General Ferrari, was regarded as one of the great triumphs of the Art Squad.

"Now I know why the general refused to release the name of the owner," Gabriel said.

"He did so at my request. We were afraid we would be targeted again if the thieves knew the quality of the pieces contained in our collection."

"There were reports at the time that the owner played a significant role in the painting's recovery."

"You have a good memory, Mr. Allon. I personally conducted the ransom negotiations. In fact, I didn't even tell General Ferrari the painting had been stolen until after the deal had been struck. He arrested the thieves when they tried to collect the money. They weren't terribly professional."

"I remember," said Gabriel. "I also remember that they were killed not long after their arrival at Regina Coeli Prison."

"Apparently, it was the result of some sort of struggle over prison turf."

Or perhaps you had them killed for stealing from the boss, thought Gabriel. "Is there something in particular you wanted to show me?" he asked.

"This," Carlo said, inclining his head toward the large canvas at the farthest end of the gallery. The image, a depiction of the Adoration of the Shepherds, was scarcely visible beneath a dense layer of surface grime and a coat of heavily discolored varnish. Carlo illuminated the painting with the flick of a light switch. "I assume you recognize the artist."

"Guido Reni," replied Gabriel, "with considerable help from one or two of his better assistants, if I'm not mistaken."

"You're not. It's been in my family's collection for more than two centuries. Unfortunately, it's been many years since it was restored. I was wondering whether you would consider taking it on after you've finished the Caravaggio."

"I'm afraid I have a prior commitment."

"So I've heard." Carlo looked at Gabriel. "I know that Monsignor Donati has asked you to investigate Claudia's death." Lowering his voice, he added, "The Vatican is nothing if not a village, Mr. Allon. And villagers like to gossip."

"Gossip can be dangerous."

"So can sensitive investigations at the Vatican."

Carlo lowered his chin and stared at Gabriel unblinkingly. Most men tended to avoid looking directly into his eyes, but not Carlo. He possessed a cool, aristocratic assurance that bordered on arrogance. He was also, Gabriel decided, a man without physical fear.

"The Vatican is like a labyrinth," Carlo continued. "You should know there are forces within the Curia who believe Monsignor Donati has unwittingly opened a Pandora's box that will further damage the Church's reputation at a time when it cannot afford it. They also resent the fact that he has chosen to place this matter in the hands of an outsider."

"I assume you share their opinion."

"I am officially agnostic on the question. But I've learned from experience that, when it comes to the Vatican, it's often better to let sleeping dogs lie."

"What about dead women?"

It was a deliberate provocation. Carlo appeared impressed by Gabriel's nerve. "Dead women are like bank vaults," he responded with surprising candor. "They almost always contain unpleasant secrets." He removed a business card from a silver case. "I hope you'll reconsider my offer on the Reni. I can assure you I'll make it well worth your while."

As Gabriel slipped the card into his pocket, there came the sound of a chime summoning the guests to dinner. Carlo placed a hand at the small of Gabriel's back and guided him toward the staircase. A moment later, he was taking his seat next to Chiara. "What did he want?" she asked quietly in Hebrew.

"I think he was trying to put me on the Marchese family pay-roll."

"Is that all?"

"No," said Gabriel. "He wanted to make sure I wasn't carrying a gun."

They emerged from the palazzo shortly after midnight to find the air filled with soft, downy snowflakes the size of Eucharistic wafers. A Vatican sedan waited curbside; it followed slowly behind as Donati, Gabriel, and Chiara made their way along the deserted pavements of the Via Veneto. Chiara held Gabriel's arm tightly as the snow whitened her hair. Donati walked wordlessly next to her. A moment earlier, as he bade farewell to Veronica with a formal kiss on her cheek, he had been smiling. Now, faced with the prospect of a long, cold night in an empty bed, his mood was noticeably gloomy.

"Was it my imagination," Gabriel asked, "or were you actually enjoying yourself tonight?"

"I always do. It's the hardest part about spending time with her."

"So why do you do it?"

"Veronica is convinced it's a little-known Jesuitical test of faith, that I deliberately place myself in the proximity of temptation to see whether God will reach down and catch me if I fall."

"Do you?"

"It's not as Ignatian as all that. I simply enjoy her company. Most people can never see past the Roman collar, but Veronica doesn't see it at all. She makes me forget I'm a priest."

"What happens if you fail your test?"

"I would never allow that to happen. And neither would Veronica." Donati signaled for his car. Then he turned to Gabriel and asked, "How was your meeting with Carlo?"

"Businesslike."

"Did he mention my name?"

"He spoke of you only in the most glowing of terms."

"What did he want?"

"He thinks it would be a good idea if I dropped the investigation."

"I don't suppose he confessed to killing Claudia Andreatti."

"No, Luigi, he didn't."

"What now?"

"I'm going to find something irresistible," answered Gabriel. "And then I'm going to smash it to pieces."

"Just make sure it isn't my Church—or me, for that matter."

Donati made two solemn movements of his long hand, one vertical, one horizontal, and disappeared into the back of his car.

By the time Gabriel and Chiara reached the Via Gregoriana, the snowfall had ended. Gabriel paused at the base of the street and peered up the hill toward the Church of the Trinità dei Monti. The streetlamps were doused, yet another effort by the government to preserve precious resources. Rome, it seemed, was receding into time. Gabriel would have scarcely been surprised to see a chariot clattering toward them through the gloom.

The cars were parked tightly against the narrow pavements, so they walked, like most Romans, in the center of the street. The engine block of a wrecked Fiat ticked like cracking ice, but otherwise there was no sound, only the rhythmic tapping of Chiara's heels. Gabriel could feel the heavy warmth of her breast pressing against his arm. He imagined her lying nude in their bed, his private Modigliani. A part of him wanted to keep her there until a child appeared in her womb, but it was not possible; the case had its hooks in him. To abandon it would be tantamount to leaving a masterpiece partially restored. He would pursue the truth not for General Ferrari, or even for his friend Luigi Donati, but for Claudia Andreatti. The image of her lying dead on the floor of the Basilica now hung in his nightmarish gallery of memory—*Death of the Virgin*, oil on canvas, by Carlo Marchese.

Dead women are like bank vaults. They almost always contain unpleasant secrets. . . .

The buzz of an approaching motorcycle dissolved the image in Gabriel's thoughts. It was speeding directly toward them, the beam of its headlight quivering with the vibration of the cobbles. Gabriel nudged Chiara closer to the parked cars and trained his gaze toward the helmeted figure atop the bike. He was piloting the machine with one hand. The other, the right, was inserted into the front of his leather jacket. When it emerged, Gabriel saw the unmistakable silhouette of a gun with a suppressor screwed into the barrel. The gun moved first toward Gabriel's chest. Then it swung a few degrees and took aim at Chiara.

Gabriel felt a sudden hollowness at the small of his back where he usually carried his Beretta. As a student of Krav Maga, the Israeli martial arts discipline, he was trained in the many techniques of neutralizing an armed opponent. But nearly all involved an opponent standing in close proximity, not one riding at high speed on a motorbike. Gabriel had no choice but to rely upon one of the central tenets of Office tradecraft—when confronted with few decent options, improvise, and do it quickly.

Using his left hand, he forced Chiara to the paving stones. Then, with a violent blow of his right elbow, he snapped a side view mirror off the nearest parked car. The throw, while lacking in velocity, was remarkably accurate. The assassin instinctively swerved to avoid the projectile, thus shifting the gun off its target line for a crucial second or two. Gabriel immediately dropped into a crouch. Then, with the bike bearing down on him, he drove his shoulder into the visor of the assassin's helmet, separating man, bike, and gun. The assassin crashed to the cobblestones, the gun a few inches beyond his reach. Gabriel broke the man's wrist, just to be on the safe side, and kicked the helmet from his head. The killer had the complexion of a Calabrian. His breath stank of tobacco and fear.

"Do you have any idea who I am?" asked Gabriel calmly.

"No," the assassin gasped, clutching his broken limb.

"That means you are the dumbest contract killer who ever walked the earth." Gabriel picked up the gun, a Heckler & Koch .45-caliber, and pointed it at the assassin's face. "Who sent you?"

"I don't know," the assassin replied, panting. "I never know."

"Wrong answer."

Gabriel placed the end of the suppressor against the assassin's kneecap.

"Let's try this one more time. Who sent you?"

PART TWO

CITY

OF

GOD

17

BEN GURION AIRPORT, ISRAEL

I N THE ARRIVALS HALL OF Israel's Ben Gurion Airport is a special reception room reserved for Office personnel. As Gabriel and Chiara entered late the following afternoon, they were surprised to find it occupied by a single man. He was seated in one of the faux-leather lounge chairs with his thick legs crossed, reading the contents of a manila file folder by the glow of a halogen lamp. He wore a charcoal-gray suit, an open-neck dress shirt, and a pair of stylish silver eyeglasses that were far too small for his face. The overall impression was of a busy executive catching up on a bit of paperwork between flights, which was not far from the truth. Since taking control of the Office, Uzi Navot had spent a great deal of time on airplanes.

"To what do we owe the honor?" asked Gabriel.

Navot looked up from the file as if surprised by the interruption. "It's not every day someone tries to kill a pair of Office agents in the middle of Rome," he said. "In fact, it only seems to happen whenever you're in town."

Navot placed the file in his secure briefcase and rose slowly to his feet. He was several pounds heavier than the last time Gabriel had seen him, evidence he was not adhering to the strict diet and exercise regime imposed by his demanding wife, Bella. Or perhaps, thought Gabriel, looking at the additional gray in Navot's cropped hair, he was merely feeling the stress of his enormous job. He had a right to. The State of Israel was confronted by an Arab world in turmoil and faced threats too numerous to count. Topping the list was the prospect that Iran's nuclear program was about to bear fruit despite the secret war of sabotage and assassination waged by the Office and its allies.

"Actually," Navot said, raising one eyebrow, "you don't look half bad for someone who narrowly survived an assassination attempt."

"You wouldn't say that if you could see the bruises on my shoulder."

"That's what you get for walking into the home of a man like Carlo Marchese without a gun in your pocket." Navot pulled a disapproving frown. "You should have had a word with Shimon Pazner before accepting that invitation. He could have told you a few things about Carlo that even your friend Monsignor Donati doesn't know."

"Such as?"

"Let's just say the Office has had its eye on Carlo for some time."

"Why?"

"Because Carlo's never been terribly discerning about the company he keeps. But we're getting ahead of ourselves," Navot added. "The Old Man wants to tell you the rest. He's been counting the minutes until your arrival."

"Is there any chance you would let us get on the next plane out of the country?"

Navot placed his heavy hand on Gabriel's shoulder and squeezed. "I'm afraid you're not going anywhere," he said. "At least, not yet."

In the heart of Jerusalem, not far from the Old City, was a quiet, leafy lane known as Narkiss Street. The apartment house at Number 16 was small, just three stories in height, and partially concealed behind a sturdy limestone wall. An overgrown eucalyptus tree shaded the tiny balconies; the garden gate screeched when opened. In the foyer was an intercom panel with three buttons and three corresponding nameplates. Few people ever called upon the occupants of the unit on the top floor, for they were rarely there. The neighbors had been told that the husband, a taciturn man with ash-colored temples and vivid green eyes, was an artist who traveled often and jealously guarded his privacy. They no longer believed that to be true.

The sitting room of the apartment was hung with paintings. There were three canvases by Gabriel's grandfather, the renowned German Expressionist Viktor Frankel, and several more works by his mother. There was also a three-quarter-length portrait, unsigned, of a gaunt young man who appeared haunted by the shadow of death. Gazing up at it, as though lost in memories, was Ari Shamron. He was dressed, as usual, in pressed khaki trousers, a white oxford cloth shirt, and a leather jacket with an unrepaired tear in the left shoulder. As Gabriel, Chiara, and Navot entered, he hastily crushed out his filterless Turkish cigarette and placed the butt in the decorative dish he was using as an ashtray.

"How did you get in here?" asked Gabriel.

Shamron held up a key.

"I thought I took that away from you."

"You did," answered Shamron with a shrug. "Housekeeping was good enough to give me another copy."

Housekeeping was the Office division that managed safe houses and other secure properties. The apartment on Narkiss Street had once fallen into that category, but Shamron had bequeathed it to Gabriel as payment for services rendered—an act of generosity that, in Shamron's opinion, entitled him to enter the apartment whenever he pleased. He slipped the key into his pocket and scrutinized Gabriel with his rheumy blue eyes. His liver-spotted hands were bunched atop the crook of his olive wood cane. They looked as though they had been borrowed from a man twice his size.

"I was beginning to think we would never see each other again," he said after a moment. "Now it seems Carlo has reunited us."

"I didn't realize you two were on a first-name basis."

"Carlo?" Shamron squeezed his deeply lined face into an expression of profound disdain. "Carlo Marchese has occupied a special place in our hearts for some time. He's the transnational threat of tomorrow, a criminal without borders, creed, or conscience who's willing to do business with anyone as long as the money keeps rolling in."

"Who are his partners?"

"As you might expect, Carlo prefers his crime organized. He's also something of a globalist, which I admire. He does business with the Russian *mafiya*, the Japanese *yakuza*, and the Chinese gangs that control Hong Kong and Taiwan. But what concerns us most are his ties to numerous criminal gangs from southern Lebanon and the Bekaa Valley. Their members come almost entirely from the Shiite branch of Islam. They also happen to be affiliated with the world's most dangerous terrorist group."

"Hezbollah?"

Shamron nodded slowly. "Now that I have your attention, I'm wondering whether you will indulge me by listening to the rest of the story."

"I suppose that depends on the ending."

"It ends the way it always ends."

Shamron gave a seductive smile, the one he reserved for recruitments, and ignited another cigarette.

Housekeeping had taken the liberty of provisioning the depleted pantry with all the supplies required for a war party. Chiara saw to the coffee while Gabriel prepared a tray of cookies and other assorted sweets. He placed it directly in front of Navot and then pushed open the French doors leading to the terrace. The chill afternoon air smelled of eucalyptus and pine and faintly of jasmine. He stood there for a moment, watching the shadows lengthening in the quiet street, as Shamron described the origins of the unholy alliance between Carlo Marchese and the Shiite fanatics of Hezbollah.

It began, he said, shortly after the brief but destructive war between Israel and Hezbollah in 2006. The conflict left Hezbollah's military forces in ruins. It also destroyed much of the extensive social infrastructure—the schools, hospitals, and housing—that Hezbollah used to purchase the support of Lebanon's traditionally impoverished Shiites. Hezbollah's leadership needed a large infusion of money to quickly rebuild and rearm. Not surprisingly, they turned to their two most reliable patrons, Syria and Iran.

"The money poured in for a while," Shamron continued, "but then the ground shifted suddenly under Hezbollah's feet. The so-called Arab Spring came to Syria with a vengeance. And the international community finally decided it was time to impose real sanctions on Iran over its nuclear program. The mullahs were forced to pinch their pennies. Once they had funded Hezbollah to the tune of two hundred million dollars a year. Now it's a fraction of that."

Shamron lapsed into silence. He was seated with his arms folded across his chest and his head cocked slightly to one side, as though he had just heard a familiar voice outside in the street. Navot was seated next to him in an identical pose. But unlike Shamron, who was staring at Gabriel, Navot was gazing down at a plate of Viennese butter cookies with an expression of studied indifference. Gabriel shook his head slowly. It had been many months since his last operation with the Office, yet in his absence it seemed nothing had changed except the color of Navot's hair.

"Hezbollah realized it had a serious long-term problem," Navot said, picking up where Shamron had left off. "Since it could no longer count on the benevolence of its patrons, it had to develop an independent, reliable means of financing its operations. It didn't take long for them to decide how to proceed."

"Crime," said Gabriel.

"Big-time crime," said Navot, snatching one of the cookies from the tray. "Hezbollah is like the Gambino family on steroids. But they tend to operate like limpets."

"Meaning they attach themselves to other criminal organizations?"

Navot nodded and treated himself to another cookie. "They're involved in everything from the cocaine trade in South America to diamond smuggling in West Africa. They also do a brisk business in counterfeit goods ranging from Gucci handbags to pirated DVDs."

"And they're good at it," Shamron added. "Hezbollah is now

in possession of at least eighty thousand rockets and missiles capable of reaching every square inch of Israel. You can rest assured they didn't get them by clipping coupons. Its rearmament is being funded in large part by a global crime wave. And Carlo is one of Hezbollah's most reliable partners."

"How did you find out about him?"

Shamron studied his hands before answering. "About six months ago, we were able to identify a senior operative in Hezbollah's criminal fund-raising apparatus. His name is Muhammad Qassem. At the time, he was employed by something called the Lebanon Byzantine Bank. We lured him to Cyprus with a woman. Then we put him in a box and brought him back here."

Shamron slowly crushed out his cigarette. "Under questioning, Qassem gave us chapter and verse on Hezbollah's criminal enterprises, including its partnership with a heretofore unknown Italian organized crime figure named Carlo Marchese. According to Qassem, the relationship is multifaceted, but it's centered on the trade in looted antiquities."

"What does Hezbollah bring to the relationship?"

"You're the expert in the dirty antiquities trade. You tell me."

Gabriel recalled what General Ferrari had told him during their meeting in the Piazza di Sant'Ignazio, that the network was receiving looted goods from someone in the Middle East. "Hezbollah brings a steady stream of product to the relationship," he said. "It's active in some of the most archaeologically significant lands in the world. Southern Lebanon alone is a treasure trove of Phoenician, Greek, and Roman antiquities."

"But those antiquities aren't worth much unless they can be brought to market with an acceptable provenance," Shamron said. "That's where Carlo and his network come in. Apparently, both sides are doing quite well for themselves."

"Does Carlo know who he's doing business with?"

"Carlo is, as we say, a man of the world."

"Who runs the Hezbollah side of the operation?"

"Qassem wasn't able to tell us that."

"Why haven't you gone to the Italians with what you know?"

"We did," replied Uzi Navot. "In fact, I did it personally."

"What was their response?"

"Carlo has friends in high places. Carlo is close to the Vatican. We can't touch a man like Carlo based on the word of a Hezbollah banker who was handled in a rather extrajudicial manner."

"So you let it go."

"We needed Italian cooperation on other issues," Navot replied. "Since then, I'm afraid we've had only limited success in interdicting the flow of money from Hezbollah's criminal networks. They're incredibly adaptive and resistant to outside penetration. They also tend to operate in countries that are not exactly friendly to our interests."

"Which means," Shamron said, "your friend Carlo has presented us with a unique opportunity." He stared at Gabriel through a cloud of cigarette smoke. "The question is, are you willing to help us?"

And there it was, thought Gabriel—the open door. As usual, Shamron had left him no choice but to walk through it.

"What exactly do you have in mind?"

"We'd like you to eliminate a major source of funding for an enemy who has sworn to wipe us off the face of the earth."

"Is that all?"

"No," said Shamron. "We think it would be best for everyone involved if you put Carlo Marchese out of business, too."

18

JERUSALEM

THE NEXT DAY WAS A FRIDAY, which meant Jerusalem, God's fractured citadel upon a hill, was more jittery than usual. Along the eastern rim of the Old City, from Damascus Gate to the Garden of Gethsemane, metal barricades sparkled in the sharp winter sun, watched over by hundreds of blue-uniformed Israeli police. Inside the walls, Muslim faithful crowded the portals to the Haram al-Sharif, Islam's third-holiest site, waiting to see whether they would be permitted to pray at the al-Aqsa Mosque. Due to a recent string of Hamas rocket attacks, the restrictions were tighter than usual. Females and middle-aged men were allowed to pass, but *al-shabaab*, the youth, were turned away. They seethed in the tiny courtyards along Lions' Gate Street or outside the walls on the Jericho Road. There a bearded Salafist imam assured them that their days of humiliation were numbered, that the Jews, the former and current overlords of the twice-promised land, were once again living on borrowed time.

Gabriel paused to listen to the sermon and then set out along the footpath leading into the basin of the Kidron Valley. As he passed Absalom's Tomb, he saw an extended family of Arabs coming toward him from the East Jerusalem neighborhood of Silwan. The women all were veiled, and the eldest boy bore a striking resemblance to a Palestinian terrorist whom Gabriel had killed many years earlier on a quiet street in the heart of Zurich. The family was walking four abreast, leaving no room for Gabriel. Rather than provoke a religious incident, he stepped to the side of the path and allowed the family to pass, an act of public etiquette that elicited not so much as a glance or nod of thanks. The veiled women and the patriarch climbed the hill toward the walls of the Old City. The boys remained behind, in the makeshift radical mosque on the Jericho Road.

By now the amplified prayers from al-Aqsa were echoing across the valley, mingling with the tolling of church bells on the Mount of Olives. As two of the city's three Abrahamic faiths engaged in a quarrel of profound beauty, Gabriel gazed across the endless headstones of the Jewish cemetery and debated whether he had the strength to visit the grave of his son, Daniel. Twenty years earlier, on a snowy January night in Vienna, Gabriel had wrenched the child's lifeless body from the inferno of a bombed car. His first wife, Leah, miraculously survived the attack despite suffering catastrophic burns over most of her body. She lived now in a psychiatric hospital atop Mount Herzl, trapped in a prison of memory and a body destroyed by fire. Afflicted with a combination of post-traumatic stress syndrome and psychotic depression, she relived the bombing constantly. Occasionally, however, she experienced flashes of lucidity. During one such interlude, in the garden of the hospital, she had granted Gabriel permission to marry Chiara. *Look at me, Gabriel. There's nothing left of me. Nothing but a mem-*

ory. It was just one of the visions that stalked Gabriel each time he walked the streets of Jerusalem. Here in a city he loved he could find no peace. He saw the endless conflict between Arab and Jew in every word and gesture, and heard it on the edge of every muezzin's call to prayer. In the faces of children, he glimpsed the ghosts of the men he had killed. And from the gravestones of the Mount of Olives, he heard the last cries of a child sacrificed for a father's sins.

It was that memory, the memory of Daniel dying in his arms, that compelled Gabriel into the cemetery. He remained at the grave for nearly an hour, thinking about the kind of man his son might have been, whether he would have been an artist like his ancestors or whether he would have found something more practical to do. Finally, as the church bells tolled one o'clock, he placed stones atop the grave and made his way across the Kidron Valley to Dung Gate. A group of Israeli schoolchildren from the Negev waited at the security checkpoint, their brightly colored knapsacks open for inspection. Gabriel briefly joined them. Then, after speaking a few words into the ear of a policeman, he slipped around the magnetometers and entered the Jewish Quarter.

Directly before him, across a broad plaza, rose the honey-colored Herodian stones of the Western Wall, the much-disputed remnant of the ancient retaining barrier that had once surrounded the great Temple of Jerusalem. In AD 70, after a ruthless siege lasting many months, the Roman Emperor Titus ordered the Temple destroyed and the rebellious Jews of Roman Palestine obliterated. Hundreds of thousands perished in the bloodletting that followed, while the contents of the Holy of Holies, including the great golden menorah, were carried back to Rome in one of history's most infamous episodes of looting. Six centuries later, when the Arabs conquered Jerusalem, the ruins of the Temple were no longer visible—and the Holy Mountain, the place regarded by Jews as the dwelling place of God on Earth, was little more than an elevated garbage dump. The Arabs erected the golden Dome of the Rock and the great al-Aqsa Mosque, thus establishing Islamic religious authority over the world's most sacred parcel of real estate. The Crusaders seized the Mount from the Muslims in 1099 and turned the shrines into churches, a tactical mistake the Israelis chose not to repeat after capturing East Jerusalem in 1967. Israeli authorities now maintained tight control over access to the Mount, but administration of the Muslim holy sites, and the sacred land beneath them, remained in the hands of the Islamic religious authority known as the Waqf.

The portion of the Western Wall visible from the plaza was 187 feet wide and 62 feet high. The actual western retaining wall of the Temple Mount plateau, however, was much larger, descending 42 feet below the plaza and stretching more than a quarter mile into the Muslim Quarter, where it was concealed behind residential structures. After years of politically and religiously charged archaeological excavations, it was now possible to walk nearly the entire length of the wall via the Western Wall Tunnel, an underground passageway running from the plaza to the Via Dolorosa. Waiting for Gabriel at the entrance was a young woman dressed in the modest skirt and headscarf of an Orthodox Jew. "He's been working nonstop at a spot near the Cave," she said in a confiding tone. "Apparently, he's found something important, because he's a complete wreck."

"How can you tell?"

The woman laughed and then led Gabriel to the top of a narrow aluminum staircase. It bore him downward beneath the Old City and backward through history. He paused for a moment beneath Wilson's Arch, the bridge that had linked the Temple Mount and Jerusalem's Upper City in the time of Jesus, and then set out along a newly paved walkway at the base of the wall. The massive foundation stones were aglow with lamplight and cool to the touch. Just a few feet above were the chaotic market streets of the modern Muslim Quarter, but here in the basement of time the silence was absolute.

The section of the tunnel known as the Cave was actually a tiny grotto-like synagogue, set against the portion of the wall thought to be the nearest point to the ancient location of the Holy of Holies. As usual, a small group of Orthodox women were praying in the synagogue, their fingers pressed reverently to the stone. Gabriel slipped quietly past them and made his way toward a tarpaulin curtain hanging a few yards away. A small handwritten sign warned of danger and instructed visitors to stay away. Gabriel parted the curtains and peered down into an excavation trench approximately twenty feet deep. At the bottom, bathed in the glow of harsh white lights, a single archaeologist picked gently at the black earth with a tiny hand trowel.

"What is it?" Gabriel asked, his voice echoing into the void.

"It's not an *it*," replied Eli Lavon. He moved aside to reveal the focus of his labors—the shoulder, arm, and hand of a human skeleton. "We call her Rivka," he said. "And unless I'm mistaken, which is highly unlikely, she died the same night as the Temple."

"Proof, Professor Lavon," Gabriel said, challenging him playfully. "Where's the proof?"

"It's all around her," said Lavon, pointing to the rectangular stones embedded in the soil. "They're from the Temple itself, and they're lying here because the Romans hurled them over the wall the night they laid waste to the House of God. The fact that Rivka's remains lie amid the stones rather than under them suggests she was thrown over the wall at the same time. So do the fractures all over her body."

Lavon gazed respectfully at the remains for a moment without speaking. "According to Josephus, our only source for what happened that night, several thousand Jews rushed into the Temple after the Romans set it ablaze. I suspect Rivka was one of them. Who knows?" he added with a sigh. "It's possible she saw Titus himself entering the Holy of Holies to claim his sacred loot. After that . . . it was hell on earth."

"Titus wasn't the world's first looter," Gabriel said. "And, unfortunately, he wasn't the last."

"So I hear." Lavon looked up. "I also hear someone tried to take a shot at you the other night in Rome."

"Actually, I think he was aiming for my wife."

"That was rather unwise. Is he still alive?"

"For the moment."

"Any idea who sent him?"

Gabriel dropped the shard of Greek pottery into the excavation pit. Lavon snatched it deftly out of the air before it could shatter on the stones of the Temple and examined it in the glow of his work lamps.

"Red-figure Attic, fifth century BC, probably by the Menelaos Painter."

"Very impressive."

"Thank you," replied Lavon. "But don't ever drop it again."

The Old City of Jerusalem was once again connected to the new by a footbridge. It stretched from the Jaffa Gate to the sparkling Mamilla Mall, one of the few places in the country where Arab and Jew mingled with relatively little tension. As usual, Gabriel and Lavon bickered over where to eat before finally settling on a fashionable European-style café. The Israel of their youth had been a land without television. Now it had all the creature comforts of the West, everything except peace.

The volume of the techno-pop music made conversation impossible inside, so they sat on the sunlit terrace at a table with a gunner's view of the Old City walls. Lavon's wispy hair moved in the breeze. He popped an antacid tablet before touching his food.

"Still?" asked Gabriel.

"It's eternal, just like Jerusalem."

Gabriel smiled. Sometimes even he found it hard to imagine that the bookish, hypochondriacal figure seated before him was regarded as the finest street surveillance specialist the Office had ever produced. He had worked with Lavon for the first time during Operation Wrath of God. For three years, they had been near-constant companions, killing both at night and in broad daylight, living in fear that at any moment they would be arrested by European police. When the unit finally disbanded, Lavon was afflicted with numerous stress disorders, including a notoriously fickle stomach. He settled in Vienna, where he opened a small investigative bureau called Wartime Claims and Inquiries. Operating on a shoestring budget, he managed to track down millions of dollars' worth of looted Holocaust assets and played a significant role in prying a multibillion-dollar settlement from the banks of Switzerland. But when a bomb destroyed his office and killed two of his employees, Lavon returned to Israel to pursue his first love, archaeology. He now served as an adjunct professor of biblical archaeology at Jerusalem's Hebrew University and regularly took part in digs around the country, such as the one in the Western Wall Tunnel.

"It's almost hard to remember what this place was like before the Six-Day War," Lavon said, gesturing toward the valley beneath the terrace. "My parents used to bring me here to see the barbed wire and the Jordanian gun emplacements along the 'forty-nine armistice line. Jews weren't allowed to pray at the Western Wall or visit the cemetery on the Mount of Olives. Even Christians had to present proof of baptism before they were allowed to visit their holy sites. And now our friends in the West would like us to surrender sovereignty over the Wall to the Palestinians." Lavon shook his head slowly. "For the sake of peace, of course."

"It's a pile of stones, Eli."

"Those stones are drenched in the blood of your ancestors. And it's because of those stones that we have a right to a homeland here. The Palestinians understand that, which explains why they like to pretend the Temple never existed."

"Temple Denial," said Gabriel.

Lavon nodded thoughtfully. "It's a first cousin to Holocaust Denial, and it's now just as widespread in the Arab and Islamic world. The calculus is quite simple. No Holocaust, no Temple . . ."

"No Jews in Palestine."

"Precisely. But it's not just talk. Using the religious authority of the Waqf, the Palestinians are systematically trying to erase any evidence that there was ever an actual temple on the Temple Mount. We're fighting an archaeological war here in Jerusalem every day. One side is trying to preserve the past, and the other is trying to destroy it, primarily under the guise of construction projects like the Marwani Mosque."

Capable of accommodating more than seven thousand worshipers, the mosque was located in the southeastern corner of the Temple Mount, in an ancient underground chamber known as Solomon's Stables. The massive construction project had destabilized the sacred plateau and created a precarious bulge in the southern wall. Under a negotiated agreement between the Israeli government and the Waqf, an engineering firm from Jordan had made the repairs, leaving behind an unsightly patch of white that was clearly visible from across the city.

"Naturally," Lavon continued, "a construction project the size of the Marwani Mosque displaced several tons of earth and debris. And what do you suppose the Waqf did with it?" Lavon quickly answered his own question. "They took it to the municipal dump or simply threw it over the walls into the Kidron Valley. I was part of the team that sifted through it. We found hundreds of artifacts dating from the First and Second Temples. They lacked proper archaeological context, of course, because they'd been ripped from their original settings." He paused, then added, "Just like that shard of Greek pottery you're walking around with."

"A man like you can often tell a great deal from a single fragment."

"Where did you get it?"

"From the home of a tomb raider in Cerveteri."

"Roberto Falcone?"

Gabriel nodded.

"Please tell me you weren't the one who pushed him into that vat of hydrochloric acid."

"Acid isn't my style, Eli. It's far too slow."

"And messy," Lavon added with a nod. "I suppose the next thing you're going to say is that there's a link between Falcone and the woman who fell from the dome of the Basilica."

"His name is Carlo Marchese," Gabriel said. "Carlo controls the global trade in looted antiquities. He's also in bed with Hezbollah. We're going to put him out of business."

"We?"

"I can't do it alone, Eli. I need an archaeologist who can read a balance sheet and knows how to track dirty money. It would also be nice if he can handle himself on the street."

"I thought you were retired."

"So did I," Gabriel said, "but for some reason I never seem to stay retired."

Lavon looked out at the walls of the Old City.

"What are you thinking about, Eli?"

"It's not a what. It's a who."

"Rivka?"

Lavon nodded.

"She's waited for two thousand years," Gabriel said. "She can wait a little longer."

19

KING SAUL BOULEVARD, TEL AVIV

THERE WAS ANOTHER THING THAT had not changed in Gabriel's absence: King Saul Boulevard. It was drab, featureless, and, best of all, anonymous. No emblem hung over its entrance, no brass lettering proclaimed the identity of its occupant. In fact, there was nothing at all to suggest it was the headquarters of one of the world's most feared and respected intelligence services. A closer inspection of the structure, however, would have revealed the existence of a building within a building, one with its own power supply, its own water and sewer lines, and its own secure communications system. Employees carried two keys. One opened an unmarked door in the lobby; the other operated the lift. Those who committed the unpardonable sin of losing one or both of their keys were banished to the Judean Wilderness, never to be seen or heard from again.

Gabriel had come through the lobby just once, the day after his first encounter with Shamron. From that point forward, he had only entered the building "black," through the underground garage. He did so again now, with Chiara and Eli Lavon at his side. They made their way down three flights of stairs, then followed an empty corridor to a doorway marked 456C. The room on the other side had once been a dumping ground for obsolete computers and worn-out furniture, often used by the night staff as a clandestine meeting place for romantic trysts. It was now known throughout King Saul Boulevard only as Gabriel's Lair. The keyless cipher lock was set to the numeric version of his date of birth. According to one Office wit, it was the most closely guarded secret in all of Israel.

"What's wrong?" Eli Lavon asked when Gabriel's hand hesitated over the keypad.

"A senior moment."

"You can't remember your own birthday?"

"No," said Gabriel, punching in the code. "I just can't believe it was that long ago."

He entered the room, switched on the overhead lights, and looked around at the walls. They were littered with the debris and the ghosts of operations past. All had resulted in innocent lives being saved, and all were soaked in blood, much of it Gabriel's. He went to the chalkboard, the last chalkboard in the entire building, and saw faint traces of his own handwriting—the outlines of an operation known by the code name Masterpiece. It had resulted in the successful sabotage of Iran's uranium enrichment facilities, and had purchased Israel and the West several years of critical time. Now it seemed that time was running out. The Iranians were once again on the doorstep of realizing their nuclear dreams. And it appeared they intended to punish anyone who tried to stand in their way, using Hezbollah, their eager proxy, as their instrument of vengeance.

"If the Office ever builds a museum," Lavon said, "it won't be complete unless it contains a replica of this room."

"What would they call the exhibit?"

"The village of the damned."

The response had come not from Lavon but from the tall, tweedy figure standing in the doorway, a thin file folder beneath his arm. Yossi Gavish was a senior officer from Research, the Office's analytical division. Born in London and educated at All Souls, he still spoke Hebrew with a pronounced English accent and was incapable of working without a steady supply of Earl Grey tea and McVitie's digestive biscuits.

"I can't believe I'm back here again," he said.

"Neither can I." Gabriel nodded toward the file and asked, "What have you got there?"

"The sum total of what the Office currently knows about Carlo Marchese." He dropped the file onto one of the worktables and looked around. "Does Uzi expect the four of us to take on Carlo and Hezbollah on our own?"

"Don't worry," Gabriel said, smiling. "The others will be here soon."

It took the better part of the morning for Personnel to track down the remaining members of Gabriel's team and cast them downward into his windowless little dungeon. For the most part, the extractions went smoothly, but in a handful of cases they encountered unexpectedly stiff local resistance. All complaints were forwarded directly to Uzi Navot, who made it clear he would tolerate no dissent. "This is not the Arab world," he told one disgruntled division chief. "This is the Office. And we are still totalitarians."

They arrived at irregular intervals, like members of an infiltration team returning to base after a successful night raid. First came Yaakov Rossman, a pockmarked former counterterrorism officer from Shabak, Israel's internal security service, who was now running agents in Syria and Lebanon. Then it was a pair of all-purpose field hands named Oded and Mordecai, followed by Rimona Stern, a former military intelligence officer who now dealt with issues related to Iran's nuclear program. A Rubenesque woman with sandstone-colored hair, Rimona also happened to be Shamron's niece. Gabriel had known her since she was a child. His fondest memories of Rimona were of a fearless young girl on a kick scooter careening down the steep drive of her famous uncle's house.

Next there appeared in the doorway a petite, dark-haired woman named Dina Sarid. A human database, she could recite the time, place, perpetrators, and casualty toll of every act of terrorism committed against Israeli and Western targets, including the long list of atrocities carried out by the highly skilled murderers of Hezbollah. For many years, she focused her considerable analytic skills on Imad Mughniyah, Hezbollah's military commander and high priest of terror. Indeed, thanks in large measure to Dina's work, Mughniyah met his much-deserved end in Damascus in 2008 when a bomb exploded beneath his car. Dina marked Mughniyah's demise by paying a visit to the graves of her mother and two of her sisters. They were killed on October 19, 1994, when a suicide bomber from Hamas, Iran's other proxy, detonated himself on a Number 5 bus in Tel Aviv's Dizengoff Street. Dina was seriously wounded in the attack and still walked with a slight limp.

As usual, Mikhail Abramov arrived last. Lanky and fair with a fine-boned face and eyes the color of glacial ice, he had immigrated to Israel from Russia as a teenager and joined the Sayeret Matkal, the IDF's elite special operations unit. Once described by

Ari Shamron as "Gabriel without a conscience," he had personally assassinated several of the top terror masterminds from Hamas and Palestinian Islamic Jihad. He now carried out similar missions on behalf of the Office, though his enormous talents were not limited strictly to the gun.

Within the corridors and conference rooms of King Saul Boulevard, the nine men and women gathered in Room 456C were known by the code name "Barak"—the Hebrew word for lightning—for their ability to gather and strike quickly. They had fought together, often under conditions of unbearable stress, on secret battlefields stretching from Moscow to the Caribbean to the Empty Quarter of Saudi Arabia. Gabriel had been lucky to survive their last operation, but now he stood before them once again, looking none the worse for wear, holding them spellbound with a story. It featured a museum curator whose father had been a tomb robber, a priest with a dangerous secret, and a glorified mobster named Carlo Marchese who was doing business with the world's most dangerous terrorist group. The goal of the operation, said Gabriel, would be simple. They were going to assemble a dossier that would destroy Carlo and in the process blow a hole in Hezbollah's bottom line. But it wouldn't be sufficient simply to prove that Carlo Marchese was a criminal. They were going to find the *cordata*, the rope, linking him directly to Hezbollah. And then they were going to wrap it around his neck.

They were a family of sorts, and like all families there were petty jealousies, unspoken resentments, and various other forms of sibling dysfunction. Even so, they managed to divide themselves into subunits and settle down to work with a minimum of bickering. Yossi, Chiara, and Mordecai saw to Carlo, while responsibility for

Hezbollah's criminal fund-raising networks fell to Dina, Rimona, Yaakov, and Mikhail. Gabriel and Eli Lavon floated somewhere in between, for it was their task to find the nexus between the two organizations—or, as Lavon put it, the wedding band that joined Carlo and Hezbollah in criminal matrimony.

Before long, the walls of Room 456C reflected the unique nature of their undertaking. On one side were the outlines of Carlo Marchese's overt business empire; on the other, the known elements of Hezbollah, Inc. It had but one task—to supply a steady stream of money to the most dangerous terrorist group the world had ever known. It was Hezbollah, not al-Qaeda, that first turned human beings into bombs, and Hezbollah that first developed a truly global capability. Indeed, on two occasions, it was able to reach its tentacles across the Atlantic and attack targets in Buenos Aires—first in 1992, when it bombed the Israeli Embassy, killing twenty-nine people, and again in 1994, when it destroyed the AMIA Jewish community center, leaving another ninety-five dead. Hezbollah's ranks were filled with several thousand highly trained terrorists, many hidden within the worldwide Lebanese diaspora, and its vast arsenal of weaponry included several Scuds, making it the only terrorist group in the world to possess ballistic missiles. In short, Hezbollah had the ability to carry out a cataclysmic terrorist attack at the time and place of its choosing. All it required was the blessing of its Shiite clerical masters in Tehran.

It was Allah who provided Hezbollah's inspiration, but mere mortals saw to its financial needs. Their faces scowled from Dina's side of the room. At the center of the web she placed the Lebanon Byzantine Bank. Then, with the help of Unit 8200, she assembled a communication matrix and phone tree that stretched from Beirut to London to the lawless Tri-Border Area of South America. Lebanon Byzantine Bank—or LBB in the lexicon of the team—was the glue that held it all together. Thanks to the cybersleuths from Unit 8200, the team perused its ledger sheets at will. Indeed, Yaakov joked that he knew more about LBB's operations and investments than even the bank's president. It quickly became apparent that the institution—"And I do use that term loosely," scoffed Yaakov—was little more than a front for Hezbollah. "Follow the money," Gabriel instructed the team, "and with a bit of luck, it will lead us to Hezbollah's man inside the network."

For the most part, Gabriel spent those days putting himself through a crash course on the global trade in illicit antiquities—specifically, how glittering treasures from the past made their way from the dirty hands of tomb robbers and thieves onto the legitimate market. Much of the work involved a mind-numbing review of monographs, catalogues, museum databases, auction house records, and published inventories of antiquities dealers around the world. But occasionally he would head over to the Rockefeller Museum with Eli Lavon in tow to sit at the feet of a looting expert from the Israel Antiquities Authority. In addition, he phoned an old friend in the London art world who had a number of acquaintances who dabbled in what he liked to call "the naughty end of the trade." Finally, he quietly renewed contact with General Ferrari, who immediately sent along copies of some of his most closely guarded files, despite the fact that Gabriel pointedly refused to identify his target. It was now an operation, and operational rules applied.

And so it went for twelve days and twelve seemingly endless nights, as each group labored to assemble its piece of the puzzle. Lavon, the biblical archaeologist, couldn't help but compare the quest to the construction of the ancient underground aqueduct beneath the City of David that linked the Gihon Spring with the Pool of Siloam. More than seventeen hundred feet in length, it had been hastily carved out of the bedrock in the eighth century BC as the city prepared itself for a siege by the approaching Assyrian army. To speed the process, King Hezekiah ordered two separate teams to tunnel toward each other simultaneously. Somehow they managed to meet in the middle, and the life-saving water flowed into the city.

The team experienced a similar episode shortly after midnight on the thirteenth day, when Gabriel's team took delivery of the nightly packet of material from Unit 8200. It included a list of all cash wire transfers that had flowed to and from the accounts of Lebanon Byzantine Bank that day. The document revealed that, at 4:17 p.m., LBB received a transfer of one and a half million euros from the Galleria Naxos of St. Moritz, Switzerland. Then, a few minutes after five o'clock Beirut time, a sum of one hundred and fifty thousand euros, ten percent of the original payment, was forwarded from LBB to an account at the Institute for Religious Works, otherwise known as the Vatican Bank. Eli Lavon would later describe the atmosphere in the room as a bit like the moment Hezekiah's workmen first heard each other chiseling through the bedrock. Gabriel ordered his own teams to dig a little more, and by dawn they knew they had their man.

20

KING SAUL BOULEVARD, TEL AVIV

H E CALLS HIMSELF DAVID GIRARD. But like almost everything else about him, it's a lie."

Gabriel dropped the file folder onto Uzi Navot's preposterously large executive desk. It was fashioned of smoked glass and stood near the floor-to-ceiling bulletproof windows overlooking downtown Tel Aviv and the sea. Hazy sunlight filtered through the vertical blinds, imprisoning Navot in bars of shadow. He left the file untouched and with a wave of his hand invited Gabriel to elaborate.

"His real name is Daoud Ghandour. He was born in the village of Tayr Dibba in southern Lebanon, the same town as Imad Mughniyah, which means they probably knew each other when they were growing up."

"How did he get from a shithole like Tayr Dibba to an antiquities gallery in St. Moritz?"

"The Lebanese way," replied Gabriel. "In 1970, when Arafat

and the PLO set up shop in southern Lebanon, the Ghandour family moved to Beirut. Apparently, Daoud was an exceptionally bright child. He went to a good school and learned to speak French and English. When it came time for him to attend university, he moved to Paris to study ancient history at the Sorbonne."

"Is that when Daoud Ghandour became David Girard?"

"That wasn't until he moved on to Oxford," Gabriel answered. "After completing his PhD in classical archaeology, he went to work in the antiquities department of Sotheby's in London. He was there in the late nineties when Sotheby's was accused of selling unprovenanced antiquities. He left London under something of a cloud."

"And went into business for himself?"

Gabriel nodded.

"How much does it cost to open a gallery in St. Moritz?"

"A lot."

"Where did he get the money?"

"Good question."

Gabriel removed a photograph from the file and dealt it across the desktop. It showed a slender figure in his late forties leaning against a glass display case filled with Greek and Etruscan pottery. He wore a dark pullover and a dark blazer. His gaze was soft and thoughtful. His posed smile managed to appear genuine.

"Handsome devil," said Navot. "Where'd you get the photo?"

"From the Web site of the gallery. His official bio has a couple of glaring holes in it, such as his given name and place of birth."

"What flavor passport is he carrying these days?"

"Swiss. He has a Swiss wife, too."

"Which variety?"

"German speaker."

"How cosmopolitan." Navot frowned at the photograph. "What do we know about his travel habits?"

"Like most people in the antiquities trade, he spends a great deal of time on airplanes and in hotel rooms."

"Lebanon?"

"He pops into Beirut at least twice a month." Gabriel paused, then added, "He also spends a fair amount of time here in Israel."

Navot looked up sharply but said nothing.

"According to Eli's friends over at the Israel Antiquities Authority, Daoud Ghandour, aka David Girard, is a frequent visitor to the Temple Mount. Actually," Gabriel corrected himself, "he spends most of his time *under* the Mount."

"Doing what?"

"He's an unpaid adviser to the Palestinian Authority and the Waqf on issues related to archaeological matters. By the way, that's not in his official bio, either."

Navot stared at the photo for a moment. "What's your theory?"

"I think he's Hezbollah's man in Carlo's network. He sells looted goods out of his gallery in St. Moritz, sends the profits back home through LBB, and gives a ten percent cut to his godfather Carlo Marchese."

"Can you prove it?"

"Not yet. Which is why I'm proposing we go into business with him."

"How?"

"I'm going to offer him something irresistible, and see if he bites."

"I probably shouldn't ask," Navot sighed, "but just where do you intend to get something so irresistible?"

"I'm going to steal it, of course."

"Of course," said Navot, smiling. "Is there anything you need from me?"

"Money, Uzi. Lots of money."

Office doctrine dictates that field agents departing for missions abroad spend their final night in Israel at a safe flat known as a jump site. There, free from the distractions of spouses, lovers, children, and pets, they assume the identities they will wear like body armor until they return home again. Only Gabriel and Eli Lavon chose not to participate in this enduring operational ritual, for by their own calculation, they had spent more time living under false names than their own.

As it turned out, both chose to pass at least part of that last evening in the company of damaged women. Lavon headed to the Western Wall Tunnel to spend a few hours with his beloved Rivka, while Gabriel made a pilgrimage to the Mount Herzl Psychiatric Hospital to see Leah. As usual, he arrived after normal visiting hours. Leah's doctor was waiting in the lobby. A rabbinical-looking man with a *kippah* and a long gray beard, he was the only person in Israel not connected to the Office who knew precisely what had happened that night in Vienna.

"It's been a while since your last visit." The doctor gave a forgiving smile. "She's looking forward to seeing you."

"How is she?"

"The same. At this stage of her life, that's the best we can hope for."

The doctor took Gabriel by the arm and guided him along a corridor of Jerusalem limestone to a common room with windows overlooking the hospital's garden. It was there, in the shade of a stone pine, that Gabriel had sought Leah's permission to marry

Chiara. The moment was only partially imprinted in Leah's watery memory. At times, she seemed to realize that Gabriel was no longer her husband, but for the most part she remained a prisoner of the past. In Leah's bewildered mind, there was nothing unusual about Gabriel's long absences. Thanks to Shamron, he had always entered and departed her world with little or no warning.

She was seated in her wheelchair with the twisted remnants of her hands resting in her lap. Her hair, once long and dark like Chiara's, was now cut institutional short and shot with gray. Gabriel kissed the cool, firm scar tissue of her cheek before lowering himself into the armless little chair the doctor had placed at her side. Leah seemed unaware of his presence. She was staring sightlessly into the darkened garden.

"Do you love this girl?" she asked suddenly, her gaze still straight ahead.

"Which girl?" asked Gabriel. And then, when he realized Leah was merely reliving the conversation that had dissolved their marriage, his heart gave a sideways lurch. "I love you," he said softly, squeezing her frozen hands. "I'll always love you, Leah."

A smile briefly graced her lips. Then she looked directly at Gabriel for a moment with an expression of wifely disapproval. "You're working for Shamron again," she said.

"How can you tell?"

"I can see it in your eyes. You're someone else."

"I'm Gabriel," he said.

"Only a part of you is Gabriel." She turned her face toward the glass.

"Don't go yet, Leah."

She came back to him. "Who are you fighting this time? Black September?"

"There is no Black September anymore."

"Who is it then?"

"Hezbollah," he answered after a moment's hesitation. "It's Hezbollah, Leah."

The name appeared to mean nothing to her. "Tell me about it," she said.

"I can't."

"Why not?"

"Because it's secret."

"Like before?"

"Yes, Leah, like before."

Leah frowned. She hated secrets. Secrets had destroyed her life.

"Where will you go this time?"

"Paris," Gabriel replied truthfully.

Her expression darkened. "Why Paris?"

"There's a man there who can help me."

"A spy?"

"A thief."

"What does he steal?"

"Paintings."

She seemed genuinely troubled. "Why would a man like you want to work with someone who steals paintings?"

"Sometimes it's necessary to work with bad people to accomplish good things."

"Is this man bad?"

"Not really."

"Tell me about him."

Gabriel could see no harm in it, so he complied with her request. But after a moment, she appeared to lose interest, and her face turned once again toward the window.

"Look at the snow," she said, gazing at the cloudless evening sky. "Isn't it beautiful?"

"Yes, Leah, it's beautiful."

Her hands began to tremble. Gabriel closed his eyes.

———

When Gabriel returned to Narkiss Street, he found Chiara stretched on the couch in the half-light, a glass of red wine balanced on her abdomen. She offered him the wine and watched him carefully as he drank, as though searching for evidence of betrayal. Then she led him into the bedroom and wordlessly removed her clothing. Her body was feverishly warm. She made love as though it were for the last time.

"Take me with you to Paris."

"No."

She didn't press the issue. She knew there was no point. Not after what had happened in Rome. And not after what had happened in Vienna before that.

"Did she remember you this time?"

"She remembered."

"Which version of you?"

"Both," he answered.

Chiara was silent for a moment. Then she asked, "Does she know you love me, Gabriel?"

"She knows."

A pause. "*Do* you?" she asked.

"What?"

"Love me."

"*Chiara* . . ."

She turned her back to him. "I'm sorry," she said after a moment.

"For what?"

"The baby. If I hadn't lost the baby, you wouldn't be going to Paris without me."

Gabriel made no reply. Chiara climbed slowly atop his body.

"Do you love me?" she asked again.

"More than anything."

"Show me."

"How?"

She kissed his lips and whispered, "Show me, Gabriel."

21

RUE DE MIROMESNIL, PARIS

Antiquités Scientifiques occupied a lonely outpost at the end of rue de Miromesnil where tourists rarely ventured. There were some in the Parisian antiques trade who had urged its owner, the fastidious Maurice Durand, to relocate to the rue de Rivoli or perhaps even the Champs-Élysées. But Monsieur Durand had always resisted for fear he would spend his days watching overweight Americans pawing his precious antique microscopes, cameras, spectacles, barometers, and surveyors, only to depart the shop empty-handed. Besides, Durand had always preferred his tidy little life at the quiet end of the arrondissement. There was a good brasserie across the street where he took his coffee in the morning and drank his wine at night. And then there was Angélique Brossard, a seller of glass figurines who was always willing to change the sign in her window from OUVERT to FERMÉ whenever Durand came calling.

But there was another reason why Maurice Durand had resisted the lure of Paris's busier streets. Antiquités Scientifiques, while reasonably profitable, operated largely as a front for his primary occupation. Durand specialized in conveying paintings and other objets d'art from homes, galleries, and museums into the hands of collectors who did not care about meddlesome details such as a clean provenance. There were some in law enforcement who might have described Durand as an art thief, though he would have quibbled with that characterization, for it had been many years since he had actually stolen a painting himself. He now operated solely as a broker in the process known as commissioned theft—or, as Durand liked to describe it, he managed the acquisition of paintings that were not technically for sale. His clients tended to be the sort of men who did not like to be disappointed, and Durand rarely failed them. Working with a stable of Marseille-based professional thieves, he had been the linchpin in some of history's greatest art heists. Topping his list of achievements, at least in monetary terms, was Van Gogh's *Self-Portrait with a Bandaged Ear*. Stolen from the Courtauld Gallery in London, it was now hanging in the palace of a Saudi sheikh who had a penchant for violence involving knives.

But it was Maurice Durand's link to a lesser-known work— *Portrait of a Young Woman*, oil on canvas, by Rembrandt van Rijn—that had led to his unlikely alliance with the secret intelligence service of the State of Israel. After accepting a commission to steal the painting, Durand had discovered that hidden within it was a list of numbered Swiss bank accounts filled with looted assets from the Holocaust. The list had allowed Gabriel to blackmail a Swiss billionaire named Martin Landesmann into sending a shipment of sabotaged industrial centrifuges to his steady customers in the Islamic Republic of Iran. At the conclusion of the operation,

Gabriel had decided to take no action against Durand lest the Office ever require the services of a professional thief.

All of which goes some way to explaining why, twenty-four hours after arriving in Paris, Eli Lavon presented himself at the entrance of the little shop at 106 rue de Miromesnil. The buzzer, when pressed, emitted an inhospitable howl. Then the deadbolts snapped open with a thud, and Lavon, shaking the rain from his sodden overcoat, slipped inside.

"Stolen anything lately, Monsieur Durand?"

"Not even a kiss, Monsieur Lavon."

The two men appraised each other for a moment without speaking. They were roughly equals in height and build, but the similarities ended there. While Lavon wore an outfit he called Left Bank revolutionary chic, Durand was impeccably attired in a somber chalk-stripe suit and lavender necktie. His bald head shone like polished glass in the restrained overhead lighting. His dark eyes were expressionless and unblinking.

"How can I assist you?" he asked, as though helping Lavon was the last thing in the world he wished to do.

"I'm looking for something special," Lavon replied.

"Well, then, you've certainly come to the right place." Durand walked over to a display case filled with microscopes. "This just arrived," he said, running his hand over one of the instruments. "It was made by Nachet & Sons of Paris in 1890. The optics and mechanics are all in good condition. So is the walnut case."

"Not that kind of something, Monsieur Durand."

Durand's hand had yet to move from the oxidized surface of the microscope. "It seems my debt has come due," he said.

"You make us sound like blackmailers," Lavon said, hoisting his most benevolent smile. "But I assure you that's not the case."

"What do you want?"

"Your expertise."

"It's expensive."

"Don't worry, Maurice. Money isn't the problem."

The rain chased them across the Place de la Concorde and along the Seine embankments. It was not the pleasing Parisian rain of songwriters and poets but a frigid torrent that clawed its way through their overcoats. Durand, thoroughly miserable, pleaded for the warmth of a taxi, but Lavon wanted to make certain they were not being followed, and so they slogged on. Finally, they entered the foyer of a luxury apartment building overlooking the Pont Marie and climbed the spiral staircase to a flat on the fourth floor. Seated in the living room, looking comfortable and relaxed, was Gabriel. With only a slight movement of his emerald-colored eyes, he invited Durand to join him. The Frenchman hesitated. Then, after receiving a nudge from Lavon, he approached with the slowness of a condemned man being led to the gallows.

"You obviously recognize me," Gabriel said, watching Durand intently as he settled into his seat. "That's usually a liability in our business. But not in this case."

"How so?"

"Because you know I'm a professional, just like you. You also know I'm not someone who would waste valuable time by making idle threats."

Gabriel looked down at the coffee table. On it were two matching attaché cases.

"Time bombs?" asked Durand.

"Your future." Gabriel placed his hand on one of the attaché cases. "This one contains enough evidence to put a man in prison for the rest of his life."

"And the other?"

"One million euros in cash."

"What do I have to do for it?"

Gabriel smiled. "What you do best."

22

QUAI DES CÉLESTINS, PARIS

THERE WAS A BOTTLE OF Armagnac on the sideboard. After hearing Gabriel's proposal, Maurice Durand poured himself a very large glass. He hesitated before drinking it.

"Don't worry, Maurice," said Gabriel reassuringly. "We save the poisoned brandy for special occasions."

Durand took a guarded sip. "There's one thing I don't understand," he said after a moment. "Why not just steal this object yourself or borrow an item from one of your museums?"

"Because I'm going to tell a story," replied Gabriel. "And like all good stories, it requires verisimilitude. If an object of great value were to appear suddenly out of thin air, our target would rightly suspect a trap. But if he believes the object has recently been stolen by a band of thieves with a long track record . . ."

"He will assume he's dealing with professional criminals rather than professional spies."

Gabriel was silent.

"How clever," Durand said, raising his glass a fraction of an inch in a mock toast. "What exactly are you looking for?"

"A red-figure Attic vessel, fourth or fifth century BC, something large enough to turn heads on the illicit market."

"Would you like it to come from a public source or private?"

"Private," replied Gabriel. "No museums."

"It's not as difficult as you think."

"Robbing a museum?"

Durand nodded.

"But it would be bad manners."

"Suit yourself." Durand sat down and stared into his drink thoughtfully. "There's a villa outside Saint-Tropez. It's located on the Baie de Cavalaire, not far from the estate that used to be owned by that Russian oligarch. His name escapes me."

"Ivan Kharkov?"

"Yes, that's him. Know him?"

"Only by reputation."

"He was killed outside his favorite restaurant in Saint-Tropez. Very messy."

"So I heard. But you were telling me about his neighbor's house."

"It's not as big as Ivan's old place, but its owner has impeccable taste."

"Who is he?"

"Belgian," said Durand disdainfully. "He inherited an industrial fortune and is doing his level best to spend every last centime of it. A couple of years ago, we relieved him of a Cézanne. It was a replacement job."

"You left a copy behind."

"Quite a good one, actually. In fact, our Belgian friend apparently still believes the painting is genuine because to my knowledge he's never reported the theft to the police."

"What was it?"

"The House of the Jas de Bouffan."

"Who handled the forgery?"

"You have your secrets, Mr. Allon, I have mine."

"Go on."

"The Belgian has several other Cézannes. He also has a very impressive collection of antiquities. One piece in particular is quite lovely, a terra-cotta hydria by the Amykos Painter, fifth century BC. It depicts two young women presenting gifts to two nude male athletes. Very sensual."

"You obviously know your Greek pottery."

"It is a passion of mine."

"How often is the Belgian at the villa?"

"July and August," Durand said. "The rest of the year it's unoccupied except for the caretaker. He has a small cottage on the property."

"What about security?"

"Surely a man such as yourself realizes there's no such thing as security. As long as there are no surprises, my men will be in and out of the house within a few minutes. And you will have your Greek pot in short order."

"I think I'd like a Cézanne, too."

"Verisimilitude?"

"It's all in the details, Maurice."

Durand smiled. He was a detail man himself.

He made but one request, that they resist the temptation to monitor his movements as he went about the business of fulfilling their contract. They readily agreed, despite the fact they had absolutely no intention of living up to their end of the bargain. Maurice Durand had once stolen several hundred million dollars' worth of paintings in the span of a single summer. One could utilize the services of a criminal like Durand, but only a fool would ever turn his back on him.

For three days, he kept to his *beau quartier* at the northern end of the eighth arrondissement. His schedule, like his shop, was filled with pleasant oddities from another time. He drank two café crèmes each morning at the same table of the same brasserie with no company other than a stack of newspapers, which he purchased from the same *tabac*. After that, he would cross the narrow street and, at the stroke of ten, disappear into his gilded little cage. Occasionally, he was obliged to open its doors to a client or a deliveryman, but for the most part Durand's confinement remained solitary. Lunch was taken at one and lasted until half past two, when he would return to the shop for the remainder of the afternoon. At five, he would pay a brief visit to Madame Brossard. Then it was back to his table at the brasserie for a glass of Côtes du Rhône, which he drank always with an air of supreme contentment.

For those unlucky souls who were forced to keep watch over this seemingly charmed life, Maurice Durand was the subject of both endless fascination and passionate resentment. Not surprisingly, there were a few members of the team, most notably Yaakov, who believed that Gabriel had erred by placing the opening stage of the operation in the hands of such a man. "Look at the watch reports," Yaakov demanded over dinner at the team's primary safe flat near the Bois de Boulogne. "It's obvious that Maurice has salted away our million euros and has no intention of ever delivering the goods." Gabriel, however, was unconcerned. Durand had shown himself in the past to be a man of some principle. "He's also a natural thief," said Gabriel. "And there's nothing a thief enjoys more than stealing from the very rich."

Gabriel's faith was rewarded the following morning, when Unit 8200 overheard Durand booking first-class accommodations on the midday TGV train to Marseille. Yaakov and Oded made the trip with him, and at five that evening, they observed their quarry make a mildly clandestine meeting in the Old Port with a local fisherman. Later, they would identify the "fisherman" as Pascal Rameau, leader of one of Marseille's many criminal organizations.

It was at this point that the operation appeared to gather its first momentum, for within twenty-four hours of Durand's visit, members of Rameau's crew were casing the Belgian's lavish villa. Gabriel knew this because two members of his own crew, Yossi and Rimona, had taken a short-term lease on a villa in the hills above the property and were watching it constantly with the help of long-lens cameras and video recorders. They never saw Rameau's men again. But two nights later, as a violent storm laid siege to the entire length of the Côte d'Azur, they were awakened by the wail of sirens along the coast road. For the next several hours, they watched blue lights flashing despondently in the drive of the Belgian's seaside palace. The police scanner told them everything they needed to know. One Cézanne, one Greek vase, no arrests. *C'est la vie.*

It was in all the papers, which is exactly what they had hoped for. The Cézanne was the main attraction; the Greek vase, a lovely hydria by the Amykos Painter, a mere afterthought. The distraught Belgian owner offered a substantial reward for information leading to the recovery of his goods, while his insurers, the great Lloyd's of London, quietly let it be known that they would consider making a ransom payment. The French police knocked on a few doors and questioned a few of the usual suspects, but after a week they decided they had more important things to do than chase down a swath of canvas and a very old lump of clay. Besides, they had dealt with this band of thieves before. These men were pros, not adventurers, and when they stole something, it never reappeared.

The theft sent the usual tremors of apprehension through the art galleries of Paris, but in Maurice Durand's world it was but a pebble cast upon an otherwise tranquil surface. They overheard him discussing the case with his favorite waitress at the brasserie, but otherwise his life moved at the same monotonous rhythm. He opened his shop at ten. He lunched at one. And at five o'clock sharp, he treated himself to the pleasures of Madame Brossard and then drank his red wine for the sake of his guiltless little heart.

Finally, a week after the theft, he rang Gabriel on a prearranged number to say the items he had requested—an early twentieth-century Swiss pocket barometer and a brass-and-wood telescope by Merz of Munich—had arrived safely. At Gabriel's request, Durand delivered the items that evening to the flat overlooking the Pont Marie and departed as quickly as he could. The painting, a landscape of Cézanne's beloved Mont Saint-Victoire, had been expertly removed from its stretcher and placed in a cardboard tube. The hydria was packed into a nylon Adidas sports bag. Eli Lavon removed it and placed it carefully on the kitchen table. Then he sat there for several minutes with Gabriel at his side, staring at the image of the Greek maidens attending to the nude athletes.

"Someone has to do it," Lavon said finally, "but it's not going to be me."

"I'm a restorer," said Gabriel. "I couldn't possibly."

"And I'm an archaeologist," Lavon replied defensively. "Besides, I've never been one for the rough stuff."

"I've never assassinated a vase."

"Don't worry," Lavon said. "Unlike your previous work, it will only be temporary."

Gabriel exhaled heavily, returned the hydria to the Adidas sports bag, and gently pushed it over the edge of the table. The sound it made on impact was like the shattering of bone. Lavon slowly opened the zipper and peered mournfully inside.

"Murderer," he whispered softly.

"Someone had to do it."

The Cézanne, however, received no such maltreatment. Indeed, during the final hours of the team's stay in Paris, Gabriel ministered tenderly to its wounds as though it were a patient in intensive care. His goal was to stabilize the image so that the painting could one day be returned to its owner in the same condition in which it had been found. No ordinary art thief would ever have taken such a step, but Gabriel's commitment to operational verisimilitude went only so far. He was a restorer first and foremost, and caring for the Cézanne helped to relieve his guilt over breaking the vase.

He briefly considered returning the canvas to a stretcher, but ruled out such a procedure on the grounds it would make the painting too difficult to move securely. Instead, he adhered a protective layer of tissue paper to the surface using a rabbit-skin glue that he concocted in the kitchen of the Bois de Boulogne safe flat. Next morning, when the glue had dried, he returned the canvas carefully to its cardboard tube and ferried it to the Israeli Embassy at 3 rue Rabelais. The Office station chief was understandably apprehensive about accepting stolen property, but he relented after receiving a phone call from Uzi Navot. Gabriel tucked the painting into a moisture-free corner of the station's vault and set the thermostat to a comfortable sixty-eight degrees. Then he headed to the Gare de Lyon and boarded the midday train for Zurich.

He passed the four-hour journey plotting the next phase of the operation, and by six that evening, he was guiding a rented Audi sedan down the graceful sweep of Zurich's Bahnhofstrasse. Seated next to him, the Adidas sports bag between his feet, was Eli Lavon. "Switzerland," he said, staring glumly out his window. "Why does it always have to be Switzerland?"

23

ST. MORITZ, SWITZERLAND

B Y THEN IT WAS MARCH, which meant that St. Moritz, the quaint former spa town in the Upper Engadine valley, was once more in the grip of madness. On the Via Serlas, perhaps the world's costliest shopping street, faded aristocrats wandered aimlessly from Chopard to Gucci to Chanel to Bulgari, along with film stars, supermodels, politicians, tycoons, and all their entourages and assorted hangers-on. They fought over the best tables at La Marmite or the Terrace and at night smiled their way into the private rooms at Dracula or the King's Club. Only a handful ever bothered to put on a pair of skis. In St. Moritz, skiing was the pastime of those who didn't have something better to do.

But tucked away on a quiet side street like an island of reason was the stately old Jägerhof Hotel. She was dowdy and dour and, most of all, unfashionable, which troubled her not one whit. Indeed, she seemed to revel in it. Her restaurants were without note; her amenities, such as they were, were second to everyone. She had no spa or indoor swimming pool and no nightclub to lure those who liked to see their names in boldface. The only music one ever heard at the Jägerhof was the sound of the string quartet that sawed away in the salon each afternoon during the drowsy lull euphemistically referred to as après ski.

Her rooms, like her manners, were dusty relics from another time. Returning guests tended to request the lower floors because the lift was forever breaking down, while those seeking a bargain gravitated to the cramped garrets. Staying in one was a tall, lanky Russian with gray eyes and bloodless skin the color of the snow atop the Piz Bernina. Sadly, he had severely twisted his knee on the first day of his holiday and had been largely confined to his room ever since. Occasionally, he would sit in the tiny arrow slit of a window and gaze longingly into the street, but for the most part he remained in his bed with his injured leg elevated. To pass the time, he watched movies and listened to music on his notebook computer. The chambermaids described him as polite to a fault, which was unusual for a Russian.

The same could not be said, however, of the doctor who appeared at the Jägerhof four days after the Russian's unfortunate accident. He was of medium height and build with a full head of silvery hair and watchful brown eyes that were partially concealed by thick spectacles. Those members of the Jägerhof staff who were unfortunate enough to encounter him during his brief visit would later remark that he seemed better suited to inflicting wounds than healing them.

"How's your knee?" asked Gabriel.

"It still hurts if I put too much weight on it."

"It doesn't look so good."

"You should have seen it two days ago."

The knee was propped upon a pair of pillows embroidered with the Jägerhof's discreet crest. Gabriel winced mildly as he inspected the swelling.

"Where did all those bruises come from?"

"I had to hit it a few times."

"With what? A sledgehammer?"

"I used the bottle of complimentary champagne."

"How was it?"

"As a blunt instrument, it was fine."

Gabriel went to the window and peered down at the postcard-perfect Swiss square. On one side, a limousine was docking with the slowness of a luxury liner at the doorway of one of the resort's pricier hotels. On the other, three fur-drenched women were posing for a photograph next to a horse drawn carriage. After a moment, the carriage moved off to the gentle clatter of snow-muffled hoof beats, revealing the understated entrance of Galleria Naxos. Through the large front display window, Gabriel could see David Girard speaking to a customer about one of the gallery's better pieces, a first-century Roman statue of a now-limbless adolescent boy posed in recline. The soundtrack of the conversation, which was being conducted in German, issued softly from the speakers of Mikhail's notebook computer.

"Where's the transmitter hidden?"

"On his desk."

"How did you manage that?"

"During my one and only visit to the shop, I left behind a very costly gold pen. Monsieur Girard has been good enough to hold on to it for me until I have a chance to drop by again. The only problem is that it's right next to the telephone. Every time someone calls the gallery, it sounds like a fire alarm is going off."

"How's business?"

"Slow. He generally sees one or two customers in the morning and a few more in the late afternoon when the slopes start to close down. By five o'clock, the place is dead."

"Any employees?"

"The wife usually spends a couple of hours in the gallery after she drops off Hansel and Gretel at the daycare center. They live a few miles from St. Moritz in a town called Samedan. Nice place. I have a feeling Daoud is the only member of Hezbollah who lives there."

"His name is David," Gabriel said pointedly. "And for the moment, we can't prove he's a member of anything except the Swiss Association of Dealers in Art and Antiques."

"Until he sees that pretty Greek pot."

"It's possible he won't bite."

"He'll bite," Mikhail said assuredly. "Then we'll burn him to a crisp and turn him around, just the way you drew it up on the chalkboard at King Saul Boulevard."

"Sometimes operations don't go as planned."

"Tell me about it." Mikhail examined Gabriel for a moment. "Maybe it's not such a good idea for you to be playing footsy with someone from Hezbollah right now."

"I barely recognize myself in this getup."

"Your famous face isn't the only reason you should think twice about walking into that gallery."

Gabriel turned and looked at Mikhail directly. "You don't think I'm up to it? Is that what you're saying?"

"It hasn't been that long since Nadia al-Bakari died in your arms in the Empty Quarter. Maybe you should let someone else go in there and dangle the bait."

"Like who?"

"Me."

"You can barely walk."

"I'll take some aspirin."

"How much do you know about red-figure Attic vases?"

"Absolutely nothing."

"That might be a problem."

Mikhail was silent.

"Are we finished?" asked Gabriel.

"We're finished."

Gabriel opened the aluminum attaché case he had brought with him into the hotel. Inside was a single fragment of the hydria, carefully wrapped in baize cloth, along with several eight-by-ten photographs of the remaining pieces of the vase. With the flip of a small interior switch, Gabriel activated the case's audio and video transmission system. Then he closed the case and looked at Mikhail.

"Are you picking up the signal?"

"Got it."

Gabriel walked over to the mirror and inspected the unfamiliar face reflected in the glass. Satisfied with his appearance, he departed the room without another word and headed downstairs to the Jägerhof's dreary lobby. By the time he stepped into the street, he was no longer the taciturn physician who had come to treat an injured Russian; he was Anton Drexler of Premier Antiquities Services, Hamburg, Germany. Ten minutes later, having performed a thorough check for surveillance, he presented himself at the entrance of Galleria Naxos. In the window lay the limbless Roman boy, looking perversely like the victim of a roadside bomb. Herr Drexler examined the statue for a moment with the discerning gaze of a professional. Then, after ringing the bell and announcing his intentions, he was admitted without further delay.

24

ST. MORITZ, SWITZERLAND

THE EXHIBITION ROOM WAS BRILLIANTLY lit and artfully staged to avoid the impression of clutter—here a selection of Greek kraters and amphorae, here a litter of Egyptian bronze cats, here a gathering of marble amputees and disembodied heads, price available on request. In the back corner of the gallery was a Chinese lacquer-finished table where David Girard, aka Daoud Ghandour, sat waiting to receive him. He wore a dark blazer, a zippered sweater, and trim-cut trousers that looked as though they were made of velvet. A sleek black telephone was wedged between his shoulder and his ear, and he was scribbling something illegible on a piece of paper using Mikhail's expensive gold pen. Gabriel could only imagine the scraping sound it was making in the garret room of the Jägerhof Hotel.

Finally, Girard murmured a few words of French into the phone and replaced the receiver. He appraised his visitor in silence for a moment with his soft brown eyes, then, without rising, asked to see a business card. Gabriel wordlessly granted his wish.

"Your card has no address and no telephone number," Girard said in German.

"I'm something of a minimalist."

"Why haven't I heard of you?"

"I try not to make waves," Gabriel responded with a docile smile. "High seas make it harder for me to do my job."

"Which is what, exactly?"

"I find things. Lost dogs, loose change behind the couch cushions, hidden gems in cellars and attics."

"You're a dealer?"

"Not like you, of course," Gabriel said with as much modesty as he could muster.

"Who sent you?"

"A friend in Rome."

"Does the friend have a name?"

"The friend is like me," Gabriel said. "He prefers calm waters."

"Does he find things, too?"

"In a manner of speaking."

Girard returned the business card and, with a movement of his eyes, asked to see the contents of Herr Drexler's attaché case.

"Perhaps you have some place a bit more private," suggested Gabriel, glancing briefly toward the gallery's large window overlooking the crowded square.

"Is there a problem?"

"Not at all," answered Gabriel in his most reassuring tone. "It's just that St. Moritz isn't what it used to be."

Girard studied Gabriel before rising to his feet and walking over to a cipher-protected door. On the other side was a climate-controlled storage room filled with inventory that had yet to find its way onto the gallery's main exhibition floor, and probably never would. Gabriel led himself on a brief tour before popping the combination locks of the attaché case. Then he unveiled the fragment of the hydria with a magician's flourish and laid it carefully on an examination table so Girard could see the image clearly.

"I don't deal in fragments," he said.

"Neither do I."

Gabriel handed him the stack of photographs. The last showed the hydria pieced loosely together.

"It's missing a few small surface fragments here and there," Gabriel said, "but it's nothing that can't be repaired by a good restorer. I have a man who can do the work if you're interested."

"I prefer to use my own restorer," Girard responded.

"I assumed that would be the case."

Girard pulled on a pair of rubber gloves and examined the fragment of pottery with a professional-grade magnifier. "It looks to me like the work of the Amykos Painter. Probably about 420 BC."

"I concur."

"Where did you find it?"

"Here and there," answered Gabriel. "Most of the pieces came from old family collections in Germany and here in Switzerland. It took me five years to track them all down."

"Really?"

Girard returned the fragment and without another word walked over to a computer. After a few keystrokes, a single sheet of paper came shooting out of the color printer. It was an alert, issued by the Swiss Association of Dealers in Art and Antiques. The subject was a red-figure Attic hydria by the Amykos Painter that had been stolen two weeks earlier from a private home in the South of France. Girard placed the alert on the table next to the photos and looked to Herr Drexler for an explanation.

"As you know," Gabriel said, reciting words that had been written for him by Eli Lavon, "the Amykos Painter was a prolific artist who created numerous stock figures that appear many times throughout his body of work. My hydria is simply a copy of the vessel that was stolen in France."

"So it's coincidental?"

"Entirely."

Girard emitted a dry, humorous laugh. "I'm afraid your friend in Rome has led you astray, because this gallery does not trade in stolen or looted antiquities. It is a violation of our association's code of ethics, not to mention Swiss law."

"Actually, Swiss law allows you to acquire a piece if you believe in good faith that it's not stolen. And I am giving you my assurance, Herr Girard, that this hydria is the result of five years' work on my part."

"Forgive me if I'm not willing to accept the word of a man who has no address and no telephone number."

It was an impressive performance but flawed by the fact that David Girard's eyes were now fixed on the fragment of pottery. Gabriel had spent enough time around art dealers to see that his target was already calculating an offer. All he needed, thought Gabriel, was a small crack of the whip.

"In fairness, Herr Girard," Gabriel said, "I should tell you that other parties are interested in acquiring the hydria. But I came to St. Moritz because I was told you had the ability to move merchandise like this with a single phone call."

"I'm afraid you overestimate my abilities."

Gabriel smiled as if to say he was having none of it. "Your list of Middle Eastern clients is legendary in the trade, Herr Girard. Surely, you have the means to produce a provenance that will satisfy one of them. By my estimate, the reassembled and restored hydria is worth four hundred thousand Swiss francs. I'd be willing to accept one hundred thousand for the fragments, leaving you a profit of three hundred thousand." Another smile. "Not bad for the price of a long-distance call to Riyadh or Dubai."

The dealer lapsed into a contemplative silence, thus surrendering any pretense that he was unwilling to handle the hydria. "Fifty thousand," he countered, "payable on completion of the sale."

Gabriel returned the fragment to its baize blanket. "If you want the hydria, Herr Girard, you will pay me the money up front. The price is not negotiable."

"I need some time."

"You have twenty-four hours."

"How do I reach you?"

"You don't. I'll call you tomorrow at five for your answer. If it is yes, I will deliver the fragments at six and expect payment in full. If the answer is no, I will hang up, and you will never hear from me again."

For their safe house, they had rented a handsome, timbered chalet on a snow-covered mountainside above the village, a bargain at five thousand Swiss francs a night. When Gabriel arrived, the entire team greeted him with a standing ovation. Then they played a recording of a phone call David Girard had just placed to a colleague in Hamburg, looking for information about a bottom feeder named Anton Drexler. "I could be mistaken," Eli Lavon said, smiling, "but it sounds as if we are most definitely in play."

It seemed no one had ever heard of him. Not a rumor in Zurich. Not a whisper in Geneva. Not so much as a peep in Basel or New

York. In fact, the closest thing David Girard found to an actual sighting of a creature called Anton Drexler was a blurry story about someone matching his description trying to sell a couple of forged Greek goddesses to Sotheby's a few years back. "Or did he call himself Dresden? Sorry I can't be of more help, David. Lunch next time you're in town?"

Finding nothing to discourage him from moving forward, Girard began making inquires of a different kind, namely, trying to locate a potential buyer for his potential new acquisition. As Gabriel had predicted, it took but a single phone call to Riyadh, where a lowly prince immediately threw his *ghutra* into the ring for three hundred thousand Swiss francs. Not content to rest there, Girard then rang a collector in Abu Dhabi who said he was in for three-twenty. A subsequent call to Moscow brought in a Russian oil trader at three-forty, at which point the real bidding began. It ended a few hours later with the Saudi prince reigning supreme at four and a quarter, payable on delivery.

It was then Girard phoned his man at the St. Moritz branch of Bank Julius Baer to request one hundred thousand Swiss francs in cash. He collected the money at four and by four-fifteen was back at the gallery, tapping the tip of Mikhail's expensive gold pen nervously against the surface of his desk. In the garret room of the Jägerhof Hotel, it sounded like a jackhammer.

"How long do you think he's going to do that?" Mikhail groaned.

"I suppose until I call him at five o'clock," answered Gabriel.

"Why don't you just get it over with?"

"Because Herr Drexler is a man of his word. And he said he would call at five."

And so they sat together, Mikhail propped on the bed, Gabriel perched in the arrow slit window, David Girard banging away at his desk in anticipation of Herr Drexler's call. Finally, at the stroke of five, Gabriel dialed the gallery on a disposable cell phone and in terse German posed a simple question.

"Yes or no?" After hearing Girard's answer, he said, "I'll be there in an hour. Make sure no one is around when I arrive."

Gabriel severed the connection and removed the SIM card from the phone. For a moment, there was silence in the room. Then the staccato tapping started up again, even louder than before.

"If he doesn't stop," Mikhail said, "I'm going to walk over there and shoot him."

"We need him to get inside Hezbollah's funding network," said Gabriel. "Then you can shoot him."

During the next sixty minutes, Gabriel and Mikhail would be granted two reprieves from the tapping. The first occurred at 5:10, when Girard's Swiss wife dropped by unexpectedly for a glass of champagne to celebrate the sale of the hydria. The second came at 5:40, when a guest from the adjacent hotel, apparently having nothing better to do, asked whether he might have a look at the merchandise. He was tall, French speaking, and deeply tanned, and dangling on his arm like a piece of jewelry was a ravishing young girl with short dark hair and a face that looked as though it had been painted by El Greco. They remained inside for fifteen minutes, though the girl spent most of that time studying her re-flection in Girard's windows. Leaving the gallery, they seemed to quarrel briefly until a few words whispered directly into the girl's ear brought a smile to her childlike face. As they set off arm in arm across the square, they walked past Herr Anton Drexler, dealer of suspect antiquities, as though he were invisible.

After making one final check of his wristwatch, Gabriel presented himself at the entrance of Girard's gallery and, at six precisely, placed his thumb upon the call button. He expected to hear the soothing purr of Girard's buzzer but instead saw a flash of blinding white light. Then the limbless Roman boy came hurtling toward him through a wall of fire, and together they descended into darkness.

25

ST. MORITZ, SWITZERLAND

T HE BOMB HAD BEEN EXPERTLY assembled and planted with care. Initially, the Swiss Federal Police concluded it had been detonated with a timing device, only to discover later it had been set off by a cell phone. The explosion blew out hundreds of windows in the center of the village, triggered a series of avalanches on the highest ski slopes, and collapsed a display of Dom Pérignon bottles in the ornate lobby of the Badrutt's Palace Hotel. The broken glass was removed with typical Swiss efficiency, and order soon restored. Even so, everyone agreed that St. Moritz, the quaint former spa town in the Upper Engadine valley, would never be the same.

Despite the power of the explosion, only three people lost their lives, including the owner of the antiquities gallery where the bomb had been planted. An additional fifty-four people were wounded, including the president of a major Swiss bank, a famous English footballer, and a Czech supermodel who had come to St. Moritz to console herself after the dissolution of her third marriage. Most of the injured sustained only minor cuts and bruises, but there were numerous broken bones suffered by those blown from their feet by the force of the blast wave.

One of the most seriously injured victims could not be identified. He had been carrying no passport or credit cards at the time of the explosion and afterward could not seem to recall his name or why he was in St. Moritz to begin with. Suffering from numerous lacerations and a severe concussion, he remained hospitalized for several days after the incident, unaware, or so it seemed, that he was the subject of intense interest on the part of the Swiss police.

There was, for a start, the video footage showing him standing at the entrance of the gallery at the time the bomb exploded, wearing a wig and false eyeglasses, and holding an aluminum attaché case—all of which were eventually recovered by crime-scene investigators. And then there was the tall, gray-eyed man with a Russian accent who had tried to carry him from the square before being stopped by police. And the large, multilingual group of tourists who had fled a luxury slope-side chateau just three nights into a weeklong booking. A thorough search of the chateau produced not a single scrap of paper that would indicate the names and identities of those who had stayed there. The same was true of the Russian's garret room at the Jägerhof Hotel.

The most intriguing piece of evidence, however, was the injured man's distinctive face, which revealed itself slowly as the swelling receded and the bruising began to fade. It was well known to Swiss intelligence; in fact, there was an entire shelf in the file rooms of the DAP, the Swiss security service, devoted solely to his exploits on the soil of their blessed little land. And now, at long last, he had been delivered helpless into their hands. There were some who wanted to throw a net over him lest he slip through their fingers yet again, but cooler heads prevailed. And so they stood watch outside his door and waited for his injuries to heal. And when he was fit enough to leave the hospital, they placed him in handcuffs and took him away.

They bundled him into a helicopter without bothering to tell the local *kantonspolizei* and flew him at high speed to the headquarters of the Swiss Federal Police on the Nussbaumstrasse in Bern. After fingerprinting him and photographing his face from every conceivable angle, they locked him away in a holding cell. It had a small flat-screen television, a writing desk stocked with pens and stationery, and a comfortable bed with starched linens. Even the Swiss police, thought Gabriel, were excellent hoteliers.

They left him alone for several hours to ponder his predicament, then, without warning or legal representation, brought him handcuffed to an interrogation room. Waiting there was the officer in charge of Gabriel's case. He called himself Ziegler. No first name, no rank, no small talk—just Ziegler. He was tall and Alpine, with the broad, square shoulders of a cross-country skier and a ruddy complexion. Arrayed on the table before him were many photographs of Gabriel at different stages of his career, and in various levels of disguise. They showed him entering and leaving banks, crossing hotel lobbies and borders, and, in one, walking along the embankment of a leaden Zurich canal in the company of the renowned Swiss violinist Anna Rolfe. Ziegler seemed especially proud of the display. Obviously, he had put a great deal of thought into it.

"We have a theory," he began as Gabriel sat.

"I can hardly wait."

Ziegler's face remained as placid as a bottomless Swiss lake. "It seems that before coming to St. Moritz, you made a brief stop in France, where you stole a painting by Cézanne and a two-thousand-year-old Greek hydria. You then transported the vase in pieces across the border and attempted to sell it to David Girard of the Galleria Naxos. What Girard didn't realize, however, is that you never had any intention of delivering the vase, since the true purpose of your little ruse de guerre was to kill him."

"Why would I want to kill a Swiss antiquities dealer?"

"Because, as you already know, that antiquities dealer wasn't Swiss. Well," Ziegler added with a xenophobic frown, "not *truly* Swiss. He was born in southern Lebanon. And from what we've learned, he was apparently still doing plenty of business there. Which is why Israeli intelligence wanted him dead."

"If we'd wanted him dead, we would have done it in a way that didn't kill two innocent people in the process."

"How noble of you, Herr Allon."

"You seem to be forgetting one other minor detail," said Gabriel wearily.

"What's that?"

"That bomb nearly killed *me*."

"Yes," Ziegler replied matter-of-factly. "Perhaps the legendary Gabriel Allon has lost a step."

Gabriel was returned to his holding cell and fed a proper Swiss meal of potato raclette and breaded veal. Afterward, he watched the evening news in German on SF 1. Fifteen minutes elapsed before they got around to a follow-up report on the bombing in St. Moritz. It was a feature piece about how the affair had adversely impacted holiday bookings. The story made no mention of David Girard's connections to Hezbollah. Nor did it refer to any arrests in the case, which Gabriel regarded as an encouraging sign.

After dinner, a doctor silently inspected his cuts and changed a few of his bandages. Then he was taken back to the interrogation room for an evening session. This time, Ziegler was nowhere to be found. In his place was a thin officer with the pallor of a man who had no time for outdoor pursuits. He introduced himself as Christoph Bittel of the DAP's counterterror division, which meant he was more spy than policeman. It was another encouraging sign. Policemen made arrests. Spies made deals.

"Before we begin," he said evenly, "you should know that Ziegler and the Federal Department of Justice and Police intend to file formal charges against you tomorrow morning. They have more than enough evidence to ensure that you spend the rest of your life in a Swiss jail. You should also know that there are numerous people here in Bern who would love to be granted the honor of escorting you to your cell."

"I had nothing to do with planting that bomb."

"I know."

Bittel picked up a remote control and pointed at a video monitor in the corner of the room. A few seconds later, two figures appeared on the screen—the tall French-speaking man and the girl with an El Greco face. Gabriel watched again as the man whispered intimately into her ear.

"These are the real bombers," Bittel said, pausing the video. "The girl concealed the device in the gallery's powder room while her colleague kept Girard busy."

"Who are they?"

"We were hoping you'd be able to tell us."

"I'd never seen them before that night."

Bittel scrutinized Gabriel dubiously for a moment before switching off the video monitor. "You are a very lucky man, Allon. It seems you have a number of friends in high places. One of them has interceded on your behalf."

"So that's it? I'm free to go?"

"Not quite yet. You *did* violate numerous laws prohibiting foreign espionage activity—laws we take very seriously. We are a welcoming country," he added, as though he were sharing highly classified information, "but we insist that visitors show us the courtesy of signing the guestbook on the way in, preferably under their own names."

"And what would you have done if we'd asked for your help?"

"We would have sent you away and dealt with it ourselves," Bittel said. "We're Swiss. We don't like outsiders meddling in our affairs."

"Neither do we. But unfortunately we have to put up with it on a daily basis."

"I'm afraid that's what it means to be an Israeli," Bittel said with a philosophical nod. "History dealt you a lousy hand, but that doesn't mean you have the right to treat our country as some sort of intelligence resort."

"My visits to your country were never all that enjoyable."

"But they were always productive. And that's all that counts. You're industrious, Allon. We admire that."

"So what do you want from me?"

"We would like you to close out your Swiss accounts."

"Meaning?"

"I ask questions about your past operations, and you answer them. Truthfully, for a change," he added pointedly.

"That could take a while."

"I have nowhere else to go. And neither do you, Allon."

"And if I refuse?"

"You will be formally charged with espionage, terrorism, and murder. And you will spend your hard-earned retirement here in Switzerland."

Gabriel made a momentary show of thought. "I'm afraid it's not good enough."

"What's not good enough?"

"The deal," said Gabriel. "I want a better deal."

"You're in no position to make demands, Allon."

"You'll never put me on trial, Bittel. I know far too much about the sins of your bankers and industrialists. It would be a public-relations disaster for Switzerland, just like the Holocaust accounts scandal." He paused. "You remember that, don't you? It was in all the papers."

This time it was Bittel who made a display of deliberation. "All right, Allon. What do you want?"

"I think it's time to open a new chapter in Israeli-Swiss relations."

"And how might we do that?"

"You'd obviously been monitoring David Girard for some time," Gabriel said. "I want copies of your files, including all the telephone and e-mail intercepts."

"Out of the question."

"It's a brave new world, Bittel."

"I'll need the approval of my superiors."

"I can wait," Gabriel replied. "As you said, I have nowhere else to go."

Bittel rose and left the interrogation room. Two minutes later, he returned. The Swiss were nothing if not efficient.

"I think it would be easier if we did this in reverse chronological order," Bittel said, opening his notebook. "A few months ago, a resident of Zurich was beheaded in a hotel room in Dubai. We were wondering whether you could tell us why."

Many years earlier, a Swiss dissident named Professor Emil Jacobi had given Gabriel a sound piece of advice. "When you're dealing with Switzerland," he explained, "it's best to keep one thing in mind. Switzerland is not a real country. It's a business, and it's run like a business."

Therefore, it came as no surprise to Gabriel that Bittel conducted the debriefing with the cold formality of a financial transaction. His manner was that of a private banker—polite but distant, thorough but discreet. He did his due diligence, but not with undue malice. Gabriel had the distinct impression the security man wanted nothing on the books that might cause him a problem later, that he was merely checking boxes and tallying up a ledger. But then, that was the way of the Swiss banker. The banker wanted the client's money, but he didn't necessarily care to know where it had come from.

The two men worked their way backward in time until they arrived at the Augustus Rolfe affair, Gabriel's first foray into the deplorable conduct of the Swiss banks during the Second World War. He was careful to say nothing incriminatory, and even more careful not to betray Office sources or tradecraft. When pushed by Bittel to reveal more, he gently pushed back. And when threatened, he issued threats of his own. He offered no apology for his actions and sought no absolution. His was a confession without guilt or atonement. It was a business transaction, nothing more.

"Have I left anything out?" asked Bittel.

"You don't really expect me to answer that, do you?"

Bittel closed the notebook and summoned a warder to take Gabriel back to his cell. A proper Swiss breakfast was waiting, along with a toiletry kit and a change of clothing. He ate while watching the morning news. Once again, there was no mention of his detainment. In fact, the only news from St. Moritz had to do with an important World Cup ski race.

After breakfast, he was escorted to the showers and told he had one hour to bathe and dress. Bittel was waiting when he returned to his cell. He had two aluminum attaché cases of Swiss manufacture. In one was the material Gabriel had requested. In the other were the fragments of the broken hydria. "If you prefer," Bittel offered, "we can tell the French police we found it in an airport locker."

"Thanks," Gabriel said, "but I'll take care of it."

"Sooner rather than later," Bittel admonished. "Let's go. Your ride is here."

They headed upstairs to the main lobby of the building. Outside a Mercedes sedan waited in the drive, its tailpipes gently smoking. Bittel shook Gabriel's hand warmly, as if they had spent the night watching old movies together. Then Gabriel turned and ducked into the back of the car. Seated opposite, a mobile phone pressed to his ear, was Uzi Navot. He looked at the bandages on Gabriel's face and frowned.

"Looks like they gave you a good going-over."

"It was worth it."

"What did you get?"

"A suitcase full of help from my new best friends in the DAP."

"Good," Navot said. "Because at this moment, we need all the help we can get."

26

BERN, SWITZERLAND

GABRIEL AND NAVOT ASSUMED the Swiss had planted transmitters in both attaché cases, so they said nothing more until they were safely inside the Israeli Embassy. It was located in a brooding old house in the diplomatic quarter, on a narrow street that was closed to normal civilian traffic. In anticipation of their arrival, the staff had filled the secure communications room with finger sandwiches and Swiss chocolates. Navot swore softly to himself as he lowered his thick frame into a chair.

"When Shamron was running the Office, the local station chiefs always made certain to have a few packs of his Turkish cigarettes on hand. But whenever I arrive, they put out a platter of food. Sometimes I get the distinct impression I'm being fattened up for slaughter."

"You're the most popular chief since Shamron, Uzi. The troops adore you. More important, they respect you. And so does the prime minister."

"But all that could change in the blink of an eye if I don't get Iran right," Navot said. "Thanks to you, we were able to slow them down for a while, but sabotage and assassinations won't work forever. At some point in the near future, the Iranians will cross a red line, beyond which it will be impossible to stop them from becoming a nuclear power. I'm supposed to tell the prime minister when that's about to happen. And if I'm wrong by so much as a few days, we'll have no choice but to live under the threat of an Iranian bomb." Navot looked at Gabriel seriously. "How would you like to have that hanging over your head?"

"I wouldn't. That's why I told Shamron to make you the chief instead of me."

"Any chance you might reconsider?"

"I'm afraid I'd be a letdown after you, Uzi."

"I appreciate the vote of confidence." Navot pushed the tray of food toward Gabriel. "Eat something. You must be starving after everything you went through."

"Actually, they took good care of me."

"What did they feed you?"

Gabriel told him.

"Was it any good?"

"The raclette was delicious."

"I've always loved raclette."

"It's potatoes smothered in cheese. What's not to love?"

Navot plucked an egg and watercress sandwich from the tray and popped it into his mouth. "I'm sorry about having to leave you behind in St. Moritz, but I figured it would be easier to get one agent out of Swiss custody than nine. Thankfully, we had some help."

"Who?"

"Your friends at the Vatican."

"Donati?"

"Higher up."

"Please don't tell me you got His Holiness involved in this."

"I'm afraid he involved himself," Navot said.

"How?"

"He had Alois Metzler of the Swiss Guard place a few discreet calls to Bern. Once Metzler got involved, it was only a matter of time before they let you out. The Office was able to stay entirely on the sidelines."

"I had to pay a toll to get out."

"How heavy?"

Gabriel told him about the debriefing.

"Was any of what you said actually true?"

"A little."

"Good boy." Another sandwich disappeared into Navot's mouth.

"I don't suppose you've managed to identify the two people who arrived at the gallery before me."

"Of course we have," Navot said, brushing the crumbs from his fingertips. "The girl is a fresh-faced newcomer, but her boyfriend is well known to us. His name is Ali Montazeri."

"Iranian?"

Navot nodded. "Ali is a proud alumnus of the Qods Force. He's now employed by VEVAK as a hired gun and assassin. He's responsible for the murder of dozens of Iranian dissidents in Europe and the Middle East. In fact, he actually tried to kill *me* once when I was working out of Paris."

"Why would the Iranians send one of their best assassins to Switzerland to kill a Hezbollah operative?"

"Good question." Navot was silent for a moment. "While you were eating veal and raclette in your Swiss jail cell, the Office was overwhelmed with a new wave of intelligence suggesting Hezbollah is about to hit us. We're talking about something big, Gabriel."

"How big?"

"Nine-eleven big," said Navot. "Big enough to start a war. And based on what we're seeing in southern Lebanon, it looks like Hezbollah is preparing for one. They're deploying their battle-hardened fighters close to our border. Their missiles are on the move, too."

"Do we know anything more about potential targets?"

"All the chatter still points to Europe, which is why the timing of David Girard's death is so interesting. Dina has a funny feeling there might be a connection."

"I get nervous when Dina has a funny feeling."

"So do I."

"How certain are you that the man who planted that bomb was Ali Montazeri?"

"One hundred percent."

"I suppose we should probably tell our new friends the Swiss about this."

"It would be the honorable thing to do," Navot said. "But for the moment, I'd rather borrow a page from the Iranian playbook."

"Which one?"

"*Khod'eh.*"

"Tricking one's enemies into a misjudgment of one's true position?"

"Correct."

"What do you have in mind?"

"First we deceive the Iranians into thinking they got away with one in St. Moritz. Then we take that load of material the Swiss gave us back to King Saul Boulevard and put it in Dina's hands."

"There's something else we should do," said Gabriel.

"What's that?"

"Find someone to put that Greek vase back together."

"Can't you do it?"

"Apples and oranges."

Navot looked down at the plate of sandwiches. "You sure you're not hungry? They're really quite good."

"You go ahead, Uzi."

"Maybe we should wrap them up for the ride home. The food on El Al isn't what it used to be."

They made the 12:45 flight out of Zurich's Kloten Airport, and by half past five they were touching down at Ben Gurion. Navot's armored Peugeot limousine was waiting on the tarmac, surrounded by twice the usual number of bodyguards. Leaning against the hood, her blue-jeaned legs crossed at the ankles, her arms folded beneath her breasts, was Chiara. She held Gabriel silently for a long time, her tearstained face buried against the side of his neck. Then she kissed his lips and gently touched the bandages on his cheeks.

"You look terrible."

"Actually, I feel much worse."

"I'd tell you to go home and get a few hours of sleep, but I'm afraid there isn't time for that."

"What's wrong?"

She handed a slip of paper to Navot. He read it by the glow of the limousine's headlamps.

"Hezbollah's military commander is telling his forces to prepare for a massive Israeli retaliation within the next two weeks." Navot squeezed the message into a ball. "That means it's for real. They're going to hit us, Gabriel. Very hard. And very soon."

As it happened, Gabriel's interrogator from the Swiss security service was true to his word, and then some. Eli Lavon likened the treasure trove of intelligence to the discovery of a hill town from a previously unknown civilization. What made it all the more remarkable, he said, was that it had been supplied by a service that had always been profoundly hostile to Israel's interests, even its very existence. "Perhaps we're not alone after all," he told the team over dinner that night. "If the Swiss can open their doors to us in our hour of need, anything is possible."

It seemed that David Girard, aka Daoud Ghandour, had popped up on the DAP's internal radar not long after he was granted the bright red Swiss passport that allowed him to enter and leave the countries of the Middle East at will. Included in the material was the original memo from the chief of Onyx, Switzerland's sophisticated electronic eavesdropping service, raising concerns about the phone and e-mail traffic of the Galleria Naxos, not to mention its financial transactions. The DAP was good enough to include the attached report, along with all subsequent updates from Onyx. When added to the intelligence already in the team's possession, the material provided incontrovertible proof that Galleria Naxos had been little more than a fund-raising front for Hezbollah. Just as clear, however, was the link between the gallery and Carlo Marchese. The team was able to trace no fewer than fifty wire transfers that had flowed from David Girard, through the Lebanon Byzantine Bank, and eventually to accounts controlled by Carlo at the Vatican Bank. Here was the *cordata* that Gabriel had been looking for—the rope linking Carlo to the terrorists of Hezbollah. The Swiss had the proof all along. They simply didn't possess the key to unlock the code.

For the moment, however, Carlo was of secondary concern to the team, because with each passing day it became evident that

David Girard had been involved in more than just fund-raising. There was the phone call he made, six months earlier, to a number in the Bekaa Valley of Lebanon that the Office had linked to a local Hezbollah chieftain. And the one he made, two weeks after that, to a number in Cairo linked to one of the numerous Hezbollah cells that had taken root in chaotic postrevolutionary Egypt. And the two hundred thousand dollars he paid to a dealer of Thai antiquities in Bangkok, a hotbed of Hezbollah activity in Southeast Asia.

"If I had to guess," said Dina, "the late David Girard was a postman. He was using his job in the antiquities biz as cover to deliver secret mail to Hezbollah cells scattered around the world."

"So why would the Iranians want him dead?"

"Maybe the mail he was carrying had something to do with the attack that's coming. Or maybe . . ."

"What, Dina?"

"Maybe it had a Tehran postmark."

In the end, it was not Swiss high technology that would provide the answer, but a good old-fashioned surveillance photograph. Snapped with a concealed camera, it showed David Girard riding a streetcar in Zurich, apparently alone. For three days, it hung on a cluttered wall in Room 456C, more for decoration than anything else, until Dina passed by it on her way to the file rooms and froze suddenly in her tracks. Ripping the photo from the wall, she stared not at Girard but at the lightly bearded figure seated next to him. The man's head was turned away from Girard, as were his powerfully built shoulders, and the sun streaming through the streetcar's windows appeared to set fire to the crystal of the heavy dive watch he was wearing on his right wrist. As a result, it drew Dina's eyes to the back of his hand, and it was then she noticed the bandage. "It's him," she whispered. "It's none other than the devil himself."

They compared the photograph of the man on the Zurich streetcar to every known image they had of him in the library, but the
computers said there was insufficient data to make a positive identification. Dina lifted her delicate chin resolutely and declared the
computers mistaken. It was him; she was certain of it. She would
stake her career on it. "Besides," she added, "don't look at the face.
Look at the hand." The hand that had been pierced by an Israeli
round in Lebanon when he was helping to turn a ragtag bunch of
Shiites into the world's most formidable terrorist force. The hand
that was drenched in blood. It was Massoud, she said. Massoud,
the lucky one.

And so Gabriel marched her upstairs and allowed her to state
her case directly to Uzi Navot. Her words drained the color from
his face and caused his eyes to move involuntarily toward the latest stack of intelligence suggesting an attack was imminent. At the
conclusion of the briefing, Navot asked for recommendations, and
Gabriel gave him only one. There were obvious risks, he said, but
they far outweighed the risks of doing nothing.

Navot hurried up the hill to Jerusalem to seek the approval
of the prime minister, and within an hour he had his operational
charter. All that remained was the obligatory courtesy call on the
Americans, a job he happily assigned to Gabriel. "Whatever you
do," he said during the drive to Ben Gurion, "don't ask for their
permission. Just find out whether there are any landmines that are
going to blow up in our face. This is not some faction of the PLO
we are talking about. This is the fucking Persian Empire."

27

HERNDON, VIRGINIA

IT HAD BEEN FARMLAND ONCE, but long ago it had been swallowed up by metropolitan Washington's seemingly unstoppable westward expansion. Now the only things that grew there were large tract homes of shrinking value and wholesome-looking children who spent far too much time roaming the darkest corners of the Internet. The names of the meandering cul-de-sacs spoke of boundless American optimism—Sunnyside and Apple Blossom, Fairfield and Crest View—but they could not conceal the fact that America, Israel's last friend in the world, had entered a state of decline.

The two-story brick home near the end of Stillwater Court differed from the adjacent residences only in that its windows were bulletproof. For many years, the neighbors had been led to believe that the man who lived there worked in one of the high-tech companies that lined the Dulles Corridor. Then came the promotion that required him to travel in an armored Escalade, and before long the neighbors realized they had a spy in their midst. But not just any spy; Adrian Carter was the chief of the National Clandestine Service, the CIA's operational division. In fact, Carter had served in the post longer than any of his predecessors, a feat he attributed more to stubbornness than talent. But then, that was typical of Carter. One of the last Agency executives to come from New England Protestant stock, he believed vanity was a sin exceeded only by cheating at golf.

Despite the fact it was only March, a warm sun baked Gabriel's neck as he crossed Carter's broad lawn, a CIA minder at his side. Carter was waiting in the open doorway. He had the tousled, thinning hair of a university professor and a mustache that had gone out of fashion with disco music, Crock-Pots, and the nuclear freeze. His tan chinos were in need of a pressing. His cotton crewneck pullover was starting to fray at the elbow.

"Forgive me for dragging you to my home," he said, shaking Gabriel's hand, "but this is my first day off in a month, and I couldn't face going to Langley or to one of our safe houses."

"I'd be happy to never see the inside of another safe house again."

"So why are you back?" Carter asked seriously. "And what the hell happened to your face?"

"I was standing too close to a Swiss antiquities gallery when a bomb exploded inside."

"St. Moritz?"

Gabriel nodded.

"I knew this was going to be good."

"You haven't heard the best part yet."

Carter smiled. "Come inside," he said, closing the door behind them. "I sent my wife out for a long walk. And don't worry. She took Molly with her."

"Who's Molly?"

"Woof, woof."

A buffet lunch waited on the screened-in porch overlooking Carter's green patch of the American dream. Gabriel dutifully filled his plate with cold cuts and pasta salad but left it untouched as he recounted the strange journey that had taken him from St. Peter's Basilica to the home of America's most senior spy. At the conclusion of the briefing, he handed over two photographs. The first showed Ali Montazeri and the El Greco girl departing the Galleria Naxos in St. Moritz. The second showed the gallery's owner sitting in the carriage of a Zurich streetcar, apparently alone.

"Look carefully at the man seated to his left," said Gabriel. "Do you recognize him?"

"Can't say I do."

"How about now?"

Gabriel gave Carter another photograph of the man. This time, it showed him entering the Iranian Embassy in Berlin.

Carter looked up sharply. "Massoud?"

"In the flesh."

The son of an Episcopal minister, Carter swore under his breath.

"Our sentiments exactly."

Carter placed the photograph on the table next to the others and stared at it in silence. Massoud Rahimi was one of those rare inhabitants of the secret world who required no introduction. In fact, most never bothered with his family name. He was just Massoud, a man whose fingerprints were on every major act of terrorism linked to Iran since the bombing of the Marine barracks in Beirut in 1983. These days, Massoud worked from the Iranian Embassy in Berlin, which doubled as VEVAK's main Western forward-operating base for terror. He carried a diplomatic passport under another name and claimed to be a low-level functionary in the consular section. Even the Germans, who maintained uncomfortably close trade relations with Iran, didn't believe a word of it.

"So what's your theory?" asked Carter.

"Let's just say we don't believe it was a coincidence that Massoud and David Girard were riding the same streetcar in Zurich."

"Do you think Massoud ordered the bombing in St. Moritz?"

"That's Massoud's way," said Gabriel. "He's never been shy about inflicting a little martyrdom on his own side when he has an important secret to protect."

"And now you want to find out the nature of that secret."

"Exactly."

"How?"

"We were hoping Massoud would agree to tell us himself."

"You're thinking about trying to buy him off?"

"Massoud would sooner slit his own wrists than accept money from Jews."

"A coerced defection?"

"There isn't time."

Carter fell into a heavy silence. "I don't need to remind you that Massoud carries a diplomatic passport," he said after a moment. "And that makes him untouchable."

"No one is untouchable. Not when lives are at stake."

"Massoud is," Carter responded. "And if you touch so much as a hair on his head, it will be open season on every Israeli diplomat in the world."

"In case you haven't noticed, Adrian, it already is. Besides," Gabriel added, "I didn't come here for advice."

"So why *are* you here?"

"I want to know whether the playing field is clear."

"I can state categorically that the Agency is nowhere near the field," said Carter. "But you should know that the Germans thought about making a run at him a couple of years ago."

"What kind of run?"

"Apparently, Massoud has a taste for the finer things in life. He routinely skims a bit off the top of his operational budget and squirrels it away in banks all over Europe. The BND had him cold. They were planning to sit down with Massoud for a little chat, at the end of which they would give him a simple choice: work for us, or we'll tell your masters in Tehran that you're embezzling state funds."

"How do you know about this?"

"Because the Germans came to me and asked whether the Agency wanted in. They even gave me a copy of the evidence they had against him."

"What happened?"

"Nothing," Carter said. "It was during the period when the White House thought it could sweet-talk the Iranians into giving up their nuclear program. The president and his team didn't want to do anything that might make the Iranians angry. As it turned out, neither did the German chancellor. She was afraid it might interfere with all the business her firms were doing in Iran."

"So it died," said Gabriel. "And a murderer sits in Berlin plotting an attack on my country."

"So it would appear."

"Where's that batch of material from the BND?"

"Locked away in the file rooms of Langley."

"I want it."

"You can have it," Carter replied, "but it'll cost you."

"How much?"

"I have a long list of questions I'd like answered."

"Why don't you just join us for the fun?"

"Because I don't want to be within a hundred miles of the fun."
Carter looked at Gabriel seriously. "Will you allow me to give you
two pieces of advice?"

"If you must."

"Invent a good cover story," said Carter. "And whatever you
do, don't screw it up. Otherwise, there's a very good chance you're
going to start World War Three."

Carter requested the German documents in a way that left only a
wispy contrail in Langley's atmosphere, and within an hour they
were delivered to his doorstep by an Agency courier. Since Carter
could not hand over the documents and still maintain any plausible
deniability, Gabriel spent the remainder of that warm afternoon
on Carter's porch, committing the details of Massoud's financial
misdeeds to memory. Carter walked him through some of the
finer points but devoted most of his time to the list of questions
he wanted put to Massoud. He wrote them in longhand and then
burned the unused pages of his yellow legal pad. Carter was a spy's
spy whose devotion to tried-and-true tradecraft was absolute. According to the wits at Langley, he left chalk marks on the bedpost
when he wanted to make love to his wife.

It was approaching four when Gabriel finished reviewing all
the documents, leaving him barely enough time to catch the evening Lufthansa flight to Berlin. As they headed outside to the
waiting Escalade, Carter seemed disappointed that Gabriel was
leaving. Indeed, he was so oddly attentive that Gabriel was somewhat surprised when he didn't remind him to buckle his seat belt.

"Something bothering you, Adrian?"

"I was just wondering whether you're really up for this."

"The next person who asks me that is—"

"It's a fair question," Carter said, cutting Gabriel off. "If one of my men went through what you did in the Empty Quarter, he'd be on permanent vacation."

"I tried."

"Maybe you should try harder next time." Carter shook Gabriel's hand. "Drop me a postcard from Berlin. And if you happen to get arrested, please try to forget where you got the information about Massoud's extracurricular activities."

"It will be our little secret, Adrian. Just like everything else."

Carter smiled and closed the door. Gabriel saw him one last time, standing curbside with his arm raised as though he were hailing a taxi. Then the Escalade rumbled round a bend, and Carter was gone. Gabriel gazed out the tinted windows at the manicured lawns and the young trees swollen with blossoms, but in his thoughts there were only numbers. The numbers of Massoud's secret accounts. And the hours remaining until Massoud made the streets run red with blood.

28

WANNSEE, BERLIN

A MONG THE OPERATION'S MANY ENDURING mysteries was how the team's Berlin safe house came to be located in the district of Wannsee. The head of Housekeeping would claim it was a mere coincidence, that he had chosen the property simply for reasons of availability and function. Only later, when the official history of the affair was being chiseled into stone, would he admit that his decision had been influenced by none other than Ari Shamron. Shamron had wanted to remind Gabriel and the team of what had happened in Wannsee in January 1942, when fifteen senior Nazis gathered over lunch in a lakeside villa to thrash out the bureaucratic details of the extermination of a people. And perhaps, all agreed, he had wanted to remind the team of the potential price of failure.

The safe house itself stood about a half-mile to the south of the site of the Wannsee Conference, on a densely wooded lane aptly named the Lindenstrasse. Two high walls surrounded it, one of crumbling brick, the other of overgrown greenery. The empty rooms smelled of damp and dust and faintly of brandy. Fat calico carp dozed beneath the ice cap of the fishpond.

The members of the team posed as employees of something called VisionTech, a Montreal-based firm that existed only in the imagination of a desk officer at King Saul Boulevard. According to their cover story, they had come to Berlin to launch a joint venture with a German firm, which explained the unusual number of computers and other pieces of technical equipment they had in their possession. They kept most of it in the large formal dining room, which served as their ops center. Within hours of their arrival, its walls were covered with large-scale maps and with surveillance photos of a man who pretended to be a low-level clerk at the Iranian Embassy but was in fact his country's top mastermind of international terror.

Dina happily accepted the assignment of preparing the questions for Massoud's long-overdue interrogation, and to enter her workspace was to enter a classroom dedicated to the evolution of modern terrorism. Massoud Rahimi had been at the center of it, beginning in November 1979, when he had been among the students and militants who stormed the American Embassy in Tehran. Several of the fifty-two hostages would later identify him as the cruelest of their tormentors. Mock executions were his favorite form of entertainment. Even then, Massoud enjoyed nothing more than seeing an American beg for his life.

His next star turn came in Lebanon in 1982, when he began working with a new Shiite militant group known as the Organization of the Oppressed on Earth. It was said that Massoud was instrumental in shortening the group's name to the Party of God, or Hezbollah. It was also said that he personally helped to assemble the twelve-thousand-pound truck bomb that destroyed the U.S.

Marine barracks at Beirut Airport at 6:22 a.m. on October 23, 1983. The explosion, the largest non-nuclear detonation since the Second World War, killed 243 American servicemen and forever changed the face of global terror. More attacks followed. Planes were hijacked, hostages were taken, embassies were bombed. All had one thing in common. They were carried out at the behest of the man who now worked from the Iranian Embassy in Berlin, protected by the shield of a diplomatic passport.

But how to convince a man such as Massoud to relinquish his most murderous secrets? And how to take possession of him in the first place? They would have to engage in the time-honored Shiite practice known as *taqiyya*, displaying one intention while harboring another. They were not going to kidnap Massoud, said Gabriel. They were going to be his saviors and protectors. And when they were finished wringing him dry, they were going to let him go his merry way. Catch and release, he called it. No harm, no foul.

They would have preferred to watch him for a month or more, but it wasn't possible; the red lights were flashing at King Saul Boulevard, with all the intelligence pointing to a major attack in a week or less. They had to take Massoud into custody before the bombs exploded, or before Tehran found an excuse to summon him home. That was Gabriel's greatest fear, that VEVAK would put Massoud on ice before the attack, leaving him beyond the reach of the Office or anyone else. And so Gabriel set a deadline of three days—three days to plan and execute the abduction of an Iranian diplomat in the heart of Berlin. When Eli Lavon placed their odds at just one in four, Gabriel took him into Dina's makeshift office to see the photographs of what might happen if they failed. "I don't want odds," said Gabriel. "I want Massoud."

Their assignment was made slightly easier by the fact that Massoud obviously felt secure on German soil. His schedule—at least in the brief time they were able to observe it—was strictly regimented. He spent most of his time inside the VEVAK station at the embassy, which was coincidentally located next door to the German Archaeological Institute, a good omen, in the opinion of the team. He arrived no later than eight a.m. and remained until late in the evening. His apartment was two miles to the north of the embassy, in the section of Berlin known as Charlottenburg. His official car appeared unarmored, though that was not true of the VEVAK-issue thug who served as his driver and bodyguard. The task of neutralizing the bodyguard on the night of the snatch fell to Mikhail. Not that he needed much convincing. After spending years dodging Iranian-supplied bullets while serving in the IDF, he was anxious to return the favor.

But where to do it? A busy street? A quiet one? A traffic signal? Massoud's doorstep? Gabriel decreed that the spot would be determined by just one factor. It had to offer them a clear route of escape in the event of either success or failure. If they chose a spot too close to the Iranian embassy, they might find themselves in a shootout with the German police who guarded it day and night. But if they let Massoud get too close to his apartment, they could become ensnarled in Charlottenburg's heavy traffic. In the end, the choice was clear to everyone. Gabriel marked the location on the map with a blood-red pin. To Eli Lavon, it looked like a gravestone.

With that, the operation settled into the phase the team referred to as "final approach." They had their target, they had their plan, they had their assignments. Now all they had to do was get the aircraft on the ground without killing themselves and everyone else on board. They had no computers to guide them, so they would have to do it the old-fashioned way, with instincts and nerve and perhaps a bit of good fortune as well. They tried to keep their reliance on providence to a bare minimum. Gabriel believed that operational luck was something to be earned, not counted upon. And it usually came about as a result of meticulous planning and preparation.

In the lexicon of the Office, the operation was "wheel heavy," meaning it would require several vehicles of different makes and models. Transport, the Office division that saw to such matters, acquired most from friendly European rental agents in ways that could not be traced back to any member of the team. The most important vehicle, however, was Office owned. A Volkswagen van with a concealed human storage compartment, it had played a starring role in one of Gabriel's most celebrated operations—the seizure of Nazi war criminal Erich Radek from his home in the First District of Vienna. Chiara had been behind the wheel that night. Radek still made regular appearances in the worst of her nightmares.

Much to her dismay, Chiara was not among those present in Berlin, though her role in the operation remained central. Her task was to coordinate the elaborate piece of *taqiyya* that would cover the team's tracks and, if successful, throw both the Germans and the Iranians off its scent. Like all good lies, it was plausible and contained elements of truth. And perhaps, said Gabriel, it also contained a thread of hope for the future—a future where Iran was no longer in the grip of a cabal of religious madmen. The mullahs and their henchmen in the Revolutionary Guard were not rational actors. They were unpredictable and apocalyptic. And the Middle East would never know true peace until they were ushered into history.

There were other lies as well, such as the canvas rucksack filled with cream-colored clay, wires, and timing devices, and the small limpet-style mine that was far more sound than fury. But they would all be for naught unless they could extract Massoud from his car with a minimum of violence. After much deliberation, it was decided that Yaakov would serve as the sharp end of the sword, with Oded, a blunt object of a man, playing a supporting role. An experienced interrogator of terrorists, Yaakov had a face and demeanor that left little doubt he meant what he said. More important, Yaakov was a descendant of German Jews and, like Gabriel, spoke fluent German. It would be Yaakov's job to talk Massoud out of the car. And if words didn't work, Oded would bring down a very large hammer.

They didn't dare rehearse in public, so they conducted countless miniature dry runs within the confines of the Wannsee safe house. In the beginning, Gabriel's demeanor was businesslike, but as the practice sessions dragged on, his mood grew brittle. Mikhail feared he was suffering an operational hangover from the bombing in St. Moritz, or perhaps from the nightmare in the Empty Quarter. But Eli Lavon knew otherwise. It was Berlin, he said. For all of them, Berlin was a city of ghosts, but it was especially true for Gabriel. It had been the home of his maternal grandparents. And in all likelihood, it would have been Gabriel's home, too, were it not for the band of murderers who had gathered in the lakeside villa just up the road.

And so they listened with admirable patience as he challenged every aspect of the plan for what seemed like the hundredth time. And they treated themselves to a small smile when he gave Yaakov and Oded a thorough dressing-down after a particularly dreadful final walk-through. And they were careful not to creep up on him when he was alone because, despite a lifetime in the trade, he was suffering from an unusual bout of nerves. And finally, on their last afternoon in Berlin, when they could bear his ill temper no more, they darkened his distinctive gray temples and concealed his unforgettable green eyes behind a pair of glasses. Then they bundled him in a coat and scarf and, with a gentle nudge, cast him out of the safe house to walk among the souls of the dead.

The field man in him wanted to see it all at least once with his own eyes—the embassy, the watch posts, the fallback positions, the snatch point. Afterward, he boarded an S-Bahn train that bore him across Berlin to the Brandenburg Gate. Now on the old East German side of the city, he made his way along the Unter den Linden, beneath the bare limbs of the lime trees. At the Friedrichstrasse, the center of Berlin's debauched nightlife during the 1920s, he turned right and headed into the district known as Mitte. Here and there he glimpsed a relic of the neighborhood's Stalinist past, but for the most part the architectural stains of communism had been scrubbed away. It was as if the Cold War, like the real war that preceded it, had never happened. In modern Mitte, there were no memories, only prosperity.

At the Kronenstrasse, Gabriel turned right again and followed the street eastward until he arrived at a modern apartment house with large square windows that shone like slabs of onyx. Long ago, before communism, before the war, the spot had been occupied by a handsome neoclassical building of gray stone. On the second floor had lived a German Expressionist painter named Viktor Frankel, his wife, Sarah, and their daughter, Irene, Gabriel's mother. Gabriel had never seen a photograph of the apartment, but once, when he was a young boy, his mother had tried to sketch it for him before breaking down in tears. Here was the place where they had lived a charmed bourgeois life filled with art, music, and afternoons in the Tiergarten. And here was the place they had stayed as the noose tightened slowly around their necks. Finally, in the autumn of 1942, they were herded by their fellow country-men aboard a cattle car and deported east to Auschwitz. Gabriel's grandparents were gassed upon arrival, but his mother was sent to the women's work camp at Birkenau. She never told Gabriel of her experiences. Instead, she committed them to paper and locked them away in the archives of Yad Vashem.

I will not tell all the things I saw. I cannot. I owe this much to the dead. . . .

Gabriel closed his eyes and saw the street as it had been before the madness. And then he saw himself as a child, coming to visit grandparents who had been allowed to grow old. And he imagined how different his life might have been had he been raised here in Berlin instead of the Valley of Jezreel. And then a cloud of acrid smoke blew across his face, like the smoke of distant crematoria, and he heard a familiar voice at his back.

"What were you hoping to find here?" asked Ari Shamron.

"Strength," said Gabriel.

"Your mother gave you strength when she named you," Sham-ron said. "And then she gave you to me."

29

BERLIN

S HAMRON HAD REGISTERED AT THE ADLON under the name Rudolf Heller, one of his favorite European aliases. Gabriel wanted to avoid the security cameras of the famous old hotel, so they walked along the edge of the Tiergarten instead. The air had turned suddenly frigid, and the wind was whistling through the columns of the Brandenburg Gate. Shamron was wearing a cashmere overcoat, a fedora, and tinted eyeglasses that made him look like the sort of businessman who made money in shady ways and never lost at baccarat. He paused at Berlin's new Holocaust memorial, a stark landscape of rectangular gray blocks, and frowned in consternation.

"They look like containers waiting to be loaded into a cargo ship."

"The architect wanted to create an atmosphere of discomfort and confusion. It's supposed to represent the orderly extermination of millions amid the chaos of war."

"Is that what you see?"

"I see a small miracle that such a memorial even exists on this spot. They could have tucked it away in a field in the countryside. But they put it here, in the heart of a reunited Berlin, right next to the Brandenburg Gate."

"You give them too much credit, my son. After the war, they all pretended they hadn't noticed their neighbors disappearing in the middle of the night. It wasn't until we captured the man who worked right over there that Germany and the rest of the world truly understood the horror of the Holocaust."

He was pointing across the Tiergarten, in the general direction of the Kurfürstenstrasse. It was there, in an imposing building that had once housed a Jewish mutual aid society, that Adolf Eichmann had made his headquarters. Gabriel's eyes, however, were still fixed on the gray boxcar-shaped stones of the memorial.

"You should write it all down." He paused and looked at Shamron. "Before it's too late."

"I'm not going anywhere yet."

"Even *you* won't live forever, Ari. You should spend some time with a pen in your hand."

"I've always found the memoirs of spies to be tedious reading. Besides, what good would it do?"

"It would remind the world why we live in Israel instead of Germany and Poland."

"The world doesn't care," Shamron responded with a dismissive wave of his hand. "And the Holocaust isn't the only reason we have a home in the Land of Israel. We're there because it was ours in the beginning. We *belong* there."

"Even some of our friends aren't so sure of that anymore."

"That's because the Palestinians and their allies have managed to convince much of the world that we are appropriators of Arab land. They like to pretend that the ancient kingdoms of Israel were a myth, that the Temple of Jerusalem was nothing but a Bible story."

"You sound like Eli."

Shamron gave a brief smile. "In his own way, your friend Eli is waging war in those excavation trenches beneath the Western Wall. Our Muslim brothers have conveniently forgotten that their great Dome of the Rock and al-Aqsa Mosque are built on the ruins of the First and Second Jewish Temples. The political battle for Palestine is now a religious war for Jerusalem. And we have to prove to the world that we were there first."

A gust of wind moaned amid the stones of the memorial. Shamron turned up his coat collar and rounded the corner into a street named for Hannah Arendt, the philosopher and political theorist who coined the phrase "the banality of evil" to describe Eichmann's role in the extermination of six million European Jews. Shamron, who had spent hours alone with the murderer in a Buenos Aires safe house, regarded the characterization as misguided at best. He entered a coffeehouse, then, after noticing the No Smoking sign, sat at a table outside.

"Healthy Germans," he said, lighting a cigarette. "Just what the world needs."

"I thought you'd forgiven them."

"I have," Shamron said, "but I'm afraid I'll never forget. I also wish their government would consider putting some distance between itself and the Islamic Republic of Iran. But I learned long ago not to pray for impossible things."

Shamron fell silent as the waitress, a beautiful girl with milk-white skin, delivered their coffee. When she was gone, he looked around the busy street and treated himself to a smile.

"What's so funny?" asked Gabriel.

"When you came out of that Saudi prison, you told me you would never do another job for the Office. And now you're about to carry out one of our most daring operations ever, all because some girl took a nasty fall in St. Peter's Basilica."

"She had a name," Gabriel replied. "And she didn't fall. She was pushed by Carlo Marchese."

"We'll deal with Carlo when we're finished with Massoud."

"I assume you've reviewed the plan?"

"Thoroughly. And my instincts tell me you have no more than thirty seconds to get Massoud into the first car."

"We've rehearsed it at twenty. But in my experience, things always go faster when they're live."

"Especially when you're involved," Shamron quipped. "But tonight you'll only be a spectator."

"A very nervous spectator."

"You should be. If this goes wrong, it will be a diplomatic disaster, not to mention a major propaganda victory for the Iranians. The world doesn't seem to notice or care that they target our people whenever it suits them. But if we respond in kind, we're branded as rogue gunslingers."

"There are worse things they could call us."

"Like what?"

"Weak," replied Gabriel.

Shamron nodded in agreement and stirred his coffee thoughtfully. "Getting Massoud out of his car and into yours is going to be the easiest part of this operation. Convincing him to talk is going to be another thing altogether."

"I'm sure you have a suggestion. You wouldn't be here otherwise."

Shamron acknowledged the remark with a nod of his head. "Massoud isn't the sort of man who scares easily. The only way you'll succeed is to present him with a fate worse than death. And then you have to throw him a lifeline and hope that he grasps it."

"And if he does?"

"The temptation will be to get every drop of information you can. But in my humble opinion, that would be a mistake. Besides," he added, "there isn't time for that. Get the intelligence you need to stop this attack. And then . . ."

Shamron's voice trailed off. Gabriel finished the thought for him.

"Let him go."

Frowning, Shamron nodded slowly. "We are not our enemies. And that means we do not kill men who carry diplomatic passports, even if they have the blood of our children on their hands."

"And even if we know he will kill again in the future?"

"You have no choice but to make a deal with the devil. Massoud has to believe you won't betray him. And I'm afraid trust like that can't be earned using blindfolds and balaclavas. You'll have to show him that famous face of yours and look him directly in the eye." Shamron paused, then added, "Unless you would like someone else to take your seat at the interrogation table."

"Who?"

Shamron said nothing.

"You?"

"I'm the most logical choice. If Massoud looks across the table and sees you, he'll have good reason to fear he might not survive the ordeal. But if he sees me instead . . ."

"He'll feel warm all over?"

"He'll know he's dealing with the very top levels of the Israeli government," Shamron answered. "And it just might make him more willing to talk."

"I appreciate the spirit of the offer, Abba."

"But you have no intention of accepting it." Shamron paused, then asked, "You realize that he's going to spend the rest of his life trying to kill you."

"He'll have to get in line."

"You could always move back to Israel."

"You never give up, do you?"

"It's not in my nature."

"What would I do for a living?"

"You could help me write my book."

"We'd kill each other."

Shamron slowly crushed out his cigarette, signaling the time had come to leave. "It's rather appropriate, don't you think?"

"What's that?"

"That your last operation should take place here in the city of spies."

"It's a city of the dead," Gabriel said. "And I want to get out of here as quickly as possible."

"Take Massoud as a souvenir. And whatever you do, don't get caught."

"Shamron's Eleventh Commandment."

"Amen."

They parted beneath the Brandenburg Gate. Shamron headed to his room at the Hotel Adlon; Gabriel, to the footpaths of the Tiergarten. He remained there until he was certain he was not being followed, then returned to the safe house in Wannsee. Entering, he found the members of his team going through a final checklist. At dusk, they began slipping out at careful intervals, and by six o'clock they were all at their final holding points. Gabriel scoured the rooms of the old house, searching for any trace of their presence. Afterward, he sat alone in the darkness, a notebook computer open on his lap. On the screen was a high-resolution shot of the Iranian Embassy, courtesy of a miniature camera concealed in a car parked legally across the street. At twelve minutes past eight o'clock, the embassy's security gate slid slowly open, and a black Mercedes sedan nosed into view. It turned left and passed within a few inches of the camera—so close, in fact, that Gabriel felt as though he could reach out and pluck the single passenger from the backseat. Instead, he lifted a radio to his lips and informed his team the devil was heading their way.

30

BERLIN

THE *TAQIYYA* BEGAN TWO MINUTES later, at 8:14 p.m. local time, when the Berlin police received a call concerning a suspicious package found inside the Europa Center, the indoor shopping mall and office complex located next to the remnants of the Kaiser Wilhelm Memorial Church. The package was actually a battered canvas rucksack of the sort often carried by goths, skinheads, anarchists, radical environmentalists, and other assorted troublemakers. It had been placed at the foot of a bench a few feet from the center's famous water clock, a popular gathering spot, especially for young children. Later, witnesses would describe the person who left it behind as a Muslim woman in her early thirties. They were correct about her age, but not her ethnicity. They were to be forgiven for the mistake, for she had been wearing a *hijab* at the time.

The caller who reported the suspicious rucksack described the contents as looking like an explosive device, and the first uniformed police officers to arrive concurred. They immediately ordered an evacuation of the area around the water clock, followed soon after by the entire mall and all the surrounding buildings. By 8:25, several thousand people were streaming into the streets, and police units were converging on the scene from every quarter of Berlin.

Even within the serene and stately confines of the Hotel Adlon, it was clear Berlin was in the grips of a citywide emergency. In the famed lobby bar and lounge, where senior Nazi henchmen had once held court, nervous guests sought explanations from management, and a few stepped outside onto the sidewalk to watch the police cruisers roaring down the Unter den Linden. One guest, however, appeared oblivious to all the excitement. A well-dressed gentleman of advanced years, he calmly signed for a whisky he had scarcely touched and rode an elevator to his suite on the hotel's uppermost floor. There he stood in the window, watching the light show as if it all had been arranged for his private amusement. After a moment, he pulled a mobile phone from the breast pocket of his suit and auto-dialed a number that had been preloaded for him by a child who understood such things. He heard a series of clicks and tones. Then a male voice greeted him with little more than a grunt.

"What am I looking at?" asked Ari Shamron.

"The prelude," replied Uzi Navot.

"When does the curtain rise on the first act?"

"A minute, maybe less."

Shamron severed the connection and gazed out at the blue lights flashing across the city. It was a beautiful sight, he thought. By way of deception, thou shalt do war.

At that same moment, some three miles to the west of Shamron's unique observation post, Yossi Gavish and Mikhail Abramov sat

astride a pair of motorcycles at the edge of a small park on the Ha-
genstrasse. At that hour, the park was long deserted, but warm
lights burned in the bottle-glass windows of the miniature Teutonic
castles lining the street. Mikhail was rubbing his sore knee. Yossi
was so motionless he looked as though he had been cast in bronze.

"Relax, Yossi," Mikhail said softly. "You have to relax."

"You're not the one with a bomb in your pocket."

"It's not going to explode until ten seconds after you attach it to
the car."

"What if it malfunctions?"

"They never do."

"There's always a first time."

A green-and-white police van flashed past, siren screaming.
Yossi had yet to move a muscle.

"Breathe," Mikhail ordered. "Otherwise, the police are liable to
think you're about to kidnap an Iranian diplomat."

"I don't know why I have to attach the bomb."

"Someone has to do it."

"I'm an analyst," Yossi said. "I don't blow up cars. I read books."

"Would you rather take out the driver instead?"

"And how am I supposed to do that? Dazzle him with my wit
and intellect?"

Before Mikhail could respond, he heard a crackle in his miniature earpiece, followed by three short bursts of tone. Looking
up the street, he saw the headlights of an approaching Mercedes.
As it swept past their position, he could see Massoud in the backseat, catching up on a bit of paperwork by the glow of his executive
reading lamp. A few seconds later came a BMW, Rimona driving,
Yaakov and Oded seated ramrod straight in back. Finally, Eli Lavon rattled past in a Passat station wagon, clutching the wheel as
though he were piloting an oil tanker through icy seas. Mikhail

and Yossi eased into the trailing position and waited for the next signal.

They had come to the point that Shamron liked to describe as the operational fork in the road. Until now, no line had been crossed and no crime committed, save for a minor bomb scare in the Europa Center. The team could still abort, regroup, reassess, and try another night. In many respects, it was the easier decision to make—the decision to sheathe the sword rather than swing it. Shamron called it "the coward's escape hatch." But then, Shamron had always believed that far more operations had been sunk by hesitation than by recklessness.

On that night, however, the decision was not Shamron's to make. Instead, it was in the hands of a battered secret warrior sitting alone in an empty house in Wannsee. He was staring at the screen of his computer, watching his team and his target as they approached the point of no return. It was the Königsallee, a street running from the parkland of the Grunewald to the busy Kurfürstendamm—and once Massoud crossed it, he would be beyond their reach. Gabriel keyed into his secure radio and asked whether anyone had any last-minute objections. Hearing nothing, he gave the order to proceed. Then he closed his eyes and listened to the sirens.

Afterward, there were some at King Saul Boulevard who would bemoan the fact that no videotape had been made. Shamron, however, took the opposite view. He believed that operational videotapes, like suicide missions, should be left to Israel's enemies.

Besides, he said, no piece of video could capture the perfection of the maneuver. It was a piece of epic poetry, a fable to be told to successive generations by the glow of a desert campfire.

It began with an almost imperceptible movement of two vehicles—one driven by Rimona, the other by Eli Lavon. Simultaneously, both slowed and moved slightly to the right, leaving Yossi a clear pathway to the rear bumper of the Mercedes. He took it with a twist of his throttle and within a few seconds was staring over the devil's left shoulder. Carefully, he reached into his coat pocket and flipped the activation toggle on the magnetic grenade. Then he stared straight ahead and waited for the girl to step into the street.

She was wearing a neon-green jacket with reflective stripes on the sleeves and pushing a bicycle with a lamp aglow on the handlebars. An hour earlier, she had been carrying the canvas rucksack that had caused so much distress in central Berlin. Now, as she entered a well-lit pedestrian crosswalk, limping slightly, she carried nothing but a false passport and a boundless hatred for the man riding in the backseat of the approaching Mercedes sedan.

For an instant, they all feared that Massoud's driver intended to use his diplomatic immunity to run her down. But finally, he slammed on the brakes, and the big black car came skidding to a halt amid a cloud of blue-gray smoke. Yossi swerved to his left to avoid the car's rear bumper and then shouted a few obscenities through the driver's-side window before covertly attaching the grenade inside the front wheel well. By now, the girl had safely reached the other side of the street. Massoud's driver actually gave her a small wave of apology as he drove off. The girl accepted it with a smile, all the while moving away with what seemed to be inordinate haste.

Six seconds later, the device exploded. Its carefully shaped and calibrated charge sent the entire force of the detonation inward, leaving no chance of collateral damage or casualties. Its bark was definitely worse than its bite, though the blast was powerful enough to shred the car's left-front tire and blow open its hood. Now blinded and confused, the driver lurched the car instinctively to the right. It bounded over the curb and smashed through an iron fence before beaching itself in the Hagenplatz, a small triangle of green that the team affectionately referred to as Ice Cream Square.

If the plan had a weakness, it was the bus shelter located a few feet away from the intersection. On that evening, five people waited there—an elderly German couple, two young men of Turkish descent, and a woman in her twenties who was so thin and pale she might have just stumbled from a building that had been bombed by the Allies. What they saw next appeared to be nothing more than an act of kindness carried out by three good Samaritans who just happened upon the scene. One of the men, a tall, slender motorcyclist, immediately rushed to the aid of the stricken driver—or so it seemed to the witnesses in the bus shelter. They did not notice, however, that the motorcyclist quickly removed a pistol from the driver's shoulder holster. Nor did they notice that he injected a dose of powerful sedative into the driver's left thigh.

The other good Samaritans focused their attention on the man riding in the backseat of the Mercedes. Owing to the fact that he was not wearing a seat belt, he was left heavily dazed by the force of the collision. An injection of sedative worsened his condition, though the witnesses did not see that, either. What they would remember was the sight of the two men lifting the injured passenger from his ruined car and placing him tenderly in their own. Instantly, the car shot forward and turned left toward the wilds of the Grunewald—odd, since the nearest hospital was to the right.

The motorcyclist followed, as did a Passat station wagon driven by a meek-looking soul who appeared oblivious to the entire episode. Later, when questioned by police, the witnesses would realize that the operation had been carried out in near silence. In fact, only one of the good Samaritans, a man with dark hair and pockmarks on his cheeks, had spoken to the injured passenger. "Come with us," he had told him. "We will protect you from the Jews."

As Gabriel predicted, the snatch had taken less time than expected—just thirteen seconds from beginning to end, with the extraction of Massoud from the car requiring only eight. Now, alone in the Wannsee safe house, he listened as the team made the first vehicle change of the night and then watched the lights of their beacons streaking northward along the E51 Autobahn. Time was now a precious commodity. They needed every drop, every granule, they could find. A few seconds here and there could mean the difference between success and failure, between life and death. Gabriel could do nothing more. He had already set the city of his nightmares alight. Now all he could do was watch it burn.

He sent a flash message to King Saul Boulevard confirming the first phase of the operation had gone as planned. Then he stepped outside and climbed into an Audi sedan. After driving past the haunted lakeside villa where the murder of his grandparents had been planned, he headed for the Autobahn. The Berlin police were still streaming toward the Europa Center. But for how long?

On the top floor of the Hotel Adlon, Ari Shamron stood alone in his window, watching the blue police lights swirling beneath his feet. For the past several minutes, all had been streaking toward the same point in western Berlin. But at 8:36 p.m., he noticed a distinct change in the pattern. He didn't bother to ask King Saul Boulevard for an explanation. The deception was over. Now it was a race for the border.

PART THREE

THE
WELL
OF
SOULS

31

BERLIN-NORTHERN DENMARK

THE IRANIAN LIBERATION ARMY, a previously unknown group dedicated to the overthrow of the country's theocratic rulers, appeared for the first time on Western radar screens—or anywhere else, for that matter—late the following morning, when it claimed responsibility for the abduction of Massoud Rahimi, a senior Iranian intelligence agent based in the German capital of Berlin. It did so in a printed manifesto delivered clandestinely to the BBC in London, and on a Web site that popped up within hours of the abduction. Among its laundry list of demands were a cessation of Iran's nuclear weapons program and the release of all those jailed for reasons of politics, religion, conscience, or sexuality. The mullahs had just seventy-two hours to comply; otherwise, the group vowed, it would grant Massoud the violent death he had given to so many innocent victims. As if to illustrate its seriousness, it posted a photo of the captive flanked by two men wearing balaclava helmets. Massoud was staring straight into the camera with his hands bound behind his back. His heavy face showed no signs of violence, though his eyes appeared somewhat groggy.

The dramatic emergence of a new Iranian opposition movement caught many in the media by surprise, and during the first hours of the crisis, reporters in Europe and America were left with no choice but to speculate wildly as to the ILA's origins and aims. Gradually, however, a portrait emerged of a small, tightly knit group of secular Iranian intellectuals and exiles who wished to drag their country from the Dark Ages into the modern world. By that evening, terrorism experts and foreign policy analysts on both sides of the Atlantic were talking about a new force that posed a clear threat to the Iranian regime's grip on power. And not one realized that every shred of information they were imparting with such authority had been invented by a group of people working out of a basement office in Tel Aviv.

A few of the better terrorism experts were familiar with the name Massoud Rahimi, while those old enough to recall the Iranian hostage crisis took a small measure of joy in his predicament. That was not the case, however, in Tehran, where the Iranians reacted with predictable fury. In an official statement, they denied the existence of a group called the Iranian Liberation Army, denied that Massoud Rahimi was an agent of Iranian intelligence, and denied he was in any way linked to terrorism. Furthermore, they accused Israel of creating the group out of whole cloth in order to cover up its involvement in the affair. The Israeli prime minister took to the floor of the Knesset to denounce the Iranian claims as the ravings of depraved zealots. Then he took a not-so-subtle poke at the Germans for allowing Massoud, a known murderer with the blood of hundreds of innocent people on his hands, to masquerade as a diplomatic functionary on German soil. The German chancellor called the remarks "unhelpful" and pleaded with the prime minister to take steps to lower the temperature. Privately, she told her intelligence chiefs that she believed the Israelis were almost certainly involved.

Not surprisingly, given the sophistication of the operation, there were many within the German police and security services who agreed with their chancellor, though they had no evidence to support such an allegation. A frustrated interior minister fumed to his closest aides that it *had* to be the Israelis because no other intelligence service in the world was clever enough—or, frankly, devious enough—to even conceive of such an operation. Wisely, the minister's aides counseled their master to leave such sentiments out of his next press briefing.

To their credit, the German police threw everything they had into the search for the missing Iranian. They scoured the country from east to west, from the mountains of Bavaria to the rocky gray shores of the Baltic. They looked for him in cities and in towns large and small. They made contact with their sources and informants inside Germany's large community of radical Islamists and tapped every phone and e-mail account they thought might yield a clue. After twenty-four hours, however, they had nothing to show for their efforts. That evening, the interior minister informed the Iranian ambassador that, as far as the German police were concerned, his colleague had vanished from the face of the earth. It was not true, of course. They were simply looking for him in the wrong place.

At the northern tip of Denmark is a narrow cat's claw of a peninsula where the North Sea and the Baltic collide in a war without end. On the Baltic side of the peninsula, the sand is flat and desolate, but along the North Sea it rises into windswept dunes. Here lies the tiny hamlet of Kandestederne. In summer, it is filled with Danish holidaymakers, but for the rest of the year it feels as though it has been abandoned to the plague.

At the fringes of the village, hidden in the swale of a large dune, stood a handsome wooden cottage with a large porch facing the sea. It had four bedrooms, an airy kitchen filled with stainless steel appliances, and two open sitting rooms furnished in the minimalist Danish style. It also boasted a wine cellar in the basement, which Housekeeping had quietly converted into a soundproof holding cell. Inside sat the man for whom the German police were so desperately searching—blindfolded, gagged, stripped to his underwear, and shivering violently with cold. In twenty-four hours, he had been given nothing to eat or drink and no care other than a small dose of tranquilizer to keep him quiet. No one had spoken to him. Indeed, as far as Massoud knew at that moment, he had been left alone to die a slow, agonizing death of starvation. It was a punishment he deserved. Providence, however, had chosen another path for him.

The next leg of Massoud's journey began in the twenty-sixth hour of his captivity, when Mikhail and Yaakov escorted him blindfolded upstairs to the dining room. After securing him tightly to a metal chair, they removed the blindfold and gag. Massoud blinked rapidly several times before surveying the walls. They were hung with several enlarged photographs of his handiwork—here the ruins of the U.S. Marine barracks in Beirut, here the charred hull of a Tel Aviv bus, here the shattered remnants of the Jewish community center in Buenos Aires. He managed to contort his heavy features into an expression of disbelief, but when his gaze finally settled on the man seated directly across the table, he recoiled in fear.

"You were expecting someone else?" asked Gabriel calmly in English.

"I have no idea who you are," Massoud responded in the same language.

"Bullshit."

"You won't get away with this."

"We already have."

Three items lay on the table in front of Gabriel: a manila file folder, a BlackBerry, and a loaded Beretta 9mm. He moved the Beretta a few inches with studied care and then pushed the Black-Berry across the table so Massoud could see the screen. On it was the front page of the BBC's mobile news site. The lead story was about a bold kidnapping in the heart of Berlin.

"You have committed a gross violation of the Vienna Convention on Diplomatic Relations," Massoud said after a moment.

"Your abduction was carried out by the Iranian Liberation Army. It says so right there on the BBC," Gabriel added, tapping the screen. "And as you know, the BBC is never wrong."

"Well played," said Massoud.

"It wasn't that hard," replied Gabriel. "We just borrowed a page from your playbook."

"Which one?"

"*Taqiyya.*"

"There's no such thing as *taqiyya*. It is nothing but a slur spread by the enemies of Shia Islam."

"You engage in *taqiyya* every day when you assure the world that your nuclear program is strictly for peaceful purposes."

"Is that what this is about?"

"No." Gabriel retrieved the BlackBerry and then flipped slowly through the contents of the manila file folder. "You stand accused of masterminding multiple acts of terrorism that have resulted in the deaths of hundreds of innocent people. You also stand accused of conspiring to commit future acts of terrorism and of providing material support to a group that has as its goal the physical annihilation of my people." He looked up from the file and asked, "How do you plead?"

"I am a third secretary in the consular section of the Iranian Embassy in Berlin."

"How do you plead?" Gabriel asked again.

"You are in violation of all diplomatic norms and customs."

"How do you plead?"

Massoud raised his chin and said, "I plead not guilty."

Gabriel closed the file folder. Court adjourned.

They brought him back for two more hearings that night, each with the same result. After that, they kept him awake with regular bastings of freezing seawater and recordings of ear-shattering noise that were piped into the soundproof chamber for Massoud's private listening enjoyment. Gabriel was reluctant to employ physical coercion—he knew that with enough sleep and sensory deprivation, Massoud would admit to being the Cat in the Hat—but he had no choice. Two clocks were now ticking. On one was the time they had left before the attack; on the other, the time they had left before they were discovered. Gabriel had set a deadline of seventy-two hours to be out of Denmark. The chief of the Danish security service was a friend, but he wouldn't be for long if he found out Gabriel had brought a man like Massoud Rahimi onto Danish soil.

And so, as that second day dragged on, they gradually turned up the pressure on their prize. The noise grew louder, the water colder, and the threats whispered into his ear became ever more terrifying. When he asked for food, they offered him a bowl of sand. And when he pleaded for drink, they drenched him with a bucket of briny water straight from the sea. Sleep was out of the question, they assured him, unless he agreed to cooperate.

Slowly, with each passing hour, Massoud's strength ebbed, as did his will to resist. More than anything, though, he seemed to realize that this unfortunate episode did not necessarily have to end with his death, that perhaps there was a deal to be made. But how to convince him to accept the outstretched hand? And who to extend it in the first place?

"Why me?" asked Eli Lavon incredulously.

"Because you're the least threatening person in this house," Gabriel said. "And because you haven't laid a finger on him."

"I don't interrogate people. I just follow them."

"You don't have to ask him anything, Eli. Just let him know that I'm willing to discuss a generous plea bargain."

Lavon spent five minutes alone with the monster and then came back upstairs.

"How did it go?"

"Other than the part about threatening to kill me, I thought it went as well as could be expected."

"How long should we give him?"

"An hour should be enough."

They gave him two instead.

The next time Massoud was escorted into the makeshift court-room, he was shivering uncontrollably, and his lips were blue with cold. Gabriel seemed not to notice. He had eyes only for the file that was open before him on the table.

"It has come to our attention that during your time in Berlin, you have been less than forthright in your use of VEVAK operational funds," Gabriel said. "Obviously, this is of no concern to us. But as fellow tradesmen, we feel duty bound to report it to your superiors in Tehran. When we do, I'm afraid they'll want to secure your release for reasons other than your personal well-being."

"More Jewish lies," Massoud responded.

Gabriel smiled and then proceeded to recite a series of account numbers and corresponding values.

"Those are all legitimate accounts used for legitimate purposes," Massoud replied calmly.

"So you have no objection to us telling your superiors at VEVAK about them?"

"I don't work for VEVAK."

"Yes, you do, Massoud. And that means you have a way out of your current circumstances." Gabriel paused, then added, "If I were in your position, I'd take it."

"Perhaps I'm not as talkative as you, Allon."

"Ah," said Gabriel, smiling, "so you recognize me after all."

"You do have a way of getting your face into the newspaper."

Gabriel turned a page in his file. "You face serious charges, Massoud. How do you plead?"

"Not guilty."

"How do you plead?"

"Not guilty."

"How do you plead?"

Silence . . .

Gabriel looked up from the file.

"How do you plead, Massoud?" he asked gently.

"What do you want from me?"

"I want you to answer a few questions."

"Then what?"

"If you tell me the truth, you'll be released. If you lie to me, I'll tell your superiors in Tehran that you've been stealing money from them. And then they'll put a bullet in your head."

"Why should I trust you?"

"Because at this moment, I'm your only friend in the world."

The Iranian made no reply.

"How do you plead, Massoud?"

"What do you want to know?"

32

KANDESTEDERNE, DENMARK

THEY GAVE HIM A HOT shower at gunpoint and dressed him in a blue-and-white tracksuit, extra large to fit his bulky frame. A plate of food awaited him in the dining room, along with a cup of sweetened Persian tea. Despite his intense hunger, and the fact that they gave him no utensils other than a harmless plastic spoon, he managed to eat with dignity.

"Nothing for you?" he asked, nodding toward the empty table in front of Gabriel.

"I wouldn't be able to keep it down."

"Don't be so judgmental, Allon. We're professionals, you and I."

"You're a murderer."

"So are you."

Gabriel glanced at Yaakov, and the food was removed. Massoud showed no anger.

"First rule of interrogation, Allon. Don't let the subject get under your skin."

"Second rule, Massoud. Don't piss off the interrogator."

"I'd like to smoke."

"No."

"Then perhaps you would be good enough to allow me to pray."

"If you must."

"I must," replied Massoud. "What time is it?"

"Isha."

"Which direction is Mecca?"

Gabriel pointed to the right. Massoud smiled.

"Third rule of interrogation, Allon. Don't tell the subject where he is."

"You're in hell, Massoud. And the only way you're going to get out is to tell me the truth."

He prayed for thirty minutes. When he was finished, Mikhail and Yaakov started to secure him to the metal chair, but Gabriel intervened and in Hebrew said the restraints would not be necessary. Massoud furrowed his brow, as though he did not understand, which Gabriel suspected was not the case. He permitted the Iranian to eat the remainder of his dinner. Then, afterward, he gave him a fresh glass of warm tea.

"How beneficent of you," remarked Massoud.

"I assure you my motives are entirely selfish," Gabriel responded. "We have a long night ahead of us."

"Where would you like to start?"

"The beginning."

"In the beginning," Massoud recited, "God created the heavens and the earth. Then he created the Jews and ruined the whole thing."

"Let's advance the calendar a few years, shall we?"

"How far?"

"David Girard," answered Gabriel, "aka Daoud Ghandour."

It was not possible to tell the story of Daoud Ghandour, he said, without first telling the story of Israel's ill-fated occupation of Lebanon. At first, Gabriel was reluctant to give Massoud a platform to engage in triumphalist breast-beating, but he quickly realized it was a rare opportunity that could not be spurned. And so he sat patiently, his hands folded on the table, as Massoud recounted how the Iranians had skillfully exploited the chaos in Lebanon to create a death trap for hundreds of Israeli soldiers. "You came to Lebanon to destroy the PLO," he said, taunting Gabriel ever so slightly, "and in its place you left Hezbollah."

As Massoud continued, he shed the mantle of the aggrieved political hostage and adopted the air of a university professor leading a small seminar. Watching him, Gabriel understood why he had prospered in the cutthroat world of the Revolutionary Guard and VEVAK. In a parallel universe, Massoud might have been a renowned jurist or a statesman from a decent country. Instead, the turbulent history of Islam and the Middle East had conspired to turn him into a facilitator of mass murder. Even so, Gabriel couldn't help but feel a grudging respect for him. To anesthetize himself, he glanced frequently at the enlarged photographs of Massoud's handiwork. So did Massoud. He seemed proudest of one in particular—the one that showed smoke rising from the U.S. Marine barracks in Beirut. The event, he said, had been a watershed in the history of American involvement in the Middle East. It had shown America to be a paper tiger that would cut and run at the first sight of blood. And it had made a profound impression on a young Lebanese Shiite named Daoud Ghandour.

"Within a few hours of the attack, he went to see the Hezbollah recruiter in his neighborhood in south Beirut. But there was one problem," Massoud added. "Ghandour had just been accepted at the Sorbonne in Paris. He said he wanted to stay in Lebanon to fight the Jews and the Americans instead. The recruiter had a better idea. He told Ghandour to get his education. And then he called me."

"So Ghandour was an Iranian asset from the beginning?"

"You're being far too linear in your thinking, Allon. Remember, we were active at nearly every level of Hezbollah from the beginning. Hezbollah itself was an Iranian asset."

"Who ran him?"

"Our station in Paris. When he wasn't studying, he helped us keep tabs on all the Iranian exiles and dissidents who set up shop in France after the fall of the Shah."

"And when he went to England?"

"London handled him while he finished his doctorate at Oxford. By the time he started working at Sotheby's, I'd shed my fatigues and was a respectable diplomat."

"You took control of him?"

Massoud nodded. "But now, he was no longer Daoud Ghandour, a poor boy from southern Lebanon. He was David Girard, an antiquities expert who traveled the world on behalf of a respected international auction house."

"Your dream come true."

"Yours, too, I imagine."

"How did you use him?"

"Carefully. He could go places I couldn't go and talk to people who couldn't come within a mile of me."

"So you used him as a courier?"

"He was my own private Federal Express. If VEVAK wanted a Hezbollah cell in, say, Istanbul to carry out an attack, we could do it at arm's length through David. He would serve as the conduit for communications with the cell and see to its financial needs. In some cases, he even coordinated the shipment of explosives and other weapons. It was perfect." Massoud paused. "And then there was the money."

"From trading in illicit antiquities?"

Massoud nodded. "David came up with the idea while he was working at Sotheby's. He knew there was a great deal of money to be made by those willing to ignore the law. He also knew that much of the trade was controlled by one man."

"Carlo Marchese."

"Friend of the Vatican," Massoud added contemptuously. "But Carlo's organization had one flaw. It was very strong in Europe, but it needed product from the Middle East."

"Product that Hezbollah was able to supply."

"Not only Hezbollah. Many of the antiquities were pieces from the Persian Empire that had come out of the ground in Iran. Within a short time, the operation was generating several million dollars a month, all of which went directly into Hezbollah's coffers."

"Then a curator at the Vatican started asking too many questions."

"Yes," Massoud agreed. "And the party was over."

When Massoud requested a cigarette a second time, Gabriel relented and gave him one of Yaakov's Marlboros. He smoked it slowly, as though he suspected he would not receive another, and was careful to direct his exhalations away from Gabriel. VEVAK, it seemed, was aware of Gabriel's aversion to tobacco.

But that was not all it knew about him. It knew, Massoud boasted, that Monsignor Luigi Donati, private secretary to His Holiness Pope Paul VII, had asked Gabriel to investigate the death of Claudia Andreatti. It also knew that Gabriel had discovered the body of a tomb raider named Roberto Falcone. It knew this, Massoud said, because Carlo Marchese had told his business partner David Girard.

"Carlo was aware of your investigation from the very beginning," Massoud explained. "And he believed correctly that you were a threat to him. When the other members of the network started to get jumpy, he told them not to worry, that he would find an Italian solution to the problem."

"Killing me?"

Massoud nodded. "But first, he wanted to get a sense of how much you knew about his operation. So he threw a dinner party in your honor. Then he tried to kill you as you were walking home." He shook his head slowly. "Frankly, we weren't surprised when the attempt on your life failed. The man Carlo sent to do the job might have been good enough to earn a living in Italy, but not in our world."

"So you decided to do it yourself."

"We looked upon the situation as a unique opportunity to cause a scandal for your service at a time it could least afford one. We also regarded it as a chance to exact some revenge over the damage you did to our nuclear program."

"How did you know we would find Girard?"

"Let's just say that we had great faith in your ability, though we never imagined you'd have a stolen Greek amphora in your back pocket. That was a masterstroke, Allon."

"I can't tell you how much your approval means to me," Gabriel said. "But you were about to explain how the two professional assassins you sent to St. Moritz to kill me muffed the job."

"We felt it was important that your body be clearly recognizable. If you'd been blown to bits, your service would have been able to deny you were ever there."

"How thoughtful of you."

The Iranian shrugged off Gabriel's sarcasm.

"So you killed one of Hezbollah's top operatives in order to kill me under circumstances that were embarrassing to our service?"

Massoud nodded. "Once Hezbollah's links to Carlo's smuggling network had been exposed, Girard had outlived his usefulness. He was expendable."

"So are you," Gabriel replied. "We know a big attack is coming, and you're going to help me stop it. Otherwise, I'm going to do to you what I did to those secret uranium-enrichment plants. I'm going to blow you to bits. And then I'm going to send you home to your masters in Tehran in a box."

He tried to wriggle out of the noose, but then, Gabriel expected nothing less. He denied, he deferred, he deflected, and, finally, he spun several fabrications that he hoped would satisfy his small but attentive audience. With his expression, Gabriel made it plain he had seen such performances before. His demands were clear and unyielding. He wanted verifiable details of the pending attack—the time, the place, the target, the weapons, the members of the action cell. Once the attack had been interdicted, Massoud would be quietly released. But if he refused to provide the information, or if he attempted to run out the clock, Gabriel would destroy him.

"As your only friend in the world," said Gabriel, "I would advise you to accept our generous offer. All you have to do is surrender the details of a single attack. In return, you'll be free to maim and murder to your heart's content."

"Rest assured, you'll be at the top of my list, Allon."

"That's why I would also advise you to accept a desk job at VEVAK headquarters in Tehran," Gabriel countered. "Because if you ever set foot outside Iran again, my friends and I are going to hunt you down and kill you."

"How can I be sure you won't kill me in any case?"

"Because we're not like you, Massoud. When we enter into an agreement, we mean it. Besides," Gabriel added, "killing hostages in cold blood has never been our style."

Massoud's gaze traveled over the photographs of his handiwork before settling once again on Gabriel.

"I have no idea what day it is."

"It's Friday," answered Gabriel.

Massoud's expression darkened. "What time on Friday?"

"That depends."

"Central European."

Gabriel woke his BlackBerry and looked at the screen. "Two-twelve a.m."

"Good," Massoud said. "That means there's still a bit of time."

"When is the attack?"

"Tonight, shortly after sundown."

"The Sabbath?"

Massoud nodded.

"What's the target?"

"A city you know well, Allon. In fact," the Iranian said, smiling, "we chose it in your honor."

33

VIENNA

THERE WAS A SIX-THIRTY A.M. flight from Copenhagen that arrived in Vienna midmorning. After entering Austria on an American passport that he had conveniently forgotten to return to Adrian Carter, Gabriel went to an airport café and read the morning papers for an hour until he spotted Mikhail, Oded, Yaakov, and Eli Lavon crossing the arrivals hall. He followed them outside and watched as they climbed into four separate taxis. Then he walked over to a black sedan with Vienna registration and ducked into the back. Seated on the opposite side was Ari Shamron. He had shed the tailored worsted-and-silk clothing of Herr Heller and was once again dressed in khaki, oxford cloth, and leather. He tossed his cigarette out the window as the car lurched forward.

"You look as though you haven't slept in a week."

"I haven't."

"Just a few more hours, my son. Then it will all be over."

The car turned onto the A4 Ost Autobahn and headed toward central Vienna. The weather was miserable, windblown rain mixed with ice pellets and snow.

"How much have we told the Austrians?" asked Gabriel.

"Uzi woke Jonas Kessler, the chief of the Austrian security service, early this morning and told him that his country was to be the target of a terrorist attack it had done nothing to provoke."

"How did Kessler take it?"

"After delivering the obligatory lecture about how Israel is making the world less safe by its actions, he demanded to know the origin of the intelligence. As you might expect, Uzi was rather vague in his response, which didn't sit well with Kessler."

"Does he know the time frame?"

"He knows we're talking about hours rather than days, but Uzi insisted on telling him the rest in person. Actually," Shamron added, "we thought it might be a good idea if you handled the briefing."

"Me?"

Shamron nodded. "Some of our fickle allies here in Europe are under the impression that we feed them information about potential plots simply to bolster our own standing. But if the warning comes from you, it would send a clear message that we're serious. *Deadly* serious."

"Because they know I wouldn't set foot here unless lives were at stake?"

"Exactly."

"And when they ask about the source of the intelligence?"

"You say that a little bird told you. And then you move on."

Gabriel was silent for a moment. "If Massoud is telling us the truth," he said finally, "the situation is probably beyond the capabilities of the Austrians. This needs to be handled properly, Ari. Otherwise, people will die. Lots of people."

"Then perhaps we can come to an equitable solution."

"How equitable?"

"We'll save the lives, and they'll take the credit."

Gabriel smiled. Then he closed his eyes and was instantly asleep.

As usual, there was an inter-service spat over the venue. Uzi Navot wanted to hold the conference in a secure room at the Israeli Embassy, but Jonas Kessler chose an imposing government building in Vienna's elegant Innere Stadt, just around the corner from the State Opera House. A temporary sign in the lobby declared the premises were to be used that day for a conference having something to do with sustainable agriculture, but at the entrance to the main salon was a plastic bin where arriving guests were instructed to deposit their mobile phones and other electronic devices. The chamber itself was a Hapsburg monstrosity hung with gold curtains and crystal chandeliers that floated overhead like candlelit clouds. As Gabriel and Shamron entered, Navot was hovering over a buffet table piled high with Viennese cakes and cream-filled tarts. Kessler, an angular figure with dark hair combed close to the scalp, stood on the opposite end of the room, surrounded by a protective cordon of aides. He was staring at his watch, as if wondering whether he could wrap things up in time for his midday workout.

At Kessler's suggestion, they took their assigned seats at a formal rectangular table that looked more suited to Cold War summitry than a gathering of spies. Gabriel, Shamron, and Navot sat on one side, the Austrians on the other. Most were from the counterterrorism division of the security service, but there were also several senior officers from the Bundespolizei, Austria's national police force. Kessler didn't bother with introductions. Nor were there any issues regarding language; Gabriel, Shamron, and Navot all spoke fluent German. In fact, Navot's had the faint trace of a Viennese accent. His ancestors had lived in Vienna when the Germans annexed Austria in 1938. Those who managed to escape were first robbed of everything—everything but their Viennese accents.

"We're honored to have so many distinguished officers from your service here today," Kessler said without conviction, tapping a silver spoon against the rim of his china coffee cup like a gavel. "Especially you, Herr Allon. It's been a long time since your last visit to Vienna."

"Not as long as you think," Gabriel remarked.

Kessler managed a tight smile. "I was working the night the PLO set off that bomb beneath your car," he said after a moment. "I remember it all as though it were yesterday."

"So do I," Gabriel replied evenly.

"I imagine," said Kessler. "I was also working the night you kidnapped Erich Radek from his home in the First District and smuggled him back to Israel."

"Radek agreed to go to Israel voluntarily."

"Only after you took him to the scene of the crime at Treblinka. But that, as they say, is ancient history." Another forced smile. "Herr Navot tells me that Hezbollah has set its sights on Vienna."

Gabriel nodded.

"When will this attack occur?"

"Shortly after sundown."

"The target?"

"The Stadttempel synagogue and community center. If the terrorists are successful, more than a hundred people could die tonight. If, on the other hand, we work together . . ." Gabriel's voice trailed off, the thought unfinished.

"Yes?"

"Only the four terrorists will die."

"We haven't agreed to work with you, Herr Allon. And we're certainly not going to engage in some sort of targeted killing operation."

"When I finish telling you what you're up against, you'll realize you have no other option."

"Perhaps you would be good enough to tell us the source of your information."

"Rule number one about working with the Office," said Gabriel. "Don't ask too many questions."

If Gabriel's unorthodox opening remarks had one effect, it was to render his audience speechless. Indeed, as he relayed the information that had been given to him by Massoud, the Austrians emitted no sound except for the occasional gasp of disbelief. Gabriel could scarcely blame them, for at that moment a four-member team of Hezbollah operatives was holed up in an apartment at Koppstrasse 34, preparing to carry out the worst terrorist attack in Austria's history. Each member of the cell would be armed with a semiautomatic pistol and a suicide vest filled with dozens of pounds of explosives and lethal shrapnel. They would use their pistols to overpower the security guards who stood watch over the historic complex during services. Once the guards were neutralized, the team would split in half—two for the synagogue, two for the community center located directly across the narrow street. They intended to detonate their explosives simultaneously. *Allahu Akbar.*

"Why shouldn't we simply move in and arrest them now?" asked Kessler.

"Because they're not amateurs from the Muslim slums of Western Europe. These are hardened Hezbollah terrorists who cut their teeth fighting the Israeli military in southern Lebanon."

"Meaning?"

"They went fully operational several hours ago. If you try to enter that apartment, they'll detonate their explosives. The same thing will happen if you try to quietly evacuate the building or try to take them into custody at any stage along their journey to Paradise."

"Why not simply cancel services this evening?"

"Nothing would make us happier. But if the terrorists arrive to find the synagogue closed, they'll go in search of another target. At that hour, I'm sure they won't have any trouble finding one. In fact, if I had to guess, they'll go to the Kärntnerstrasse and kill as many innocent Austrians as they can."

The Kärntnerstrasse was a busy pedestrian boulevard that ran from the State Opera House to the Stephansdom cathedral. The economic and social heart of Vienna, the street was lined with cafés, exclusive shops, and department stores. On a Friday evening, an attack there would be devastating. Jonas Kessler understood that, of course, which explained why he looked as though he had just swallowed his cuff links. When he finally spoke again, his voice contained none of its previous sarcasm. In fact, Gabriel thought he could detect the slightest trace of gratitude.

"What are you suggesting, Herr Allon?"

"I'm afraid there's only one possible course of action."

"And that is?"

"We wait for the terrorists to approach the synagogue and declare their intentions. And then we put them down before they can hit their detonation switches."

"Kill them?"

Gabriel made no response. Neither did Shamron or Navot.

"We have a highly capable tactical police unit that is more than up to a job like this."

"Einsatzkommando Cobra," Shamron interjected. "Better known as EKO Cobra."

Kessler nodded. "They've trained for just this kind of scenario."

"With all due respect, Herr Kessler, when was the last time a member of EKO Cobra shot a living, breathing terrorist through the brain stem so he couldn't detonate his bomb with a dying twitch of his fingers?"

Kessler was silent.

"I thought so," Shamron said. "Do you happen to recall when EKO Cobra was formed, Herr Kessler?"

"It was shortly after the Munich Olympics massacre."

"That's correct," Shamron said. "And I was there *that* night, Herr Kessler. We begged the Germans to let us handle the rescue operation at Fürstenfeldbruck Air Base, but they refused. I had to listen to the screams of my people as they were being butchered. It was . . ." Shamron's voice trailed off, as though he were searching for the appropriate word. Finally, he said, "It was unbelievable."

"The people who will enter that synagogue tonight are Austrian citizens."

"That's true," Shamron said. "But they're also Jews, which means that we are their guardians. And we're going to make sure they come out of that synagogue alive."

34

VIENNA

AFTER THAT, THE DEBATE ENDED, and the two sides settled down to the business of hammering out an operational accord. Within a few minutes, they had the broad outlines of an agreement. Gabriel and Mikhail would see to the takedown; EKO Cobra, the surveillance. At Kessler's insistence, the Austrians reserved the right to move against the terrorists at any point prior to their arrival in the Jewish Quarter if the opportunity presented itself. Otherwise, they were to give the Hezbollah team a wide berth—or, as Shamron put it, they were to quietly escort them to death's door. Gabriel made the Austrians' job easier by telling Kessler the exact route the terrorists would take to the synagogue, including the streetcars they would use. Kessler was clearly impressed. He suggested a café on the Rotenturmstrasse that Gabriel could use as a staging post. Gabriel smiled and said he would use the one next door instead.

"Why?"

"Better view."

"When exactly was the last time you were in Vienna?"

"It slips my mind."

Which left only the rules of engagement. On this point, there was no room for debate. Gabriel and Mikhail were to take no lethal action until the terrorists drew their guns—and if they killed unarmed men, they would be prosecuted to the full extent of Austrian law, and any other law Kessler could think of. Gabriel agreed to the provision and even signed his name to a hastily drafted document. After adding his own signature to the agreement, Kessler handed over several miniature radios preset to the frequency the EKO Cobra teams would be using that night.

"Weapons?" asked Kessler.

"It's a little too early in the day for me," said Gabriel.

Kessler frowned. "Your intelligence is very precise," he said. "Let us hope it is also accurate."

"It usually is. That's how we've managed to survive in a very dangerous neighborhood."

"Are you ever going to tell me your source?"

"It would only complicate matters."

"I don't suppose this has anything to do with that missing Iranian diplomat."

"What missing diplomat?"

By then, it was approaching noon. Shamron gave Gabriel a cardkey to a hotel room in the Innere Stadt and told him to get a few hours of rest. Gabriel wanted to survey the battlefield in daylight first, so he set out on foot along the Kärntnerstrasse, trailed not so discreetly by a pair of oafs from Kessler's service. In the Stephansplatz, large crowds wandered a Lenten street fête. Gabriel briefly considered entering the cathedral to see an altarpiece he had once restored. Instead, he sliced his way through the colorful stalls and made his way to the Jewish Quarter.

Before the Second World War, the tangle of narrow streets and alleys had been the center of one of the most vibrant and remarkable Jewish communities in the world. At its height it numbered 192,000 people, but by November 1942 only 7,000 remained, the rest having fled or been murdered in the extermination camps of Nazi Germany. But the Holocaust was not the first destruction of Vienna's Jews. In 1421, the entire Jewish population was burned to death, forcibly baptized, or expelled after a scurrilous charge of ritual murder swept the city. The Austrians, it seemed, felt compelled to slaughter their Jews from time to time.

The heart of the Jewish Quarter was the Stadttempel synagogue. Built in the early nineteenth century, when an edict by Emperor Joseph II required non-Catholic houses of worship to be hidden from public view, it was tucked away behind a façade of old houses on a tiny cobbled lane called the Seitenstettengasse. On Kristallnacht, the organized spasm of anti-Jewish violence that swept Germany and Austria in November 1938, the synagogues of Vienna went up in flames as firefighters looked on and did nothing. But not the Stadttempel. Setting it alight would have destroyed the neighboring structures, so the mobs had to be content with merely smashing its windows and vandalizing its glorious sanctuary. It was the only synagogue or prayer room in the entire city to survive that night.

Gabriel approached the synagogue along the same route the terrorists would take later that evening. At sunset, most of the congregants would be gathered inside, but a few would surely be clustered around the entrance. Protecting them from collateral harm would be Gabriel's primary challenge. It meant that he and Mikhail would have to be extremely accurate and rapid in their use of firepower. Gabriel reckoned they would have only two seconds to act once the terrorists drew their weapons—two seconds to render four battle-hardened terrorists harmless. It was not the sort of thing that could be taught in a classroom or on a firing range. It took years of training and experience. And even then, an instant of hesitation could mean the difference between life and death, not only for the targets of the attack but for Gabriel and Mikhail as well.

He remained in the street until he had committed every crack and cobble to memory, then made his way to a quaint square lined with restaurants. One was the Italian restaurant where he had eaten his last meal with Leah and Dani, and in an adjacent street was the spot where their car had exploded. Gabriel stood motionless for a long moment, paralyzed by memories. He tried to control them but could not; it was as if he had contracted Leah's merciless affliction. Finally, he felt a gentle tap on his elbow and, turning sharply, saw the powdered face of an elderly Austrian woman. He calculated her age. It was his other affliction.

"Are you lost?" she asked in German.

"Yes," he replied forthrightly.

"What are you looking for?"

"Café Central," he answered without hesitation.

She pointed to the southwest, toward the Hofburg Quarter. Gabriel walked in that direction until he was out of the woman's sight. Then he turned and made his way back toward the cathedral. The hotel where the Office had booked a room for him was one street over. As Gabriel entered, he saw Yaakov and Eli Lavon drinking coffee in the lobby. Ignoring them, he walked over to the concierge to say he would be going upstairs to his room.

"Your wife arrived a few minutes ago," the concierge said.

Gabriel felt as though a stone had been laid over his heart. "My wife?"

"Yes," the concierge said. "Tall, long dark hair, dark eyes."

"Italian?"

"Very."

Gabriel felt himself breathe again. Turning, he walked past Yaakov and Lavon without a word and headed upstairs to his room.

A Do Not Disturb sign hung from the door latch. Gabriel inserted his cardkey into the slot and slipped quietly inside. From the bathroom came the sound of water splashing in the shower. Chiara was singing softly to herself. The tune was melancholy, her voice low and sultry. Gabriel padded over to the foot of the bed, where a change of his own clothing lay in a neat pile. Next to it was a gun, a sound suppressor, a box of ammunition, and a shoulder holster. The gun was a .45-caliber Beretta, larger than the 9mm he generally preferred but necessary for a quick and decisive kill. The ammunition was hollow-point, which would help to alleviate the threat of collateral casualties due to overpenetration. Gabriel loaded ten rounds into the magazine and inserted it into the butt. Then he screwed the suppressor into the end of the barrel and, extending his arm, checked the weapon for balance.

"What do you suppose normal people do when they come to Vienna?" Chiara asked.

"They have coffee and listen to music."

Gabriel lowered the Beretta and looked at her. She was leaning against the doorjamb of the bathroom, her body wrapped in a toweling robe, her face flushed from the heat of the shower.

"I thought I told you to stay in Jerusalem."

"You did."

"So why are you here?"

"I didn't want you to have to come back here alone."

Gabriel ejected the magazine from the Beretta and unscrewed the suppressor.

"Why are you doing this?" she asked.

"Because the Austrians have never dealt with a scenario like this before. And even if they had, I wouldn't be willing to entrust them with Jewish lives."

"Is that the only reason?"

"Why else would I be doing it?"

Chiara sat on the edge of the bed and studied him carefully. "You look dreadful," she said.

"Thank you, Chiara. You look lovely as always."

She ignored his remark. "I don't know what that night was really like," she said, "but I have a fairly good idea. You relive it in your dreams more often than you realize. I hear everything. I hear you weeping over Dani's body. I hear you telling Leah that the ambulance will be there soon."

She lapsed into silence and brushed a tear from her cheek. "But sometimes," she continued, "everything turns out differently. You kill the terrorists before they can set off the bomb. Leah and Dani are unharmed. You live happily ever after. No explosion. No funeral for a child." She paused. "No Chiara."

"It's just a dream."

"But it's how you wish things had turned out."

"You're right, Chiara. I do wish Dani hadn't been killed that night. And I do wish Leah—"

"I don't blame you, Gabriel," she said, cutting him off. "I knew that when I fell in love with you. I always knew I would only have part of your heart. The rest would always belong to Leah."

Gabriel reached down and touched her face. "What does any of this have to do with tonight?"

"Because you're right about one thing, Gabriel. It is only a dream. Killing those terrorists tonight won't bring Dani back to life. And it won't make Leah the way she was. In fact, the only thing you might achieve is getting yourself killed in the same city where your son died."

"The only people who are going to die tonight are the terrorists."

"Maybe," she said. "Or maybe you'll make a mistake, and I'll leave Vienna a widow." She smiled in spite of herself. "Wouldn't that be poetic?"

"I'm not a poet. And I'm not going to make a mistake."

She exhaled heavily in capitulation and pulled the robe tightly across her breasts. "I don't suppose you have room for one more person on your team tonight?"

Gabriel stared at her blankly.

"I thought that would be your answer." She took hold of his hand. "How will I know, Gabriel? How will I know if you're alive or dead?"

"If you hear explosions, you'll know I'm dead. But if you hear sirens . . ." He shrugged.

"What?"

"It will all be over." He kissed her lips and whispered, "And then we'll go home and live happily ever after."

———————

Gabriel showered and tried to sleep, but it was no good. His mind was aflame with too many memories of the past, his nerves too brittle with anxiety about what the next few hours would bring. And so he lay quietly next to Chiara as the afternoon shadows grew thin upon the bed, listening to the chatter over the radio that Jonas Kessler had given to him. EKO Cobra had established an observation post outside the apartment house on the Koppstrasse and, using a thermographic camera, had confirmed the presence of at least four people inside. Additional EKO Cobra teams were posted at various points along the route from the Koppstrasse to the Innere Stadt. It meant the terrorists would be running a gauntlet—a gauntlet that would lead them directly to the guns of Gabriel and Mikhail.

Sunset that evening was at 6:12. At half past four, Gabriel drank two cups of coffee—enough to make him alert, but not enough to make his hands shake—and dressed in the clothing that Chiara had brought from Jerusalem. Faded blue jeans, a dark woolen pullover, a shoulder holster: the uniform of a soldier of the night. He reassembled and loaded the Beretta and inserted it into the holster. Then, as Chiara looked on in silence, he repeatedly practiced drawing the weapon and firing two shots in rapid succession, both at a sharp upward trajectory.

When he felt ready, he holstered the gun and pulled on his leather jacket. Then he removed his wedding band and handed it to Chiara. She didn't ask why; she didn't need to. Instead, she kissed him one last time and tried not to cry as he slipped silently out the door. When he was gone, she stood alone in the window, her face wet with tears, and prayed for the screaming of sirens.

35

VIENNA

AUSTRIA'S FEDERAL MINISTRY OF THE INTERIOR occupied a magnificent old Hapsburg palace at Herengasse 7. Deep within the massive structure was a crisis center and situation room that had been constructed in the tense days after 9/11, when everyone in Europe, including the Austrians, assumed they were next on al-Qaeda's hit list. Fortunately, Jonas Kessler had set foot in the crisis center only one time. It was the night Erich Radek was captured by the same man who now held Kessler's career in the palm of his hand.

The center was arranged like a small amphitheater. On the lower level, in a space the staff referred to as "the pit," liaison officers from the various branches of the Austrian Federal Police and security services sat at three common tables crowded with phones and computers. The more senior staff sat in an ascending staircase of workstations, with the uppermost deck reserved for chiefs, ministers, and, if necessary, the federal chancellor himself.

At 5:35, Jonas Kessler settled into his assigned seat, with the interior minister on one side and Uzi Navot on the other. Next to Navot was Ari Shamron. He was twirling his old Zippo lighter between his fingertips and staring at the largest image on the video display wall. It showed the exterior of the apartment house at Koppstrasse 34. At 5:50, the exact time Gabriel had predicted, four young Lebanese men emerged from the entrance. Each wore a heavy woolen overcoat. Their faces were clean-shaven, a sign they had ritually prepared themselves for the virginal delights that awaited them in Paradise.

The four Arabs walked two blocks to the Thaliastrasse and descended into a U-Bahn station. At 5:55, they boarded a train—separate carriages, just as Gabriel had said they would. Watching them on the video monitors, Kessler swore softly beneath his breath. Then he looked at Navot and Shamron.

"I don't know how to thank you," he said.

"Then don't," Shamron replied darkly. "Not until it's over."

"Bad karma?" asked Kessler.

Shamron made no reply other than to twirl his lighter nervously between his fingertips. He didn't believe in karma. He believed in God. And he believed in his angel of vengeance, Gabriel Allon.

Regrettably, this was not the first time Arab terrorists had targeted Vienna's historic Stadttempel. In 1981, two people were killed and thirty were wounded when Palestinian militants attacked a Bar Mitzvah party using machine guns and hand grenades. As a result of the attack, those wishing to enter the synagogue now had to pass through a cordon of youthful Israeli-born security guards. Members of the local Jewish community were usually admitted without delay, but visitors had to endure a maddening cross-examination and a search of their belongings. It was about as pleasant as boarding an El Al airplane.

Most of the guards were veterans of the diplomatic protection arm of Shabak, Israel's internal security service. As a result, the two on duty that night recognized Yaakov Rossman as he approached the synagogue, trailed by Oded and Eli Lavon. Yaakov pulled the two guards aside and, as calmly as possible, told them that the synagogue was about to be attacked. Then he rattled off a quick set of instructions. The two guards immediately entered the offices of the Jewish community center, leaving Yaakov and Oded to handle security in the street. Eli Lavon, a former member of the community, covered his head with a *kippah* and entered the synagogue. Old habits die hard, he thought, even in wartime.

As usual, a small crowd of congregants was milling in the foyer. Lavon picked his way through them and entered the beautiful oval sanctuary. Looking up toward the women's gallery, he saw faces aglow with candlelight between the Ionic columns. Their male relatives were now settling into their seats on the lower level. As Lavon walked past them and mounted the *bimah*, several heads turned in bewilderment. Then a few smiles appeared. It had been a long time since they had seen him.

"Good evening, ladies and gentlemen," Lavon began, his voice calm and pleasant. "It's quite possible that some of you might remember me, but that's not important right now. What *is* important is that you all leave the sanctuary through the back door as quickly and quietly as possible."

Lavon had been expecting a Talmudic debate on why such a step was necessary, or even whether it was possible on the Sabbath. Instead, he watched in wonder as the congregants rose to their feet and followed his instructions to the letter. In his earpiece, he could hear a voice in German saying the four Hezbollah operatives had just changed onto a Number 3 U-Bahn train bound for the Innere Stadt. He looked at his watch. The time was 6:05. They were right on schedule.

At the far end of the Rotenturmstrasse, just a few paces from the banks of the Donaukanal, is a café called Aida. The awning that shades its tables is Miami pink, as is the exterior of the building, making it, arguably, the ugliest café in all of Vienna. In another lifetime, under another name, Gabriel had brought his son to Aida most afternoons for chocolate gelato. Now he sat there with Mikhail Abramov. Four members of EKO Cobra were huddled around a nearby table, as inconspicuous as a Times Square bill-board. Gabriel had his back turned to the street, the weight of the .45-caliber Beretta tugging at his shoulder. Mikhail was drum-ming his fingers nervously on the tabletop.

"How long do you intend to do that?" asked Gabriel.

"Until I see those four boys from Hezbollah."

"It's giving me a headache."

"You'll live." Mikhail's fingers went still. "I wish we didn't have to let him go."

"Massoud?"

Mikhail nodded.

"I gave him my word."

"He's a murderer."

"But I'm not," said Gabriel. "And neither are you."

"What if he wasn't telling you the truth? Then you wouldn't have to live up to your end of the bargain."

"If four suicide bombers from Hezbollah come walking up that street in a few minutes," Gabriel said, nodding toward the win-dow, "we'll know he was telling us the truth."

Mikhail started drumming his fingers again. "Maybe we don't actually have to *kill* him," he said philosophically. "Maybe we could just . . . forget him."

"What does that mean?"

"It means that Yossi and the others could just drive away from that house in Denmark with Massoud still chained to the wall. Eventually, someone would find his skeleton."

"A dishonest mistake? Is that what you're suggesting?"

"Shit happens."

"It would still be murder."

"No, it wouldn't. It would be death by negligence."

"I'm afraid that's a distinction without a difference."

"Exactly." Mikhail opened his mouth to continue, but he could see Gabriel was listening to the radio.

"What is it?"

"They're getting off the train."

"Where?"

"The Stephansplatz."

"Right where Massoud said they would."

Gabriel nodded.

"I still think we should kill him."

"You mean *forget* him."

"That, too."

"We're not murderers, Mikhail. We are *preventers* of murder."

"Let's hope so. Otherwise, they're going to have to pick us off the street with tweezers."

"It's better to think positive thoughts."

"I've always preferred to dwell upon the worst-case scenario."

"Why?"

"Motivation," said Mikhail. "If I imagine a rabbi soaking up my blood for burial, it will motivate me to do my job properly."

"Just wait until the guns appear. We can't kill them until we see the guns."

"What if they don't draw their guns? What if they just detonate themselves in the street?"

"Positive thoughts, Mikhail."

"I'm a Jew from Russia. Positive thoughts aren't in my nature."

The waitress placed a check on the table. Gabriel gave her a twenty and told her to keep the change. Mikhail glanced at the four EKO Cobra men.

"They look more nervous than we do."

"They probably are."

Mikhail turned his gaze to the street. "Have you given any thought to what you're going to do next?"

"I'm going to sleep for several days."

"Make sure you turn the phone off."

"This is the last time, Mikhail."

"Until some terrorist comes along who decides he wants to reduce the world's population of Jews by a few hundred. Then we'll be right back here again."

"I'm afraid you're going to have to do it without me next time."

"We'll see." Mikhail looked at Gabriel. "Are you really sure you're up for this?"

"If you ask me that one more time, I'm going to shoot you."

"That would be a very bad idea."

"Why?"

"Look out the window."

In the crisis center of the Austrian Interior Ministry, Ari Shamron stared at the video monitors, watching intently as the four Hezbollah terrorists turned into the narrow cobbled alley leading to the synagogue, followed by Gabriel and Mikhail. And at that moment, he had a chillingly clear premonition of disaster unlike any he had ever experienced before. It was nothing, he assured himself. The Stadttempel had survived Kristallnacht; it would survive this night, too. He ignited the Zippo lighter and stared at the jewel-like flame. Two seconds, he thought, maybe less. Then it would be done.

They had arranged themselves in a boxlike formation, with two in front and the other two trailing a few steps behind. Gabriel couldn't help but admire their tradecraft. With their winter coats and false casual demeanor, they looked like four young men out for an evening in Vienna's famed Bermuda Triangle—anything but four Hezbollah suicide bombers who were minutes from death. Gabriel knew a great deal about them. He knew each of their names, the villages where they had been born, and the circumstances of their recruitments. For now, though, they were simply Alef, Bet, Gimel, and Dalet—the first four letters of the Hebrew alphabet. Alef and Bet belonged to Gabriel; Gimel and Dalet, to Mikhail. *Alef, Bet, Gimel, Dalet* . . . Then it would be done.

The street rose at a pitched angle and curved slightly to the right. After a few more paces, Gabriel could see Yaakov and Oded standing in a pool of white light outside the synagogue's entrance. Oded was cross-examining a pair of American Jews who wished to attend Shabbat services in the city of their ancestry, but Yaakov was watching the four young men coming toward him up the street. He stared at them for an appropriate interval before forcing himself to look away. Oded seemed not to notice them. Having admitted the two Americans, he was now working his way through the rest of the small line of congregants waiting to enter. A dozen more, including a pair of young children, stood in the street, unaware of the horror that was approaching.

From the moment Gabriel and Mikhail had left the café, they had been gradually closing the distance between themselves and their targets. Twenty-five feet now separated them—four terrorists, two secret soldiers, each committed to his mission, each certain of his cause and his God. Tonight the ancient war for control of the Land of Israel would once again be played out on a pretty Viennese street. Gabriel couldn't help but feel the weight of history pressing down upon his shoulders as he climbed the sloping cobbles—his own history, the history of his people, *Shamron* . . . He imagined Shamron in his youth stalking Adolf Eichmann along a desolate lane north of Buenos Aires. Shamron had tripped over a loose shoelace that night and nearly fallen. After that, he had always double-knotted his laces whenever he went into the field. Gabriel had done the same tonight in Shamron's honor. No loose shoelaces. No nightmare of blood and fire at a synagogue in Vienna.

Gabriel and Mikhail quickened their pace slightly, closing the gap further still. As the terrorists passed through a cone of lamplight, Gabriel noticed the wire of a detonator switch running along the inside of Alef's wrist. All four of the terrorists wore their overcoats tightly buttoned, and, not coincidentally, all four had their right hands in their pockets. That's where the guns would be. *Draw them*, thought Gabriel. Two seconds, maybe less. *Alef, Bet, Gimel, Dalet* . . . Then it would be done.

Gabriel quickly glanced over his shoulder and saw the EKO Cobra team trailing quietly behind. Yaakov and Oded had managed to usher most of the crowd inside, but a few congregants were still milling about in the street, including the two young children. Mikhail drew several long, heavy breaths in an attempt to slow his racing heart, but Gabriel didn't bother. It wouldn't be possible. Not tonight. And so he stared at Alef's right hand, his heart beating in his chest like a kettledrum, and waited for the gun to emerge. In the end, though, it was one of the children, a young boy, who saw it first. His scream of terror set fire to the back of Gabriel's neck.

There would be no explosion.

There would be no funeral for a child.

Just a pair of fallen angels rushing forward with their arms extended.

Two seconds, maybe less.

Alef, Bet, Gimel, Dalet . . .

Then it was done.

Chiara never heard the gunshots, only the sirens. Alone in her room, she thought it was the most beautiful sound she had ever heard. She listened for several minutes, then snatched up her mobile phone and dialed Uzi Navot at the Interior Ministry. She could barely hear his voice over the background noise.

"What's going on?"

"It's over," he said.

"Was anyone else hurt?"

"Only the bad guys."

"Where is he?"

"The Austrians have him."

"I want him back."

"Don't worry," Navot said. "He's all yours now."

36

VIENNA-TEL AVIV-VATICAN CITY

L IKE MOST LIES, IT WAS not altogether convincing. Shamron found no fault in this; in fact, he wholeheartedly approved. Lying, he said, was a distinctly human endeavor, even when it was being done by professionals. And a lie that was too well told was one not easily believed.

Initially, there was confusion over precisely what had occurred at sunset in the narrow street outside the Stadttempel. The first bulletins on Austrian radio reported that a pair of gunmen had killed four Jewish men outside the synagogue in what appeared to be an act of right-wing extremist violence. The situation was muddied further when an obscure neo-Nazi group proudly claimed responsibility for the deed. Jonas Kessler's first instinct was to quickly correct the story. But Shamron and Uzi Navot prevailed upon him to let it linger until nine that evening, when he finally appeared in the Interior Ministry's press briefing room to reveal the truth—or at least the truth as he saw it. Yes, Kessler began, there had indeed been a shooting at the synagogue, but the four dead were suicide bombers from Hezbollah who had come to Vienna to carry out a murderous terrorist attack. The Austrian authorities, he said, had been alerted to the presence of the cell in Vienna by a foreign intelligence service that Kessler, for understandable reasons, could not identify. As for the successful operation outside the synagogue, it was a strictly Austrian affair carried out by the EKO Cobra division of the Federal Police. It was, Kessler concluded with admirable sincerity, "EKO Cobra's finest hour."

Naturally, the press was drawn to the one aspect of the story where Kessler had been most evasive—the source of the intelligence that had led to the successful operation. Kessler and the rest of the Austrian security establishment held fast to their refusal to comment, but within forty-eight hours, numerous unnamed "intelligence sources" were quietly giving credit to the CIA. Once again, the television terrorism analysts questioned the accuracy of the reports, saying it was far more likely that the information had come from Israel. On the record, the Israelis refused to comment. Privately, however, they swore it wasn't true.

The matter did not die there. In fact, it took on new life the very next morning when *Die Presse*, one of Austria's most respected papers, published a detailed account of the operation, based in large part on eyewitness testimony. The most intriguing aspect of the story was the description of the smaller of the two gunmen. And then there was the unkempt figure who had overseen the evacuation of the interior of the synagogue in the minutes preceding the attack. There were some who thought he bore an uncanny resemblance to a man who used to run a small Holocaust restitution agency in Vienna called Wartime Claims and Inquiries. An Israeli newspaper immediately reported that the man in question—Professor Eli Lavon of Hebrew University—was working on a dig near the Western Wall Tunnel at the time and that he had no known links to Israeli intelligence, neither of which was true.

Needless to say, much of the Islamic world was soon boiling over with a sacred rage directed at Israel, its intelligence service, and, by extension, their new friends the Austrians. Newspapers across the Middle East declared the killings a wanton act of murder and challenged the Austrians to produce the bomb vests allegedly worn by the four "martyrs." When Kessler did just that, the Arab press declared the vests fraudulent. And when Kessler released carefully edited photographs of the bodies that clearly showed the four men laden with bombs, the Arab world declared those fraudulent, too. It saw the hidden hand of Israel in the killings, and for once it was absolutely and entirely correct.

It was against this unsettled backdrop that Massoud Rahimi, Iran's kidnapped diplomat, was found wandering handcuffed and blindfolded in a pasture in the far north of Germany. He told the German police that he had escaped from his captors, but in a statement, the Iranian Liberation Army said they had released Massoud for "humanitarian reasons." The next morning, looking a few pounds thinner but otherwise in good health, Massoud appeared before the cameras in Tehran, flanked by the Iranian president and the chief of his service. Massoud offered few details about his time in captivity, except to say that, in general terms, he was well treated. His chief appeared somewhat skeptical, as did the Iranian president, who vowed that those behind the kidnapping would be severely punished.

The threat of Iranian retaliation was not taken lightly, especially within the corridors of King Saul Boulevard. For the most part, though, the Office celebrated the success of the operation. Lives had been saved, an old adversary had been severely compromised, and a lucrative fund-raising network for Hezbollah lay in ruins. If there was one factor that diminished their mood, however, it was the fact that His Holiness Pope Paul VII was scheduled to land at Ben Gurion Airport in less than a week. Given the overall turbulence in the region, Uzi Navot thought it might be wise for the Vatican to consider postponing the trip, a sentiment shared by the prime minister and the rest of his fractious cabinet. But who was going to tell the pope not to come to the Holy Land? They had but one candidate. A fallen angel in black. A sinner in the city of saints.

Father Mark was waiting for Gabriel just inside the Bronze Doors. He escorted him up the steps of the Scala Regia, across the cobblestones of the Cortile di San Damaso, and, eventually, upstairs to the private apartments of the pope. Donati was seated behind the desk in his office. It was a simple, high-ceilinged room with whitewashed walls and shelves lined with books on canon law. Framed photographs stood in neat rows atop the credenza. Most showed Donati standing discreetly at the side of his master at historic moments of the papacy. One photo, however, seemed curiously out of place—a younger version of Donati, soiled and smiling without reservation, his arm flung across the shoulder of a bookish young priest.

"That's Father José Martinez," Donati explained. "We'd just finished building a schoolhouse in our village in El Salvador. It was taken a week before his murder." He studied Gabriel's face for a moment and then frowned. "You look the way I did when I came out of El Salvador one step ahead of the death squads."

"It's been a busy few weeks since I left Rome."

"So I've been reading," Donati said. "An art theft in France, an explosion at a gallery in St. Moritz, a kidnapped Iranian diplomat, and a dramatic counterterrorism operation in the heart of Vienna. To the uninitiated, these events might appear unrelated. But to someone like me, they appear to have one thing in common."

"*Two* things, actually," said Gabriel. "One is the Office. And the other is Carlo Marchese."

It was approaching six o'clock, and the sun was dipping below the rooftops and domes of Rome's historic center. As Gabriel spoke, the soft sienna light drained slowly from the office until it was cloaked in a confessional gloom. Dressed in his black cassock, Donati might have been invisible were it not for the ember of his cigarette. At the conclusion of Gabriel's account, he sat for several minutes in a penitential silence before walking over to the window. Directly below was the Bastion of Nicholas V, the medieval tower that now served as headquarters of the Vatican Bank.

"Can you prove any of it?"

"There's the kind of proof that will stand up in a court of law. And then there's the kind of proof that's good enough to make a problem go away."

"What are you suggesting?"

"A conversation," answered Gabriel. "I'll tell Carlo everything I know. And then I'll tell him that you and His Holiness would like him to resign his position on the supervisory council of the Vatican Bank effective immediately. I'll also tell him that if he ever darkens the Bronze Doors again, he'll have to answer to me."

"It seems an awfully small price to pay for two murders."

"But it's what you wanted." Gabriel looked at Donati's silhouette in the window. "It *is* what you wanted, isn't it, Luigi?"

"The moral thing to do would be to tell General Ferrari every-thing you know."

"Perhaps. But if the Italian government brings charges against Carlo for dealing in looted antiquities, money laundering, and murder, it will be a public-relations disaster for the Church. And for you, Luigi. Everything will come out. You'll be destroyed." Gabriel paused, then added, "And so will Veronica."

"And if Carlo refuses to leave quietly?"

"I'll make it clear he doesn't have a choice. Trust me," Gabriel added, "he'll get the message."

"I won't countenance a murder. *Another* murder, I should say."

"No one's talking about killing anyone. But if there's anyone who deserves—"

Donati silenced Gabriel by raising his long hand. "Just talk to Carlo."

"When?"

"Next week. That way, there will be no chance of anything leaking to the press before the trip to Israel." He glanced over his shoulder and asked, "I don't suppose you've had a moment to look over the security arrangements?"

"Actually, I've reviewed them in great detail."

"And?"

"I have only one recommendation."

"What's that?"

"Take a rain check, Luigi."

Donati turned slowly. "Are you telling me to cancel the trip?"

"No. We just want you to postpone it until things cool down."

"*We?*"

"This comes from the top."

"The prime minister?"

Gabriel nodded.

"Unless your prime minister is prepared to formally ask the leader of one billion Roman Catholics *not* to come to Israel, there's no way we're going to cancel."

"Then someone needs to tell the Holy Father how we feel."

"I agree," Donati said, smiling. "But it's not going to be me."

The Vatican Gardens were in darkness when Gabriel emerged from the Belvedere Palace. He walked past the Fountain of the Sacrament and the Ethiopian College, then made his way toward the spot along the Vatican wall where several Swiss Guards in plainclothes stood like statues. Slipping past them without a word, he mounted a flight of stone steps and climbed slowly toward the parapet. Pietro Lucchesi, otherwise known as His Holiness Pope Paul VII, waited there alone. Rome stirred beneath his feet— dusty, dirty, eternal Rome. Gabriel never tired of looking at it. Neither did the Holy Father.

"I remember the first time we came to this spot together," the pope said. "It was after the Crux Vera affair. You saved my papacy, not to mention my life."

"It was the least we could do, Holiness," Gabriel said. He was staring across the Tiber toward the cupola of the Great Synagogue of Rome, and for an instant he saw Pietro Lucchesi standing atop the *bimah*, speaking words no pontiff had ever uttered before.

"For these sins, and others soon to be revealed, we offer our confession, and we beg your forgiveness . . ."

"It took enormous courage for you to do what you did that day, Holiness."

"It wouldn't have been possible without you. But my work isn't finished when it comes to healing the wounds between our two faiths, which is why it is essential that I make this trip to Jerusalem."

"No one wants you to come to Israel more than I do."

"But?"

"We don't believe it's safe at this time."

"Then do whatever it takes to *make* it safe. Because as far as I'm concerned, the matter is closed."

"Yes, Holiness."

The pope smiled. "That's all, Gabriel? I expected more of an argument from you."

"I try not to make a habit of arguing with the Vicar of Christ."

"Good. Because it is my wish that you serve as my personal bodyguard during the trip."

"It would be my honor, Holiness. After all, it's a role I've played before."

"To considerable acclaim."

The pope smiled briefly as the wind moved in his cassock. The air had lost the edge of winter; it smelled of pine and warm earth. His Holiness seemed not to notice. He was clearly preoccupied by matters weightier than the changing of the seasons.

"Is it true that Carlo Marchese had something to do with the death of that poor girl from the museum?" he asked finally.

Gabriel hesitated.

"Is something wrong, Gabriel?"

"No, Holiness. But it might be better if—"

"I was shielded from the unpleasant details?" The pope gave a conspiratorial smile. "I'll let you in on a little secret, Gabriel. The Vicar of Christ doesn't hold press conferences. And he doesn't have to answer a subpoena, either. It's one of the few fringe benefits of the job."

"What about the luxury apartment in the middle of Rome?"

"Actually, I've never enjoyed living above the store." The pope looked out at the hills of Rome. The city looked as though it were lit by a million candles. "Cleaning up the mess at the Vatican Bank was one of my top priorities. Now it seems a man with long-standing ties to the Vatican has undone all of our good work."

"He'll be gone before you know it."

"Do you require anything from me?"

"Stay as far away as possible."

A companionable silence settled between them. The pope examined Gabriel carefully, as Donati had before him.

"Have you given any thought to what you're going to do next?"

"I have a Caravaggio to finish."

"And then?"

"I'm going to do my very best to make my wife happy."

"And to think you would have let her slip through your fingers if it wasn't for me," the pope said. "Perhaps you should devote some of your time to having a child."

"It's complicated."

"Is there anything I can do to help?"

It was Gabriel's turn to smile. "What do you have in mind?"

"As leader of the Roman Catholic Church, I'm afraid my options are limited to prayer."

"Your prayers would be deeply appreciated."

"And what about my advice?"

Gabriel was silent. The pope scrutinized him a moment before speaking.

"You've been wandering for many years, Gabriel. Perhaps the time has come for you to go home."

"My work is here in Europe, Holiness."

"Paintings?"

Gabriel nodded.

"There are some things in life more important than art," the pope said. "I fear your country faces dark days ahead. My sleep has been troubled by dreams of late. I've been having . . . visions."

"What kind of visions, Holiness?"

"It would probably be better if I didn't answer that question," the pope replied, placing his hand on Gabriel's arm. "But listen carefully. Finish that Caravaggio, Gabriel. And then go home."

37

EAST JERUSALEM

A T THAT SAME MOMENT IN East Jerusalem, Imam Hassan Darwish guided his dented station wagon up the steep ramp leading from the Jericho Road to the Lions' Gate. As usual, the Israeli policeman on duty gave the car only a cursory inspection before allowing the imam to enter the Muslim Quarter of the Old City. Imam Darwish was a descendant of a family of Palestinian notables from the West Bank town of Hebron. More important, he was a member of the Supreme Council of the Islamic Waqf, the official caretakers of the Temple Mount plateau since Saladin recaptured it from the Crusaders in 1187. The position meant that Darwish was as close to untouchable as an Arab could be in East Jerusalem, for with only a few words of incitement, he could turn the Holy Mountain into a seething cauldron. In fact, on numerous occasions, he had done just that.

He left the station wagon in the small Waqf car park off Lions' Gate Street and entered his office at the northern edge of the

Temple Mount esplanade. A tower of phone messages beckoned from his old Ottoman desk. As the unofficial spokesman for the Waqf, he received dozens of calls each day for interviews on issues related to the Temple Mount and the other sacred sites in Jerusalem. Most he ignored, especially those from American and Israeli reporters—and not without good reason. Working first with Yasir Arafat, then with his successor, Mahmoud Abbas, Darwish had waged a relentless campaign to weaken the Jewish claim on Palestine by denying the existence of the Jewish Temple of Jerusalem. But Darwish's war on the truth had extended beyond mere words. Using the cover of construction projects, he had systematically stripped the Holy Mountain of all evidence of the ancient Temple. His unofficial adviser in the endeavor, an antiquities expert from Switzerland, had recently been martyred in an explosion at his gallery. Darwish hoped he would not meet the same fate. While he routinely spoke about the beauty of martyrdom, he much preferred to leave the dying to others.

As usual, Darwish quickly dispensed with the interview requests by dropping them unceremoniously into his rubbish bin. All that remained was a single mundane-looking message from a Mr. Farouk saying that an order of Korans had arrived from the printing presses of al-Azhar University in Cairo. Darwish stared at the message for several minutes, wondering whether he had the courage, or the faith, necessary to go through with it. Then he took a ring of keys from the top drawer of his desk and headed out onto the sacred mount.

The Darwish family had been linked to the Jerusalem Islamic Waqf for centuries, and as a child Hassan Darwish had passed his days memorizing the Koran in the shade trees at the northern edge of the Noble Sanctuary. But even now, in middle age, he could not walk past the Dome of the Rock without feeling as though Allah and the Prophet Muhammad were walking beside him. At the center of the colorful octagonal structure was the Foundation Stone, sacred to all three of the Abrahamic faiths. For Jews and Christians, it was the place where the Archangel Gabriel prevented Abraham from slaying his son Isaac; for Muslims, it marked the spot where Gabriel accompanied Muhammad on his Night Journey into heaven. Beneath the stone itself was a natural cave known as the Well of Souls, the place where Muslims believed the souls of the damned are temporarily held before being cast into hell. As a boy, Darwish used to sneak into the cave alone late at night. There he would sit for hours on the musty prayer rugs, pretending he could hear the souls wailing in anguish. In his imagination, they were never Muslims, only the Jews whom God had punished for stealing the land of Palestine.

For a time, Darwish believed it was possible for Jews and Muslims to divide the land and live side by side in peace. Now, after decades of crushing Israeli occupation and broken promises, he had come to the conclusion the Palestinians would never be free until the Zionist state was annihilated. The key to the liberation of Palestine, he believed, was the Temple Mount itself. The Israelis had foolishly allowed the Waqf to retain its authority over the Haram after the Six-Day War. In doing so, they had unwittingly sealed their own fate. A scholar of ancient Middle Eastern history, Darwish understood that conflict between Arabs and Jews was more than simply a struggle over land; it was a religious war, and the Haram was at the center of it. Arafat had used the Temple Mount to ignite the bloody Second Intifada in 2000. Now, Imam Hassan Darwish intended to use it to start another. But this intifada, the third, would dwarf the two that had come before. It would be cataclysmic, a final solution. And when it was over, there would not be a single Jew left in the land of Palestine.

With images of the coming apocalypse vivid in his thoughts, the imam passed beneath the freestanding archway of the Southwest Qanatir and set out across a broad courtyard toward the silver-domed al-Aqsa Mosque. On the eastern side of the massive structure was the newly built entrance to the underground Marwani Mosque. Darwish descended the terrace-like steps and, using one of his keys, unlocked the main door. As always, he felt slightly apprehensive about entering. As director of the construction project, Darwish knew how badly the removal of several tons of earth and debris had weakened the Haram. The entire southern half of the plateau was in danger of collapse. Indeed, on Ramadan and other important holy days, Darwish could almost hear the Holy Mountain groaning under the weight of the faithful. All it would take was one small shove, and a large portion of the most sacred place on earth would collapse into the Kidron Valley, taking the al-Aqsa Mosque, the third-holiest shrine in Islam, with it. *And what would happen then?* The armies of Islam would be on Israel's borders within hours, along with tens of millions of enraged Muslim faithful. It would be a jihad to end all jihads, an intifada with but one purpose—the complete annihilation of the State of Israel and its inhabitants.

For now, the enormous subterranean mosque, with its twelve avenues of Herodian pillars and arches, was deathly silent and aglow with a soft, divine light. Alone, Darwish padded quietly along a vaulted passage until he came to a heavy wooden door sealed fast with a thick padlock. The imam had the only key. He unlocked the door and heaved it open, revealing a flight of stone steps. At the bottom was yet another locked door. Darwish possessed the single key to this one as well, but when he opened it, the darkness beyond was absolute. He removed a small Maglite from the pocket of his *thobe* and, switching it on, illuminated the first fifty feet of an ancient tunnel no wider than the width of a man's shoulders. Dug during the time of the First Jewish Temple, it was but one of many ancient wonders unearthed by Palestinian workers during the construction of the mosque. Darwish had informed neither the Israel Antiquities Authority nor the United Nations of the tunnel's existence. No one knew about it—no one but Imam Hassan Darwish and a handful of laborers who had been sworn to secrecy.

Some men might be naturally apprehensive about entering an ancient tunnel at night, but not Darwish. As a child, he had spent countless hours happily exploring the Noble Sanctuary's hidden caves and passages. This one descended at a treacherously steep angle for several hundred feet before finally leveling off. After that it ran largely straight and flat for approximately a quarter-mile and then rose sharply once again. At the terminus was a newly installed steel ladder. Slightly winded from the arduous walk, Hassan Darwish took hold of the handrails and climbed slowly toward the wooden trapdoor at the top. Opening it, he found himself in the bedroom of an apartment in Silwan, the neighborhood of East Jerusalem adjacent to the City of David. On one wall was a poster of a French soccer star; on another, a photograph of Yahiya Ayyash, the master Hamas bomb maker known as the Engineer. Darwish opened the closet. Inside were the "Korans" that Mr. Farouk had mentioned in his message—several hundred pounds of high explosives and detonators that had been smuggled across the Egyptian border by Hezbollah and Hamas and carried into Israel by Bedouin tribesmen. There was more elsewhere in Silwan. Much more.

Darwish closed the closet door. Then he slipped out of the bedroom and made his way through the cramped rooms of the apartment to a tiny balcony overlooking the Kidron Valley. On the opposite side, floating above the soaring honey-colored walls of Herodian stone, were two enormous domes, one silver, the other gold. *"Allahu Akbar,"* the imam said softly. "And may he have mercy on my soul for what I am about to do in His name."

38

VATICAN CITY

FOR THE NEXT WEEK, GABRIEL'S turbulent life settled into a pleasant if cloistered routine. With the flat on the Via Gregoriana now off-limits, he took refuge in a small priestly apartment inside the Apostolic Palace, one floor below Donati and the pope. He rose early each morning, ate breakfast with the Holy Father's household nuns, and then headed over to the conservation lab to spend a few hours working on the Caravaggio. Antonio Calvesi, the chief restorer, rarely strayed from Gabriel's grottolike workspace. On the second day, he finally screwed up the nerve to ask about the reason for Gabriel's absence.

"I was visiting a sick aunt."

"Where?"

"Palm Beach."

Calvesi gave a skeptical frown. "Rumor has it you're going to accompany *il Papa* on his pilgrimage to the Holy Land."

"Actually, we prefer to call it Israel," said Gabriel, tapping his paintbrush gently against the flowing red mantle of John the Evangelist. "And, yes, Antonio, I'm going with him. But don't worry, I'll finish the Caravaggio when we get back."

"How long?"

"Maybe a week, maybe a month."

"Do you do that just to annoy me?"

"Yes."

"Let us hope your *aunt* remains healthy."

"Yes," said Gabriel. "Let us hope."

At ten o'clock sharp, Gabriel would depart the lab and walk over to the Swiss Guard barracks for a daily briefing on the security arrangements for the pope's trip. At first, Alois Metzler seemed annoyed by Gabriel's presence. But his misgivings quickly evaporated when Gabriel pointed out several glaring problems with the protection plan that no one else seemed to have noticed. At the conclusion of one particularly long meeting, he invited Gabriel into his office.

"If you're going to serve with us," he said, glancing at Gabriel's blue jeans and leather jacket, "you're going to have to dress like us."

"Pantaloons make me look fat," said Gabriel. "And I've never been able to figure out how to get a halberd through an airport metal detector."

Metzler pressed a button on his intercom. Ten seconds later, his adjutant entered carrying three dark suits, three white shirts, three ties, and a pair of lace-up dress shoes.

"Where did you get my measurements?" asked Gabriel.

"Your wife." Metzler opened the top drawer of his desk and removed a 9mm pistol. "You're also going to need one of these."

"I *have* one of those."

"But if you're going to pass for Swiss Guard, you have to carry a standard-issue Swiss Guard sidearm."

"A SIG Sauer P226."

"Very impressive."

"I've been around the block a time or two."

"So I've heard." Metzler smiled. "You'll just need to pass a range proficiency exam before I can issue the weapon."

"You're joking."

"I'm Swiss, which means I never joke." Metzler rose. "I assume you remember the way."

"Take a right at the suit of armor and follow the corridor to the courtyard. The door to the firing range is on the other side."

"Let's go."

The walk took less than two minutes. When they entered the range, four Swiss boys in their early twenties were blasting away, and the air was thick with smoke. Metzler ordered them to leave before giving Gabriel the SIG Sauer, an empty magazine, and a box of ammunition. Gabriel quickly inserted fifteen rounds into the magazine and rammed it into the butt of the gun. Metzler put on ear and eye protection.

"You?" he asked.

Gabriel shook his head.

"Why not?"

"Because if someone is trying to kill the Holy Father, I won't have time to protect my eyes and ears."

Metzler hung a target on the line and ran it twenty yards down the range.

"Farther," said Gabriel.

"How far?"

"All the way."

Metzler did as he was told. Gabriel raised the gun in a classic triangular firing position and poured all fifteen rounds through the eyes, nose, and forehead of the target.

"Not bad," said Metzler. "Let's see if you can do it again."

Metzler ran another target to the end of the range while Gabriel quickly reloaded the weapon. He emptied it in a matter of seconds. This time, instead of fifteen holes grouped around the face, there was just a single large hole in the center of the forehead.

"Good Lord," said Metzler.

"Good gun," said Gabriel.

At midday, Gabriel would slip the bonds of the Vatican in the back of Donati's official sedan and make his way to the Israeli Embassy to review the daily intelligence from King Saul Boulevard. Time permitting, he would return to the conservation lab for a few more hours of work. Then, at seven, he would join Donati and the pope for supper in the private papal dining room. Gabriel knew better than to raise the issue of security again, so he used the extraordinary opportunity to help prepare the pope for what would be one of the most important foreign trips of his papacy. The Secretariat of State, the rough equivalent of the Vatican foreign ministry, had written a series of predictably safe statements for the pope to issue at the various stops he planned to make in both Israel and the territories under Palestinian authority. But with each passing day, it became apparent that the pope intended to radically reshape the historically tense relationship between the Holy See and the Jewish State. The trip would be more than just a pilgrimage; it would be the culmination of the process the pope had set in motion almost a decade earlier with his act of contrition at the Great Synagogue of Rome.

On the final night, Gabriel listened as the Holy Father wrestled with the remarks he intended to deliver at Yad Vashem, Israel's museum and memorial to the Holocaust. Afterward, a restless Donati insisted on walking Gabriel back to his apartment. A detour brought them to one of the doorways leading to the Sistine Chapel. Donati hesitated before turning the latch.

"It's probably better if you go in without me this time."

"Who's in there, Luigi?"

"The one person in the world who can give Carlo the punishment he deserves."

Veronica Marchese was standing behind the altar, her arms folded defensively, her eyes on *The Last Judgment.* They remained there as Gabriel went quietly to her side.

"Do you think it will look like this?" she asked.

"The end?"

She nodded.

"I hope not. Otherwise, I'm in serious trouble."

She looked at him for the first time. He could see she had been crying. "How did it happen, Mr. Allon? How did a man like you become one of the world's finest restorers of Christian art?"

"It's a long story."

"I think I need one," she said.

"I was asked to do things for my country that left me incapable of painting. So I learned how to speak Italian and went to Venice under an assumed identity to study restoration."

"With Umberto Conti?"

"Who else?"

"I miss Umberto."

"So do I. He had a ring of keys that could open any door in Venice. He used to drag me out of my bed late at night to look at paintings. 'A man who is pleased with himself can be an adequate restorer,' he used to say to me, 'but only a man with a damaged canvas of his own can be a truly great restorer.' "

"Have you managed to repair it?"

"Portions," Gabriel answered after a reflective silence. "But I'm afraid parts are beyond repair."

She said nothing.

"Where's Carlo?"

"Milan. At least, I think he's in Milan. Not long ago, I discovered that Carlo doesn't always tell me the truth about where he is or who he's meeting with. Now I understand why."

"How much did Donati tell you?"

"Enough to know that my life as I knew it is now over."

A leaden silence fell between them. Gabriel recalled how Veronica had appeared that afternoon at the Villa Giulia museum, how she could have passed for a much younger woman. Now, suddenly, she looked every one of her fifty years. Even so, she was remarkably beautiful.

"You must have realized your husband wasn't what he appeared to be," he said at last.

"I knew Carlo made a great deal of money in ways I didn't always understand. But if you're asking whether I knew he was the head of an international criminal organization that controlled the trade in illicit antiquities . . ." Her voice trailed off. "No, Mr. Allon, I did not know that."

"He used you, Veronica. You were his door into the Vatican Bank."

"And my reputation in the antiquities world gave him a patina of respectability." Her hair had fallen across her face. Deliberately, she moved it aside, as though she wanted Gabriel the restorer to assess the damage done by Carlo's treachery.

"Why did you marry him?" he asked.

"Are you judging me, Mr. Allon?"

"I wouldn't dream of it. I was just wondering how you could choose a man like him after being in love with Luigi."

"You don't know much about women, do you?"

"So I've been told."

Her smile was genuine. It faded quickly as she listed the reasons why she had married a man like Carlo Marchese. Carlo was handsome. Carlo was exciting. Carlo was rich.

"But Carlo wasn't Donati," Gabriel said.

"No," she replied, "there's only one Luigi. And I would have had him all to myself if it wasn't for Pietro Lucchesi."

Her tone was suddenly bitter, resentful, as though His Holiness were somehow to blame for the fact she had married a murderer.

"It was probably for the better," said Gabriel carefully.

"That Luigi returned to the priesthood instead of marrying me?"

He nodded.

"That's easy for you to say, Mr. Allon." Then she added softly, "You weren't the one who was in love with him."

"He's happy here, Veronica."

"And what happens when they remove the Fisherman's Ring from Lucchesi's finger and place his body in the crypt beneath the Basilica? What will Luigi do then?" She quickly answered her own question. "I suppose he'll teach canon law for a few years at a pontifical university. And then he'll spend the last years of his life in a retirement home filled with aging priests. So lonely," she added after a moment. "So terribly sad and lonely."

"It's the life he chose."

"It was chosen for him, just like yours. You two are quite alike, Mr. Allon. I suppose that's why you get along so well."

Gabriel looked at her for a moment. "You're still in love with him, aren't you?"

"That's not a question I care to answer—at least not in here."
She tilted her face toward the ceiling. "Did you know that Claudia
called my office at the Villa Giulia the night of her death?"

"At 8:47," he said.

"Then I assume you also know she placed a call to a different
number one minute before that."

"I do know that. But we were never able to identify it."

"I could have helped you."

She handed him one of her business cards. The number Claudia
had dialed was for Veronica's mobile.

"I'd left the office by the time she called me there, and I didn't
realize until the next day that she'd called my BlackBerry."

"Why not?"

"Because it was missing all day. I found it the next morning on
the floor of my car. I didn't think anything of it until the day you
came to see me at the museum. Then I realized how Carlo had
done it. After I left you standing in that downpour, I drove into
the Villa Borghese and cried for an hour before going home. Carlo
could see something was wrong."

"Why didn't you tell me the night of the dinner party?"

"I was afraid."

"Of what?"

"That my husband would kill me, too." She looked at Gabriel,
then at *The Last Judgment*. "I hope it's as beautiful as this."

"The end?"

"Yes."

"Somehow," said Gabriel, "I doubt we'll be so lucky."

He told her as much as he could and then saw her to the Bronze
Doors. As she melted into the colonnades, he imagined Donati

walking beside her—not a Donati bound by vows of chastity, but Donati as he might have been had God not called him to become a priest. When she was gone, he started back toward his rooms, but something drew him back to the chapel. Alone, he stood motionless for several minutes, his eyes roaming over the frescoes, a single verse of scripture running through his thoughts. *"The House which King Solomon built for the Lord was sixty cubits long, twenty cubits wide, and thirty cubits high . . ."*

39

VATICAN CITY–JERUSALEM

A S LEADER OF A SOVEREIGN country, the pope has a post office, a mint, a small army, a world-class state museum, and ambassadors stationed at embassies around the world. He does not, however, have an airplane. For that, he must rely on the kindness of Alitalia, Italy's troubled national carrier. For the flight to Israel, it lent him a Boeing 767 and rechristened it *Zion* in honor of the trip. His private compartment had four executive swivel chairs, a coffee table piled with the morning papers, and a satellite television that allowed the pope to watch his departure from Fiumicino Airport live on RAI, the Italian television network.

The pope's Curial entourage and security detail sat directly behind him in the business-class section of the aircraft, while the Vatican press corps was confined to economy. As they clambered aboard laden with their cameras and luggage, several were wearing black-and-white-checkered Palestinian kaffiyehs as scarves. The second stop on the pope's busy itinerary would be the refugee camp of Dheisheh. Apparently, the Vaticanisti felt it was important to make a favorable impression on their hosts.

Despite the early-morning departure, Alitalia served a sumptuous in-flight lunch. The priests and bishops devoured the meal as if they had not seen food in days, but Gabriel was far too preoccupied to eat. Seated next to Alois Metzler, he reviewed the protection plans one final time, making a mental list of everything that could possibly go wrong. When the number of nightmare scenarios reached twenty, he closed the briefing book and stared out the window as the aircraft swept low over the Mediterranean toward Israel's verdant Coastal Plain. Five minutes later, as the wheels thudded onto the runway at Ben Gurion Airport, a member of the Vaticanisti shouted, "Welcome to Occupied Palestine!" To which a doctrinaire archbishop from the Secretariat of State murmured, "Amen to that." Clearly, thought Gabriel, there were some within the Curia who were unhappy over the pope's decision to spend Eastertide in a Holy Land controlled by Jews.

At Donati's direction, Gabriel was to be part of the pope's core protection unit, meaning he would never be more than a few feet from the pontiff's side. And so it was that, as His Holiness Pope Paul VII, the Bishop of Rome, Pontifex Maximus, and successor to St. Peter, stepped off his borrowed airplane, he was trailed by the only child of Holocaust survivors from the Valley of Jezreel. Following in the tradition set by his predecessor, the pope immediately lowered himself to his hands and knees and kissed the tarmac. Rising, he walked over to the waiting Israeli prime minister and gave him a vigorous handshake. The two men exchanged pleasantries for a few minutes, surrounded by concentric rings of security. Then the prime minister escorted the pope to a helicopter. Gabriel climbed in after him and sat between Donati and Alois Metzler.

"So far, so good," Donati said as the helicopter rose swiftly into the air.

"Yes," said Gabriel. "But now the fun begins."

They headed eastward into the Judean Hills, above the winding staircase-like gorge separating Jerusalem from the sea. Gabriel pointed out some of the villages that had seen the worst fighting during Israel's War of Independence; then Jerusalem appeared before them, floating, as though held aloft by the hand of God. The pope peered intently out his window as they crossed the city from west to east, new to old. As they passed over the Temple Mount, the golden Dome of the Rock sparkled in the midday sun. Gabriel showed the pope the Church of the Holy Sepulchre, the Church of the Dormition, and the Garden of Gethsemane.

"And your son?" asked the pope.

"There," said Gabriel as they passed over the Mount of Olives.

The helicopter banked gently to the south and flew along the 1949 Green Line, now commonly referred to as the pre-1967 border. From the air, it was plain to see how the border had effectively dissolved after more than forty years of Israeli occupation. In the span of a few seconds, they passed over the mixed Jerusalem neighborhood of Abu Tor, the small West Bank Jewish settlement of Har Homa, and the Arab village of Beit Jala. Adjacent to Beit Jala was Bethlehem. Manger Square was easily visible from the distance, for it was crammed with several thousand people, each one waving a small Palestinian flag. On the roads leading into the city, not a car moved, only the trucks and jeeps of the IDF.

"This is where things are going to get political," Gabriel told Donati. "It's important to keep things moving, especially since the guest of honor will be the only male dressed entirely in white from head to toe."

As the helicopter set down, President Mahmoud Abbas and the leadership of the Palestinian Authority waited on a dais outside the Church of the Nativity. "Welcome, Your Holiness, to the ancient land of Palestine," Abbas exclaimed, loudly enough for the remark to be heard by the reporters standing nearby. "And welcome to Bethlehem and Jerusalem, the eternal and indivisible capital of Palestine." The pope responded with a noncommittal nod and then greeted the rest of the delegation. Most were clearly pleased to be in his presence, but one, Yasser Abed Rabbo, a former leader of the terrorist Popular Front for the Liberation of Palestine, seemed far more intrigued by the bodyguard who never strayed more than a few inches from the pope's shoulder.

Entering the church, the pope spent a few minutes in silent prayer at the Altar of the Nativity. Then he asked Abbas to show him the damage that had been done to the church in 2002, when a group of Palestinian terrorists seized the sacred Christian site in an effort to evade capture. At the conclusion of the ninety-three-day standoff, Israeli forces discovered forty explosive devices concealed within the church, while Franciscan clerics held hostage during the siege described how the Palestinian terrorists looted the church of gold icons and used pages of the Christian Bible for toilet paper. All this, however, was apparently news to Mahmoud Abbas. "The only damage done to the church," he insisted, "was done by the Israelis. As you know, they are profoundly anti-Christian."

"If that is the case," the pope replied coolly, "why has the Christian population of Bethlehem fallen from ninety-five percent to just one-third? And why are Christians fleeing the territory controlled by the Palestinian Authority at an alarming rate?"

Abbas smiled weakly and looked at his wristwatch. "Perhaps, Your Holiness, it might be a good time to pay a visit to Dheisheh."

The camp was located about a mile to the south of Bethlehem on a patch of land leased from the Jordanian government after the conclusion of the War of Independence. Originally, some three thousand Palestinians, mainly from Jerusalem and Hebron, lived there in tents. Now, more than sixty years later, the tents had been replaced by cinderblock structures, and the population of the camp had grown to nearly thirteen thousand registered refugees. With unemployment rampant, most were permanent wards of the United Nations, and the camp was a hotbed of militant activity. Even so, the residents cheered the pope as he walked the narrow streets with Gabriel at his side.

At the conclusion of the tour, in the camp's dusty central square, the pope lamented what he described as "the terrible suffering of the Palestinian people." But in an abrupt departure from his prepared text, he pointedly criticized the failure of three generations of Arab leadership to achieve a just and viable solution to the refugee crisis. "Those who would perpetuate human suffering in the service of politics," he said solemnly, "must be condemned as strongly as those who would inflict it in the first place."

With that, the pope blessed the crowd with a sweeping sign of the cross and climbed into an armored limousine for the short drive to Jerusalem. Entering the Jewish Quarter through the Dung Gate, he inserted a plea for peace between the stones of the Western Wall before making his way on foot through the streets of the Muslim Quarter to the Chain Gate, one of the eastern entrances to the Haram al-Sharif. A sign posted by the chief rabbinate of Israel warned that, in its opinion, Jews were forbidden to set foot on the Mount due to its sacredness.

"I never realized," said the pope.

"It's complicated, Holiness," said Gabriel. "But in Israel, most things are."

"Are you sure you want to come with me?"

"I've been here before."

The pope smiled. "I shudder to think what would have happened to poor little Isaac if it wasn't for you."

"It was God who spared the boy. The Archangel Gabriel was only his messenger."

"I hope he sees fit to spare me, too."

"He will as long as you listen to me," said Gabriel. "Things can go wrong here in a hurry. If I see something I don't like—"

"We leave," said the pope, cutting him off.

"Quickly," said Gabriel.

Though the Waqf controlled the Noble Sanctuary itself, it did not control the entrances, which meant the Israeli government had been able to enforce the Vatican's request that the Haram be closed for the pope's brief visit. As a result, the delegation of Islamic dignitaries waiting on the steps leading to the Dome of the Rock numbered just forty. They included the Grand Mufti, the members of the Waqf's Supreme Council, and several dozen armed security guards, many of whom had links to Palestinian and Islamic militant groups. Within minutes of the pope's arrival, the mufti invited him to pray inside the Dome of the Rock, despite the fact the Waqf had assured the Vatican that no such invitation would be forthcoming. The pope diplomatically declined and then spent several minutes marveling at the building's glorious mosaics and windows. Gabriel quietly pointed out the Arabic-language inscriptions that openly mocked Christian belief and invited all Christians to convert to Islam, which Muslims considered the final and decisive revelation of the word of God.

"Do you read Arabic?" the mufti asked.

"*Nein*," Gabriel replied in German.

The tour complete, the pope and the mufti adjourned to the garden for tea. Alone with the most powerful religious figure in the world, the keeper of Islam's third-holiest shrine used the opportunity to expound upon his oft-stated theory that the Holocaust had never happened and that the Jews were secretly plotting to destroy the Dome of the Rock with the help of fundamentalist Christians from America. The pope listened in stoic silence, but in his public remarks afterward, he called the conversation "most enlightening." Then, after delivering his planned apology for the murderous excesses of the Crusades, he pointed out that the Israelis were the first conquerors in the history of Jerusalem to leave the status quo of the Holy Mountain unchanged. As a result, he declared, Islam had a special duty to not only care for the mosques that stood on the surface of the Noble Sanctuary, but to protect the sacred ruins that lay beneath it as well.

"All in all," the pope said, climbing into his limousine on Lions' Gate Street, "I think that went quite well."

"I'm not sure the mufti would agree," said Gabriel, smiling.

"He's lucky I didn't lose my temper. You should have heard the things he said to me."

"We hear it every day, Holiness."

"But I don't," the pope replied. "I can only imagine that God made me sit through that drivel for a reason."

Looking down at a copy of the Holy Father's itinerary, Gabriel couldn't help but wonder whether it was true.

The next stop was Yad Vashem.

Donati had set aside one hour for the visit, but ninety minutes elapsed before the pope finished his private tour of the newly designed Holocaust history exhibit. From there, he went to the Hall of Names, the somber repository of information about the dead, and then walked along the Avenue of the Righteous Among Nations and through the Valley of the Communities. In the Children's Memorial, a dark, haunting place of reflected candlelight, he became momentarily disoriented. "This way," said Gabriel softly. And when the pope emerged once more into the brilliant Jerusalem sunlight, his cheeks were streaming with tears. "Children," he said. "Why in God's name would they murder little children?"

"Do you need a minute to collect your thoughts?"

"No," said the pope. "It's time."

They made their way past the soaring Pillar of Heroism to the Hall of Remembrance. In the plaza outside, several hundred Israeli dignitaries and Holocaust survivors sat facing the simple podium where the pope would deliver the most important remarks of his trip. Owing to the somber location, the mood was funereal. No flags waved, and there was no applause as the pope entered the hall. Following him into the cool shadows, Gabriel felt a sense of peace for the first time since their arrival on Israeli soil. Here in this hallowed chamber of memory, the Holy Father was safe.

The flame of remembrance had been temporarily extinguished. With Donati's assistance, the pope reignited it and then knelt for several moments in silent, agonized prayer. Finally, he rose and made his way outside to the plaza where the crowd was now stirring in anticipation. As the pope approached the podium, Donati removed the black binder containing the prepared text and in its place left a single sheet of ruled white paper. On it were the handwritten notes the Holy Father had made during his final conversation with Gabriel in the Apostolic Palace. The pope was about to deliver one of the most important pronouncements of his papacy without a script.

He stood at the podium for a long moment as though Yad Vashem's unique combination of horror and beauty had rendered him incapable of speech. Having helped the Holy Father from the Children's Memorial, Gabriel knew it was genuine. But he also knew that His Holiness was about to begin his homily with a point about words versus deeds. His silence, therefore, had purpose.

"In this place of unbearable pain," he began at last, "mere words cannot possibly describe the depths of our sorrow or our shame. This beautiful garden of memory is more than just a ceremonial gravestone to the six million children of God and Abraham who perished in the fires of the Holocaust. It is a reminder that evil, true evil, is present in the world. It is a reminder, too, that as Christians we accept a portion of the responsibility for what occurred during the Holocaust, and we must beg forgiveness. A decade ago, in the Great Synagogue of Rome, we spoke of our complicity in the crime that Yad Vashem commemorates. And today, we reaffirm our sorrow, and once again we beg forgiveness. But now, in this time of escalating tension in the Middle East, our sorrow is mixed with fear. It is a fear that it could happen again."

The line sent a murmur through the crowd. Several of the reporters from the Vatican press corps were now staring bewildered at their copies of the speech. The pope sipped his water and waited for silence. Then he glanced briefly at Gabriel and Donati before resuming his homily.

"Since our appearance at the Great Synagogue of Rome, the Church has taken great steps toward eliminating anti-Jewish sentiment from our teaching and texts. We asked our Islamic brethren to undertake a similar soul-searching, but, sadly, this has not occurred. Across the Islamic world, Muslim holy men routinely preach that the Holocaust did not occur, while at the same time, radical jihadists promise to bring about another one. The contradiction is amusing to some, but not to me—not when a nation that has sworn to wipe Israel from the face of the earth is relentlessly developing the capability to do just that."

Again, the audience stirred in anticipation. Gabriel's eyes swept over the perplexed members of the Curial delegation before settling on the diminutive figure in white who was about to make history.

"There are some leaders who assure me that Israel can live with an Iran armed with a nuclear weapon," the pope continued. "But to someone who lived through the madness of the Second World War, they sound too much like those who said the Jews had nothing to fear from a Germany led by Hitler and the Nazis. Here in this sacred city of Jerusalem, we are reminded at every turn that great empires and great civilizations can vanish in the blink of an eye. Their antiquities fill our museums, but all too often, we fail to learn from their mistakes. We are tempted to think that we have reached the end of history, that it can never happen again. But history is made every day, sometimes by men of evil. And all too often, history repeats itself."

Several of the reporters were now whispering into mobile phones. Gabriel suspected they were informing their editors that His Holiness had just taken a newsworthy departure from what was supposed to be a routine speech of remembrance at Yad Vashem.

"And so," the pope resumed, "on this solemn occasion, in this sacred place, we do more than remember the six million who suffered and died in the Holocaust. We renew our bond with their descendants, and we assure them that we will do everything in our power to make certain it never happens again."

The pope paused one final time, as if signaling to the reporters that the most important line of his address was yet to come. When he spoke again, his voice was no longer tinged with sorrow, only resolve.

"To that end," he said, his arms spread wide, his amplified words echoing through the monuments of Yad Vashem, "we pledge to the people of Israel, our elder brothers, that this time, as you confront a challenge to your existence, the Roman Catholic Church will stand by you. We offer our prayers and, if you are willing to accept it, our counsel. We ask only that you proceed with the utmost caution, for your decisions will affect the entire world. The soil of this sacred city is filled with the remnants of empires that miscalculated. Jerusalem is the city of God. But it is also a gravestone to the folly of man."

With that, the audience erupted into a thunderous ovation. Gabriel and the rest of the security detail quickly went to the pope's side and escorted him to the waiting limousine. As the motorcade headed down the slope of Mount Herzl toward the Old City, the pope handed Gabriel the notes for the address.

"Add that to your collection."

"Thank you, Holiness."

"Still think I should have canceled the trip?"

"No, Holiness. But you can be sure the Iranians are putting a bounty on your head as we speak."

"I always knew they would," he said. "Just make sure no one manages to collect it before I leave Jerusalem."

40

JERUSALEM

ONATI AND THE HOLY FATHER were spending the night near the Jaffa Gate, at the residence of the Latin Patriarch. Gabriel saw them to the door, made a final check of security, then headed westward across Jerusalem through the late-afternoon shadows. Rounding the corner into Narkiss Street, he immediately saw the armored Peugeot limousine parked outside the apartment house at Number 16. Its owner was standing at the balustrade of the third-floor balcony, partially concealed by the drooping limbs of the eucalyptus tree, a sentinel on a night watch without end.

As Gabriel entered the apartment, he smelled the unmistakable aroma of eggplant with Moroccan spice, the specialty of Shamron's long-suffering wife, Gilah. She was standing in the kitchen next to Chiara, a flowered apron around her waist. Chiara wore a loose-fitting blouse with an embroidered neckline. Her hair hung about her shoulders, and her lips, when kissed, tasted of honey. She adjusted the knot of Gabriel's tie before kissing him again. Then she nodded toward the television and said, "It seems you and your friend have caused quite a stir."

Gabriel looked at the screen and saw himself, following a few feet behind the pope as he emerged from the Hall of Remembrance at Yad Vashem. A news analyst in London was talking about a wholesale realignment of the Vatican's policies toward the State of Israel. As Gabriel switched from news channel to news channel, it was more of the same. It seemed His Holiness Pope Paul VII had fundamentally altered the dynamic of the conflict in the Middle East, with the Vatican now squarely on the side of the Israelis in the conflict against Iran and radical Islam. And what made it all the more remarkable, the commentators agreed, was that the Vatican had managed to conceal the Holy Father's intentions prior to his departure from Rome.

Gabriel switched off the television and went into the bedroom to change. Then, after accepting two glasses of Shiraz from Chiara, he headed out onto the little terrace. Shamron was in the process of lighting a cigarette. Gabriel plucked it from his lips before sitting.

"You really have to stop, Ari."

"Why?"

"Because they're killing you."

"I'd rather die from smoking than by the hand of one of my enemies."

"There *are* other options, you know." Frowning, Gabriel crushed out the cigarette and handed Shamron a glass of wine. "Drink it, Ari. They say it's good for the heart."

"I put mine in storage when I joined the Office. And now that

I'm in possession of it again, it's giving me no end of grief." He drank some of the wine as a breath of wind moved in the eucalyptus tree. "Do you remember what I said to you when I gave you this flat?"

"You told me to fill it with children."

"You have a good memory."

"Not as good as yours."

"Mine isn't what it once was, which I suppose is fortuitous. I've done many things in my life I'd rather forget, most of them involving you." He looked at Gabriel seriously and asked, "Did it help at all?"

"What?"

"Vienna."

"I didn't do it for myself. I did it so someone else wouldn't have to bury a child or visit a loved one in a psychiatric hospital."

"You just answered my question in the affirmative," Shamron said. "I'm only sorry we had to send Massoud back to Tehran. He deserved to die an ignoble death."

"We did the next best thing by burning him."

"I only wish the flames could have been real instead of allegorical." Shamron drank some of his wine and asked Gabriel what it was like being on the Temple Mount.

"It's changed since my last visit."

"Did you feel close to God?"

"Too close."

Shamron smiled. "The visit didn't go exactly as planned, at least from the mufti's point of view. But from ours . . ." Shamron's voice trailed off. "The pope's words of support couldn't have come at a more opportune time. And we have you to thank for it."

"They were his words, Ari, not mine."

319

"But I'm not sure he would have spoken them if it wasn't for your friendship. I just hope he stands by us when the inevitable becomes a reality."

"You mean an attack on Iran?"

Shamron nodded.

"How much longer do we have?"

"Your friend Uzi will have to make that decision. But if I had to guess, it will be some time in the next year. In my opinion," Shamron added, "we've waited too long already."

"But even you're not sure whether an attack on their facilities will be successful."

"But I *am* certain of what will happen if we do nothing," Shamron said. "It's not a nuclear attack that I fear the most. It's that our enemies will use the protection of an Iranian nuclear umbrella to make our daily lives unlivable. Rockets from Gaza, rockets from Lebanon, entire sections of the country left uninhabitable. Then what? People get nervous. They slowly start to leave. And then the beautiful country that I helped to create and defend collapses."

"It's possible you're being too pessimistic."

"Actually," Shamron said, "I was giving you my best-case scenario."

"And the worst case?"

He turned his head a few degrees and gazed in the direction of the Old City. "It could all go up in a ball of fire, like the night Titus laid siege to the Second Temple."

The sound of Chiara's laughter filtered from the kitchen onto the terrace. It softened Shamron's dark mood.

"Have there been any developments on the child front?"

"The pope is praying for us."

"So am I," Shamron said. "I read an interesting article about

infertility not long ago. It said frequent travel can sometimes interfere with conception. It also said that the couple should remain at
home as often as possible, surrounded by family and loved ones."

"Have you no shame?"

"None whatsoever." Shamron smiled and placed a hand on Gabriel's arm. "Are you happy, my son?"

"I will be as soon as I put His Holiness back on his airplane."

"I assume you're planning to accompany him?"

Gabriel nodded. "I need to have a word with Carlo Marchese. I
also have to finish that Caravaggio."

"Never a dull moment."

"Actually, I'd kill for one."

"And when you're finished in Rome? What then?"

Gabriel smiled. "Drink your wine, Ari. They say it's good for
the heart."

As Shamron predicted, the pope's remarks during his visit to the
Temple Mount did not go over well in the Muslim world. On Al
Jazeera that evening, one commentator after another branded them
an affront that could not go unanswered. Watching the coverage
from his office, Imam Hassan Darwish found the outrage mildly
amusing. He knew that in just a few hours' time, the pope's words
would seem like a bit of loose talk by an old man in white. With his
eyes fixed on the screen, he reached for the phone and dialed. The
man he knew as Mr. Farouk answered instantly.

"Yes?"

"Deliver the Korans to the address I gave you."

"Allahu Akbar."

Darwish replaced the receiver and headed across the esplanade to the Dome of the Rock—not to the main hall of the shrine, but to the cave just beneath the Foundation Stone known as the Well of Souls. There he knelt on a musty prayer rug, listening to the wailing of the dead. Soon they would be free, he thought, because soon there would be no Well of Souls. In fact, if Allah allowed everything to go according to plan, there would be nothing at all.

41

THE OLD CITY, JERUSALEM

I T WAS GOOD FRIDAY, which meant Jerusalem, God's fractured citadel upon a hill, was in a state of near hysteria. In the predominantly Jewish districts of the New City, the morning proceeded with the usual last-minute preparations for the coming Shabbat. But in East Jerusalem, thousands of Muslims were making their way to the Haram al-Sharif for Friday prayers, while at the same time, a multitude of Catholics from around the world were preparing to commemorate the crucifixion of Christ with the man they believed to be his representative on earth. Not surprisingly, police and medical personnel reported an unusual surge in cases of Jerusalem Syndrome, the sudden religious psychosis brought on by exposure to the city's countless sacred sites. In one incident, a guest of the King David Hotel appeared in the lobby wearing only a bedsheet, proclaiming the end of days was near.

"Where is he now?" asked Donati.

"Resting comfortably under heavy sedation," replied Gabriel. "He's expected to make a full recovery."

"Is he one of ours or one of yours?"

"Yours, I'm afraid."

"Where's he from?"

"San Francisco."

"And he had to come all the way to Jerusalem to have a psychotic break?"

Smiling, Donati lit a cigarette. They were seated in the formal parlor of the Latin Patriarch's residence. On the table between them was a large-scale map of the Old City with the Via Dolorosa, the Way of Grief, marked in red. A narrow Roman road with steep, cobbled stairs in places, it ran two thousand feet across the Old City, from the former Antonia Fortress to the Church of the Holy Sepulchre, regarded by Christians as the place of Christ's crucifixion and burial. Like most Israelis, Gabriel avoided the street because of the aggressive Palestinian shopkeepers who tried to ensnare every passing soul, regardless of their faith. Usually, the shops remained open on Good Friday, but not today. Gabriel had ordered them all closed.

"I have to admit that this is the day that worries me the most," he said, staring at the map. "The pope has to walk along a very narrow street and stop at fourteen of the most famous places in religious history."

"I'm afraid there's nothing we can do about the route—or the story, for that matter. His Holiness *has* to walk the same route that Christ walked on the way to his crucifixion. And he insists on doing it with as much dignity as possible."

"Will he at least reconsider the Kevlar vest?"

"No."

"Why not?"

"Because Our Lord did not wear a bulletproof vest on the way to his death. And neither will my master."

"It's just a reenactment, Luigi."

"Not for him. When the Holy Father sets foot on the Via Dolorosa, he will be the embodiment of Jesus Christ in the eyes of his flock."

"With one important difference."

"What's that?"

"His Holiness is supposed to survive the day."

The pope came down from his rooms ten minutes later, his gleaming white soutane covered by a scarlet vestment, and climbed into the back of his limousine. It bore him around the northern edge of the Old City, past an endless throng of delirious Christian pilgrims, and eventually to the Lions' Gate. The Vaticanisti waited there, along with a large delegation of clergy and Catholic dignitaries who would follow in the pope's footsteps as he walked the stations of the cross. As Gabriel and Donati helped the Holy Father from the car, the crowd burst into rapturous applause. It was quickly drowned out, however, by the sound of the midday sermon blasting from the towering minaret of the al-Aqsa Mosque.

"What's he saying?" Donati asked.

"It wouldn't survive translation," Gabriel answered.

"That bad?"

"I'm afraid so."

The first station of the cross was located on a small flight of steps at the Umariya Elementary School, an Islamic *madrassa* where the notorious Palestinian terrorist Abu Nidal was once a student. It was on that spot, according to the Gospels and Christian tradition, where Pontius Pilate, prefect of what was then the Roman-ruled province of Judea, condemned Jesus to death by crucifixion. Now, almost two millennia later, His Holiness Pope Paul VII stood on the same spot, his eyes closed, and said, "We adore thee, O Christ, and we praise thee." Donati and the rest of the delegation surrounding the pope immediately genuflected and responded, "Because by thy holy cross thou hast redeemed the world." Gabriel looked at his watch. It was five minutes past noon. One down, thirteen to go.

The office of Imam Hassan Darwish had two windows. One looked south toward the Dome of the Rock and the al-Aqsa Mosque; the other faced west toward the Via Dolorosa and the domes of the Church of the Holy Sepulchre. Usually, Darwish kept the shades tightly drawn in the second window so he would not have to see what he regarded as a revolting temple of polytheism. But now, on the most tragic day on the Christian liturgical calendar, he stood there alone, watching the foolish little man in red and white leading a procession of apes and pigs along the street of sorrows. A moment later, when the pope entered the Church of the Flagellation, Darwish closed the blinds with a satisfying snap and walked over to the other window. The Dome of the Rock, the symbol of Islam's ascendancy over the city of God, filled the horizon. Darwish cast a glance at his wristwatch. Then he twirled his prayer beads nervously round his fingers and waited for the earth to move.

At King Saul Boulevard, Dina Sarid was keeping a tense vigil of a far different kind. The room where she worked had no windows and no view of anything except for its walls. At the moment, they were cluttered with the fragments of the operation that had just ended successfully in Vienna. It was all there, laid out from beginning to end, step by step, link by link—Claudia Andreatti to Carlo Marchese, Carlo Marchese to David Girard, David Girard to Massoud Rahimi, Massoud Rahimi to the four Hezbollah terrorists who died outside the Stadttempel synagogue. But was the Iranian-Hezbollah operation truly over? And had the historic Stadttempel synagogue in Vienna been its real target? After hours of frenzied research and analysis, Dina now feared the answer to both questions was a resounding no.

Her quest had begun shortly after seven the previous evening, when Unit 8200 had intercepted and decoded a priority transmission from VEVAK headquarters to all Iranian stations and bases worldwide. The message contained just three words: BLOOD NEVER SLEEPS. The words had meant nothing to the mathematicians and computer geniuses at the Unit, but Dina, a scholar of Islamic history, immediately recognized the Iranians had borrowed the phrase from none other than Saladin. Spoken to his favorite son, Zahir, they were meant as a warning against the use of unnecessary violence. "I warn you against shedding blood, indulging in it and making a habit of it," Saladin had said, "for blood never sleeps."

Like most fathers, however, Saladin did not always heed his own advice. After defeating the Crusaders in the Battle of Hattin near the shores of the Sea of Galilee, he offered two hundred of the defeated knights the chance to save themselves by converting to Islam—and when they refused, he looked on happily as mystics and scholars from his court put them clumsily to the sword. Upon entering Jerusalem three months later, he immediately ripped down the Christian cross that had been placed atop the Dome of the Rock and dragged it through the city. His first instinct was to lay waste to the Church of the Holy Sepulchre—he referred to it as "the Dungheap"—but in the end he allowed it to remain open so long as its bells remained silent. Indeed, until the nineteenth century, the tolling of church bells in Jerusalem was forbidden by Muslim edict. The creation of the State of Israel—and the capture of the Old City in the 1967 Six-Day War—upended the Islamic ascendancy in Jerusalem that Saladin's conquest had brought about. Yes, the Haram al-Sharif remained under the control of the Waqf. But it was fundamentally a walled fortress of Islam within a majority Jewish city.

Blood never sleeps. . . .

But why had the Iranians used the phrase in a coded transmission? And what did it mean? Was it a not-so-veiled threat against the pope? Perhaps, but Dina was troubled by something else. Why had the Jerusalem Islamic Waqf, keepers of the third-holiest shrine in Sunni Islam, retained a Shiite Muslim from southern Lebanon to serve as its adviser on issues related to the Temple Mount's archaeological past? It was possible the Waqf didn't know David Girard was actually Daoud Ghandour. It was also possible that Girard's connection to the Waqf was a coincidence—possible, thought Dina, but unlikely. Like all good Office analysts, she always assumed the worst. And the worst possible explanation for Girard's frequent visits to the Temple Mount was that he had been sent there by his Iranian control officer, Massoud, the lucky one.

He could go places I couldn't go and talk to people who couldn't come within a mile of me. . . . He was my own private Federal Express. . . .

It was this gnawing concern that compelled Dina to ask Unit 8200 to urgently subject all the electronic intelligence related to David Girard to steganographic analysis—steganography being the practice of hiding important coded messages inside a seemingly harmless vessel. Its use pre-dated even Saladin. The word "steganography" was Greek in origin, and the first uses of "concealed writing" dated to the fifth century BC, when Demartus, king of Sparta, hid his secret correspondence beneath a layer of beeswax. In the digital age, secret messages could be transmitted instantly over the Internet disguised as something entirely harmless. Casing photos for a terrorist attack could be hidden within pictures of girls in swimsuits; a message to an active terror cell inside a recipe for *boeuf bourguignon*. Decoding was a simple process that involved removing the proper number of bits from the color component of the cloaking image. Press a few buttons on a computer keyboard and the pretty girls became pictures of government buildings or subway platforms in New York City.

After 9/11, Israeli high-tech firms had been at the forefront of developing sophisticated software capable of quickly searching massive amounts of data for steganographic material. As a result, it took the Unit only a few hours to find two intriguing images that had been sent to the same Gmail address on the very same day. The first, hidden inside an apparently harmless photo of an Egyptian bronze cat, showed David Girard standing before a pair of ancient pillars in a darkened chamber, an imam at his side. The second image, hidden inside a snapshot of his wife, was a photograph of a trapezoid drawn freehand on a yellow legal pad. The trapezoid was empty except for a single small circle in the lower third. Next to the circle was a three-digit number: 689.

The trapezoid bore a vague resemblance to the outer boundaries of the Temple Mount plateau, which made the three-digit number all the more interesting; 689 was the year 'Abd al-Malik, the fifth Umayyad caliph, had begun construction of the Dome of the Rock. Dina ran through several possible scenarios involving the number, but none made any sense to her. Then she placed the two images side by side and posed a simple question. What if the number had nothing to do with history and everything to do with location—specifically, the altitude of the chamber where Girard was standing? The Temple Mount plateau stood 2,428 feet above sea level, or 740 meters. Six hundred eighty-nine meters would therefore be 51 meters, or 167 feet, *beneath* the Temple Mount.

Now, alone in the team's subterranean lair, she stared at the secret photograph of David Girard standing in his. And at the faces of the four Hezbollah terrorists who had been killed in Vienna. And at Massoud Rahimi riding a streetcar in Zurich. And at the text of the priority message that had gone out the previous evening to all Iranian intelligence stations and bases. Then, finally, she stared at the team's battered television, where a small man in white was making his way slowly down the Via Dolorosa toward the church that Saladin had referred to as "the Dungheap."

Blood never sleeps. . . .

And then she understood. She couldn't prove any of it, just as she couldn't prove that the man on the streetcar had been Massoud, but she *knew* it. And so she snatched up the receiver of her phone and dialed the extension for Uzi Navot's office. Orit, his unhelpful executive secretary, answered after the first ring. Inside King Saul Boulevard, she was known as "the Iron Dome" because of her unrivaled ability to shoot down requests for a moment with the chief.

"Not possible," she said. "He's completely swamped."

"It's urgent, Orit. I wouldn't be calling if it wasn't."

Navot's secretary knew better than to ask what it was about. "I can give you two minutes," she said.

"That's all I need."

"Get up here. I'll squeeze you in as soon as I can."

"Actually, I need him to come to me."

"You're pushing it, Dina."

"Tell him if he wants there to be an Israel next week, he'll drop everything and get down here right away."

Dina hung up the phone and stared at the television. The pope had just arrived at the sixth station of the cross, the spot where Veronica wiped the face of Jesus.

"We adore thee, O Christ, and we praise thee."

Blood never sleeps. . . .

42

TEL AVIV–JERUSALEM

ARE YOU JOKING, DINA?"

With her expression, she made clear she wasn't.

"Walk me through it," Navot said.

"There isn't time."

"Make time."

She pointed to a photo of the ruined Galleria Naxos in St. Moritz.

"What about it?"

"According to Massoud, David Girard knew that Gabriel was investigating the murder of Claudia Andreatti at the Vatican and that Gabriel had gotten too close to Carlo Marchese."

"Go on."

"Why was Girard still in Europe? Why didn't he pull up stakes and head back to Hezbollah Land?"

"Because they wanted to leave him there as bait for Gabriel."

"Correct. But *why*?"

"Because they wanted to kill him for blowing up their centri-fuges."

"It's possible, Uzi. But I don't think so. I think they wanted Ga-briel to come to St. Moritz for another reason."

"What's that?"

"*Taqiyya.*" Dina pointed to another photo—the Iranian assas-sin named Ali Montezari and the El Greco girl who served as his accomplice. "They gave the job to someone we would recognize. They *wanted* us to know they were behind it."

"Why?"

"Because they also wanted us to find this." She was point-ing to another photo—Massoud and Girard, side by side on a Zurich streetcar. "I checked the weather in Zurich on the day this picture was taken. The sun was shining, but it was bitterly cold."

"Why is the weather important?"

"Because Massoud isn't wearing gloves." She pointed to the bandage on the back of his right hand. "He wasn't wearing gloves because he wanted us to see it." She paused, then whispered, "He wanted *me* to see it."

"You're saying Massoud *wanted* us to know he was linked to David Girard and the bombing of the gallery?"

"Exactly."

"Why?"

"*Taqiyya,*" she said again.

Navot's expression had lost any trace of skepticism. "Keep go-ing."

"The Iranians dangled Massoud in front of us and left us no choice but to bite by bombarding us with chatter about a com-ing terrorist attack and putting Hezbollah's forces on the move in

southern Lebanon. It was a classic feint. And it had but one purpose. *Taqiyya*."

"Displaying one intention while harboring another."

Dina nodded.

"But the cell in Vienna was real."

"True. But it was never going to be allowed to carry out its assignment. Massoud always planned to reveal its existence to us in
dramatic fashion, leaving just enough time for us to act."

"You're saying the cell was *taqiyya*?"

She nodded. "It was like General Patton's ghost army during
the Second World War, the one the Allies put in East Anglia to
make the Germans think the invasion of France would come at
Calais instead of Normandy. The British and American deception
officers filled the airwaves with false signals because they knew
the Germans were listening. Even after the first troops landed on
the beaches, the German army was paralyzed by indecision because they believed the decisive battle of the war would be fought
at Calais."

"So under your scenario, Vienna was Calais."

"It's not my scenario. It's Massoud's."

"Prove it."

"I can't."

"Do the best you can, Dina."

She showed Navot the two steganographic images that had been
discovered by Unit 8200. Navot furrowed his brow.

"David Girard standing in a cave, and a map that looks as
though it was drawn by a five-year-old."

"But look what happens when you compare that crude map to
this."

Using her computer, Dina superimposed the image over a map
of the Temple Mount.

"Close," Navot said.

"Close enough." Dina quickly explained her theory about the significance of the number 689, that it represented the depth of the underground cavern where David Girard was standing in the photo.

"Are you certain he sent those images to Massoud?"

"No. But we have no choice but to assume that was the case."

"Why would he?"

"Because he's a classical archaeologist, not a geologist or an engineer. He needed someone with the right background to run the numbers for him."

"What numbers?"

"He needed to know how much high explosive he would need to bring down the Temple Mount."

Navot's face was now ashen. "Who's the other man in the photograph?"

"Imam Hassan Darwish," Dina said. "He oversaw the expansion of the Marwani Mosque. He's also regarded as the most radical member of the Waqf."

Dina held up the VEVAK message that had gone out the previous night.

Blood never sleeps. . . .

"Saladin?" asked Navot.

Dina nodded. "I think it's a signal to prepare for the violent uprising that would sweep the Islamic world the instant the Dome of the Rock and the al-Aqsa Mosque are destroyed. If anything happens to those buildings . . ." Her voice trailed off. "It's over, Uzi. It's lights out."

"Even the Iranians aren't *that* crazy," Navot said dismissively. "Why would the mullahs blow up two of Islam's most important shrines?"

"Because they're not *their* shrines," Dina answered. "The Noble Sanctuary is a Sunni sanctuary, and we all know how Sunnis and Shiites feel about each other. All the Iranians would need is one apocalyptic maniac inside the Waqf to help them."

"You think Darwish is their maniac?"

"Read his file."

Navot lapsed into a thoughtful silence. "You can't prove a word of it," he said at last.

"Are you willing to bet I'm wrong?"

He wasn't. "How long do we have?"

She looked at the television. "If I had to guess, the Temple Mount will come down at three o'clock while His Holiness is inside the Sepulchre."

"The hour that Christ died on the cross?"

"Precisely."

Navot looked at his watch. "That leaves us ninety minutes."

"Tell Orit to put me through next time I call."

Navot ran a hand anxiously over his cropped gray hair. "Do you know how many people are atop the Temple Mount right now."

"Ten thousand. Maybe more."

"And do you know what will happen if we go up there and start looking for a bomb? We'll start the third intifada."

"But we don't have to *look* for the bomb, Uzi. We already know where it is."

"One hundred and sixty-seven feet beneath the surface, somewhere between the Dome of the Rock and the al-Aqsa Mosque?"

Dina nodded.

"Is Eli Lavon still working in the Western Wall Tunnel?"

"He hasn't left since we got back to town."

"Do phones work down there?"

"Sometimes."

Navot exhaled heavily. "I can't send Eli into the Temple Mount without the prime minister's authority."

"Then perhaps you should call him," Dina said. "And you might want to think about getting Eli some help."

Navot looked at the television screen and saw Gabriel walking a step behind the pope along the Via Dolorosa. Then he reached for the phone.

Gabriel felt his mobile phone vibrate as the pope arrived at the eighth station of the cross, the spot where Christ paused to comfort the women of Jerusalem. He checked the number on the caller ID screen, then quickly raised the phone to his ear.

"We might have a problem," Navot said.

"The pope?"

"No."

"Where, Uzi?"

"The one place in Jerusalem we can't afford one."

"What are you talking about?"

"Start walking toward the Western Wall Tunnel. Dina will tell you the rest on the way."

43

THE OLD CITY, JERUSALEM

GABRIEL DID NOT WALK FOR LONG. In fact, by the time he reached the Church of the Redeemer, he was running as fast as his legs would carry him. In the narrow alleys of the Christian Quarter, pilgrims blocked his way at every turn, but once he crossed into the Jewish Quarter, the crowds thinned. He wound his way eastward—up and down stone steps, beneath archways, and across quiet squares—until he arrived at one of the portals to the Western Wall. Because it was a Friday, the plaza was more crowded than usual. Several hundred people, men and women, were praying directly against the Wall, and Gabriel reckoned there were at least a hundred more inside the synagogues of Wilson's Arch. Pausing, he tried to imagine what would happen if even one of the giant Herodian ashlars broke loose. Then he walked over to the highest-ranking police officer he could find.

"I want you to close the Wall and plaza."

"Who the hell are you?" the police officer asked.

Gabriel raised his wraparound sunglasses. The officer almost snapped to attention.

"I can't close it down without a direct order from my chief," he said nervously.

"As of this moment, I am your chief."

"Yes, sir."

"Close the plaza and Wilson's Arch. And do it as quietly as possible."

"If I tell those *haredim* they have to leave, it won't be quiet."

"Just get them out of here."

Gabriel turned without another word and headed toward the entrance of the Western Wall Tunnel. The same Orthodox woman was there to greet him.

"Is he down there?" Gabriel asked.

"Same place," the woman said, nodding.

"How many other people are in the tunnel?"

"Sixty tourists and about twenty staff."

"Get everyone out."

"But—"

"Now."

Gabriel paused briefly to download an e-mail from Dina onto his BlackBerry. Then he followed the path downward into the earth and backward through time, until he was standing at the edge of Eli Lavon's excavation pit. Lavon was crouched over the bones of Rivka in a pool of blinding white light. Hearing Gabriel, he looked up and smiled.

"Nice suit. Why aren't you with His Holiness?"

Gabriel dropped the BlackBerry into the void. Lavon snatched it deftly out of the air and stared at the screen.

"What's this?"

"Get out of that hole, Eli, and I'll tell you everything."

A mile to the west, at the apartment in Narkiss Street, Chiara was watching live coverage of the Good Friday procession on Israeli television. A few moments earlier, as the pope was leading the delegation in prayer at the eighth station of the cross, she had noticed Gabriel holding a mobile phone to his ear. Now, as the Holy Father made his way solemnly from the eighth station to the ninth, Gabriel was no longer at his side. Chiara stared at the screen a few seconds longer before snatching up the phone and dialing Uzi Navot's office at King Saul Boulevard. Orit answered.

"He was just about to call you, Chiara."

"What's happening?"

"He's on his way to Jerusalem. Hold on."

Chiara felt her stomach churning as Orit put her on hold. Navot came on the line a few seconds later.

"Where is he, Uzi?"

"It's complicated."

"Damn it, Uzi! Where is he?"

Though Navot did not know it, Gabriel was at that moment perched at the edge of the excavation pit with Eli Lavon at his side. Beneath them glowed the chalky white bones of Rivka, witness to the Roman siege of Jerusalem and the destruction of Herod's Second Temple. For now, Lavon was oblivious to her; he had eyes only for the tiny image on the screen of Gabriel's BlackBerry. It showed David Girard, aka Daoud Ghandour, standing in an underground chamber of some sort at the side of Imam Hassan Darwish, the Muslim cleric from the Supreme Council of the Jerusalem Waqf.

"Are those pillars in the background?"

"The pillars aren't the concern right now, Professor."

"Sorry."

Lavon inspected the second image—the trapezoid with the mark and the number 689 in the lower third.

"It would make sense," he said after a moment.

"What's that?"

"That the chamber where they're standing is located in that portion of the Mount. The ground beneath the Dome of the Rock and the entrance to the al-Aqsa Mosque is riddled with conduits, shafts, and cisterns."

"How do we know that?"

"Because Charles Warren told us so."

Sir Charles Warren was the brilliant officer from the British Royal Engineers who conducted the first and only survey of the Temple Mount between 1867 and 1870. His meticulously detailed maps and drawings remained the standard resource for modern archaeologists.

"Warren found thirty-seven underground structures and cisterns beneath the Temple Mount," Lavon explained, "not to mention numerous aqueducts and passageways. The largest ones were located around the spot indicated on this map. In fact, there's an enormous cistern in that area called the Great Sea that was carved from the limestone bedrock. It was illustrated contemporaneously by an artist named William Simpson." Lavon looked up. "It's possible David Girard and the imam are standing right there."

"Can we get to it?"

"Simpson's illustration clearly shows the presence of at least three large aqueducts leading to other cisterns and structures within the complex. But it's also possible the Waqf has dug new tunnels and passageways under the guise of their construction projects."

"Is that a *yes* or a *no*, Eli?"

"You're asking me questions I can't possibly answer," Lavon replied. "The truth is, we have no idea what's *really* under the Mount because we're forbidden to set foot there."

"Not anymore."

"Do you know what will happen if the Waqf finds us up there?"

"Actually, I'm more concerned about what will happen if a bomb goes off in an underground cavern between the Dome of the Rock and the al-Aqsa Mosque."

"Point taken."

"What *would* happen, Eli?"

"I suppose that depends on the size of the bomb. If it were the size of the average suicide vest, the Holy Mountain wouldn't feel a thing. But if it were something big . . ."

"Massoud destroyed the Marine barracks in Beirut with the biggest non-nuclear explosion the world had seen in a generation. He knows how to make things fall down."

Lavon rose to his feet and walked over to the giant ashlars of the Western Wall. The tourists had been evacuated; the tiny synagogue known as the Cave was empty. They were entirely alone.

"I always hoped I would have a chance to see what was on the other side," he said, his eyes searching the stone. "But I never imagined it would come about because of something like this."

"Surely you've found something more down here than some old bones, Professor."

"Surely," Lavon replied distantly.

"Can you get us in there, Eli?"

"Inside the Temple Mount?" Lavon smiled. "Right this way."

They headed past the Cave and then took a flight of steps down to an ancient stone archway sealed with gray brick and mortar. Next to it an illuminated modern sign read WARREN'S GATE.

"It's named for Charles Warren, of course," Lavon explained. "During the time of the Second Temple, it led from the street where we're standing now into an underground passageway. That passageway led to a flight of steps. And the steps—"

"Led to the Temple."

Lavon nodded. "In 1981, the chief rabbi of the Western Wall foolishly ordered workmen to reopen the gate, but as soon as they started digging, the sound of the hammers carried through the passages and into the cisterns up on the Mount. The Arabs could hear it very clearly. They immediately stormed into the tunnels, and a small battle broke out. The Israeli police had to come onto the Mount to restore order. After that, Warren's Gate was sealed, and it remains sealed today."

"But obviously, it's not the *only* underground passage onto the Mount."

"No," Lavon answered, shaking his head. "There's at least one other tunnel that we know of. We found it a couple of years ago. It's about fifty yards that way," he said, pointing northward along the wall. "And it's identical in design to Warren's Gate."

"Why was it never made public?"

"Because we didn't want to start another riot. A handful of Israeli archaeologists were allowed to spend a few minutes inside before it was sealed."

"Were you one of them?"

"I would have been, but I had a previous engagement."

"Where?"

"Moscow."

"Ivan?"

Lavon nodded.

"How thick is the seal on the new tunnel?"

"Not like this one," Lavon said, patting the coarse brickwork. "Even an archaeologist with a fickle stomach could get through it without a problem. For a tough guy like you, it won't take more than a couple swings of a hammer."

"What about the noise?"

"The sermon should cover it," said Lavon. "But there is another problem."

"What's that?"

"If that bomb goes off while we're inside the Temple Mount, we're going to end up like Rivka."

"There are worse places to be buried, Eli."

"I thought you said this place was nothing but a pile of stones."

"I did," said Gabriel. "But they're my stones."

Lavon lapsed into silence.

"What are you thinking about?"

"The pillars."

"Get me a hammer and a flashlight, Eli, and I'll take you to see the pillars."

44

JERUSALEM

T HE DRIVE FROM KING SAUL BOULEVARD to the Prime Minister's Office in Jerusalem usually took a half-hour, but on that afternoon, Uzi Navot's motorcade accomplished it in just twenty-two minutes door to door. By the time Navot entered the building, Gabriel's radio had been switched off the papal protection network onto a secure band reserved for Office security personnel. As a result, Navot was able to listen as Gabriel and Eli Lavon raided a storage room in the Western Wall Tunnel for the supplies they would need to break into the Temple Mount.

The prime minister was waiting in the cabinet room, along with the defense minister, the foreign minister, and Navot's counterpart from Shabak. Live CCTV images of the Old City flickered on the video display wall. In one, the Vicar of Christ was approaching the Church of the Holy Sepulchre. In another, several thousand Muslims were gathered atop the Haram al-Sharif. And in a third, a dozen Israeli police officers stood watch in the now-empty Western Wall Plaza. It was, thought Navot, the Good Friday from hell.

"Well?" asked the prime minister as Navot settled into his usual seat.

"They're just waiting for your order."

"A single analyst says there's a bomb in the Temple Mount that could bring down the entire plateau, and you say I have no choice but to believe her."

"Yes, Prime Minister."

"Do you know what's going to happen if the Palestinians find out that Gabriel and Eli are in there?"

"Someone's liable to get hurt," Navot said. "And then the Arab Spring comes to Jerusalem."

The prime minister stared at the video screens for a moment before nodding his head once. Navot quickly passed the order along to Gabriel. A few seconds later, he heard the sound of four sharp blows.

Alef, Bet, Gimel, Dalet . . .

Then it was done.

From the storage room, Gabriel and Lavon had taken a sledgehammer, a pickax, two coils of nylon rope, two hard hats with halogen lamps, and whatever small hand tools they could find to disarm the bomb. Before putting on his hard hat, Lavon had first covered his head with a *kippah*. Gabriel had removed his suit jacket, necktie, and shoulder holster. The SIG Sauer 9mm that Alois Metzler had given him was now tucked into the waistband of his trousers at the small of his back. He left the microphone of the miniature radio open so Navot could hear his every breath and footfall.

After breaking through the cement seal, they entered an arched passageway that bore them through the base of the western retaining wall and into the Mount itself. The paving stones of the ancient street were as smooth as glass. Three times a year—on Pesach, Shavuot, and Sukkot—Jews from the ancient kingdoms of Israel had walked over these stones on their way to the Temple. Even Gabriel, who had more on his mind than history, could almost feel the presence of his ancestors, but Eli Lavon was plunging headlong through the gloom, breathless with excitement.

"Look at the dressings on these stones," he said, running his hand along the cold wall of the passage. "There's no way these are anything but Herodian."

"We don't have time to look at stones," Gabriel said, prodding Lavon along the passage with the handle of the pickax.

"There's a very good chance that you and I are going to be the last Jews to ever set foot here."

"If that bomb goes off, we definitely will be."

Lavon quickened his pace.

"Where are we exactly?" asked Gabriel.

"If we were on the surface, we'd be passing through the Gate of Darkness heading directly toward the eastern façade of the Dome of the Rock." Lavon paused and then turned his headlamp toward a pair of columns in the stonework. "Those are Doric," he said. "They're Herodian, no question about it."

"Keep walking, Eli," Gabriel said with another nudge of the pickax.

Lavon obeyed. "At the end of this passage," he said, "there's a cistern that was discovered by Charles Wilson, the other great British explorer of ancient Jerusalem."

"As in Wilson's Arch."

Lavon's headlamp bobbed in the affirmative. "According to Wilson, the cistern is ninety-three and a half feet long, eighteen feet wide, and thirty-five feet deep. After that, we should see a series of steps."

"And if the steps are there?"

"They'll take us up closer to the surface. From there, we should be able to find our way into the network of cisterns and aqueducts. We know it's all connected because of the Warren's Gate incident in 1981. We just have to find the right connections."

"Before the bomb explodes," Gabriel added darkly.

They walked a few more paces. Then Lavon froze.

"What's wrong?"

Lavon stepped aside to reveal a coarse gray wall blocking the end of the passageway.

"Something tells me that isn't Herodian."

"No," said Lavon. "In my expert opinion, it's Palestinian, circa two thousand and ten."

"How thick is it?" the prime minister asked.

"They won't know until they start hammering," Navot said. "And if they start hammering . . ."

"The Palestinians will be able to hear them on the Mount."

Navot nodded.

It took the prime minister only a few seconds to arrive at his decision. "Tell them to break down that seal. But if they don't find that bomb by two-thirty, I'm going to order the arrest of Imam Hassan Darwish and go in heavy from the top."

"Israeli troops and police on the Temple Mount?"

The prime minister nodded resolutely.

"If you do that," Navot said, "you'll start the third intifada while the eyes of the world are on us because of the pope."

"I realize that, Uzi, but it's better than the alternative."

Navot ordered Gabriel to start hammering.

Alef, Bet, Gimel, Dalet . . .

And they'd barely made a dent.

At that same moment, Imam Hassan Darwish was standing atop the western retaining wall of the Temple Mount, staring down at the empty plaza below. Security alerts were common in Jerusalem, but the Israelis blocked access to the holiest site in Judaism only when they believed an attack was imminent. It was possible the closure was the result of an unrelated threat, but Darwish suspected otherwise. Somewhere, somehow, the plot had been compromised.

Turning, Darwish headed across the esplanade toward the Dome of the Rock. As usual, only females and old men had been allowed into the Haram for Friday prayers; Darwish bade good afternoon to a few of them with the customary greeting of peace before descending into the Well of Souls. There he passed through a locked door and followed an ancient flight of steps downward into the heart of the Holy Mountain. A moment later, he was standing in one of the largest cisterns on the Temple Mount, listening to the sound of distant tapping.

It could mean only one thing.

The Jews were coming.

For five minutes, they beat against the wall without a break, Lavon with the sledgehammer, Gabriel with the pickax. Gabriel broke through first, opening an aperture in the brickwork about the size of a fist. He removed the lamp from his hard hat and shone the beam into the void.

"What do you see?" asked Lavon.

"A cistern."

"How big?"

"Hard to say, but it looks to be about ninety-three and a half feet long and about eighteen feet wide."

"Anything else?"

"Steps, Eli. I can see the steps."

The head of security for the Jerusalem Islamic Waqf was a forty-five-year-old veteran of both Fatah and the al-Aqsa Martyrs Brigade named Abdullah Ramadan. Imam Darwish called him on his mobile and told him to come to the cistern beneath the Dome of the Rock. He didn't have to explain the meaning of the tapping sound.

"Warren's Gate?"

"It could be," Darwish answered. "Or it could be one of the new ones they've found during their illegal excavations."

"What do you want me to do about it?"

"Take three of your best men down there and find out if they're trying to gain access to the Haram."

"And if they are?"

"Punish them," said the imam.

The prime minister stared at the clock on the wall of the cabinet room. It was ten minutes past two. He looked at Navot and asked, "How big is that damn hole?"

Navot posed the question to Gabriel and then relayed his answer to the prime minister and the rest of the room.

"Not big enough."

"How much longer is it going to take?"

Again Navot relayed the question.

"They're not sure."

"Tell them they have to work faster."

"They're working as fast as they can, Prime Minister."

"*Tell* them, Uzi."

Navot passed along the prime ministerial order to pick up the pace. Then, after hearing Gabriel's response, he smiled.

"What did he say?" the prime minister asked.

"He said he's working as fast as he can, Prime Minister."

"Are you telling me the truth, Uzi?"

"No, Prime Minister."

The prime minister smiled in spite of himself and looked at the clock.

It was 2:12.

By 2:15, the hole was about a foot in diameter, and by 2:20 it was large enough to accommodate the shoulders and hips of a slender man. Gabriel shimmied through first, scraping the skin from his arms in the process, followed a few seconds later by Lavon. After returning the *kippah* and hard hat to his head, he stood stock-still for a moment, speechless with awe. Before them was the cistern, and beyond it, rising into the darkness, was the first flight of Herodian stairs.

"There's only one reason for this cistern to be here," Lavon said, dipping his hand in the water of the long, rectangular pool. "It was a *mikvah*. They would have cleansed themselves ritually before heading up to the Temple."

"This is all very interesting, Professor, but we need to keep moving."

"At least let me take a few pictures."

"We'll stop on the way out."

Lavon skirted the edge of the pool and raced up the first flight of ancient steps, the beam of his light bouncing over the walls and ceiling of the arched passage. At the top, he froze again. "Look at this!" he said, pointing to a few lines of ancient Hebrew chiseled into the wall. "It says that gentiles are forbidden to enter the courts of the Temple. Why would there be a sign like this if there wasn't a Temple to begin with?"

It was a logical question, but at that instant, Gabriel's thoughts were elsewhere. He was wondering why four large Arab men with flashlights were coming toward them down the next flight of steps. Then the first bullet came scorching past his ear, and he had his answer. It seemed the neighbors had heard the pounding. It was hardly surprising, thought Gabriel. Blood never sleeps.

45

JERUSALEM

I T LASTED JUST FORTY-FOUR SECONDS, but later, Uzi Navot would swear it seemed like an hour or more. From his limited vantage point, it sounded as though Gabriel and Eli Lavon were under attack from an Arab legion. What struck Navot most, however, was the sound of Gabriel's breathing. Not once did it break its normal rhythm. Nor did he speak except to twice tell Lavon to keep his head down.

The recordings would indicate that Gabriel did not begin to return fire until almost twenty seconds into the engagement. After his first shot, there was an agonized wail that seemed to rise from the very depths of the Well of Souls. Five seconds later, Gabriel fired a second shot, after which the intensity of the opposing gunfire decreased sharply. His third and fourth shots were fired with double-tap quickness, and once again there was a scream of pain from somewhere in the passage. Two more shots followed in rapid succession. Then the gunfire ended, and there was only the sound of an Arab man pleading for mercy.

"Who sent you down here?" Navot heard Gabriel ask calmly.

"Go to hell!" a voice shouted back in Arabic.

Navot heard another shot, followed by a scream.

"Who sent you?" Gabriel repeated.

"The imam," the Arab replied through gritted teeth.

"Which imam?"

"Darwish."

"Hassan Darwish?"

"Yes . . . it was . . . Hassan."

"Where's the bomb?"

"What bomb?"

"Where is it, damn it?"

"I don't know anything . . . about a bomb!"

"Are you telling me the truth?"

"Yes!"

"Are you?"

"Yes! I swear."

Navot heard one more shot. Then there was nothing but the sound of Gabriel's steady breathing.

"Are we still in business?" asked the prime minister.

"For the moment," replied Navot.

"I suppose that answers the question about whether there's really a bomb somewhere up there."

"Yes, Prime Minister, I suppose it does. But we now have another problem."

"What's that?"

"Gabriel Allon is inside the Temple Mount with only Eli Lavon for protection."

"Do you know what's going to happen if they get their hands on them?"

"Yes, Prime Minister," Navot said, staring at the CCTV images of the crowds pouring out of the al-Aqsa Mosque. "They're going to tear them both to pieces."

"Should we order them out?"

"I'm afraid it's too late."

They had just entered the first aqueduct. It was 2:23.

It was no wider than a phone booth and scarcely tall enough for them to walk fully upright. Here and there, rivulets of water wept from tiny seams in the walls, but otherwise the bedrock was as dry as the bones of Rivka. Lavon navigated by compass. Softly, he counted their steps.

The channel wound its way through the limestone in a serpentine pattern, which meant they had only a vague idea of what lay ahead. Despite the fact they were now only a few feet beneath the surface of the Mount, they could hear no sound other than their own footfalls and Lavon's steady counting. At two hundred paces exactly, they reached the next cistern. Lavon paused and looked around in wonder. Then he raised a forefinger to his lips to tell Gabriel to keep his voice down.

"Do you recognize it?" Gabriel whispered.

Lavon nodded his head vigorously. "The T shape is consistent with a cistern that Warren found here," he answered, his voice a hoarse whisper. "It was probably dug during the time of Herod. The stone quarried from this spot might very well have been used for the Temple itself."

"Where are we on the Mount?"

"Just outside the entrance to al-Aqsa." He pointed down the length of the horizontal portion of the T. "There should be another small T-shaped cistern right over there. And then—"

"The Great Sea?"

Lavon nodded his head and then led Gabriel across the upper portion of the ancient cistern. At the opposite side was the mouth of another aqueduct, narrower than the last. As he expected, it bore them into the next cistern. This time, they made their way to the foot of the T and entered the next aqueduct. After a few paces, the vast cathedral-like chasm of the Great Sea opened before them.

And it was entirely empty.

"Well?" asked the prime minister.

Navot shook his head.

"What are they going to do now?"

"They're working on it."

At the roof of the chamber was an opening, like the oculus at the top of the Pantheon in Rome. Through it streamed a shaft of brilliant sunlight and the sound of the amplified sermon blasting from the minaret of the al-Aqsa Mosque.

"How far below the surface are we?" asked Gabriel in a whisper.

"Forty-three feet."

"Or thirteen meters," Gabriel pointed out.

"Thirteen point *ten* meters," Lavon corrected him.

"If Dina is right," Gabriel said, "the bomb would be in a chamber more than a hundred feet beneath us."

"Which would make sense," Lavon said.

"Why?"

"Because if I were going to take down the Temple Mount pla-teau, I'd want to place the charge lower than this."

"Is there a way down from here?"

"No one's ever been below this—at least no one we know about." He turned and studied the distant wall of the cavern. There were three more aqueducts, each leading in a slightly differ-ent direction. "Pick one," he said.

"I'm an art restorer, Eli. You pick."

Lavon closed his eyes for a few seconds and then pointed to the aqueduct on the right.

At that same moment, Imam Hassan Darwish was less than one hundred feet away, in the cistern beneath the Well of Souls. In his hand was the Makarov pistol that Abdullah Ramadan had given to him before heading into the depths of the Noble Sanctuary to con-front the invading Jews. The sound of the brief but intense battle had carried through the aqueducts, directly to Darwish's ears. He had heard everything, including the sound of his own name being shouted in agony. Now he could hear the soft, muffled footfalls of at least two men approaching the chamber that Darwish had secretly carved from the Holy Mountain. It was there he had hid-den the bomb that would destroy it and thus destroy the State of Israel. But there was something else inside the chamber other than explosives—a secret that no one, especially the Jews, could be al-lowed to see.

He looked at his watch: 2:27. At Darwish's instructions, the man known as Mr. Farouk had set the timing device on the weapon to go off at three o'clock. He had chosen the time, the supposed hour of Christ's death on the cross, as a calculated insult to the whole of Christianity, but it was not the only reason. By three o'clock, the

Friday prayer services in al-Aqsa would be over, and the crowds of Muslim faithful would be departing the Noble Sanctuary. But for the moment, the three hundred and eighty thousand square feet of the great mosque were filled to capacity with more than five thousand people. Darwish had no choice but to turn them all into holy martyrs. And himself as well.

He remained in the cistern beneath the Well of Souls for a moment longer, reciting the final prayers of the *shahid*. Then, with the Makarov pistol in one hand and a flashlight in the other, he set out along a narrow, ancient passage. It bore him downward into the earth and backward through time. It was the time before Islam and the Prophet. The time of ignorance, he thought. The time of the Jews.

The first aqueduct terminated after about fifty feet in a small fishbowl of a cistern, so they quickly retraced their steps to the Great Sea and entered the second channel. After just a few steps, Lavon came upon an aperture in the right side that led to still another passage. The ground was littered with fragments of loose limestone. Lavon inspected them in the glow of his headlamp and then ran his hand over the edges of the opening.

"This is new."

"How new?"

"*New* new," Lavon said. "It looks as though it was cut quite recently."

Without another word, he set off down the conduit, Gabriel at his heels. After a few paces, there appeared a flight of wide, curving steps that were obviously carved by modern stone-cutting tools. Lavon plunged downward in a rage, with Gabriel a few steps behind, struggling to keep pace. At the bottom of the steps was an archway with a few characters of Arabic script carved into the stone above the apex. They shot past it without a glance. Then, awestruck, they came suddenly to a stop.

"What the hell is that?" asked Gabriel.

Lavon seemed incapable of speech.

"Eli, what is it?"

Lavon took a few tentative steps forward. "Don't you recognize them, Gabriel?"

"Recognize *what*, Eli?"

"The pillars," he said. "The pillars that were in the photograph."

"And where are the pillars from?"

Lavon smiled, breathless. "'The House which King Solomon built for the Lord was sixty cubits long, twenty cubits wide, and thirty cubits high.'"

"What is it, Uzi?" the prime minister asked.

"You wouldn't believe me if I told you."

"Try me."

"Eli thinks he just found remnants of the First Temple. And by the way," Navot added, "they also found the bomb."

The prime minister looked up at the video monitor and saw thousands of Muslims streaming out of the al-Aqsa Mosque. Then he looked at the men seated around him and gave the order to send in the police and the IDF.

"It's better than the alternative," Navot said, watching as the first Israeli forces entered the Noble Sanctuary.

"We'll see about that."

46

THE TEMPLE MOUNT, JERUSALEM

T HE CAVERN WAS THE SIZE of a school gymnasium. Tilting his headlamp skyward, Gabriel noticed the crude light fixtures hanging from the roof and the power line that snaked down one wall to an industrial-grade switch. Throwing it, he flooded the vast space with a heavenly white light.

"My God," gasped Eli Lavon. "Don't you see what they've done?"

Yes, thought Gabriel, running his hand over the glassy smooth surface of the freshly hewn wall. He could indeed see what they had done. They had carved a massive hole in the heart of God's mountain and turned it into a private museum filled with all the archaeological artifacts that had been unearthed during the years of reckless construction and secret excavations—the building stones, capitals, columns, arrowheads, helmets, shards of pottery, and coins. And now, for motives even Gabriel could scarcely comprehend, Imam Hassan Darwish intended to blow it all to bits—and the Temple Mount along with it.

For the moment, though, Eli Lavon seemed to have all but forgotten about the bomb. Entranced, he was making his way slowly through the artifacts toward the two parallel rows of broken pillars that formed the centerpiece of the exhibit. Pausing, he consulted his compass.

"They're oriented east to west," he said.

"Just like the Temple?"

"Yes," he said. "Just like the Temple."

He walked to the eastern end of the pillars, touched one reverently, and then walked a few steps farther. "The altar would have been here," he said, gesturing with his small hand toward an empty space at the edge of the cavern. "Next to the altar would have been the *yam*, the large bronze basin where the priests would wash before and after a sacrifice. Kings Seven describes it in great detail. It was said to be ten cubits across from brim to brim and five cubits high. It stood upon twelve oxen."

" 'Three facing north,' " said Gabriel, quoting the passage, " 'three facing west, three facing south, and three facing east, with the tank resting upon them.' "

" 'Their haunches were all turned inward,' " said Lavon, completing the verse. "There were ten other smaller basins where the sacrifices were washed, but the *yam* was reserved for the priests. The Babylonians melted it down when they burned the First Temple. The same was true of the two great bronze columns that stood at the entrance of the *ulam*, the porch."

" 'One to its right and one to its left,' " said Gabriel.

" 'The one to its right was called Jachin.' "

" 'And the one to the left, Boaz.' "

Gabriel heard a crackle in his earpiece followed by the voice of Uzi Navot.

"We're trying to get to you as quickly as possible," Navot said. "The police and IDF have entered the Temple Mount compound through the eastern gates. They're meeting resistance from the Waqf security forces and the Arabs coming out of al-Aqsa. It's getting pretty ugly right above your head."

"It's going to get a lot uglier if this bomb explodes."

"The bomb disposal teams are coming in the second wave."

"How much longer, Uzi?"

"A few minutes."

"Find Darwish."

"We're already looking for him."

As Navot fell silent, Gabriel looked at Lavon. He was staring toward the roof of the cavern.

"Jachin and Boaz were each crowned with a capital that was decorated with lilies and pomegranates," he said. "There's a debate among scholars as to whether they were freestanding or whether they supported a lintel and a roof. I've always subscribed to the second theory. After all, why would Solomon put a porch on the house of God and leave it uncovered?"

"You need to get out of here, Eli. I'll stay with the bomb until the sappers arrive."

Lavon acted as though he hadn't heard. He took two solemn steps forward, as though he were entering the Temple itself.

"The door that led from the *ulam* into the *heikhal*, the main hall of the Temple, was made from the wood of fir trees, but the doorposts were olive wood. They burned when Nebuchadnezzar put the First Temple to the torch." Lavon paused and placed a hand gently atop the ruins of one of the pillars. "But he couldn't burn these."

Gabriel walked past a trestle table heaped with coins and ancient tools and slipped between two of the pillars. He touched one and asked Lavon what had happened to them after Nebuchadnezzar destroyed the Temple.

"The Scriptures are unclear, but we always assumed the Babylonians hurled them over the walls of the Temple Mount and into the Kidron Valley." He looked at Gabriel with a rueful smile. "Sound familiar?"

"Very," said Gabriel.

Lavon moved to the next pillar. It was about eight feet in height, and one side was blackened by fire. " 'They made Your sanctuary go up in flames,' " he intoned, quoting Psalms 74, " 'they brought low in dishonor the dwelling-place of Your presence.' "

"You need to be leaving, Eli."

"Where am I going to go? Upstairs to the riot?"

"Make your way through the aqueducts back to the Western Wall Tunnel."

"And what am I supposed to do if I run into another group of Saladin's warriors? Fight them off with my pickax like a Crusader?"

"Take my gun."

"I wouldn't know what to do with it."

"You were in the army, Eli."

"I was a medic."

"*Eli,*" said Gabriel in exasperation, but Lavon was no longer listening. He was moving slowly from pillar to pillar, his expression a mixture of astonishment and anger. "They must have hauled them out of the valley in 538 BC, when the Persian Empire authorized the construction of the Second Temple. And when Herod renovated the place five centuries later, he probably used them as part of the supporting structure, which would explain why the Waqf found them when they were digging around up here. They were too big to take to the dump or throw into the Kidron Valley again, so they hid them here, along with everything else they ripped from the mountain." He looked around the vast cavern. "Even if we are able to get this material out of here, it has no proper context anymore. It's as if it was . . ."

"Looted," said Gabriel.

"Yes. Looted."

"We'll get it out, Eli, but you really should go now."

"I'm not leaving these things here alone," Lavon answered. He was drifting from pillar to pillar, his face tilted skyward. "The contemporary models and drawings of the First Temple oftentimes put a roof over the *heikhal*, but there wasn't one. It was an open courtyard with two-story chambers on three sides. And at the far western end of the structure was the *debir*, the Holy of Holies, where they kept the Ark of the Covenant."

Lavon approached the spot slowly because it was there that Imam Darwish had chosen to place the bomb. It was no ordinary bomb, thought Gabriel. It was a Western Wall of explosives, wired and primed and waiting to detonate. Were it something small, Gabriel might have been able to disarm it with a sapper whispering in his ear. But not this.

"How do you suppose they were able to do it?"

"I'm sure Imam Darwish will be happy to tell us."

Lavon shook his head slowly. "We were fools to let them have complete control of this place. Who knows? Maybe we should have behaved like every other army that conquered Jerusalem."

"Tear down the Dome and al-Aqsa? Rebuild the Temple? You don't really believe that would have been the right thing to do, Eli."

"No," he admitted, "but at a moment like this, I'm allowed to imagine what it might have been like."

Gabriel looked at his watch.

"How many minutes left?"

"If Dina is right—"

"Dina is always right," Lavon interjected.

"Twenty-five minutes," said Gabriel. "Which is why you need to get out of here."

Lavon turned his back to the bomb and lifted his arms toward the avenue of pillars. "There isn't a single authenticated artifact from the First or Second Temple. Not one. It's the reason why Palestinian leaders have been able to convince their people that the Temples were a myth. And it's the reason why they hid these pillars in a hole one hundred and sixty-seven feet beneath the surface." He looked at Gabriel and smiled. "And it's the reason why I'm not leaving this mountain until I know these pillars are safe."

"They're just stones, Eli."

"I know," he said. "But they're *my* stones."

"Are you really willing to die for them?"

Lavon was silent for a moment. Then he turned to Gabriel. "You have a beautiful wife. Maybe someday you'll have a beautiful child. *Another* beautiful child," he added. "Me . . . these stones are all I have."

"You're the closest thing in the world I have to a brother, Eli. I'm not leaving you behind."

"So we'll die together," Lavon said, "here, in the house of God."

"I suppose there are worse places to die."

"Yes," he said. "I suppose there are."

At that moment, Imam Hassan Darwish was standing in the doorway of the underground structure that had been built on his orders, listening to the two Jews speaking in their ancient language.

Darwish recognized them both. One was the noted biblical archae-ologist Eli Lavon, a critic of the Waqf and its construction projects. The other, the one with gray temples and green eyes, was Gabriel Allon, the murderer of Palestinian heroes. Darwish could scarcely believe his good fortune. The presence of the two men would make his task more difficult. But it would also make his journey to Para-dise far sweeter.

The imam turned his gaze from the men and looked at the ex-plosive device that lay within the ruins of the First Jewish Temple. The man called Mr. Farouk had built a manual override into the detonator in the event of a scenario such as this and had instructed Darwish on how to trigger it. A flick of a switch was all it would take.

Just then, Darwish heard the clatter of boots in the aqueducts. It appeared the Jews had broken through the Waqf's defenses. History was attempting to repeat itself. But not this time, thought Darwish. This time, the sacred shrines of Islam would not fall into the hands of the infidel, as they had in 1099, when the Crusad-ers besieged Jerusalem. This time would be different. A flick of a switch was all it would take.

The imam closed his eyes and, in his thoughts, recited the Verse of the Sword from the Koran: "Fight and kill the disbeliev-ers wherever you find them, take them captive, harass them, lie in wait and ambush them, using every stratagem of war." Then he charged into the museum of the ancient Jews and opened fire.

The first shots struck the ancient pillars and sent teardrops of flam-ing limestone into Gabriel's cheek. Looking up, he saw Hassan Darwish running across the floor of the cavern, his face contorted with a hatred born of faith and history and a thousand humiliations large and small. Instantly, Gabriel leveled his own weapon and charged toward the imam as bullets flashed past his ears. He fired the gun as he had in the range beneath the Vatican, shot after shot without pause, until nothing remained of the imam's face. Then, turning, he saw Eli Lavon crumpled on the ground, his arms wrapped around the base of one of the pillars. Gabriel pressed his palm against the bullet wound in Lavon's chest and held him as the life started to leave his eyes. "Don't die, Eli," he whispered. "Damn you, Eli, please don't die."

PART FOUR

EGO
TE
ABSOLVO

47

JERUSALEM

WITHIN AN HOUR OF THE Israeli incursion onto the Temple Mount plateau, the third intifada erupted in the Palestinian territories of the West Bank and Gaza Strip. Initially, the heavily armed security forces of the Palestinian Authority tried to control the violence. But as images of Israeli troops in the Haram al-Sharif spread like wildfire across the Arab world, the militiamen joined the rioters and engaged Israeli troops in running gun battles. Ramallah, Jericho, Nablus, Jenin, and Hebron all saw heavy fighting, but the worst of the clashes occurred in East Jerusalem, where several thousand Arabs tried but failed to retake the Temple Mount. By sunset, as sirens announced the arrival of the Jewish Sabbath, Islam's third-holiest shrine was under Israeli control, and the Middle East seemed precariously close to war.

The king of Jordan, himself a direct descendant of the Prophet

Muhammad, demanded the Israelis leave the Noble Sanctuary at once, but he stopped short of calling for violence to expel them. That was not the case, however, in Cairo, where the Muslim Brotherhood, the new leaders of the Arab world's most populous nation, called for a pan-Islamic jihad to avenge the outrage. Hamas, a branch of the Brotherhood's Islamist tree, immediately pummeled Beersheba and several other Israeli towns with a barrage of rockets that left ten Israelis dead. In Lebanon, however, Hezbollah remained curiously silent, as did its Shiite masters in Tehran.

Among the many challenges faced by Israeli officials during those explosive first hours was the presence of His Holiness Pope Paul VII. With the Old City of Jerusalem now a war zone, he took shelter in a monastery in Ein Kerem, the former Arab village just west of downtown Jerusalem that, according to Christian tradition, was the birthplace of John the Baptist. At the request of the Israeli prime minister, the pope agreed, albeit reluctantly, to cancel a planned Holy Saturday mass on the Mount of Beatitudes, along with Easter Sunday services at the Church of the Holy Sepulchre. Regrettably, the Holy Father had little choice in the matter. The Sepulchre, the sacred Christian shrine that Saladin had wanted to raze, was one of the main targets of Muslim rage.

There were many in the papal entourage who pleaded with the Holy Father to return to the safety of the Vatican, but he insisted on staying in the misplaced hope his presence might help to calm the situation. He spent much of his time at the Hadassah Medical Center, located not far from the monastery. Needless to say, the pope's frequent appearances at the hospital generated speculation that he was ill or had been injured in the violence. It wasn't true; he was simply ministering to a soul in need.

The patient in question had arrived at the hospital in the first minutes of the uprising, a bullet in his chest, more dead than alive. The staff was told that his name was Weiss, but was given no other information except for his approximate age and his medical history, which included numerous disorders related to stress. The blinds over his window, which looked east toward the walls of the Old City, remained tightly drawn. Two armed guards stood watch outside his door, one to its right and one to its left.

The pope was not the only dignitary to visit the wounded man. The prime minister came to see him, as did the chief of staff of the IDF, the heads of the various Israeli intelligence services, and, for reasons never made clear to the hospital staff, a large delegation of archaeologists from Hebrew University and the Israel Antiquities Authority. There was one man, however, who never moved from the patient's bedside. He made no attempt to conceal his identity, for it wouldn't have been possible—not with those distinctive gray temples and unforgettable eyes.

He drank little, ate less, and slept not at all. When one of the doctors offered him a bed and a mild sedative, he was met by a glare of disapproval. After that, no one dared to ask him to leave—even on the second night, when, for two terrible minutes, the patient's heart stopped beating. For the next twenty-four hours, the visitor remained motionless at the foot of the bed, his face illuminated by the glow of the ventilator, as if he were a figure in a painting by Caravaggio. Occasionally, the nurses could hear the figure speaking softly. His words never varied. "Don't die, Eli. Damn you, Eli, please don't die."

On Easter morning, the tolling of Jerusalem's church bells was scarcely audible over the sound of gunfire. At noon, a crude Palestinian rocket fell into the Garden of Gethsemane, and at mid-afternoon bullets raked the exterior of the Church of the Dormition. That evening, a distraught Holy Father paid one final visit to the unconscious patient before boarding his plane to return home. When he was gone, another elderly man took his place. He, too, was known to the staff of the trauma center. He was the one they spoke of only in whispers. The one who had stolen the secrets that led to Israel's lightning victory in the Six-Day War. The one who had plucked Adolf Eichmann, managing director of the Holocaust, from an Argentine street corner. *Shamron . . .*

"You need to go home and get some rest, my son."

"I will."

"When?"

"When he opens his eyes."

Shamron twirled his Zippo between his fingertips. Two turns to the left, two turns to the right.

"Must you, Ari?"

Shamron's fingers went still. "You have to prepare yourself for the possibility he's not going to make it."

"Why would I do that?"

"Because it is the likely outcome. He'd lost nearly all his blood by the time they got him onto the table. His heart—"

"Is fine."

"But it's not as young as it once was," Shamron said. "And neither is yours, my son. And I'm afraid of what will happen if it gets broken again."

"I deserve it."

"Why would you say such a thing?"

"I should have heard Darwish coming."

"You both were distracted, which was understandable. It's not every day that one has a chance to walk through the *heikhal* of the First Temple of Jerusalem."

"Do you think the pillars truly are from the First Temple?"

"We know they are," Shamron said. "We're just waiting for the right moment to show them to the world."

"Why wait?"

"Because we don't want to do anything to make the situation any worse."

"How much worse could it get?"

"There are ninety million Egyptians. Imagine what would happen if the Muslim Brotherhood convinced just ten percent of them to march on our borders. If that bomb had actually gone off . . ." Shamron's voice trailed off. "It's frightening to think how close we came—or how tenuous our existence is in this land."

"How long are we planning to stay on the Temple Mount?"

"If it were up to me, we'd never leave. But the prime minister intends to hand it back to the Waqf as soon as all the archaeological material has been safely removed."

"So we go back to the status quo?"

"Until the Islamic world is ready to accept our right to exist, I'm afraid the status quo is the best we can hope for."

"I'd like to make one change to it, if it's all right with you."

"What's that?"

"Massoud."

Shamron smiled. "The next time a bomb goes off under his car, it won't be a small one."

Gabriel took hold of Lavon's hand.

"If he dies, Ari, I'll never forgive myself."

"It wasn't your fault."

"I should have made him leave."

"There's no way Eli would have ever left that mountain without knowing those pillars were safe."

"They're just stones, Ari."

"They're Eli's stones," Shamron said. "And now they're soaked in his blood."

48

JERUSALEM

I T WOULD BE ANOTHER SEVENTY-TWO hours before sufficient order had been restored to allow the government of Israel to fully explain to the world why it had entered the Temple
Mount and what it had discovered there. To do so, it assembled a
pool of journalists and camera crews from the world's most au-
thoritative news organizations and took them down through the
network of aqueducts and cisterns, to the newly dug chamber 167
feet beneath the surface. There the chief of staff of the IDF showed
them the massive bomb, while the head of the Israel Antiquities
Authority walked them through the remarkable collection of artifacts that had been unearthed by the Waqf during years of reckless
digging. The highlight of the tour were the two rows of limestone
pillars, twenty-two in all, that had been part of the *heikhal* of King
Solomon's First Temple of Jerusalem.

As expected, the reaction to the news was mixed at best. The
video of the ancient pillars electrified the Israeli public and sent a

tremor of anticipation through the global community of archaeologists and ancient historians. Most scholars immediately accepted the pillars as authentic, but in Germany the leader of a discipline of archaeology known as biblical minimalism dismissed them as "twenty-two hunks of wishful thinking." Not surprisingly, the leadership of the Palestinian Authority seized on that statement when issuing its own response to the news. The pillars were an Israeli hoax, it said. And so was the "so-called bomb."

But what had led the Israelis to enter the Temple Mount in the first place? And who had been the ultimate mastermind of the plot to bring it down? The Israeli government, citing its long-standing refusal to comment on matters related to intelligence gathering, declined to go into specifics. But as the pillars emerged slowly from the earth, a series of stories appeared in the press that began to shed a diffuse light on the mysterious chain of events that had led to their discovery.

There was the exposé in *Le Monde* about a Sorbonne graduate named David Girard, aka Daoud Ghandour, who had advised the Waqf on archaeological matters, and who, according to unnamed law enforcement officials, was a member of a criminal antiquities smuggling network with links to Hezbollah. And the story in the *Neue Zürcher Zeitung* about an Iranian connection to the bombing of Galleria Naxos in St. Moritz. And the investigative follow-up in *Der Spiegel* that linked David Girard to one Massoud Rahimi, the Iranian terrorist mastermind who had been briefly kidnapped in Germany. Which made it all the more interesting when, just twelve days later, that same Massoud Rahimi was killed in Tehran by a limpet-style bomb planted beneath his car. The television terrorism analysts had little doubt about who was behind the assassination or what it meant. Massoud had been the mastermind of the Temple Mount plot, they proclaimed, and the Israelis had just returned the favor.

But there were many aspects of the story the press would never learn, including the fact that the affair had begun when Gabriel Allon, the wayward son of Israeli intelligence, had been summoned to St. Peter's Basilica to view the corpse of a fallen angel. Or that Gabriel had spent the last two weeks sitting beside the hospital bed of the archaeologist whose blood stained the pillars of Solomon's Temple. As a result, he was present when the archaeologist finally opened his eyes. "Rivka," Eli Lavon murmured. "Make sure someone looks after Rivka."

That same evening, a tense calm fell over Jerusalem for the first time since the beginning of the Temple Mount crisis. Gabriel went to the Mount Herzl Psychiatric Hospital to spend a few minutes with Leah before meeting Chiara for dinner at a restaurant located in the original campus of the Bezalel Academy of Art and Design. Afterward, he took her for ice cream and a walk in Ben Yehuda Street.

"Donati called this afternoon," she said suddenly, as though it had slipped her mind. "He was wondering when you were coming back to Rome to finish the Caravaggio and deal with Carlo."

"I'd almost forgotten about them both."

"That's understandable, darling. After all, you *did* save Israel and the world from Armageddon and find twenty-two pillars from the First Temple of Jerusalem."

Gabriel smiled. "I'll leave the day after tomorrow."

"I'm coming with you."

"You can't. Besides," he added quickly, "I have a job for you. *Two* jobs, actually."

"What are they?"

"I need someone to look after Eli until I get back."

"And the other?"

"The government has decided to put the pillars in a special wing at the Israel Museum. You're going to be part of the team that will design the interior of the building and the overall exhibit."

"Gabriel!" she exclaimed, throwing her arms around him. "How on earth did you manage that?"

"As one of the co-discoverers of the pillars, I have a certain amount of sway. In fact, they wanted to name the exhibit in my honor."

"What did you tell them?"

"That it should be called the Eli Lavon Wing," he said. "I'm just thankful it's not going to be the Eli Lavon *Memorial* Wing."

"Will they change anything?"

"The pillars?"

Chiara nodded.

"Did you hear what the Palestinians said about them?"

"Zionist lies."

"Temple Denial," said Gabriel. "They can't admit that we were here before them because that would mean we have a right to be here now. In their eyes, we have to remain foreign invaders, something to be driven out, like the Crusaders."

"Blood never sleeps," Chiara said softly.

"Nor is it in short supply," Gabriel added. "Our friends in the West like to think the Arab-Israeli conflict can be solved by drawing a line on a map. But they don't understand history. This city has existed in a state of almost perpetual warfare for three thousand years. And the Palestinians are going to keep fighting until we're gone."

"So what do we do?"

"Hold fast," said Gabriel. "Because the next time we lose Jerusalem, it will be for good. And then where will we go?"

"I've been asking myself the same question."

The air had turned suddenly cooler. Chiara pulled her coat tightly around her and studied a group of Israeli teenagers laughing on the other side of the street. They were sixteen or seventeen. In a year or two, they would all be in the army, soldiers in the war without end.

"It's not so easy, is it, Gabriel?"

"What's that?"

"To think about leaving at a time like this."

"It's the other form of Jerusalem Syndrome. The worse it gets, the more you love it."

"You *do* love it, don't you?"

"I love it dearly," he said. "I love the color of the limestone and the sky. I love the smell of the pine and the eucalyptus. I love it when the air turns cold at night. I even love the *haredim* who shout at me when I drive my car on Shabbat."

"But do you love it enough to stay?"

"His Holiness thinks I have no choice."

"What are you talking about?"

Gabriel told her about the conversation with the pope on the parapet of the Vatican walls, when the leader of a billion Catholics confessed he was having visions of the Apocalypse. "He thinks we've been wandering too long," he said. "He thinks the country needs me."

"The pope doesn't have to wait in hotel rooms wondering whether you're going to come back from an operation alive."

"But he *is* infallible."

"Not when it comes to matters of the heart." Chiara looked at Gabriel for a moment. "Do you know what it's going to be like if we live here? Every time we come home, Ari is going to be sitting in our living room."

"As long as he doesn't smoke, that's fine with me."

"Do you mean that?"

"He's like a father to me, Chiara. I need to take care of him."

"And when Uzi asks you to run an errand for the Office?"

"I suppose I'll just have to learn those three little words."

"Which words?"

"Find someone else."

"What will you do for work?"

"I'll find work."

"It gets claustrophobic here."

"Tell me about it."

"We'll need to travel, Gabriel."

"I'll take you wherever you want to go."

"I've always wanted to spend an autumn in Provence."

"I know just the village."

"Have you ever been to Scotland?"

"Not that I can recall."

"Will you take me skiing just once?"

"Anywhere but St. Moritz or Gstaad."

"I miss Venice."

"So do I."

"Maybe Francesco Tiepolo can give you a bit of work."

"He pays me peanuts."

"I *adore* peanuts." She leaned her head against his shoulder. Her hair smelled of vanilla. "Do you think it will hold?" she asked.

"The quiet?"

She nodded.

"For a little while," said Gabriel, "if we're lucky."

"How long will you be in Rome?"

"I suppose that depends entirely on Carlo."

"Just don't go anywhere near him without a gun in your pocket."

"Actually," he said, "I was planning on having Carlo come to me."

Chiara shivered.

"We should be going," said Gabriel. "You'll catch your death."

"No," she said, "I love it, too."

"The cold at night?"

"And the smell of the pine and eucalyptus," she said. "It smells like . . ." Her voice trailed off.

"Like what, Chiara?"

"Like home," she said. "It feels good to finally be home."

49

PIAZZA DI SANT'IGNAZIO, ROME

WHEN GABRIEL ENTERED THE PIAZZA DI Sant'Ignazio two days later, the sun shone brightly from a cloudless Roman sky, and the tables of Le Cave stood in neat rows across the paving stones. At one, shaded by a white umbrella, sat General Ferrari of the Art Squad. Near his elbow was a copy of that morning's edition of *Corriere della Sera*, which he placed in front of Gabriel. It was open to a story from Paris about the unexpected recovery of two stolen works of art. The Cézanne was the main attraction; the Greek vase, a lovely hydria by the Amykos Painter, a mere afterthought.

"I was right about one thing," the general said. "You certainly do know how to think like a criminal."

"I had nothing to do with it."

"And I still have a perfectly good right hand." The general appraised Gabriel for a moment with his one good eye before asking whether he had stolen the painting and the vase himself.

"Operational verisimilitude required me to utilize the services of a professional."

"So it was a commissioned theft?"

"You might say that."

"Does this thief ever practice his trade in Italy?"

"Every chance he gets."

"How much would I have to pay for his name?"

"I'm afraid it's not for sale."

Gabriel returned the paper to the general, who used it to wave away an approaching waiter.

"I've been reading the recent news from your country with great interest," he said, as though Gabriel's country was some place hard to find on a map. "Do you believe those pillars are truly from Solomon's First Temple?"

Gabriel nodded.

"You've seen them?"

"And the bomb they were going to use to blow them to pieces."

"Madness," said the general, shaking his head slowly. "I suppose it puts my efforts to protect Italy's cultural patrimony in a whole new light. I only have to contend with thieves and smugglers, not religious maniacs who are trying to plunge the Middle East into war."

"Sometimes the religious maniacs actually get help from the thieves and smugglers." Gabriel paused, then added, "But then, you already knew that, didn't you, General Ferrari?"

Ferrari fixed Gabriel with a glassy stare from his prosthetic eye but said nothing.

"That's why you sent me to Veronica Marchese," Gabriel continued. "Because you already knew that her husband controlled the global trade in looted antiquities. You also knew he was working with the criminal funding arm of Hezbollah. You knew all this," Gabriel concluded, "because my service told you it was so."

"Actually," the general responded, "I knew about Carlo long before your chief brought us his dossier."

"Why didn't you do anything about it?"

"Because it would have destroyed the career of a woman I admire greatly, not to mention a close friend of hers who lives next door to His Holiness on the third floor of the Apostolic Palace."

"You knew that Donati and Veronica were lovers once?"

"And so does Carlo," the general said, nodding. "He also knows that the monsignor left his order after a pair of killings in El Salvador. Which is why he wanted to be on the supervisory council of the Vatican Bank so badly."

"He knew it would be a perfect safe harbor to launder his money because Donati would never dare move against him."

The general nodded thoughtfully. "The monsignor's past made him vulnerable," he said after a moment. "That is the last thing one should be in a place like the Vatican."

"And when you heard that Claudia Andreatti had been found in the Basilica?"

"I had no doubt as to who was behind her death."

"Because your informant Roberto Falcone told you that she'd been to Cerveteri to see him," Gabriel said. "And when I found Falcone's body in the acid bath, you realized that you had a perfect solution to your Carlo problem. An Italian solution."

"Not in the strictest sense of the term, but, yes, I suppose I did." The unblinking eye scrutinized Gabriel for a moment. "And now it seems we have arrived at the place where we began. What do we do about Carlo?"

"I know what I'd *like* to do."

"How much hard evidence do you have?"

"Enough to tie a *cordata* around his scrawny neck."

"How do you want to handle it?"

"I'm going to tell him to resign his post at the Vatican Bank immediately. But first, I'm going to offer him a chance to confess his sins."

The general smiled. "I've always found that confession can be good for the soul."

After lunch, Gabriel hiked across the river, to the faded old palazzo in Trastevere that had been turned into a faded old apartment building. He still had the key. Entering the foyer, he once again checked the postbox. This time, it was empty.

He headed upstairs and let himself into the flat. It was exactly as he had left it nearly four months ago, with one exception: the electricity had been cut off. And so he sat alone at her desk, watching as the creeping afternoon shadows slowly reclaimed her possessions. Finally, a few minutes after six, he heard the scrape of a key entering the lock. Then the door swung open, and Dr. Claudia Andreatti came floating toward him through the darkness.

Her sister's death had spared the world a cataclysm, which meant that Paola Andreatti deserved to know nothing less than the complete truth about what had happened. Not the Office's version of the truth, thought Gabriel, and surely not the Vatican's. It had to be truth without evasion and without regard to the sensitivities of powerful individuals or institutions. A truth she could take to the grave of her sister and, one day, to her own.

And so Gabriel told her the entire story of his remarkable journey from the dome of St. Peter's Basilica to the hole in the heart of the Holy Mountain, where he had found the twenty-two pillars of Solomon's First Temple and the bomb that could have caused a conflict of biblical proportions. She remained silent throughout, her hands folded neatly on her lap. The eyes that watched him from the evening shadows were identical to the ones that had gazed up at him from the floor of the Basilica. The voice, when finally she spoke, was the same voice that had spoken to him briefly in the stairwell of the Vatican Museum the night of her death.

"What are you going to do about Carlo?"

Gabriel's answer seemed to cause her physical pain.

"Is that all?" she asked.

"If the Italian prosecutors bring charges against him—"

"I know how the justice system works in Italy, Mr. Allon," she said, cutting him off. "The case will drag on for years, and the chances are good he'll never see the inside of a jail."

"What do you want, Dr. Andreatti?"

"Justice for my sister."

"It's not something I can give you."

"Then why did you bring me to Rome?"

"For the truth," he said. "I wanted you to hear the truth. And not just from me. From him as well."

"When?" she asked.

"Tomorrow night."

She was silent for a moment. "If there was a God," she said finally, "he would die the same death as my sister."

Yes, thought Gabriel. If there was a God.

50

VATICAN CITY

ONATI RANG CARLO MARCHESE LATE the following afternoon and said the Vicar of Christ wanted a word.

"When?" asked Carlo.

"Tonight."

"I have something."

"Cancel it."

"What time?"

"Nine o'clock," said Donati. "The Bronze Doors."

The time had not been chosen at random, but Carlo appeared not to notice. Nor did he seem to think it was odd when he found Father Mark waiting to greet him. Carlo was the kind of man who didn't have to stop at the Permissions Desk on his way into the building. Carlo could find his own way from the Bronze Doors to the papal apartments.

"This way," said Father Mark, taking Carlo's elbow with a grip that indicated he had been lifting more than just a communion chalice. He led him up the Scala Regia and into the Sistine Chapel. There they passed beneath Michelangelo's *Last Judgment*, with its swirling vision of the Apocalypse and the Second Coming of Christ, before heading down the gray-green tube to the Basilica. As they crossed to the other side of the soaring nave, Carlo began to show his first signs of agitation. It increased sharply when Father Mark informed him they would be taking the stairs to the dome rather than the elevator. The stairs were General Ferrari's idea. He wanted Carlo to suffer, even in a small way, on his way to absolution.

The climb took slightly more than five minutes. As they reached the landing at the top of the stairs, Carlo tried to pause in order to catch his breath, but Father Mark nudged him into the gallery of the dome. A raincoated figure stood at the balustrade, peering downward toward the floor of the Basilica. As Carlo entered, the figure turned and regarded him without a word. Carlo froze and then recoiled.

"Something wrong, Carlo? You look as though you just saw a ghost."

Carlo spun round and saw Gabriel standing where Father Mark had been.

"What is this, Allon?"

"Judgment, Carlo."

Gabriel went to Paola's side. She was staring downward again, as though oblivious to Gabriel's presence.

"This is where Claudia was standing when she died. Whoever murdered her approached her from behind and broke her neck before throwing her over the barrier to make it look like a suicide. That was the easy part. The hard part was getting her up to the gallery in the first place." Gabriel paused. "But you managed to figure that out, didn't you, Carlo?"

"I had nothing to do with her death, Allon."

Carlo's declaration of innocence echoed high in the dome before dying the death it deserved. His gaze was now fixed on Paola's neck. Gabriel placed a hand gently on her shoulder.

"She was scheduled to meet with Donati that night to tell him you were running your criminal empire from the Vatican Bank. But she canceled the meeting without explanation. She *canceled* it," Gabriel added pointedly, "because someone told her to come to the dome of the Basilica. That person was going to give her the information she needed to destroy you. It was someone she trusted, someone she used to work with." Gabriel paused again. "Someone like your wife."

Carlo seemed to be trying to regain his composure, but Paola's presence wouldn't permit it. He was still staring at her neck. As a result, he didn't notice General Ferrari standing a few feet behind him.

"Sometime that evening," Gabriel resumed, "Claudia received a text message from Veronica asking her to come here. She called Veronica's cell a few minutes before nine, but there was no answer. That's because Veronica didn't have her cell. *You* did, Carlo."

"You can't prove any of this, Allon."

"Remember where you're standing, Carlo."

Paola gave Carlo an accusatory glare before setting off on a slow tour of the gallery.

"But who to trust with the job of actually killing your wife's best friend?" Gabriel asked. "It had to be someone who could get inside the Vatican without much trouble, someone who didn't have to stop at the Permissions Desk before entering the palace." Gabriel smiled. "Know anyone like that, Carlo?"

"You don't really believe I killed that poor girl with my own hands."

"I *know* you did. And so does she," Gabriel added with a glance at Paola. "Help her soul find peace, Carlo. Tell her that you killed her sister to protect your position at the Vatican Bank. Confess your sins."

Paola's presence had clearly lost its hold over Carlo. He was now staring at Gabriel with the same arrogant smile he had worn the night he tried to have Gabriel and Chiara killed. He was once again Carlo the untouchable, Carlo the man without physical fear.

"You are a member of a very small club," Gabriel said. "You are the only person who ever tried to kill my wife who is still walking this earth. If you would like to remain here with us, I would advise you to tender your resignation at the Vatican Bank immediately. But first," he added, glancing again toward Paola, "I want you to tell her why you murdered her sister."

"You can have my resignation but—"

"Your wife already knows," Gabriel said, cutting him off. "I told her everything before the Holy Father left for Jerusalem. She believed me, because she remembered that on the night of Claudia's death she couldn't find her mobile."

To bring an opponent's wife into play violated Gabriel's personal code of ethics, but the tactic had its intended effect. Carlo's face was now crimson with rage. Gabriel pressed his advantage.

"She's going to leave you, Carlo. In fact, if I had to guess, she's probably been thinking about it for some time. After all, she never loved you the way she loved Donati."

That was enough to push Carlo's anger past the point of control. He blundered toward Gabriel in a blind fury, his face unrecognizable with rage, his arms outstretched. Gabriel took a lightning step to one side, leaving Carlo to careen over the balustrade. A hand reached out, flailing. Too late, Gabriel tried to grasp it. Then he seized Paola and covered her ears tightly so she couldn't hear the sound of Carlo's body colliding with the marble below. Only when General Ferrari had taken her out onto the roof terrace did Gabriel look over the side. There he saw the pope's private secretary kneeling on the floor of the Basilica, his fingertips moving gently over Carlo's forehead. *Ego te absolvo.* And then it was done.

For the next two days, Gabriel remained a prisoner of his curtained little tomb at the far end of the restoration lab. The other members of the staff saw him rarely. He was there when they arrived in the morning, and he remained there, surrounded by a corona of brilliant halogen light, long after they left for the night. There were rumors of a disaster of some sort behind the shroud—an unexpected loss of Caravaggio's original work, or perhaps a botched retouching. Enrico Bacci, still seething over his failure to secure the assignment, demanded a staff intervention, but Antonio Calvesi refused. Calvesi had heard the stories about the endless sessions before the canvas when the end was in sight. In fact, he had personally witnessed such an ordeal in Florence many years earlier, when Gabriel, then working under an assumed identity, had labored for twenty hours without a break to complete a Masaccio before his deadline. "There's no problem," Calvesi assured his faithless staff. "He's just closing in on his target. Just be thankful it's a painting and not a man."

And so it came to pass that on the morning of the third day, when the staff came trickling into the lab, they found the curtain of his workspace hanging open and the painting propped on an easel, looking as though it had just been completed by Caravaggio himself. The only thing missing was the man who had restored it. Calvesi spent an hour fruitlessly searching for him before heading up to the palace to personally deliver the news to Monsignor Donati. The Caravaggio was finally finished, he reported. And Gabriel Allon, renowned restorer of Old Master paintings, retired Israeli spy and assassin, and savior of the Holy Father, had vanished without a trace.

AUTHOR'S NOTE

The Fallen Angel is a work of fiction. The names, characters, places, and incidents portrayed in the story are the product of the author's imagination or have been used fictitiously. Any resemblance to actual persons, living or dead, businesses, companies, events, or locales is entirely coincidental.

Those who have made the ascent to the dome of St. Peter's Basilica will surely remember there is a wire suicide barrier along the edge of the viewing gallery. I removed it in order to make a murder, and an accidental fall, more plausible. The conservation laboratory of the Vatican Picture Gallery has been accurately rendered, though in no way do I mean to suggest there are any problems of provenance regarding the Vatican's extraordinary collection of antiquities, even by today's exacting curatorial standards. The Vatican Bank, however, has a long and well-documented history of financial transgressions. The latest occurred in September 2010, when Italian authorities conducting a money-laundering probe seized $30 million from the bank and placed two of its top officers under investigation. The following month, police in Sicily announced they had uncovered a money-laundering scheme that utilized the Vatican Bank account of a priest whose uncle had been convicted on charges of Mafia association.

The headquarters of the Carabinieri's Art Squad is in fact located in Rome's Piazza di Sant'Ignazio, and the unit's role in the investigation of convicted antiquities smuggler Giacomo Medici—and the recovery of the Euphronios Krater from New York's Metropolitan Museum of Art—has been faithfully portrayed. There is indeed an antiquities gallery on a picturesque square in St. Moritz, though I am quite confident it is in no way associated with the Shiite militant group Hezbollah. The Lebanon Byzantine Bank does not exist, but the Lebanese Canadian Bank does—and it is there, according to U.S. officials, that Hezbollah launders at least a portion of the money it earns through its global criminal fund-raising operations. It was an unnamed U.S. federal agent, speaking to the *New York Times* in December 2011, who first described Hezbollah as "the Gambinos on steroids," not Uzi Navot, the fictitious chief of Israeli intelligence.

Massoud Rahimi, the Iranian intelligence officer who appears in *The Fallen Angel*, was created by the author, but his close ties to Hezbollah, a group often called the "A-team of terrorists," are based entirely on fact. Hezbollah has carried out numerous acts of terror at Iran's behest and would surely play a prominent role in Iran's response to any attack on its nuclear weapons facilities. In fact, there is ample evidence to suggest Israel is already being targeted by Hezbollah for attempting to disrupt the Iranian nuclear program with acts of sabotage and assassination. In January 2012, authorities in Azerbaijan broke up a Hezbollah terror cell that had allegedly targeted the Israeli ambassador there and a rabbi from a local Jewish school. In February, Israeli diplomats in Georgia and India came under simultaneous attack. The next day, a bomb exploded in a Bangkok apartment, exposing an Iranian-Hezbollah cell that was preparing to kill Israeli diplomats in the Thai capital. But then, none of this should come as much of a surprise. In July 2006, Hossein Safiadeen, Hezbollah's representative in Tehran, announced the group intended to murder Israelis and Jews wherever it could find them, declaring ominously, "There will be no place they are safe." Surely, the remark found favor with Iran's supreme leader, Ayatollah Ali Khamenei, who has called Israel a "cancerous tumor" that must be removed. This coming from a man who is seeking the capability to do just that with the push of a button.

The sacred plateau in Jerusalem referred to as the Temple Mount by Jews and the Haram al-Sharif by Muslims is indeed under the control of the Islamic Waqf. The southern retaining wall of the Mount did in fact develop a precarious bulge as a result of the construction of the Marwani Mosque, and the description of archaeologically rich debris being hurled into the Kidron Valley is, sadly, all too accurate. I utilized the work of the great British archaeologist Sir Charles Warren while writing the climax of the novel, though I granted myself much license to move my characters as needed. For example, the secret tunnel that Gabriel Allon and Eli Lavon used to gain access to the interior of the Mount was created by the author, and in no way was it based on truth.

Regrettably, the same cannot be said when it comes to the beliefs and opinions of some of those who serve as the caretakers of the most sacred parcel of land on earth. In 1999, Ekrima Sa'id Sabri, then the grand mufti of Jerusalem, declared that "the Jew" was plotting to destroy the Haram al-Sharif. "The Jew will get the Christian to do his work for him," explained Sabri, who holds a doctorate from Cairo's al-Azhar University, Sunni Islam's most important center of study. "This is the way of the Jews. This is the way Satan manifests himself." In 2000, shortly before Pope John Paul II made his historic pilgrimage to Israel that included a visit to the Temple Mount, Sabri denied the Holocaust had ever happened. "Six million Jews dead? No way. They were much fewer. Let's stop with this fairy tale exploited by Israel to capture international solidarity." These were not the words of a fundamentalist cleric from an insignificant Salafist mosque. They were spoken by the man who controlled the third-holiest site in Islam.

It is little wonder, then, that Holocaust Denial is now main-stream thinking in the Arab and Islamic world, as is its first cousin, Temple Denial. Virtually the entire leadership of the Palestinian Authority—even some of those regarded as "moderates" in the West—deny there was ever an actual Jewish Temple atop the Temple Mount. At the Camp David summit in 2000, when President Bill Clinton worked tirelessly to negotiate a settlement to the Arab-Israeli conflict, Yasir Arafat baldly asserted the Temple had stood not in Jerusalem but in Nablus. His outburst stunned President Clinton, who responded, "As a Christian, I, too, believe that under the surface there are remains of Solomon's Temple." Clinton's chief Middle East negotiator, Dennis Ross, would later say of Arafat's performance at the summit: "He created a new mythology by saying the Temple doesn't exist there. It was the only new idea he raised in fifteen days at Camp David."

Clinton would make several more attempts to bring peace to the Middle East during the last days of his presidency, including the so-called Clinton Parameters, which he placed before the Israelis and Palestinians during a dramatic meeting in the Cabinet Room of the White House. A non-negotiable set of terms for a final agreement, the Parameters called for the creation of a Palestinian state in the Gaza Strip and 96 percent of the West Bank. The Temple Mount plateau, sacred to the three Abrahamic faiths, would have been included in the *Palestinian* state, while the Western Wall and Jewish Quarter of the Old City would have remained under Israeli control. Israeli Prime Minister Ehud Barak accepted the terms, but Yasir Arafat, after much dithering and equivocation, did not. In his memoirs, President Clinton was remarkably candid about his feelings toward the man whose "colossal mistake" had denied him a historic foreign policy achievement. "I am a failure," he told Arafat during a bitter telephone conversation. "And you have made me one."

But did the Temple of Solomon, as described in wondrous detail in Kings I and Chronicles, truly exist? The best way to answer that question would be to conduct a thorough but careful excavation of the entire Temple Mount plateau, with Israeli and Palestinian scholars working side by side, perhaps under United Nations supervision. Given Islamic sensitivities and current political realities, that is unlikely. So, too, is a settlement of the Arab-Israeli conflict, at least in the near future. At some point soon, Middle East watchers agree, there is likely to be another eruption of violence, a third intifada. Bombs will explode, bullets will fly, and children on both sides of the long and bloody contest over the twice-promised land will die. And to think it would have ended more than a decade ago if Yasir Arafat had only found the courage to speak a single word: "Yes."

ACKNOWLEDGMENTS

THIS NOVEL, LIKE THE PREVIOUS books in the Gabriel Allon series, could not have been written without the assistance of David Bull, who truly is among the finest art restorers in the world. Each year, David spends many hours scouring my manuscripts for factual errors when he could be standing in front of an easel bringing a damaged painting back to life. David has filled our lives with art and humor, and his cherished friendship is perhaps the greatest unexpected by-product of the Gabriel Allon series.

I am deeply indebted to Father Mark Haydu, the international director of the Patrons of the Arts in the Vatican Museums, for his invaluable contribution to this project. Also, to Sara Savodello, Carolina Rea, Lorna Richardson, and Dottoressa Gabriella Lalatta, a brilliant art historian who took my family and me from the glory of the Sistine Chapel room to the basement of the Vatican Picture Gallery, where the staff restorers care for the pope's magnificent collection of paintings. There we met the remarkable Francesca Persegati, who was not at all concerned when I told her a notoriously introverted Israeli assassin would soon be working in a curtained cave beneath the loft. A special thanks to Father Kevin Lixey, who was at our side as we processed through the streets of Rome on the feast of Corpus Christi, a few feet behind Pope Benedict XVI. The meal we all shared that candlelit night was the highlight of our time in Rome.

I spoke to numerous Israeli and American intelligence officers and policymakers while preparing this manuscript, and I thank them now in anonymity, which is how they would prefer it. Fred S. Zeidman, the former chairman of the U.S. Holocaust Memorial Council, opened many doors for me in Israel and inspires me daily with his dedication to preserving the memory of those killed in the Shoah. The brilliant Maxwell L. Anderson, director of the Dallas Museum of Art, patiently answered my many questions about the curatorial hazards of acquiring antiquities under the new guidelines put in place to protect the cultural patrimony of the so-called source countries. As always, Roger Cressey, formerly of the National Security Council, now of Booz Allen Hamilton, helped me to better understand the way the world *really* works. My dear friend George Weigel gave me valuable insights into the historic visit of Pope John Paul II to the Holy Land in 2000 and influenced my thinking on relations between Roman Catholics and the State of Israel. "M" and "B" gave me tutorials on the turbulent Middle East with the sort of special insights only they could provide.

Michael Oren, the renowned Middle East scholar and writer who now serves as Israel's ambassador to the United States, taught me many important lessons about the great empires that have left their mark, and the blood of their soldiers, on the soil of modern Israel. His beautiful wife, Sally, and their three amazing children, Yoav, Lia, and Noam, were by my side at many points along the journey and were a constant source of joy and love. Our dear friends Lior and Talia opened their home to us in suburban Tel Aviv and rode to the rescue when we ran into a logistical problem at a military checkpoint outside Hebron in the West Bank. Gabriel Motzkin and Emily Bilski, who have the misfortune of living next door to the Allons on Narkiss Street, accompanied us on our first visit to Israel two decades ago, and our two families spent many pleasant evenings together during our most recent trip. Rachel and Elliott Abrams shared their extraordinary knowledge of Israeli politics over dinner in Abu Ghosh; Avner took us on a late-night safari in the Golan Heights that included several high-speed pursuits of wild boar and jackals. Yehuda Deutsch led us on an unforgettable tour of the excavations in the City of David. In fact, I can still hear him singing Leonard Cohen's majestic "Hallelujah" to steady our nerves as we walked through the dark, narrow passage of Hezekiah's Tunnel, the cool Jerusalem spring water swirling around our ankles.

A heartfelt thanks to Yitz Applbaum, Yogi Loshinsky, and Miri Sack of the Western Wall Heritage Foundation for giving us a glimpse into the astonishing world that lies submerged along the edge of the Temple Mount. The archaeologists who pick at the ancient soil near the tunnel conduct their work with great professionalism and sensitivity, and their spirit found its way into the fictitious Eli Lavon. As the international campaign to delegitimize the State of Israel gains in intensity, the archaeologists' efforts to unearth the ancient Jewish past in Jerusalem have taken on greater significance. To borrow a phrase from Ari Shamron, they are "waging war" in those tunnels. Fortunately, it is the one war in the Middle East in which no blood is shed.

I wish to thank my dear friend Doron Almog and his lovely wife, Didi, for taking such good care of us while we were in Israel. Before retiring from the Israel Defense Forces, Doron served as the chief of Southern Command and, in 1976, was the first Israeli soldier on the ground in Uganda during Operation Entebbe. But Doron is much more than one of his country's most decorated soldiers; he is a humanitarian who has dedicated his life to caring for the weakest of Israel's citizens, regardless of whether they are Arab or Jew. I will never forget the afternoon we spent together at Aleh Negev, the village he founded in southern Israel to care for the severely disabled. Nor will I forget the five members of Doron's family who were murdered by a female Palestinian suicide bomber at Maxim restaurant in Haifa on October 4, 2003. Sixteen other innocent people were killed in the attack.

I consulted hundreds of books, newspaper and magazine articles, and Web sites while preparing this manuscript, far too many to name here. I would be remiss, however, if I did not mention the extraordinary scholarship and reporting of Peter Watson and Cecilia Todeschini, Vernon Silver, Margaret M. Miles, Jason Felch and Ralph Frammolino, Sharon Waxman, Roger Atwood, Dore Gold, Paul Johnson, Hershel Shanks, Leen and Kathleen Ritmeyer, and Simon Sebag Montefiore, whose magisterial *Jerusalem: The Biography* is perhaps the finest book ever written on the history of the much-fought-over city upon a hill. Louis Toscano, my dear friend and longtime personal editor, made countless improvements to my manuscript, as did my copy editor, Kathy Crosby. Obviously, responsibility for any mistakes or typographical errors that find their way into the finished book falls on my shoulders, not theirs.

We are blessed with many friends who fill our lives with love and laughter at critical junctures during the writing year, especially Rabbi David Wolpe, Jane and Burt Bacharach, Stacey and Henry Winkler, Joy and Jim Zorn, Mollie and Jack Blades, Angelique and Jim Bell, Steve Capus and Sophia Faskianos, Enola and Stephen Carter, Andrea and Tim Collins, Margarita and Andrew Pate, Mirella and Daniel Levinas, Jane and Rob Lynch, and the greater Kobak family. Former First Lady Barbara Bush and President George H. W. Bush have been a constant source of support throughout my writing career, as has their amazing chief of staff, Jean Becker, who truly runs the world from her offices in Houston and Kennebunkport. Doug Banker made certain that the time away from my desk was filled with as much fun and music as possible. Dr. Benjamin Shaffer, Washington's preeminent orthopedic surgeon, expertly repaired a shoulder injury that made writing a novel even more painful than usual; Dr. David Jacobs, a real-life House, showed our family how medicine should always be practiced. Bob Barnett, Michael Gendler, and Linda Rappaport were a source of wise legal counsel and much laughter.

Special thanks to the remarkable team of professionals at HarperCollins, especially Jonathan Burnham, Brian Murray, Michael Morrison, Jennifer Barth, Josh Marwell, Tina Andreadis, Leslie Cohen, Leah Wasielewski, Mark Ferguson, Kathy Schneider, Brenda Segel, Carolyn Bodkin, Doug Jones, Karen Dziekonski, Archie Ferguson, David Watson, Cindy Achar, David Koral, and Leah Carlson-Stanisic.

I wish to extend my deepest gratitude and love to my children, Nicholas and Lily. Not only did they assist me with the final preparation of my manuscript, but they were at my side on a remarkable research trip that took us from the dome of St. Peter's Basilica to the Etruscan tombs in Cerveteri, to an ancient aqueduct beneath Jerusalem. Finally, I must thank my wife, the brilliant NBC News journalist Jamie Gangel, who skillfully edited each of my drafts and listened with remarkable forbearance as I worked through the plot and themes of this, the twelfth novel in the Gabriel Allon series. Were it not for her patience and attention to detail, *The Fallen Angel* would not have been completed by its deadline. My debt to her is immeasurable, as is my love.

ABOUT THE AUTHOR

D ANIEL SILVA IS THE NUMBER ONE *New York Times* bestselling author of *The Unlikely Spy*, *The Mark of the Assassin*, *The Marching Season*, *The Kill Artist*, *The English Assassin*, *The Confessor*, *A Death in Vienna*, *Prince of Fire*, *The Messenger*, *The Secret Servant*, *Moscow Rules*, *The Defector*, *The Rembrandt Affair*, and *Portrait of a Spy*. He is married to NBC News *Today* correspondent Jamie Gangel; they live in Washington, D.C., with their two children, Lily and Nicholas. In 2009 Silva was appointed to the United States Holocaust Memorial Museum Council.

www.danielsilvabooks.com